Lucifer & the Great Baltimore Brawl

GALE
A Cengage Company

Copyright © 2023 Howard Weinstein.
All original song lyrics and poems © 2023 by Howard Weinstein.
Thorndike Press, a part of Gale, a Cengage Company.

ALL RIGHTS RESERVED
This novel is a work of fiction. Names, characters, places and incidents are either the product of the author's imagination, or, if real, used fictitiously.
Thorndike Press® Large Print Hardcover Western.
The text of this Large Print edition is unabridged.
Other aspects of the book may vary from the original edition.
Set in 16 pt. Plantin.

LIBRARY OF CONGRESS CIP DATA ON FILE.
CATALOGUING IN PUBLICATION FOR THIS BOOK
IS AVAILABLE FROM THE LIBRARY OF CONGRESS.

ISBN-13: 979-8-88579-444-2 (hardcover alk. paper)

Published in 2023 by arrangement with Howard Weinstein.

Printed in Mexico
Printed Number: 1   Print Year: 2024

GALLOWAY'S GAMBLE, BOOK 2

LUCIFER & THE GREAT BALTIMORE BRAWL

HOWARD WEINSTEIN

THORNDIKE PRESS
A part of Gale, a Cengage Company

No matter how long we live, or how much we accomplish, life is inevitably an unfinished project. This novel is dedicated in memory of:
- my father-in-law Mike White, who dearly loved steam trains
- fellow writers Ann Crispin and Dave Galanter, gone too soon with too many tales untold
- eclectic, eccentric (but never dull!) journalist friend Thomas Vinciguerra
- old pal Joel Davis, who almost always found the silver lining
- Marc Wright, creative curmudgeon and longtime neighbor and friend
- Albert Palazzo, friend, inspiration and teacher extraordinaire
- David Tayman, our beloved veterinarian, benefactor, mentor and friend
- Gordon Lightfoot, my musical hero, for a lifetime of great songs.

Finally, a toast to Secretariat, arguably the greatest racehorse of all time. His epic 31-length win at the 1973 Belmont Stakes to claim the Triple Crown remains the most thrilling sports event I've ever seen. (Check it out on YouTube!) Amazingly, Big Red's speed records still stand a half-century later.

ACKNOWLEDGEMENTS

First, thanks to readers who said, "What do you mean you're not writing more *Star Trek* stories?!" — then gave me the benefit of the doubt, read *Galloway's Gamble,* and left kind reviews on the book's Amazon.com page. Many also asked for a sequel. Sorry it took so long.

Thanks to old friend Ross Lally for 19th century firearms tech support. To Terry Erdmann, Jim Rhule, Glenn Greenberg, Andrew Bergstrom, and Victoria Holzrichter for the loan of names. And to Steve Wilson for tech assistance.

A tip of the Stetson to Marshall Trimble, Arizona's official historian and longtime proprietor of the entertaining and enlightening *Ask the Marshall* column in *True West Magazine.* If you've got an Old West question, he's got the answer.

Thanks to the editors and writers at *True West* for publishing a magazine I've found truly helpful in writing historical fiction.

Finally, thanks to my smart wife Susan White for sanity-saving computer/IT support!

Howard Weinstein
April 2023

P.S. See if you can find the following "Easter eggs" I've hidden in this novel:

- *Have Gun – Will Travel* (CBS TV series)
- *Alias Smith and Jones* (ABC TV series)
- *Deadwood* (HBO TV series)
- *Gigi* (Lerner and Loewe film musical)
- Singer Tony Bennett (who left his heart, etc.)
- Legendary baseball manager Casey Stengel
- "Canadian Railroad Trilogy" (Gordon Lightfoot song)

PREVIOUSLY...

Welcome to the second volume of my recollections of the adventures me and my older brother Jake shared when we were young.

In my earlier account, I wrote of our family's frontier odyssey — ranging from our mother Cara Galloway's Philadelphia birth in 1826, to her sons being born in Arkansas in 1847 and '48, to our migration to East Texas, settling in the tiny riverside town of Serenity Falls in '49. That's where Mama was forced to protect her young sons from our violent drunk of a daddy by shooting him dead in our cabin on a winter's night in 1852, leaving her to run and improve the scruffy saloon he owned at the time.

Our rambles took Jake and me from fighting in the Civil War to Indian encounters, and from the open range to grand Mississippi riverboats as we sought our fortune at poker tables across the Old West. Although we rarely looked for trouble, trouble found us — especially in the spring of '73, when we visited Serenity Falls and found the town facing doom at the hands of land-grabbing cattle baron Wilhelm Krieg and corrupt banker Silas Atwood.

Krieg and Atwood plotted to steal for themselves a huge stretch of fertile and valuable land by evicting all the settlers who'd built homes, farms and businesses. My impulsive brother wanted to resolve the conflict with gunfire. In keeping with my philosophy that it's better to be a live coward than a dead hero, I convinced Mama, Jake, and a select few townsfolk there might be a way to outfox those scoundrels — without getting ourselves killed.

With essential help from wily mentor Mississippi Mike Morgan and resourcefully dishonest poker maestro Gideon Duvall, we wove an intricate confidence scheme that finagled Krieg into risking his vast land holdings and emptying Atwood's bank vault in order to buy up a boatload of bogus stock in a non-existent railroad. Despite perilous twists and turns, our plan worked in the end — much to our astonishment.

Our justifiable little conspiracy saved Serenity Falls, deprived two greedy men of ill-gotten gains, and eventually cost Krieg his cattle empire and Atwood his bank — with few outside our tight circle any the wiser for years. Following that righteous swindle, me and Jake left Texas to lay low far away from Krieg. We chose San Francisco as our destination, and liked it so much that we stayed for quite a spell.

Our David vs. Goliath battle against corruption taught us that life, like poker, is a chancy proposition — if you want to win, you have to be willing to lose. Our ability to apply that lesson would be tested once again by the tale told in this new book.

I promise you that the events herein are presented as seen with my own eyes, or as affirmed by faithful witnesses. It all happened pretty much this way.

James B. Galloway
December 1906

1

"Fair is foul, and foul is fair: Hover through the fog and filthy air."
~ The Witches in William Shakespeare's *Macbeth*

American Sport & Spirit,
October 6, 1873
★ DEALE'S DEAL
by HORATIO DEALE ★

Reporting, Dear Readers, from San Francisco, the Paris of the West, at the Sea Breeze Race Course — which can be quite lovely, except when the Golden City's frequent fog obscures one's view, like dank Stygian vapors wafting from the portals of Hades, and when fierce gusts blow from the deceptively named *Pacific Ocean.*

Here, at the close of the autumn horse racing meeting, under Nature's ground-girdling mists, Your Humble Correspondent is about to witness spirited combat between the marvelous Maryland Thoroughbred champion Grand Larceny (so christened due to his talent for purloining races with last-minute charges from behind) and the California-bred upstart palomino Phoenix (who truly rose from the ashes of a horrific barn fire when he was but a foal).

Will this race be merely a forgettable fogbound dash? Or something more?

Two horses. Head to head. One wins, one loses. Racing doesn't get much simpler than that. Or so I thought.

But crooks are known for seizing opportunities to do their deeds unseen, under cover of darkness — or shrouded by San Francisco's notorious fog. Though fog is much more prevalent in summer, here I am with brother Jake, standing in an October fog so thick we can't see the towering Sea Breeze grandstand a hundred feet away. Even before the horses reach the starting line, I'm on the lookout for anything shady — but what if I miss something because of the fog?

Horse racing is the country's first true national pastime. And these two horses are as good as it gets. Handsome colt Phoenix is an uncommon palomino Thoroughbred, owned and prized by Eduardo Lobo, and trained by Victoria Krieg — both young, and new to the Sport of Kings.

Eddie is a big baby-faced rancher with shoulders as broad as a mesa and a thick mop of black hair. Victoria is the brash daughter of our Texan nemesis, Wilhelm Krieg. Not quite nineteen, she's generally wise beyond her years (except for her unaccountable flirtation with my headstrong brother, which first percolated during our ensnarement of her father a few months back). With her chestnut hair, dusting of freckles across her nose and a knowing sparkle in her dark eyes, Victoria is a formidable force.

Famed and feared Maryland horseman Cortland Van Brunt III, owner of the big bay stallion Grand Larceny, is a reigning monarch of the Eastern Thoroughbred world. He almost always wears a straw planter's hat with a kettle-curled brim. With his wooly white beard, round ruddy face leathered by years of sun and wind, and a long-stemmed Dutch clay pipe clenched in his teeth, he resembles that "jolly old elf" Saint Nick himself, straight from the popular poem Mama read to us each Christmas Eve when we were kids.

In Van Brunt's case, looks are deceiving.

These two horses have already competed three times during the Sea Breeze season, with Phoenix winning them all. If Van Brunt couldn't defeat a horse, he'd only be satisfied once he *owned* that horse. So he's maneuvered Eddie Lobo into a fool's wager.

Like many bad ideas, this one sparked from boasts that kindled into argument, leading Van Brunt to challenge Eddie to a straight-up match race, with each owner putting up five thousand dollars — winner take all. But Van Brunt is rich, and knowing Eddie scarcely had a spare dime, he then suggested Eddie put up his horse against Van Brunt's cash.

Eddie should've walked away. But he didn't. Peaceable by nature, he's got a streak of stubborn pride. He believes Phoenix has already proved himself the better horse, and reckons he'll make an easy five grand, which his scrappy little operation sure could use. So he's agreed to Van Brunt's terms. In a fair race, in a fair world, the risk would be minimal. But fair isn't what Van Brunt has in mind.

Phoenix is smaller and lighter than his opponent, but well-muscled. His flaxen tail swishing with his easy stroll, he seems unperturbed. Eddie likes his chances, and his young jockey Rafael Cabrera, wearing green and white silks, is confident. Before he mounts up, Rafael bows his head, recites the Lord's Prayer in Spanish, and crosses himself for good measure.

A dark bay with a white blaze, glossy Grand Larceny struts like the world's biggest, meanest Tennessee Walking Horse. His crackerjack jockey is Champagne Charley Fly, a sinewy, seasoned black man (like so many riders of the era), resplendent in silks of white, black, yellow, and red. His grin reveals the glint of a gold front tooth.

The race will be a single lap of the one-mile oval, starting and ending in front of the grandstand. The horses come to rest. At the sharp rap of the starter's drum, they take off like rockets. Dirt flies from beneath their hooves. The damp ground muffles their galloping rumble and they disappear into the fog.

We peer into the distance, but the horses are invisible, their pace unknown. On average, they'd cover each quarter-mile in thirty-five seconds or less. Victoria keeps her eye on her stopwatch.

Tick-tick-tick . . .

"Quarter pole," she says.

Seconds sweep by. The horses remain obscured somewhere out there.

"No way Phoenix loses," Eddie says.

Vic says, "Into the back stretch."

Tick-tick-tick . . .

"Half-mile to go."

Tick-tick-tick . . .

Necks craned, eyes peeled, we strain to see the horses emerge from the fog.

"Coming into the homestretch," Vic says.

Tick-tick-tick . . .

At last, a horse materializes from the spirit realm — only it's the big bay Grand Larceny, not our golden palomino.

Tick-tick-tick . . .

Then there's Phoenix, laboring to close the gap, Rafael hunkered on his back, whipping the horse's haunches. They only trail by a length, but it might as well be a country mile.

Tick-tick-tick . . .

Grand Larceny and Champagne Charley Fly win by that measly length. Victoria clicks the watch in her hand like she wants to crush it. "One-forty-three," she mutters.

Both horses sail past the finish line, swallowed up again by the fog.

The jockeys and their mounts return at a walk. Van Brunt's camp-followers whoop and holler as they scramble and jig onto the track. One slips and pratfalls in the dirt.

Jake, who doesn't know or care much

about horses, asks, "A minute-forty-three — is that good?"

"Phoenix can run faster in his sleep," Eddie says with a mournful shake of his head.

Van Brunt waves his hat in triumph as he and his crowd parade Grand Larceny past the grandstand, back toward the paddock. We surround Rafael as he hops off his horse in a breathless tizzy of confusion.

"Eddie, we was in front — I *know* they was behind us! And then — boom! They was right alongside, like they fell outta the sky — and pullin' away. You know I hate usin' the whip." Rafael hugs the palomino's sweat-lathered neck. "I'm sorry, boy."

A Bible verse comes to mind, from Ecclesiastes: *I returned, and saw under the sun, that the race is not to the swift, nor the battle to the strong.*

Not to quibble with Scripture, but I think when a race doesn't go to the swift, somebody cheated. You don't have to be a Pinkerton to figure fog invites skullduggery.

Eddie is stunned, but Victoria is furious with him. "I told you to walk away! Did you listen?" She senses me looming and directs her fire my way: "Jamey — *don't* butt in!"

I ignore her warning. "I think something fishy happened out there. I think Van Brunt is chiseling you outta your horse."

Victoria squints at me. "How?"

"I don't know. And even if I did, I'm not sure how we'd prove it."

What I also didn't know in that moment, on that misty morning, was how me and my big mouth were about to launch us on a snakebit cross-country quest to win back a champion racehorse lost to sinister jiggery-pokery. Had a soothsayer forewarned us almost everything that *could* go wrong *would* go wrong, we might never have left San Francisco in the first place.

But off we would go, the very personification of the old saying about fools rushing in where angels fear to tread.

2

"Railroad iron is a magician's rod, in its power to evoke the sleeping energies of land and water."
~ Ralph Waldo Emerson

The Old West was an expanse of soaring peaks and searing deserts, trickling creeks and rushing rivers, grassy plains and prairies — all mostly uninhabited. With so much empty space and a scant and scattered population, the odds were against running into any particular long-lost someone.

But the majority of settlers migrated to hubs of civilization like iron filings to a magnet. And those bigger towns and cities tended to sprout either near age-old rivers washing through the wilderness, or the web of railroads beginning to span the continent. So it wasn't altogether surprising that we'd cross paths with Victoria Krieg one September evening in San Francisco. But the trail that got us there wasn't exactly a straight line.

After our slick swindle had successfully upended Wilhelm Krieg and Silas Atwood's plot to wipe Serenity Falls off the map, Mississippi Mike Morgan (our partner in righteous crime) conspired with our very own mother and Sheriff Jawbone Huggins to spirit me and Jake far from Krieg's vengeful reach, as a precaution. In fact, my brother and me got thoroughly hornswoggled by Mike's scheme, in which a convincing but fake U.S. marshal "arrested" us for stock fraud and announced he was hauling us to Texas state prison.

Instead, he took us to the Dallas railroad depot — where Mike surprised us with carpetbags packed by Mama with essentials we'd need to get us somewhere safe. Guided by a coin toss, we decided to "Go West, young man!" as *New York Tribune* editor Horace Greeley may or may not have said. So we boarded a train bound for San Francisco, which was about as far west as we could go without a boat.

Though we made do with upholstered seats rather than a sleeper compartment, any trip not on horseback was fine with big brother Jake. We found Mama had packed our satchels with clothes, cash, nuts, and dried fruit — and a letter saying how proud of us she was, and warning us we'd best write home often. We also found a short note from Mississippi Mike instructing us to find lodgings at San Francisco's Hotel Carlton, and to look up his friend Nathan Hale Boone, who lived at the hotel.

While all the newspapers glorified the new Transcontinental Railroad as history's greatest engineering feat, in truth the railroad fell short of reaching the ocean, owing to the unbridgeable obstacle of San Francisco Bay. Those choppy three-mile-wide waters separated Oakland and Alameda on the bay's east side from San Francisco to the west.

Near the end of the line, we passed extensive railroad and shipbuilding facilities sprawling across a hundred acres. On any given day at Oakland's teeming seaport, old wooden schooners and clippers, iron-hulled square-riggers, and the latest steamships delivered exotic silks and spices from the Orient, loaded up grain harvested in golden inland valleys, and transported lumber from northwestern forests to arid and treeless Southern California.

At the Pacific Railway's Oakland Long Wharf terminus, we and other newly arrived passengers boarded a side-wheeler ferry with teak decks and black smokestacks. Wind whipped across the water, so we huddled inside the ferry's elegant salon for the short harbor cruise, gawking through large windows at islands with military fortifications, the Golden Gate strait, and mountains stretching to the northern horizon.

Like Rome, San Francisco was built on seven hills. Streets swept up toward bluffs where pricey villas overlooked the rest of the city. Most buildings were made of wood and only two or three stories tall, due to occasional earthquakes that shook the region. Some newer buildings with iron beams and stone walls dared to reach higher.

Piers and warehouses ringed the north end of the San Francisco peninsula. Every slip had one ship docked, and two or three waiting at anchor to be swarmed by stevedores and longshoremen loading and unloading every imaginable cargo. The ferry tied up at the foot of Market Street, a broad boulevard leading into the city's dynamic heart. Of all the American cities we'd visited, including New Orleans and St. Louis, none pulsed with greater gusto than San Francisco.

Carriages from a dozen horse-car lines jockeyed to transport ferry passengers to hotels not far from the waterfront. "Where to?" the nearest driver called to us.

"Hotel Carlton," Jake said with a step toward the carriage.

I snagged his arm. "Not so fast. We may not be able to afford it until we start banking some poker winnings." I ignored Jake's groan of annoyance and asked a city constable in his brass-buttoned blue coat if he could direct us to cheaper lodgings.

He mentioned some boardinghouses and hotels in the Barbary Coast precinct, notorious for its dance halls, saloons, whorehouses — and violence. "Keep your eyes open, especially after dark, chances are you'll come out alive," he assured us, then resumed his patrol.

Jake scowled. "Not exactly a five-star recommendation."

"We don't have a five-star budget."

Following the constable's tip, we walked northwest, skirting Chinatown, where colorful Celestials hustled about their business amid exotic food smells wafting from open booths and pushcarts. As we zig-zagged along narrow streets, inhabitants and buildings grew seedier by the block.

Jake's eyes darted in search of lurking dangers among the gaunt, ragged men and women loitering in doorways and on corners. "I am not likin' the look of this."

"Maybe we find a cheap place for a night or two, meet Mike's friend at the Carlton, see where that leads?"

We stopped across the street from a two-story house with peeling yellow paint, and a sign over the door identifying it as the ironically named Grande Hotel. Honest to God, the place looked abandoned — until we heard shouts from inside, and two brawling men tumbled out onto the sidewalk.

A motley coven of Barbary Coast denizens scuttled from their dens and burrows, heckled the combatants and called out bets on the scuffle, as the smaller fighter snarled, "How many times I gotta tell ya — stop runnin' whores at the Grande!"

As if on cue, a half-dressed young woman flew out the hotel's front door and fled down the street, triggering the crowd's raucous laughter.

"I don't know about you," said Jake, "but I've seen enough."

"Me, too."

In rare brotherly agreement, we reversed course and abandoned the Barbary Coast.

3

"I have always been rather better treated in San Francisco than I actually deserved."
∼ Mark Twain

Kearney Street felt more welcoming, with its blocks of first-class restaurants and all manner of shops displaying stylish clothing, jewelry, silks, silver, china and other fine wares. In these more genteel parts of town, curved bay windows were a popular architectural feature on many buildings, since the city's fickle weather made sitting in a sunny bay window a better bet than shivering outdoors in a garden.

We turned onto Market Street, and there was the seven-story Hotel Carlton filling an entire square block. Dodging busy horse-drawn traffic across Market, we marched past carriages parked in the hotel's brick driveway, up the portico steps and in through etched-glass doors opened by a doorman in a royal blue uniform.

Monumental inside and out, the Carlton had only been open a year. The lobby featured palatial columns, arched windows and doorways, and a soaring atrium ringed by six levels of balconies. Ethereal sunlight filtered down through the expansive glass dome crowning the entire space. Twin marble staircases descended from the mezzanine level, framing a curved main desk where clerks and concierges saw to every need of their guests.

Bellhops and porters (some young white boys, others Chinese men) wearing gold-trimmed blue uniforms scurried back and forth like industrious ants. Plush furniture and Oriental rugs divided the grand space into intimate sitting areas. Heroic statuary, flowers and shrubs arrayed around a central fountain and murals of Western vistas made the lobby feel like a courtyard garden.

There were swanky shops on one side, and the well-appointed Market Street Tavern a few strides from the front desk. At the tavern's open entrance, a pianist in a swallowtail coat sat at a concert piano and entertained patrons and passersby with classical melodies.

With our budget in mind, we booked a

week's stay in one of the cheapest and smallest of the hotel's seven hundred rooms and suites. The clerk pointed across the lobby. "Stairs here. Elevators there."

Jake started toward the bank of four "rising rooms," as hydraulic elevators were called back when they were uncommon. We'd never seen one, much less ridden in one before.

I stopped. "Not so fast."

Jake stopped. "If you think I'm walking up three flights —"

Before we could resolve our standoff, a diminutive Chinese bellhop skittered across our path as a booming male voice called, "Hey! Boy! Bags. Over here. Now."

A fleeting hint of distress pinched the bellhop's face.

"Hey! Boy!" the voice bellowed again. The voice's owner, a fleshy man in a silk top hat and green frock coat, stood near the front desk with three enormous leather suitcases. He pounded the silver service bell five times in impatient succession.

"What's your name?" I murmured to the bellhop.

He bowed his head slightly. "Chen Ping, sir. Just Ping okay."

"Then he shouldn't call you 'boy' — it's rude."

"That is Mr. Chase," Ping said with a pained half smile. "Regular Carlton customer. As long as he tips, rude is okay with Ping."

"How much does he tip?" Jake asked.

"Four bits."

"For each suitcase?"

"For *all* suitcase."

"Well," Jake said, "how 'bout if we tip you a dollar — per bag."

The bellhop shuffled two steps toward the rich man. "So sorry, Mr. Chase. Ping already promise to help them."

He grabbed our carpetbags, led us to the elevators, and pressed the call button. Peeking into the dim elevator shaft through windows in the redwood safety doors, I heard an unsettling rattle of machinery as robust cables shuttled the cars up and down.

"I don't trust these things," I mumbled.

Ping looked up at me. "Very safe, sir. Legs appreciate."

"My baby brother's a little bit chicken," Jake confided to the bellhop.

"This," I said, "from a man afraid to ride a horse."

"Not afraid — I just don't like it."

"Never mind that riding in *this* thing can kill you."

"Ping just said it's safe."

"I'll take a horse over an elevator any day." Elevator Two arrived first. The safety doors and inner iron gate opened. Jake strode right on in. Ping followed. I grudgingly brought up the rear. I had to admit, the Otis Elevator Company had finished the cab like a refined drawing room — polished wood, scrolled trim, brass accents (including a corporate plaque too big to miss), and an overhead electric light in a crystal globe.

Jake glanced at the freckle-faced operator's engraved name badge. "Timothy . . . third floor, please. Believe it or not, this is our maiden voyage in one of these contraptions."

"Well, sir, you're in for a gravity-defying treat," Timothy said as he closed the gate with a clang, and rotated the crank handle on a control box bolted to the wall.

The car rose smoothly enough, accompanied by clickety-clanking and whirring from above. "Should it be making all that racket?" I asked.

"Don't worry, sir," Timothy said. "That means everything's working like it should." He brought us to a gentle, perfectly aligned stop at the third floor. "Here we are." He slid open the safety gate and I ducked out.

"Holy mackerel!" Jake said, too thrilled to move.

The call bell rang. "My cue, sir," Timothy said. "But I can see you want another ride. Going down?"

Jake nodded eagerly. I sighed and stepped back into the elevator. Timothy shut the gate and nudged the crank. The elevator dropped — and our stomachs did a surprise flapjack flip before settling.

Timothy grinned. "You'll get used to that."

We landed at the lobby and Timothy welcomed a wealthy older couple headed for the sixth floor. We rode all the way up, then down again to the third floor — where Jake still didn't want to leave. I wondered if our entire stay in San Francisco would consist of elevator rides.

Timothy opened the safety gate and Jake shook his hand. "Jake Galloway. My queasy brother is Jamey."

We left Timothy and followed Ping around a couple of corners to Room 310. He used his pass key, went in and set our bags down. As promised, Jake handed him two dollars.

"Thank you! You need anything, ask for Ping." With a formal little bow, he left and closed the door behind him.

Our room overlooked an alley at the rear of the building, where delivery wagons clattered in and out all day (which explained the bargain rate). The room measured sixteen feet on a side, with mahogany furniture and luxurious beds made up with floral quilts, feather pillows and downy white linens. Like every Carlton guest room, ours had a bay window, twelve-foot-high ceiling, bronze gas chandelier, fireplace, private wash-room (with a communal tub down the hall), even an electric call button to summon hotel staff — by far the grandest place we'd ever stayed.

We unpacked, then went down (by elevator) to eat at the Golden Gate Grill, a cozy restaurant in a corner of the lobby, known for fine food and newfangled electric lights. Our steak platters were worth every penny. Afterward, we stopped at the front desk and asked for Mr. Boone's room number.

The chief concierge (Mr. Nethercutt, according to his nameplate) was a thin man with a thin mustache perched over thin lips. "Sorry, gentlemen. By Carlton policy, the privacy of our guests is sacrosanct. If you'd care to leave a note for Mr. Boone, I shall have it delivered."

He provided paper, pen, and inkwell, and I wrote a short letter introducing us as Mississippi Mike Morgan's friends. I tucked it into an envelope, gave it to Nethercutt, and asked if he could direct us to any poker games at the hotel.

"Certainly, Mr. Galloway. There are several gentlemen who convene Wednesday, Friday and Saturday evenings at eight in the Sequoia Parlor, second floor near the Grand Ballroom."

"Might they welcome new players?"

"There may be an empty seat or two. Mr. Boone often attends, so you may encounter him there — if he has returned from his latest travels."

We thanked him, and since it was Friday, we set our sights on that game that evening.

4

"Everybody makes mistakes — and every mistake has a lesson to teach us."
∼ Victoria Krieg

It's a big world, and the odds of any few lives intersecting are steep. So I have to believe it was either random chance or dumb luck that set Victoria Krieg, Eddie Lobo, and the Galloway brothers on a collision course.

See, Jake and me weren't the only ones who'd taken a powder from Texas. About that same time, as Wilhelm Krieg's empire crumbled, his observant daughter Victoria sized up her father's well-deserved misfortune, and decided to escape from his self-inflicted destiny. Taking a sack filled with jewelry she'd inherited from the mother who'd died giving birth to her, and more glittering gifts given to her by her father, Victoria traveled light and pointed her white

Arabian stallion Lucifer west. Dodging trouble as they traversed almost two thousand miles, they reached San Francisco in May, a few weeks after me and my brother had arrived.

She needed to find employment fast, or she'd be forced to sell off her family treasure faster than she'd intended. So she visited all the city's riding and racing establishments in search of any kind of job working with horses — and every trainer and owner she met scoffed at the notion that this pretty little gal might be worth hiring.

Running out of options, she rode Lucifer on one drizzly day to the Bay View Race Course five miles south of town. Nevada City mining millionaire George Hearst had been the principal investor in the track and surrounding park, hotel, stables, and bulkheads to protect against the tide, all constructed during the Civil War on reclaimed marshland.

Close to calling it one more hopeless day and retreating to her seedy downtown boardinghouse, Victoria providentially witnessed one of Eduardo Lobo's horses finishing dead last in a race where the other six entries were far from noteworthy. That particular afternoon, big, tall Eddie looked as hunched and bedraggled as his horse and jockey, who'd both suffered the indignity of having mud flung into their faces while trailing from start to finish.

In fact, it was that very woebegone condition that drew Victoria's attention. "So, he's a palomino under all that dirt," she quipped, introducing herself to the dispirited owner as he and his filthy horse trudged back to their barn.

Eddie confessed to being a racing novice, and doubted he'd ever know enough about Thoroughbreds to saddle a winner. "Maybe Phoenix just doesn't have the fire."

"Oh, he's got fire," Victoria said. "What he needs is training."

"But great horses wanna win so bad, you can see it in their eyes — it's a little scary. What if he don't wanna win bad enough?"

"How badly do *you* want to win?"

"Real bad."

"Well, all I see in your eyes is sad." She kept expecting the big man to run her off. But he didn't, so she continued walking and talking. "Look, if he was really terrible, he wouldn't be this dirty."

"How do you mean?"

"Would you want to run head-on into a mud storm?"

"I reckon not."

"Me, neither. If Phoenix had no stomach

for it, he would've fallen way behind, real fast. He would've still finished last, but he'd be a lot cleaner. He never flinched or quit. Horses like him were born to run — if someone can teach him how."

"I can barely afford feed. Where am I gonna find somebody like that?"

"You're looking at her." Never short on gumption, Victoria said straight out that she'd never trained an actual racehorse before. But that didn't stop her from guaranteeing she could get *this* horse to finish in the money within a month.

Figuring he had nothing to lose, Eddie offered her a meager salary, grub, a bunk at his farm — and half their winnings as incentive. "Which, right now, is half of nothing."

"That'll change."

With a handshake to seal the deal, Victoria helped Eddie and his stable boy pack up his two horses and gear. That's when they noticed that her ornery Arabian Lucifer and affable Phoenix seemed to hit it off. With the horses in side-by-side stalls in the livestock car, they all took the train south. On the way, Victoria learned in detail how poorly Eddie's first racing season had gone, which explained his desperation.

They got off at Redwood City, a tidy village with four church steeples and two thousand residents living there in the official seat of San Mateo County. With saddles and gear transferred to a wagon, the racehorses tied behind, and Victoria riding Lucifer alongside, they drove to Fernando Farms in the green hills a few miles outside town.

Victoria expected to spend her first few days there taking stock of Eddie's undertrained horses, but no sooner had they arrived than her plans hit a brick wall named Samuel Batts, Eddie's foreman. A stooped and taciturn black man with white hair, he hobbled about on a bum leg and a hand-carved cane, barking orders at harried ranch-hands.

Victoria expected he'd also be barking at her. While she'd never allow anyone to treat her like a servant, the old foreman didn't seem to be a man who cottoned to insubordination. Raising a ruckus just to make a point could end this endeavor before it started, so she resolved to bite her tongue as much as she could stand.

That determination lasted only as long as it took for Samuel to throw the first verbal jab: "No way, no how this li'l white girl could possibly know nuthin' about training horses."

Victoria counterpunched. "From seeing

your best horse run, Mr. Batts, it appears that y'all are already experts at knowing nothing about training horses."

The old man's eyebrows danced a huffy little jig. "Why, I been tendin' horses since way before you was born —"

"And I bet I can learn a lot from you. I also bet I'll get better racing results."

Eddie gave Samuel a hangdog look. "We can't do worse."

"Why do horses run?" Victoria asked them.

"Because we tell 'em to," Samuel said, like it was obvious.

She shook her head. "Horses are too big to *tell* 'em anything."

Eddie squinted. "So, why *do* they run?"

"If you're a horse, you're fast. When you're scared, what's the safest thing to do?"

"Run?"

Victoria nodded. "Nothing feels better than feeling safe. So running feels good — the faster, the better."

"You the boss, Eddie," said Samuel before he shrugged and limped away.

"Trust me, he grows on you," Eddie said to Victoria.

"He doesn't want me here."

"But I do."

With Eddie's vote of confidence, Victoria

got to work appraising the Fernando Farms horses and jockeys. She also learned bits and pieces of Eddie's story. Not from Eddie, who didn't seem much inclined to talking about himself, but from the men who worked with him, including his top jockey Rafael Cabrera, and even from Samuel Batts.

The farm had been founded by Eddie's grandfather Fernando Lobo, who'd moved his family north from Mexico looking for a better life. Fernando first worked for a wealthy land-grant *ranchero,* and then bought enough property from his employer to start his own small *rancho* in 1839. Eddie's father Pablo took over after Fernando's death in 1850, a year after Eddie was born (which made him a little younger than me and Jake).

In addition to earning renown for raising fine riding and working horses, Pablo also began breeding Thoroughbreds. But misfortune continued dogging the Lobos — Eddie's mother Sofia died in 1859, when her boy was only ten. And eleven years later, when their main barn caught fire, Eddie's father raced in and out, saving as many horses as he could. As embers flew and beams burned, Pablo rushed in to rescue one last horse — but the roof fell in, killing him and his favorite mare.

At the age of twenty-one, Eddie found himself an orphan, in charge — and not at all sure he could carry on. He knew he owed it to his ancestors to try, and leaned on the man his beloved *papi* had trusted — Samuel Batts.

As an olive branch, Victoria also asked the old foreman about himself, and Samuel seemed appreciative. He told her how he'd been born a slave in 1824, and how his early affinity for horses earned him an apprenticeship in the stables of William Ransom Johnson's Oakland Plantation in Virginia. Known as the "Napoleon of the Turf," the silver-haired Johnson owned many of the greatest racehorses of the age. The Old Dominion State was the center of American racing at the time, and Johnson was its reigning emperor.

When Samuel turned twenty, Johnson allowed him to buy his freedom as a reward for years of stouthearted service. Working his way to northern California by 1849, he hired on with Fernando Lobo, who soon made him foreman. And Samuel had worked for the Lobo family ever since.

From then on, Victoria made a point of treating Samuel with the deference he'd earned along a hard road she couldn't even imagine. She understood she'd have to prove her worth. To his credit, Samuel in turn became less cantankerous, and let her do the job Eddie hired her for.

But she harbored her own secret self-doubts — could she actually deliver on her bold promise? And if she failed, what then? For all Eddie knew, he'd bought the proverbial pig in a poke. So much was out of her hands. All she could do was focus on the only thing under her control — doing the work.

She trained not only the horses, but also taught Rafael and two other even less experienced jockeys to better understand the animals they rode. A skinny *mestizo* (of Mexican and Indian descent) with big strong hands, Rafael in particular had great potential. Cocky but unschooled, the fearless twenty-year-old had been orphaned at twelve and taken in by Eddie's father, who raised the boys together like mismatched brothers. Pablo must have seen in Rafael then what Victoria saw now — a kid with a raw gift for riding fast horses.

He also proved to be a quick study, and told Victoria he was grateful to have someone correct his errors. "Nobody ever done that for me before."

"Everybody makes mistakes," she said,

"and every mistake has a lesson to teach us. That's how we learn to do better."

Victoria's worries eased when all three jockeys achieved ever-faster practice times, giving *rancho* morale a welcome boost. But, like they say, the proof of the pudding is in the eating — the only results that really mattered would come in actual races, with especially high hopes pinned on golden palomino Phoenix, the pride of Fernando Farms.

They got their answer ahead of a schedule that always seemed improbable, if not impossible. Only three weeks after Victoria started, Rafael steered Phoenix to a close second-place finish at Bay View. Two days later, they beat a solid field of seven for an easy win.

Victoria's training skills continued to deliver surprising success throughout the summer. Not only did Phoenix manage a string of wins against strong competition at the city's major tracks, but Victoria even coaxed money finishes from Eddie's lesser horses.

The rise of Phoenix culminated with three commanding victories at the Ocean Course on the peninsula's less developed western outskirts. When that track first opened in May of 1865, eight thousand spectators had shown up — more than any previous California sporting event — to witness an epic endurance contest of three two-mile heats between a pair of great Kentucky Thoroughbreds named Lodi and Norfolk.

Why, even Mark Twain reported in the weekly San Francisco literary journal *The Californian* that the matchup had awakened "extraordinary attention all over the Pacific coast, and even far away in the Atlantic States. I saw that if I failed to see this race I might live a century, perhaps, without ever having an opportunity to see its equal."

Doomed by its remote location, the Ocean Course never lived up to that early promise. Sparse attendance would lead to its demise by the end of 1873. But it lasted long enough for Phoenix to draw the attention of Eastern interloper Cortland Van Brunt III, whose horses were among the losers Phoenix left behind.

After his third confounding loss, Van Brunt strode up to Eddie in the paddock and offered to buy Phoenix for ten thousand dollars. "Which is not chicken feed," Van Brunt emphasized.

Eddie grinned like that was the craziest thing he'd ever heard. "Sorry, sir. Not for sale."

Van Brunt held his ground, his bandy legs

set in a wide stance. He made a pompous show of clearing his throat, as if preparing to deliver a ringing oration. "You don't know this about me, son. But when I set my sights on a thing, I get it, by hook or by —"

"He's not a thing," Victoria interrupted. "He's a horse — Eddie's horse."

"For now, li'l lady," Van Brunt said. "And aren't you a pretty bit o' calico. You two youngsters are the youth of America, by which I mean you are the future, and since you have not been at the game as long as I have, I shall do you the favor of passing along a lesson I have learned over a lengthy span of being alive." Van Brunt wagged his gnarled finger at Victoria. "The long and short of it is, never make predictions — especially about the future. And you can look that up."

Vic really wanted to snap Van Brunt's finger like a dry twig, but she managed to restrain herself long enough for him to tip his hat and walk away. "I guarantee you," she said to Eddie, "he thinks the sun rises just to hear him crow. Somebody oughta hobble that man's lip."

"Aww, he don't mean anything by it."

"I know exactly what he means. I know how rich men think."

"What makes you so sure?"

"Growing up with my father — our family motto was, 'Nobody says no to a Krieg.' Van Brunt's no different."

"Well, he can't make me sell a horse I aim to keep."

"There's more than one way to skin a cat — or get a horse. Don't underestimate him, Eddie."

"You worry too much."

"And you don't worry enough."

5

> "Remember, boys, it's a bugger-or-be-buggered world."
> ~ Leander Foley,
> Comstock Lode Silver King

After a tasty roasted chicken supper at the Golden Gate Grill, we went to find that poker game the concierge told us about. Even though we were only going up one floor, Jake insisted on taking the elevator. I wasn't in a mood to argue.

Elevator Two in Timothy's capable hands happened to be empty. "Timothy," I said, "God's honest truth now, do these things ever come crashing down?"

"They *used* to —"

"Ha!" I sneered at my brother.

"Let him finish," he jeered right back.

Timothy continued, speechifying like an elevator evangelist as we went up. "They *used* to — that is, until Mr. Elisha Otis invented the safety brake. Why, he even put on a death-defying demonstration at the New York World's Fair back in '53. The Otis safety brake saved the day, and made tall buildings possible."

"Mr. Otis was pretty sure of himself," I said.

"If he wasn't, we'd be climbing a lot more stairs."

Leaving the elevator, we passed a billiards room, peeked into the Grand Ballroom with gilded chandeliers suitable for Buckingham Palace, and found the Sequoia Parlor. An airy space with bay windows, it was furnished with armchairs and couches, and featured a well-provisioned bar (with bartender), landscape murals, and sideboards for serving food. Three tables near the windows were inlaid with mosaic chess boards and set with sculpted ivory and onyx pieces.

A pair of round poker tables dominated the center, and five rich men in their forties and fifties were in the process of gathering around one of them. Their designated dealer shuffled a deck with light-fingered proficiency. Matched stacks of poker chips towered at each seat.

"Gentlemen," I said, "may we join you?"

The slender dealer had muttonchop side-whiskers so bushy they doubled the width of his face. "Elijah Greenberg, at your service," he said with an amiable grin and a slight European accent.

"Jamey Galloway. This is my brother Jake."

Greenberg introduced his companions, all wearing flawlessly tailored suits. To help me remember their names, I paired each man with his physical attributes:

"Rufus Ambrose" — portly, clean-shaven.

"John Wilkinson" — tall and heavy-set, silver beard, bald head.

"Leander Foley" — short and spindly, his mustache flowing into his muttonchops.

"Otto Rewer" — walrus mustache and a tuft on his chin.

We shook hands and they took our measure. What they saw were two fellows in their mid-twenties, broad-shouldered Jake with his fair face and chestnut curls, me slimmer with a darker complexion, wavy black hair, and a horseshoe mustache. We did our best to present ourselves as sophisticated, and probably fell short.

"What brings you to our little game?" Rufus Ambrose asked.

I explained we were new in town and hoping to find Nathan Hale Boone. "Do you gentlemen know him?"

"We know him well," Wilkinson said. "Are

you boys friends of his?"

"Actually, we've never met him. A mutual friend told us to make his acquaintance."

Leander Foley returned to the table with a drink. "Sound advice. Nathan knows his way around the city. And, unlike we who work eight days a week, he seems to be a man of leisure."

"That is," Rewer said, "when he's not traveling on mysterious 'business' missions."

"What exactly does he do?" Jake asked.

Our hosts shared a chuckle. "Whatever it is," Ambrose said, "it pays well, since he lives like a sultan in a Carlton suite. But nobody rightly knows."

"And nobody rightly cares," dealer Elijah Greenberg said, "since he's excellent company."

"Are you boys rich?" Rewer asked us.

"We got aspirations," Jake said.

"Because *we're* all rich," Rewer said. "Not that we started out that way — we all came here in the '40s with hardly two nickels to rub together. But we nabbed opportunity by the balls. Now, here I am, a real estate developer. I knock down trees and put up buildings."

Jake thought for a second. "What if you run outta trees?"

"Then I'll knock down mountains. Wilkinson here, corporate lawyer, knows where the bodies are buried. Greenberg with the fast fingers owns the biggest department store in the city. Ambrose is a banker, so you know he's rich. And 'Little' Foley here made the biggest fortune of all from the Comstock Lode."

"So," Foley said, "are you boys rich enough to buy into our friendly little game?"

"How much?" I asked.

"A thousand each," banker Ambrose said.

"We can swing that," I said, despite the dent that would put in our bankroll.

Greenberg smiled. "Then pull up a chair."

"Remember, boys," Foley said as Greenberg dealt the first hand, "it's a bugger or be buggered world."

Over the course of the evening, we learned that they all lived in exclusive Nob Hill mansions, alongside such luminaries as former governor Leland Stanford and his three fellow founders of the Central Pacific Railroad — Mark Hopkins, Collis Huntington, and Charles Crocker. Our cordial new poker pals had all arrived in San Francisco at the start of the famous Gold Rush of 1848 and '49, when San Francisco was nothing more than an encampment of eight hundred souls.

By 1850, hordes of prospectors had transformed it into a city of twenty-five thousand. And there were indeed fortunes to be made — not from sifting for the color in the creeks, but by selling the goods and services all those new Californians needed.

A few years after the Gold Rush went bust, miners struck the Comstock Lode straddling the California-Utah Territory border, near Lake Tahoe. That celebrated silver bonanza drew not only miners, but all manner of speculators, bankers, and investors. Even though San Francisco was two hundred and fifty miles away from the Comstock Lode beehive and boomtowns like Virginia City, it was the nearest seaport, so savvy San Franciscans made a killing, and the city kept growing.

Our wealthy *compadres* weren't exactly terrible at poker, but like most gamblers in my experience they fancied themselves better than they really were. While Jake played with his usual reckless relish, I spent the first few hands taking stock of their various unwitting tendencies and tells. I could've picked their pockets clean, but I'd have felt like a spoilsport doing that to men who gambled more for fellowship and fun than profit. I also didn't want to risk making a sour first impression — which might get back to our potential benefactor, Mr. Boone.

For now, this was literally the only game in town for me and Jake, at least until we found others away from the hotel. Not only did these hospitable robber barons make us feel welcome, but by the time they called it a night around ten, we'd won enough to make us happy — and not enough to make enemies.

"You have definite promise as a poker player, son," Foley said to me.

Jake almost snorted his whiskey out his nose.

Just then, a dark-haired man in a cream frock coat and gold brocade vest entered the parlor. "It's Boone!" Foley announced. "At long last!"

"Sincere apologies, gentlemen," Nathan Hale Boone said. His genial baritone resonated with a velvety growl. "Sometimes the trains simply do not run on time."

As Mr. Boone greeted them, Elijah Greenberg confided to me, "When it comes to poker, Foley is a chowderhead, as I'm sure you noticed. You went easy on us, no?"

I was the very soul of wide-eyed innocence. "Who — me?"

Greenberg chuckled. "You are welcome any time, because you are young *mensches* who did not take advantage of *schmucks* with too much money and too little sense."

Mr. Boone overheard our exchange. "Is that true?" he asked me with a twinkle in his eye. "You didn't clean out these rich bastards when you had the chance?"

"Afraid not, sir."

"Then you boys must be Jamey and Jake Galloway. Mississippi Mike's brief description of you hit the bullseye."

Mr. Boone wasn't exceptionally big, but his powerful handshake and the fit of his custom-tailored coat across his shoulders hinted at coiled strength. He appeared to be around forty, with a precisely barbered mustache and a throaty laugh. As his friends made their exit, he held up a liquor bottle. "I can't coax you aristocrats into a sip of this excellent Cognac, fresh from St. Louis?"

"Our wives would have our heads," Wilkinson said.

"Worse," Ambrose said in mock horror, "they might ask how much we lose at these games."

After they left, Mr. Boone grabbed three glasses from the bar with one big hand, motioned us to leather wing chairs, and poured that very expensive liquor. I stopped him before he filled the third glass.

"I don't really drink, Mr. Boone . . . sir."

"This is the good stuff, kid — imported from France." He glanced at Jake. "He really doesn't drink?"

Jake shook his head. "That's 'cuz our daddy was a mean drunk, Mr. Boone, sir. When we were little, one night he held a big ol' knife to our throats. Mama had to shoot him dead."

"Well, that is a commendable if tragic reason for abstaining," Mr. Boone said with sympathy. "You stick to your guns, Jamey."

"He doesn't like guns either," Jake said with an embarrassed eyeroll.

"I can't imagine a more traumatic night for you boys. Jake, you're okay with drinking, and guns?"

"He's too thick-headed to be traumatized, Mr. Boone, sir," I said.

Boone smiled. "Mississippi Mike didn't tell me you boys were so entertaining." He noticed Jake about to gulp his drink and stopped him. "Jake! You *savor* that Cognac — as you would the company of a lovely woman."

Jake complied, and asked Mr. Boone how he happened to know Mike.

"We've tilted at some windmills and righted some wrongs together. But I've always marveled at Mike's congregation of friends from coast to coast. Did you know he's old chums with Sam Clemens?"

My eyes popped. "*Mark Twain* Sam Clemens?!?"

"Mm-hmm. They met back in the late '50s, when Mike was gambling on riverboats and Sam was a young pilot."

Now that was something I'd have to ask Mississippi Mike about someday.

"Tomorrow," Mr. Boone said, "I'll give you a proper introduction to this great city. Meet me in the lobby at ten sharp."

Next morning, we reported early, and Mr. Boone insisted that we stop addressing him as "Mr. Boone, sir," which he found much too formal. Despite his invitation to simply call him Nathan, that felt insufficiently respectful. I suggested "Mr. B," and we agreed on that.

Over the next week, he gave us a comprehensive tour of town by foot and street-car. He showed us his favorite restaurants and shops. His tailor treated us like princes. His banker opened an account for us. Florists, confectioners, booksellers, shoemakers, tobacconists, tavern-keepers — all knew him by name, and by reputation as a man who spent wisely for the finer things.

He shared our enjoyment of the booming sport of baseball, and we frequented games played at the verdant Recreation Grounds in the Mission District. We sampled the best entertainment spots — pubs and clubs; dance and music halls; and grand theatres where artists from far and wide performed classical and popular music, opera, ballet, and plays old and new.

In general, Mr. B struck an admirable balance — honoring history and tradition, yet embracing the innovations of an ever-changing world. The city and the Carlton felt more and more like home, and we wrote Mississippi Mike (who had relocated to Baltimore and resumed his long-dormant law practice) to thank him for steering us toward the hotel and Mr. Boone.

We soon felt confident enough to navigate on our own. Mr. B and his Carlton poker buddies referred us to other games around town, where I could play with less restraint — although I still avoided winnings so extravagant as to make us unwelcome. As our bank account grew, we moved to a bigger Carlton room with a better view.

Another indulgence — a couple of meals each week at the Eden Terrace, the peerless restaurant occupying much of the Carlton's top floor. Built around the hotel's extraordinary central atrium, the restaurant was renowned for superlative international cuisine, conjured by chefs who capitalized on coastal proximity for their signature catch-of-the-day seafood. The only way to get it fresher would be dining on a fishing boat.

As if ambrosial food wasn't enough, the Eden Terrace's crowning glory was its clear dome consisting of 70,000 individual glass panes, granting the lords and ladies of San Francisco's high society an awesome view of the sky's red dawns, bold blues, and golden sunsets. An Eden Terrace meal with sterling-silver cutlery chiming against crystal and gold-rimmed china was always worth the expense.

It wasn't unusual for San Francisco's weather to cycle through three seasons in a day, skipping only winter, which was fine with us. Even in blazing summer sun, sea and bay breezes tamed the heat. And on one particular Saturday evening in early September, cool air wafted through the Sequoia Parlor's windows as we played poker with Mr. B and friends.

Despite Jake's usual poker malpractice, the cards kept going his way.

"Jake has an unusual advantage," Mr. B joked. "He plays with such careless abandon, it's impossible to tell when he's bluffing."

Nobody noticed the young woman gliding into the parlor until her gloved hand grazed Jake's shoulder. "Why, 'Mr. Dilmore,' " she purred with a winsome Texas twang, "fancy meetin' you here."

Months after we'd successfully rescued Serenity Falls from Wilhelm Krieg's greedy hands, we had no reason to think we'd ever hear Jake's *nom de guerre* again. Yet, there it was, spoken by a sultry voice we recognized instantly . . .

6

> "This may be a big country,
> but it's a small world."
> ~ Victoria Krieg

We looked up to see a vision in sapphire satin — elegant, alluring Victoria Krieg and her sassy smile.

Jake tossed his cards down. "Deal me out, boys."

Silver king Leander Foley rubbed his hands together. "You have an alias! I bet there's a juicy story to be told."

"And maybe I'll tell it sometime," Jake said as he slid his chair back. "Just not tonight."

"Victoria Krieg," I said, "how did you find us?"

"Well, 'Mr. Hollister,' " she began.

"Ha! Another alias," Foley cackled. "The plot thickens!"

"I spied the two of you in the lobby one

day," Victoria said, "and found myself thinking, 'This may be a big country, but it's a small world.' I asked at the front desk if they could tell me your room, but — hotel policy and all."

"You strike me as a lady who doesn't take no for an answer," said Foley.

Victoria batted her eyelashes. "Well, sir, I did keep asking around. Eventually, that nice bellhop Ping said he knew you as true gentlemen — but not by the names Dayton Dilmore and Levi Hollister. He told me I could probably find you two playing poker — and here you are." She kissed Jake on the cheek. "Y'all don't mind my stealin' 'Mr. Dilmore' away, do you?"

"Well, he is unaccountably winning tonight," Foley said. "But there's no stopping young love."

"Thank you, gentlemen," Victoria said, taking my brother by the hand and towing him out the door.

With an amused arch of his eyebrows, Mr. B watched them go and quoted *A Midsummer Night's Dream:* " 'For aught that I ever could read, could ever hear by tale or history, the course of true love never did run smooth.' "

"The story of Jake's life," I said.

"He has no idea he's in *way* over his head

with that young lady, does he?"

"He's usually the last to know."

Without a word between them, Victoria led Jake up to her room on the fourth floor. She opened her door, gave him a toe-curling kiss, steered him inside, and bumped the door shut with her hip. Then, when he expected a second kiss, she bit his lip instead.

"Oww! What was that for?"

"For ruining my father," she said in an icy voice.

"Y-you knew?"

"I pieced it together — and not that he didn't deserve it." Victoria waltzed Jake into a backward retreat around the room, much to her amusement. "So, what *is* your real name, 'Dayton Dilmore'?"

"Like Ping told you," he said, trying to avoid tripping over furniture. "It's Jake Galloway."

"Your partner in crime?"

"My brother Jamey."

She continued her advance. "That was some inventive flimflam you two pulled on my father and brother."

"We had some help." Jake found himself backed into a corner. "I'm confused. Are you mad at me? Or not?"

She raised her hand. He flinched, expecting a slap across his face. Instead, she tilted his chin down and kissed him. "Poppa had it coming, from somebody, somewhere, sometime."

"And somebody else might've killed him," Jake pointed out in our defense.

"There's that. Y'all made a fool of him over money, and that's his own fault."

"Like our friend Mississippi Mike says, it ain't leadin' a man into temptation if he's already memorized the map."

"And y'all did it to save Serenity Falls, not to line your own pockets . . . which makes you a little bit intriguing."

Jake brightened. "And you like your fellas smart — ?"

"Not *too* smart."

"Then I'm your man."

"I'll bet you are."

She pushed Jake back onto the bed, climbed up and straddled him. And that's how they picked up where they'd left off months earlier — only, on a comfortable hotel bed instead of a saddle blanket in a grassy Texas glade, they wouldn't end up with thistles in their hair. Victoria leaned in to kiss him.

But Jake raised his hand to stop her. "Hold on. If your poppa had it coming —"

"You've got *me* — *here* — *now* . . . and you want to talk about my father?"

"Well, when you put it that way — never mind."

"Without your brazen railroad scheme," she said between soft kisses, "I might never've left Texas. And then where would we be?"

"Not here. Not now."

"Wouldn't that be a shame?"

"Yes, ma'am."

For the next day or so, that's pretty much what they did and where they did it, keeping their strength up with room service food. Over a generous Sunday breakfast, they traded tales of how they'd each ended up in San Francisco. Victoria had left Texas soon after we did, riding away from her father's ranch with her horse and her cache of treasure.

"My father bought my mother quite a lot of jewelry," she said, nibbling her omelet. "His way of trying to make up for dragging Felicity from civilized Philadelphia to the wilds of Texas."

Jake remembered from when they'd first met how Victoria referred to the mother who had died giving birth to her not as "Mama" but by her name.

"I never knew her. I had no memories of

65

her," she said. "But I inherited her jewelry — plus what my father bought me, without much thought to what a little girl needs. So I took that easy-to-carry fortune with me when I left."

"And you just up and sold it?"

"I keep it in a bank vault. Sell some as I need to."

"No sentimental value?"

A rare sadness welled up in Victoria's eyes. "Maybe if I could picture Felicity wearing her jewels, but . . . I can't. So the only value is what someone else is willing to pay for it."

"What about the jewelry he gave you?"

"I'd have traded all of it for him seeing me as *me* . . . and not a shadow of Felicity. But, in a way, he did me a favor."

"How?"

"He spent his time building his empire. My brother Wolf was expected to be part of that. I wasn't. So he hired nannies and tutors to raise me. And every chance I got, I'd escape."

"Didn't that get you in trouble?"

"My caretakers were so afraid he'd dismiss them that they didn't report my criminal mischief."

"And where'd you run off to?"

"Our stables, of course."

"You and my brother," Jake said. "What is it with y'all and horses?"

"From the first horse I ever saw, I knew they were God's best creation. So I'd sneak out to the stables and corrals, and torture the wranglers with questions. And they'd lasso me and carry me back to the house."

"And you'd escape again."

Victoria laughed. "Oh, it was so much fun! Eventually, the nannies and tutors gave up."

"And the wranglers?"

"I was the rancher's motherless waif. They were terrified of his temper — and afraid I might shatter like a fragile teacup."

Jake cocked a dubious eyebrow. "You? Fragile?"

"They eventually figured out I was sturdier than I looked. And, as you've heard, nobody says —"

"— says no to a Krieg," Jake recited along with her, recalling her family's imperious motto.

"So they started teaching me about horses, and swearing. I came to believe that's why my mother was taken away, and why I was put on Earth."

"To learn how to cuss?"

"No, silly. To be with horses."

"Your father never found out?"

"The cattle king was too busy to know

67

what I was up to, but he finally got fed up with all the nannies and tutors quitting. That's when he packed me off to the Franklin Christian Girls School in Philadelphia."

"I'm guessing they couldn't tame you either . . . ?"

"They started taking us for lessons at a riding academy a mile away."

"And you started sneaking away from school —"

"— when I should've been studying. For months, I traded stall mucking and horse brushing for riding and training lessons with the stable owner, Mr. Roberts. At least until I got caught."

"Then what happened?"

"They expelled me and sent me home."

"Is that when you got Lucifer?"

"Mm-hmm. Four years ago, I talked Poppa into taking me to a horse auction, where I saw this wild, white Arabian. It took three men hanging onto ropes for dear life to keep him under control! He should've been worth a fortune, except nobody could get near him."

"Except you?"

She smiled at the memory. "They tried to keep me away. I guess they were afraid he'd trample me. So I stood outside the fence watching, while he kicked and bucked and tossed his beautiful mane. The second our eyes met, he calmed right down. He's the only gift my father ever gave me that mattered."

"What does Lucifer think about being a city horse after life on the open range?"

"Oh, he's not really a city horse."

"Why? Where do you keep him?"

"Out where I live when I'm not here."

"You mean you don't live here at the Carlton all the time?" Jake pouted like a kid who'd just found out somebody canceled Christmas.

"I'd have to sell way more jewelry to afford that. So I stay here from time to time, when I feel like being pampered, or seeing a show, or shopping."

"Where are you the rest of the time?"

"I'll show you tomorrow."

7

"I'm not afraid of storms, for I'm learning how to sail my ship."
~ Amy in *Little Women,* by Louisa May Alcott

Monday's dawn light peeked through the curtains of our hotel room. I heard a key in the lock, and Jake tiptoed in. Nobody had laid eyes on him since he and Victoria left the poker parlor Saturday evening.

"I was about to send out a search party," I said.

Jake grinned. "Rise and shine. We got a busy day today."

"Doing what?"

"Taking a trip."

"To where?"

"Horse farm."

I squinted. "Why? You hate horses."

"Because it's Vic's horse farm."

"She owns a horse farm?" I sat up and

scratched my unkempt hair.

"No, she works there."

"Doing what?"

"Training racehorses. Let's go!" He yanked the covers off me. "We got a train to catch."

The notion of Jake voluntarily being around a bunch of cantankerous Thoroughbreds promised to be at least a little entertaining for me, if not for him. So we washed, dressed, and headed down to the lobby.

We found Victoria playing a quiet classical piece on the tavern's piano. Wearing britches, her long hair woven into a neat French braid, she had a basket of fruits, biscuits, and pastries from the Golden Gate Grill. We three raced to the railroad depot a few blocks from the hotel and caught a Southern Pacific train to Redwood City, about twenty-eight miles south of San Francisco.

During the ninety-minute ride, Vic told us how she'd come to know Eddie Lobo, and how their partnership had bloomed into a friendship. The warmth in her voice when she talked about Eddie plainly rattled Jake. He couldn't help wondering behind his frown if she and Eddie were more than business partners, and I admit I had the same thought.

When the train stopped at Redwood City, we got off and crossed the street to the livery where Vic picked up a horse and buggy and drove us to Eddie's place west of town. The lure of such pretty terrain, coupled with convenient railroad service, had already convinced a passel of San Franciscans to build sizable country "cottages" out thataway.

Vic turned our buggy through the wooden arch at the entrance to Fernando Farms and up a rutted lane. We heard the percussion of hammers and the snarl of saws chewing through wood. Among the weathered buildings, we saw a big barn in final stages of construction. A white-haired black man hobbling on a cane snapped orders at four young Mexicans cutting lumber and nailing up planks.

"With this season's winnings," Vic said, "Eddie could finally afford to replace the barn that burned down. That's Samuel — Eddie couldn't run the place without him." She waved to the foreman and hollered: "Where's Eddie?"

Samuel pointed with his cane. "Out back, workin' with the baby."

Vic kept the horses moving up the gentle slope toward a ramshackle farmhouse, barns, and corrals, with a fenced pasture and practice track beyond. "When it comes to horses, there's not much Samuel doesn't know — except training. Takes a big man to 'fess up to being wrong."

"When did he come around?" I asked. "When Phoenix finished second?"

Vic snorted. "Nope — called it beginner's luck. It took Phoenix winning his next *three* races for Samuel to admit I *might* know something he didn't."

She parked the buggy near the two older barns. Eddie came out, sleeves rolled up, a ratty straw hat on his head, and a lanky tri-color hound dog ambling by his side. A boyish grin lit his sun-bronzed face when he saw Victoria.

He reached up with hands the size of dinner plates, lifted her without effort, and set her down on the ground. They greeted each other with a hug that seemed a notch beyond friendship, and Vic introduced us. Keep in mind, me and Jake each stood right about six-foot-tall, but we felt like small fry next to Eddie. For all his imposing size, the gap between his front teeth made him look like an overgrown kid.

"Pleased to meet you," I said. "Vic's told us a lot about you."

The dog stuck her nose up in the air, and bayed a full-throated "Baaa-*roooo!*"

"That's hound for howdy," Eddie translated, smiling down at her big brown eyes. "Olivia here is a pretty good judge of character, and livin' proof animals are the best people."

"Ain't that the truth, girl," I said as I skritched her floppy brown ears. Olivia sat on my foot and leaned against my leg to show her approval.

"So, how's he doing?" Vic asked Eddie with a nod toward the barn.

"Oh, you know how he mopes when you're gone."

Victoria led us into the barn, down the center aisle to the back row of stalls, and turned left to the tune of a horse complaining loudly. "Looocifer — mama's home!" she crooned, and he quieted right down.

But the instant Jake heard the horse's name, his face blanched. I slapped him on the back. "Ain't that the horse that scared the crap outta you?"

Vic laughed. "Jake didn't get singled out. Lucifer doesn't like many, especially men."

"He tolerates me," Eddie said, "sorta."

Vic turned to me. "So Jake told you —"

"— how Lucifer terrorized him? Yes, ma'am. But Jake's not exactly a horse person."

"Gee, I hadn't noticed," she teased.

Jake wasn't amused. "Okay, smart guy," he said to me, "we'll see how much he likes you."

The white stallion reared in his stall when he saw all of us, then quickly settled down and nuzzled Vic over the gate. She touched my shoulder. "Lucifer, this is Jamey."

I approached — within biting range. Lucifer seemed steady enough, as if he sensed my affinity for horses. He was real handsome, and big for an Arabian. He had the broad forehead, large eyes and nostrils, and almost delicate muzzle typical of the breed, along with their distinctive dished profile.

I held my hand out, fingers curled under in case he decided to chomp. But all he did was snort and snuffle. He lowered his head, a sign of deference, inviting me to pet him just above his charcoal nose.

"Hey," Jake complained, "how come he likes Jamey?"

"Because," I said, "he knows a true horse person when he smells one."

Two seconds later, Lucifer swung his big, hard head and knocked me flat on my conceited ass. My noggin thumped against the soft dirt, and I saw stars. As I reset my senses, both Lucifer and the palomino in the next stall hung their heads over their doors, and had a good horse laugh at my expense.

Jake snickered. "You were saying, Mr. True Horse Person?"

Vic gave me a hand up. I dusted off my pants and my pride.

"Lucifer can be a bit fickle," she said.

"So I see."

Vic kissed the placid palomino on his nose and he answered with a contented whinny. "This sweetie-pie is Phoenix. He's our best racehorse — maybe the best in California — and he's just getting started." She turned to Eddie. "Samuel said you were working with the baby?"

"Trying to. Gettin' nowhere fast."

Vic led us out the back door of the barn to the fenced training ring. In the center, a feisty reddish-roan colt with three white stockings and a white star between his eyes stood tall. When he grew up, he'd be regal. But right then, he snorted and dug at the dirt in a display of juvenile defiance.

"Two-year-old?" I guessed.

"Nearly," Vic said. "Stardust. We call him Dusty. He's a handful, but it's time."

"For what?" Jake asked.

"Teaching him to be saddled and ridden."

Jake pretended to know more than he did, which almost never went the way he expected. "Oh, you mean broke."

Vic shook her head. "Nobody should *ever* 'break' a horse. Spirit needs direction — not crushing. Instead of trying to convince a horse I'm the boss, I teach him to be my dance partner. We learn to listen to each other, without needing words. I like to call it 'sparking.' "

She entered the ring with a long rope in her hands, and stretched out the lasso loop at one end. Dusty kept his distance.

"Never seen anything like how she can train a horse," Eddie said as we leaned on the fence rail. A few farmhands joined us to watch.

Victoria's voice stayed soft and sweet. "Heyyy, Dusty. You gonna be a good boy for me today?"

Dusty tossed his head: *I don't think so, lady.*

Vic inched closer, so gradually that the horse didn't seem to notice. "C'mon, Dusty, let me see those big brown eyes. You can do it."

He made eye contact for a few seconds before looking away again. "There ya go, Dusty." After a little more waltzing, he locked his gaze on her. "Good boy."

She knew what I'd learned training my pony Shadow when I was a kid — once you know how to read it, a horse's face is as expressive as ours. And they learn to understand human expressions, too.

Vic gave the rope a few lazy twirls, then lofted the loop over Dusty's head. Realizing he was caught, he protested with a few half-hearted bucks and kicks, then walked around the ring. Walking became trotting, and she let him run three laps around her, until he halted and took two careful steps in her direction.

"*Gooood* boy, Dusty." As Vic walked past us, Eddie handed her a light training whip, about six feet long plus another few feet of lash at the end.

"How long's this gonna take?" Jake asked.

Eddie nodded toward gear perched on the fence. "In less than an hour, she'll get that halter and saddle on him — and be ridin' him."

"No way."

"Yup."

My brother loved the sort of disagreement that led to wagers. Like Mama always said, Jake would bet on anything at the drop of a hat, even if he had to drop the hat himself. He had to know he was completely unqualified to judge Vic's chances of success — but he never let a little thing like that stop him. "Hnnh . . . under an hour? Wanna bet?"

Eddie suggested a dollar. Jake agreed.

Vic walked alongside Dusty and tickled his flank with the whip. At first, he tried to wriggle away, but she kept talking to him, brushing him with the whip, and soon he didn't mind. Then she traded the whip for a saddle blanket hanging over the fence. When she flapped it in the air, Dusty skipped sideways.

Jake said, "Let's make it five bucks."

Eddie gave him a glance. "Don't count yer chickens, Jake."

"You afraid of losing?"

"Just tryin' not to rob you. But I'll go for five."

Soon, not only was Dusty okay with the blanket on his back, he didn't fuss when Vic put a leather halter over his head in one smooth motion.

Seeing a squint of doubt on Jake's face, Eddie nudged him. "Make it ten?"

Jake exercised rare discretion. "Nahh. Five's good."

Next, Vic swung the saddle off the fence and onto Dusty's back. When she tightened the cinch, he tried to bite her.

Jake promptly forgot about discretion. "Okay, I'm in for ten."

Eddie agreed before Jake could change his mind.

Jake peeked at his pocket watch. Twenty

minutes left in Vic's hour, and there he was, rooting against the girl he *really* liked. He didn't have to wait long for his come-uppance.

Vic gripped the saddle horn, slid her left foot into the stirrup and stood herself up and down a few times. She leaned across the saddle so the horse could feel her full weight. Then she was up and sitting pretty.

At first, she let Dusty circle the ring at his own pace. Within a couple of minutes, they were trotting and then cantering at Vic's request. Her horse sense resembled the self-assurance I felt playing poker. We accepted the possibility of failure, controlled what we could, didn't fret over what we couldn't, and believed the outcome would go our way more often than not.

With ten minutes remaining, Jake forked over ten crumpled dollars.

Eddie folded the money neatly. "Not only is Vic a great trainer, she showed me how almost everything I was doin' was wrong. You shoulda had more faith in her."

He was right. And Jake knew it.

8

> "A human being has a natural desire to have more of a good thing than he needs."
>
> ~ Mark Twain

After Victoria's virtuoso training exhibition, she and Eddie showed us around the farm. When we met their best rider, Rafael Cabrera, Jake felt a little better seeing how even a jockey who rode fierce horses for a living gave Lucifer's stall a wide berth.

Eddie apologized for the dilapidated state of his modest one-story house. "Roof and windows leak. Han Mei needs a new stove. But all that'll have to wait. For now, everything goes back into the horses."

"What good are the horses if your house falls down?" Jake mumbled.

Vic rose to Eddie's defense. "Raising great horses is a rich man's sport. And they're gonna be surprised when we beat 'em at their own game."

We washed at the pump outside the back door and were about to go in for midday dinner when Rafael came running up. "Eddie — he's here!"

"Who?"

"That *estupido pendejo,* Van Brunt."

Last time they'd seen Van Brunt was a few weeks earlier at the Ocean Course, after Phoenix had won the meeting's final race by embarrassing Van Brunt's top horse, Grand Larceny. We all followed Eddie around to the front of the house.

Van Brunt's carriage and horse were hitched to the rail, but no Van Brunt. We found him in the barn, admiring serene Phoenix munching his feed. Olivia added a growl to her baying, a clear indication that this intruder didn't pass muster with her.

"Howdy, Mr. Van Brunt," Eddie said. "You came a long way just to visit Phoenix. How'd you know where to find us?"

"It's the cat's business to know where the mice are holed up." Van Brunt had his long-stemmed pipe clenched in his side teeth. "Now, I put a lot of stock in a horse's name. How did he come to be called Phoenix?"

Vic looked concerned, knowing the tragic story, but Eddie seemed fine. "Barn fire when he was a foal. My *papi* got him out safe, but Phoenix got singed." He pointed to a patch of mottled scarring on the horse's left hind leg where the hair never quite grew back.

"Rising from the ashes, indeed. Well, son, your *papi* sounds like a brave man."

"He was. He died tryin' to save the last horse."

"Well, that's a damn shame. So he left this whole kit 'n' caboodle to you?"

"Yessir."

Van Brunt paused for an ostentatious throat-clearing. "That's a heavy load on a young man's shoulders. Such a thing could wear even the best fella down, and that's the bottom fact of the matter. You'll know that, once you're as ancient as me. Most people my age are dead, at the present time. Mr. Lobo, no blatherskite — I am here to double my offer for this fine horse — *twenty* thousand. That's nothing to sneeze at."

"Still not for sale," Eddie said, still amiable.

"Y'know," Van Brunt went on, "there comes a time in every man's life, and I've had quite a few myself. Once those Sea Breeze races're done, I'll make space for him in my private horse-transport railroad car for our trip back east. He'll ride like a king. And I would have to say, he'll love

Maryland."

"He might at that," Eddie said. "And maybe we'll take him someday."

"Can't help but notice," Van Brunt said, "your house appears to be more than somewhat in a state of disrepair. You can surely use the money."

Nothing like trespassing uninvited on a man's property, insulting his home, browbeating him into selling a horse not for sale — I admired Eddie's natural gift for civility.

But that didn't keep Victoria from steaming. "Mr. Van Brunt —" she said, biting off each syllable.

Van Brunt interrupted. "I would not expect a member of the gentler sex to know much about it, but rest assured if you bred one horse like this, you'll breed others. Be sensible, son."

"Phoenix is a once-in-a-lifetime horse," Eddie said.

"There's no such thing."

"There is, and you're looking at him."

"You know the old joke," Van Brunt said. "How do you make a small fortune in horse racing?"

"Yeah," Vic said, without a smile, "start with a *large* fortune."

"Horse racing takes money, and lots of it," Van Brunt said. "To sum-totalize, this

84

here Phoenix deserves to be running against the greatest Thoroughbreds, from the greatest stables in Kentucky and Virginia, New Jersey and New York. Honor bright, he should be winning the biggest purses at the best tracks — Saratoga, Jerome Park, Pimlico, Monmouth . . ."

"Well, sir," Eddie said, "someday —"

"Not someday, son — *today.* Such hoot 'n' holler's above your bend, but I can make it happen. Much as it pains me, I'll even cut you in for twenty percent of his winnings."

"Sorry you came all this way for nothing."

"No harm. Pleasant trip." Van Brunt cast an appreciative eye on Lucifer in the next stall. The surly white Arabian snorted in displeasure. "Now, that is one grandiferous animal. If Phoenix is not for sale —"

"Neither is Lucifer," Vic said.

"Not even for ten grand?"

"Why would you want him? You can't race him."

"But I could ride him."

Vic snickered, imagining Van Brunt flying off her horse. "He's very particular."

"So am I, dearie, and I have no doubt I can bend him to my will. Plus, adding him to my Arabian breeding stock, he'd be well worth that investment and more. The long and short of it, he'd be a true treasure. As for Phoenix," Van Brunt said with an icy chuckle, "I customarily get what I want."

"By hook or by crook, I know," Eddie said.

"Well, we'll see what transpires at Sea Breeze."

"We'll be there."

They shook hands and Van Brunt left the barn. Watching him go, Rafael muttered *"El diablo,"* and crossed himself for good measure.

"Takes *cojones,*" Jake said, "trying to buffalo a man into selling his best horse."

"Not worth botherin' about," Eddie said. "But we better get on up to the house, or Han Mei'll tan my hide for lettin' all her food get cold."

We followed Eddie in the back door and took our seats around the big kitchen table. Han Mei, Eddie's stern Chinese housekeeper and cook, set out a hot meal of rice and chicken in a sauce that tasted like a savory mix of Chinese and Mexican. There were also three side dishes, none of which I could identify — and all delicious.

As we ate, Jake scrutinized even the most trifling interactions between Victoria and Eddie, while Eddie mostly concentrated on multiple helpings of everything on the table. Big as he was, he looked like a fellow who'd eat almost anything that didn't eat him first.

With each tour Han Mei made to serve or clear away plates, she cast a quick glower at Vic, which got me to wondering what that was all about. Otherwise, I passed an agreeable hour talking horses with Eddie, Rafael, and Vic.

They were excited about the impending two-week fall meeting at Sea Breeze, the new crown jewel of San Francisco horse racing. Running from Monday, September 22 to October 6, those races would close out local competition for the year — and would be the first full-fledged campaign for Fernando Farms since Vic took over training. She and Eddie had high hopes for Phoenix.

"He and Lucifer look like they're real pals," I said.

"They are," Vic said, "which surprised the hell out of me, Lucifer being Lucifer. He turned out to be a good sparring partner for Phoenix, too. They really get a kick out of racing each other for fun."

"Arabian versus Thoroughbred?" I said. "Doesn't seem fair to Lucifer."

"At two miles or under, Phoenix has the advantage — although not as much as you'd expect. Lucifer is bigger and faster than most Arabians. And once they're past two miles, he's got that Arabian stamina — if he feels like winning, he can."

After coffee and fresh-baked apple pie, it was time to catch the train back to San Francisco. We bowed and thanked Han Mei for her hospitality, and Eddie wrapped up a half-dozen muffins and put them in Vic's basket for the trip. Outside, she gave Eddie a peck on the cheek. Eddie blushed. Jake scowled. We climbed into the buggy, and I ended up squeezed in the middle of the seat between Jake and Vic.

"Be back in a couple of days," Vic said. With a shake of the reins, we bounced down the lane toward the road.

"What's Han Mei got against you?" I asked.

"It's not so much me in particular," Vic said. "She's worked for Eddie's family since before he was born. She tends to protect him like he's the world's biggest child."

"Is he?"

"Sometimes. He knows horses, but he's a babe in the woods about almost everything else. San Francisco's the furthest from home he's ever been. I get why she looks out for him. She's only known me a few months. So I've learned to stay out of her way when she mutters Chinese cusses."

"How do you know they're cusses?" Jake asked.

"Eddie translates."

Jake frowned. "Speaking of Eddie . . ."

By the look on his face, I knew he was about to say something stupid, so I tried to sidetrack him. "Hey, Jake, y'know —"

But he plowed right over me. "Vic, is there something going on between you and him?"

I slouched down in the seat as far as I could.

Taken by surprise, Vic leaned forward to glare past me and straight at Jake. "How's that any of your business?"

Not having given this line of questioning much forethought, it was Jake's turn to be caught flat-footed. "Well . . . what about all the time you and me are spending together?"

"What about it?" Vic challenged, her voice turning frosty. "Are we married?"

"No, but —"

"Is Eddie my business partner?"

"Yeah, but —"

"But *what*?"

Jake folded. "But . . . nothin'."

"That's what I thought." Victoria faced forward again. "Not that it's any of your funeral, but when I'm at Eddie's farm —

just so you know — I have a room in the barn."

My brother had a knack for blundering into messes of his own making, so I rarely felt sorry for him. But to be fair, this time he might've been onto something. Eddie showed definite signs of being smitten by Victoria, but was too bashful to speak up. And a gal with that much backbone, intent on clearing her own path in the world, could not be faulted for finding Eddie's determination to succeed in horse racing admirable.

On the other hand, my brother didn't seem to have his sights set on anything much more ambitious than having a good time. If this truly was a romantic competition, Jake might've fallen well behind the frontrunner already. Question was, could he catch up?

After we bumped down the road in prickly silence for a mile or so, he did surprise me by asking Vic a question that showed genuine curiosity: "That horse, Dusty — how'd you do that?"

Vic glanced over, trying to decide if this was Jake's way of making up for his jealousy. She gave him the benefit of the doubt. "It's all about trust."

"How do you mean?"

"Well, think about it — a rider sits pretty

much right where a mountain lion would leap onto a horse's back to try and kill him."

"But how do you convince him a human rider is different?"

"By showing him he can rely on me. Once he believes it, we've got a bond. And I make him a promise — that I'll never let anything bad happen to him."

Jake thought it over. "Trust, huh?"

"Trust."

"How did you learn all that training stuff?"

"When I was little, I'd watch the wranglers working on the ranch."

"And you copied what they did?"

"Never! When I saw how they 'broke' a horse, it broke my heart. I knew there had to be a kinder way. Mr. Roberts, the stable owner in Philadelphia, taught it to me."

"Is that how you broke — I mean, sparked — Lucifer?"

Vic nodded. "He was the first horse I trained all on my own. Then I started working with other horses on the ranch."

"What did your father think?"

Vic sighed. "I'm not sure he ever noticed."

9

"What's in a name? That which we call a rose by any other word would smell as sweet."
~ Juliet in Shakespeare's *Romeo and Juliet*

Following our visit to Fernando Farms, Victoria and Jake only had a few days together in the city before she went back to work preparing for the upcoming races. Once she left, Jake was not great company, mostly moaning and groaning about all the time she was spending with Eddie. Vic returned to the Carlton in the nick of time — one day later and I might've strangled Jake.

It was the evening of Sunday, September 21, and the Sea Breeze races would be getting underway the next day. Jake and me went down to the lobby, where he'd be meeting Vic for a romantic supper at the Eden Terrace, and I'd be joining Mr. Boone for a night at the theatre.

We found Vic seated at the tavern's grand piano, with a blissful look on her face. The regular pianist stood by, admiring how she played a precise musical cascade I recognized as Bach's "Jesu, Joy of Man's Desiring." The intricate swirl of notes brought to mind a swift mountain stream tumbling over sun-dappled rocks. When she finished, we applauded — joined by Mr. Boone and strangers who'd stopped to listen.

"*Brava,* Victoria," Mr. B said. "*Herr* Bach himself would approve."

She acknowledged our praise with a modest nod and slid off the bench. "The only thing I truly miss about my father's house is my mother's piano."

"You'll have your own piano someday," Jake said. "I'd bet on it."

Vic thanked the regular pianist, linked arms with Jake, and off they went to the elevators.

After devouring a couple of juicy sirloins at the Golden Gate Grill, me and Mr. B went across the street to the Excelsior Theatre to see acclaimed singer and actress Emmaline Rose present her one-woman evening of drama, music, and comedy. Her entire three-week run of shows had sold out months before, but Mr. B (no surprise) had access to a private opera box whenever he liked.

The twelve-hundred-seat Excelsior had quickly earned renown as one of the finest theatres in America when it opened in 1869. Patrons in full feather walked up broad granite steps, through classical columns, into an expansive lobby where heels clicked across marble floors under majestic murals of California's natural wonders.

A small army of uniformed ushers guided ticketholders to their seats. We'd be watching from the comfort of one of ten regally-appointed boxes perched along both sides of the auditorium. Furnished with six tufted armchairs, ours was closest to the stage.

Mr. B flipped a silver dollar to our lanky young attendant. "Thank you, Henry."

Henry's eyes lit up. "Thanks, Mr. Boone!" He darted out the door, calling back over his shoulder, "Enjoy the show — she's wonderful!"

While we waited, I marveled at the Excelsior's many expensive special touches. The woodworked façades of the balconies and loge boxes were decorated with more depictions of California scenery. Towering fifty feet over the maroon-velvet orchestra seats, the painted ceiling displayed classical and

Biblical tableaux like a secular Sistine Chapel.

The Excelsior claimed bragging rights as the first West Coast theatre to use calcium lighting (known as limelight) with special reflectors to illuminate the wide stage. Modern gas footlights and border lights could produce hues to match any mood, and an inventive system of moveable flats and backdrops enabled quick changes of sets and scenery.

The low buzz of voices filled the theatre until house lights dimmed. The crowd hushed in anticipation. Newspaper reviews had hailed Emmaline Rose as "a gifted Enchantress of the Stage in prose, poetry, and song," and I wondered if anyone could possibly live up to such expectations.

The first piano notes rippled from the orchestra pit, joined by tranquil strings. The curtain parted, revealing a woman in a warm pool of light, looking down from a ten-foot-high balcony above an otherwise bare stage. She wore a shimmering ivory gown that bared her milky shoulders, her Titian hair piled casually above her heart-shaped face.

Our seats were so close I was already spellbound by the sparkle in her sky-blue eyes. Applause filled the theatre and she clasped her hands over her heart in mutual salute. It's a rare performer who earns such laurels before saying a word, but she already held her rapt audience in the palm of her hand.

She turned her back and bowed her head. The audience settled into silence. When Miss Rose turned around again, she'd transformed herself by carriage and comportment into someone else entirely — a giddy schoolgirl half her actual age. Her lithe neck arched as she gazed off into some dreamy distance far beyond the theatre's confines. Ranging from quiet yearning to pouty despair and soaring passion, her beguiling voice rang out in flawless service to William Shakespeare's enduring poetry:

> O Romeo, Romeo, wherefore art thou Romeo?
> Deny thy father and refuse thy name.
> Or if thou wilt not, be but sworn my love
> And I'll no longer be a Capulet.
> 'Tis but thy name that is my enemy:
> Thou art thyself, though not a Montague.
> What's Montague? It is nor hand nor foot
> Nor arm nor face nor any other part
> Belonging to a man. O be some other name.

And then those blue eyes met mine for a lingering moment, as if Juliet's speech was meant just for me. Even after she looked away, I hung on every word from her ruby lips, and wondered: *Did that really happen?*

> What's in a name? That which we call a rose
> By any other word would smell as sweet;
> So Romeo would, were he not Romeo call'd,
> Retain that dear perfection which he owes
> Without that title. Romeo, doff thy name!
> And for that name, which is no part of thee,
> Take all myself.

The footlights came up as she seemed to float down a spiral staircase from her balcony to the stage. She transformed from character back to actress, as she would throughout that evening: "That's how Will Shakespeare's young Juliet felt, head over heels for a handsome boy she met at a dance. And that, my friends, is how I feel about spending this evening sharing my favorite tasty morsels of music and theatre — with you!"

Her arms outstretched, her smile dazzled

like the summer sun — beaming in my direction long enough for my bewitched heart to skip a beat. Or was I plumb loco? My own balcony scene played out in my head: *Was she looking at me, or wasn't she? And if she was . . . why me? What if she was really gazing at Mr. Boone? Or at nobody in particular?*

As Emmaline Rose bowed into the tide of applause washing over her, stage lights illuminated gaily painted scenery depicting a San Francisco cityscape with blue sky and white clouds. When the ovation subsided, she spoke in feigned confidence: "Is there anyone here who doesn't know the eventual fate of Juliet and her Romeo?"

Knowing laughter flittered through the house.

"Well, in case anyone has indeed missed the last three centuries of classical English theatre, I won't divulge the details. But the hopeful romance of that immortal soliloquy makes it one of my favorites, because (let's be honest, ladies) who doesn't love love? And each time I'm blessed to perform here in San Francisco, I'm reminded of how this city sparks the torch in romantics of all ages, as they seek their heart's delight among her seven hills."

The audience seconded the sentiment

with another round of applause.

"I believe lovers and poets will write odes to San Francisco as long as she overlooks the blue and windy sea — and I've written one myself. I confess to being a better librettist than composer. So I've borrowed a melody from an old folk song called 'Belle of Belfast City' or 'The Wind,' sung by children from the Emerald Isle to Boston. I call it 'The Toast of Golden City.' "

The small orchestra struck up a jaunty tune, and a young couple darted onto the stage, whirling around Emmaline in a playful polka as she sang:

Ocean winds come blowin' round, swirlin'
   up and down the town.
Shy, sweet Sam swears he loves her, all
   the boys are pinin' for her!
She is winsome, she is witty, she's the
   toast of Golden City!
Boys in town, they want her so. Please,
   sir, tell me what you know.

Who knows where she'll settle down,
   dressed in finest silky gowns.
She's the apple of Sam's eye, says he'll
   win her bye and bye.
She is winsome, she is witty, she's the
   toast of Golden City!

She goes dancin' to and fro. Please, sir,
   tell me who's her beau?

Off to church and ring the bell, Sam has
   fallen for her spell.
Wrapped around her finger small, Sam is
   happiest of all.
He's so grateful, she's so giddy, they're
   the toast of Golden City.
Oh, how fast the news has spread,
   everybody knows they're wed!
He is winsome, she is witty, they're the
   toast of Golden City!
They're a-dancin' to and fro, now we
   know she loves him so!

At the song's end, I swear Emmaline Rose's coy glance found me once again. Dismiss my claim as blarney, if you like. It would be nothing short of miraculous if an actress on a bright stage, with the audience at best dimly lit, could pick out *any* single face — let alone keep coming back to it. But, oh, how I wanted that miracle to be true.

For the first hour, Emmaline's show alternated between Shakespearean scenes and songs ranging from sublime to comedic. Some songs were well-known, including "Hard Times" and "Sweet Betsy from Pike."

Others I hadn't heard before, like a lively dance song she'd learned in New England called " 'Tis the Gift to be Simple" (sung *a capella*). Her soulful interpretation of "Battle Hymn of the Republic" wrung new grief and hope from lyrics we knew all too well, with the Civil War not yet ten years past.

Shakespeare's *grande dames* included Lady Macbeth obsessed with her "damned spot," *Hamlet*'s mad Ophelia, Beatrice falling for Benedick's false love, Helena from *All's Well That Ends Well* declaring, "My friends were poor, but honest; so's my love," and Rosalind closing out *As You Like It*.

For every segment, Miss Rose explained why each song or scene mattered to her, like she was in your front parlor with a few friends, instead of a huge theatre with every seat filled. Her supple voice ranged from intimate to stirring to saucy, befitting the temper of each piece, and never failed to reach all the way to the balcony's back row.

Mostly, she worked on a spare stage, with minimal props and scenery hinting at time or place. Emmaline herself sped through a succession of costume and hair-style changes appropriate to the musical or dramatic moment.

And, yes, there were other times when I

was dead-certain she was making eyes at me. But I didn't dare mention my fancy to Mr. B, for fear he'd laugh in my face. Not wanting to be branded a fool, I kept my mouth shut.

During intermission, while I waited in line to buy a sweet-scented apple pastry at the lobby refreshment booth, I saw our young usher Henry huddle with Mr. Boone. The kid left before I got back, and we returned to our seats.

The equally captivating second half of the show wove together a tapestry of songs — a Stephen Foster medley, "Greensleeves," "Shenandoah," "When Johnny Comes Marching Home," even a rousing singalong of "Row, Row, Row Your Boat" — and the bold choice of a woman performing speeches written for Shakespeare's most memorable *male* characters.

Not that she needed to justify anything to her enchanted audience, but Emmaline did remind us that in the days of Shakespeare's legendary Globe Theatre, women were forbidden to be actors, so men played all the female roles. "In these modern times," she said, "I am happy to turn the tables."

Even the most distinguished actors — whether the Bard's contemporary Richard Burbage, John Philip Kemble and Edmund

Kean in the 18th and early 19th centuries, or any non-homicidal Booth — would've been hard-pressed to serve up a more conflicted "To be, or not to be" Hamlet, strut and fret his hour upon the stage better than her Macbeth, or embody a more "honest Puck" apologizing "If we shadows have offended."

In the versatile voice of Emmaline Rose, every scene and song was a polished gem. With Puck's epilogue from *A Midsummer Night's Dream* bidding her audience, "Good night unto you all. Give me your hands, if we be friends, and Robin shall restore amends," she earned a thunderous ovation — which continued for a good five minutes after she'd bowed and left the stage.

What the second act did *not* include were any more fleeting glances in my direction. Believe me, I was on the lookout, and I'd have seen one if it happened. So maybe that whole silly notion was nothing more than a figment of my dewy-eyed imagination.

The curtain opened again on a darkened stage. The star glided into a single pool of light for an encore. She introduced her final song, called "The Maiden's Lament" in keeping with the evening's theme of love. "I wrote the lyrics based on my own encounters with the male of the species, set to the popular music of 'The Yellow Rose of Texas.' Ladies, you will likely recognize these experiences. And, gentlemen, I hope you'll laugh . . . but feel free to squirm, too," she said with an impish smile.

The lights went dark. The orchestra struck up the lively tune. Stage left lit up where Emmaline now stood behind a painted stage-flat schooner with masts and sails, in front of a New York City backdrop. As she sang and stepped out of the make-believe boat, a well-dressed suitor entered and pantomimed his sweet-talk in a breezy dance around her:

> I sailed up north from Georgia, to see what I could see.
> I turned away that very day from rebel treachery.
> Fresh out on the avenue, there's dandy Mr. Brown,
> who promised he would squire me all around old New York Town.
> When he vowed I was an angel, the treasure of his life,
> I blessed my lucky stars . . . we ran into his outraged wife!
>
> No, I didn't need no rascal to woo me unto woe.

> So when I got the chance, I gave ol'
> Brown the old heave-ho!
> Heave-ho! Heave-ho! He got the old
> heave-ho!

Whereupon "Mr. Brown" found himself dance-flung off into the darkness (to uproarious audience laughter). The lights went down on that side of the stage and, with barely a pause to catch her breath, Emmaline reappeared at bright stage right. She stood in the cab of a miniature locomotive flat, in front of a backdrop showing a whitewashed New England church and autumnal trees. Leaving the train, she was met by a dancing young man costumed as a black-clad pastor:

> So I rode rails up to Boston, the land of
> bean and cod.
> There I met a preacher, said he'd lead
> me straight to God.
> I soon learned Parson Billy was not a
> man to trust.
> He whimpered, wept, and wailed when I
> left him in the dust.
>
> No, I didn't need no minister to pray me
> unto woe.
> So sad-sack Reverend Billy got that very

same heave-ho!
Heave-ho! Heave-ho! He got the old heave-ho!

Parson Billy met the same fate as Mr. Brown, spun offstage as the lights went dark again. They came back up, shining like the sun on center stage. There, Emmaline pouted in mock displeasure, surrounded by Mr. Brown, Parson Billy, and two other would-be admirers, all dancing around her and wordlessly pleading for her attentions. She stiff-armed and sidestepped their comic pratfalls as she sang:

Oh, all you maidens fair and chaste,
   please heed these tales
I tell. I have much to relate to thee, so
   listen very well.
Handsome gents will hold thy hand and
   dance the waltz of love,
Pledge their hearts and promise thee the
   moon and stars above.

This world is full of lessons all young girls
   must learn,
Or right into the fires of hell you may be
   cast to burn.
So when a man beseeches thee to
   choose him as thy beau,

> Bestow on him a dainty smiiiile . . . and then the old heave ho!
> Heave-ho! Heave-ho! He got the old heave-ho!
> Heave-ho! Heeeeave-hooooo! He got the old heave-ho!

In perfect time, Emmaline's four rejected suitors fell at her feet in sequence as the song ended. "The Maiden's Lament" brought down the house, earning a standing ovation that rocked the very bones of the Excelsior. Emmaline took her bows amid a barrage of floral bouquets tossed by the audience, and disappeared backstage. But the rhythmic applause continued, along with men hollering vows of undying love.

Finally, the star sashayed out for one more bow, scooped up a bouquet, and slipped away through the curtains without so much as a nod in my direction. The show was over, and so was my fantasy.

"I guess she *wasn't* looking at me," I mumbled with a disappointed sigh. "I am such an idiot."

Mr. B laid a supportive hand on my shoulder. "Didn't Ben Franklin say, 'He that can have patience can have what he will'?"

"Patience for what?"

As if on cue, Henry the usher arrived at

our box, carrying a small silver tray with a single red rose and an ivory envelope.

I stared at him and the tray with considerable confusion. "Huh?"

The perfumed envelope was embossed with a rose and the initials *ER,* with my name written in graceful feminine script.

Now it was Mr. B's turn to be impatient. "For godsakes, Jamey — *open* it."

I fumbled with the flap, unfolded the note and read it. "Holy mackerel — she really *was* looking at me."

"She was indeed," Mr. B said with an amused twinkle.

"You knew? Why didn't you tell me?"

"You didn't ask." He handed me the flower from the tray. "Go — gather ye rosebuds."

Henry escorted me down a backstage maze to the star's dressing room. He knocked on the door and Miss Rose's slender young assistant opened it.

"Millie," Emmaline sang out, "is that Henry with my young man?" She spoke with a cheery Georgia drawl, which she'd tamed during her performance.

"Yes, Miss Emma," Millie said.

"Hello, Jamey, darlin'! Please — c'mon on in, and don't mind the unholy mess. Thank you, Henry!"

After Henry departed, I took a tentative step into the room — and understood the warning. At first glance, it looked like an entire theatre company had exploded, with costumes, props, and flowers strewn everywhere. But what looked like chaos was actually well-organized bedlam. Emmaline sat in front of a mirror, wearing a loosely-sashed pink robe, wiping makeup off her face with a cloth.

Millie flitted about with energetic efficiency, sorting things as she went. To my surprise, she lifted a high-swirled auburn wig off the actress's head and placed it on a wooden form on a table, alongside seven other wigs done up in a variety of styles, in colors from brassy blonde to raven black.

"Millie, darlin'," Emmaline said, "why don't y'all take a break?"

Millie nodded and shut the door behind her as she left, leaving the star and me alone together. I still held that single rose from the silver tray in my hand, unsure what to do with it — considering the glut of flowers swamping the room.

With costumes piled on the only other chair, there wasn't anywhere for me to sit. I was afraid if I touched anything, I'd trigger a catastrophic cave-in. And my mouth felt as parched as a dry creek bed.

Watching in her mirror, Emmaline noticed my fixation on all those wigs. "You've heard that two heads are better than one? Well... I've got eight! Nine, if you count my own."

Her quip settled my nerves and I stopped staring at the wigs. She unpinned her own copper-colored hair, shook it loose, and gave it a brisk brushing.

"Audiences love wardrobe changes," she explained. "But there's no time for a hairdresser, too, so — wigs! The magical humbug of the stage — nothin' is as it seems."

She bound her hair into a ponytail, and resumed her makeup removal. "Greasepaint is the bane of an actor's existence. I hate the way it feels. But without it, we'd look like Death itself."

"Don't you like what you do, Miss Rose, ma'am?"

"Oh, I love playin' pretend, makin' people laugh, or cry, or sing along — it's the best feeling in the world! But once the audience goes home, I'm ready to get back to bein' the girl behind all that make-believe — 'When the hurlyburly's done, when the battle's lost and won.' "

"Macbeth! Act 1, scene 1."

She smiled at me over her shoulder. "I do find a man who knows his Shakespeare irresistible — as long as he's not an actor."

Satisfied her face was clean, she stood and turned toward me. "Not too disappointed, I hope?"

"No, ma'am." As beautiful as she'd appeared during her show, she looked younger, prettier, and more petite as herself. "But if I saw you on the street, all fresh-scrubbed, I wouldn't know you were the Emmaline Rose I just saw on stage."

"That's the way I like it." She looked up into my eyes.

My mind went all fuzzy, like being cocooned in a floral cloud. "You sure have a lot of flowers in here, ma'am. Mostly roses."

"The curse of my surname," she said in mock anguish.

I was so nervous that it took me a second to catch on. "Oh . . . *ohhh*. Emmaline *Rose*."

"Gentlemen think they're bein' witty when they send *roses* to Emmaline *Rose*. So I invariably end up smothered by —" She cued me with a gesture.

"*Roses*."

"Well, Mr. Galloway, I would dearly enjoy us keepin' company in the coming days — if you don't mind."

"No, ma'am. I don't mind at all."

"Good. In that case, I have but two requests. If you should feel the urge to send me roses —"

"— *don't.* Got it. No roses, ma'am." I discarded the single rose in my hand with a casual toss over my shoulder.

She laughed. "In fact," she said with a wave around the room at the floral overabundance, "no flowers at all. But do you see what's missing?"

"Umm . . . no, ma'am."

"*Chocolates.* Nathan Boone knows my favorites."

"No roses. Yes, chocolates," I said, getting the hang of our give and take. "Was that the second request, ma'am?"

"No. My second request is . . . *please* stop calling me 'ma'am.' "

"Then what should I —"

She brushed my cheek with a feather-light touch. "My friends call me Emma."

"Well, here's to friendship."

"And maybe more . . ."

10

> "When I used to read fairy-tales, I fancied that kind of thing never happened, and now here I am in the middle of one!"
> ~ *Alice's Adventures in Wonderland*
> by Lewis Carroll

There's no quiet way to turn a key in a hotel room door lock. Believe me, I tried.

It was early the next morning, and I didn't feel like facing Jake's scrutiny about where I'd been all night. So I hoped he was asleep — or, even better, that he'd stayed in Victoria's room. I crept into the darkness and closed the door as gently as possible — causing an unfortunate metallic click that sounded to me like a thunderclap.

Then I heard my brother's sarcastic voice: "That must've been the longest show in the history of theatre."

"Shut up and go back to sleep."

"Not when you've got a tale to tell."

"And you apparently don't." I flapped the drapes open, enjoying Jake's pained squint as daylight streamed in.

"Yeah, well, Vic had to be at the track early — and spending way too much time with Eddie, for my money."

"Speaking of money, that's her job, y'know."

Jake changed the subject. "And where did you spend all night?"

Not one to spoil the suspense, first I told him all about Emmaline's amazing show, and how he had to see it.

"Yeah, yeah, I'll see the show. Now get to the good part." When he heard about the perfumed note summoning me to her dressing room, he sat up in disbelief. "Nuhh-uhh."

"Yup."

"My baby brother . . . with world-famous stage star Emmaline Rose?!"

"We just talked most of the night."

"Heh-heh . . . but not the *whole* night."

"A gentleman doesn't kiss and tell."

"Which means there's something to tell. Where's she staying?"

"A suite, upstairs. We're meeting at ten for a day on the town."

Jake shook his head in astonishment. "Well, I'll be a monkey's uncle. You . . . and

Emmaline Rose."

After washing, shaving, and changing clothes, I scurried down to the lobby for my rendezvous thirty minutes early — plenty of time to wonder if Emmaline might come to her senses in the light of day, and regret she'd ever met me. Trust me when I tell you — clockwatching does *not* make time fly faster. Nor does pacing.

By the time she made her entrance coming down the marble staircase at the stroke of ten, I'd pert near worn a rut in the rug. Dressed in a smart yellow walking suit, she greeted me with a smile and a kiss, took my hand and pulled me along. "San Francisco awaits us."

That day, we browsed some of her favorite shops, had a midday picnic on a park lawn overlooking the bay, and had a grand time "riding the rope." That's what the natives called their cable car excursions aboard the city's brand-new transportation sensation.

Emmaline surprised me with her enthusiastic knowledge of this contraption, which got built after accidents in which horses pulling heavy street-cars had slipped on rain-slicked cobblestones and skidded down steep hills, resulting in horrible injury and death to people and animals. Scottish-born engineer Andrew Hallidie had proposed a practical solution — a rail network driven by a steam-powered cable loop thousands of feet long, snaking under the cobblestones in iron tubes buried between the rails, and able to move passenger coaches safely up and down the city's steepest streets.

Just a few weeks earlier, on September 1, the Clay Street Hill Railroad Corporation was the first line to open for public use, with one set of tracks going up and one down. The mile-long route rose three hundred feet in elevation from the bottom of Nob Hill to the top.

San Franciscans quickly embraced the new cable cars. Their brightly painted coaches resembled small railroad cars, about twenty feet long, enclosed on all sides and low enough to the ground that ladies could easily step on and off unassisted.

We rode up to the Clay Street heights, where we hopped off and scampered about as Emmaline showed me vantage views of the city and bay. She pointed out Woodward's Gardens, a combination park and zoo in the Mission District that was a favorite of hers. "We'll go there soon, I promise."

Meanwhile, despite Jake's general aversion to horses, he gamely spent time at the Sea Breeze race course, rooting for Eddie and Vic's entries when they were racing, and competing for Vic's attention when they weren't. When it came to tending the horses, Jake didn't have much to contribute beyond encouragement, leaving him feeling about as useful as buttons on a bullfrog. But he deserved credit for trying.

He even developed some affinity for good-natured Phoenix, and Vic caught him petting the palomino's nose over the stall door. "Glad to see you boys're getting along," she said with a kiss on Jake's cheek.

That Monday afternoon, as Jake fed Phoenix some hay, Eddie and Victoria worked outside on another one of their horses, a gray with white socks named John Fremont. He'd won his outing earlier in the day and earned some pampering as a reward.

Vic saw Van Brunt approaching and intercepted him, keeping him a good twenty feet from Eddie. Taking a page from Eddie's book, she chose honey over vinegar this time, meeting Van Brunt with a smile and a Texas twang. "Why, Mr. Van Brunt, you know Eddie's answer hasn't changed."

"That damnable Phoenix keeps beating my Grand Larceny."

"Next time, you can always withdraw your horse."

"Because of backbone, in which I believe strongly, I will not. But I will tell you my new offer for Phoenix is twenty-*five* thousand." Van Brunt raised his voice for Eddie's benefit. "I say, *twenty-five thousand dollars*! And I would say at the present time that is more money than Eddie has seen in his entire lifetime. He's off his chump if he doesn't take it."

"Maybe so," Vic said with a shrug. "But like I told you —"

"Now, as I see it, you and Eddie may be the youth of America, handsomer than us old coots, and thinking you're holding onto a gold mine at the present time. But one wrong stride and that great stallion of yours ends up a plow horse — or worse. No telling when or where. It would be a shame if something happened to him."

Jake gave serious thought to punching Van Brunt in the nose. But Vic stayed calm. "Still not for sale."

Van Brunt smiled. "Before I head east, I will have that horse."

"Mr. Van Brunt, if I didn't know better, I'd say that sounds a li'l bit like a threat."

"More like a promise." He tipped his straw hat, and walked away.

Jake came up to Vic. "He's a pushy sonofabitch."

"Aww, thanks for sticking close in case I needed help."

"Which you didn't."

"It was sweet, just the same." She rewarded him with another quick kiss.

About the same time as I returned to our room after escorting Emmaline to the theatre, Jake came back from Sea Breeze. He flopped face down on his bed, whining about Vic's being too busy all day long to pay him much attention.

So I told him about the cable car rides — hoping he had enough irritating cussedness left in him to seize a golden opportunity to tease me.

"You expect me to believe you went tearing downhill in a cable car?" he scoffed, half-heartedly rising to the occasion.

"You think you're the only daredevil in the family?"

That balderdash got him to lift his head off the pillow. "You? A daredevil? The scaredy-cat who didn't wanna ride the danged elevator?"

"You should've seen me, hanging out of that cable car."

He sat up. "Okay, I dare you — let's go ride it again so I can see it for myself."

I accepted his challenge — without him

noticing my sneaky plot to distract him from girl troubles. Two hours together riding up and down Clay Street seemed to have the desired effect, but Jake's excitement wore off. By the time we got back to the hotel, he was down in the dumps again.

With no racing on Sunday, September 28, and Emmaline free until she had to report to the theatre by six, we lassoed our lady friends, hopped onto a horse-drawn streetcar, and set out for a bright fall day at Woodward's Gardens. Even though Emmaline was old enough to be Victoria's mother, they hit it off right away, leaving me and Jake sitting by as they chattered.

Vic gushed over Emmaline's show, which she'd seen with Jake and me one night (thanks to tickets from Mr. Boone). And Emmaline was enthralled by Vic's life story — from losing her mother in childbirth, to escaping from her father's crumbling cattle empire and blazing her own trail.

"Darlin'," Emmaline said, "it's as if y'all have lived through a medley of Shakespeare's plays! I admire such courage, leavin' home and family."

"I didn't have many choices. And Poppa had nobody to blame for his downfall but himself."

" 'The fault, dear Brutus, is not in our stars, but in ourselves.' I lived that tale, too. My daddy's undoing was his unholy allegiance to slavery. By the time I was your age, I knew he'd never turn away from the sin that built his fortune. I didn't know when war would come, but I knew it would."

"Was it hard for you to go?" Vic asked.

Emmaline sighed. "In the end, it was dreadfully simple. The only possible fate for the South, and my family, was calamity. If I couldn't change it, then I didn't have the heart to stay and witness it."

They also shared a mutual love of horses. Emmaline told of her childhood on her family's Georgia plantation, peppered Vic with horse training questions, and promised to see Phoenix race at Sea Breeze.

The street-car dropped us at the main entrance to Woodward's Gardens on Mission Street. For the bargain price of twenty-five cents apiece, we passed through a stone gateway topped with flapping pennants and entered a wonderland that would've enchanted both fictional Alice and author Lewis Carroll, creator of her fantastical adventures.

The property had been a six-acre country manor in the heart of the city, owned by wealthy Robert Woodward. After building a new mansion in scenic Napa Valley north of town, he'd transformed his city estate into a lush park. Gravel paths meandered through verdant lawns and gardens, while fountains, lakes, streams and waterfalls — even man-made grottos — captivated visitors of all ages. Flamingos, pelicans, ostriches, deer, and small barnyard critters wandered freely — and a peacock unfurling its shimmering tail plumage on a sunny hillside is a grand sight indeed.

At mid-morning, there were already hundreds of people on the grounds. By afternoon, there would be thousands. Amusements and attractions included nature and art museums, aviaries full of exotic birds, a reptile house, camel rides, and merry-go-rounds. After a midday meal at the park's excellent restaurant, Emmaline led us into a cool dark tunnel under 14th Street. Such an otherworldly chamber of echoes was the perfect place for children to shout, whoop, laugh, and screech like delighted demons at the top of their leathery little lungs.

Out the other side, we saw the biggest menagerie in the whole country, with scores of captive wild animals in cages and enclosures, including ferocious wolves, bears, and lions. Visitors to the popular monkey house were endlessly entertained by the antics of our distant Darwinian cousins.

Throughout the year, an adjacent pavilion seating five thousand presented such spectacles as fire eaters from India, Siberian reindeer, Oriental acrobats, dancing bears, chariot races, sharpshooting exhibitions, and classical and popular music. Emmaline hoped to perform there during her next San Francisco engagement.

Going back through the tunnel, childish echoes abounded — until Emmaline began to sing. Her voice rang like a crystalline bell, and even the wildest kids stopped to listen:

> 'Tis the gift to be simple, 'tis the gift to be free
> 'Tis the gift to come down where we ought to be.
> And when we find ourselves in the place just right,
> 'Twill be in the valley of love and delight.
> When true simplicity is gained,
> To bow and to bend we shan't be ashamed,
> To turn, turn will be our delight,
> Till by turning, turning we come 'round right.

Her happily surprised audience of strangers clapped and cheered. She took a bow and laughed. "Now I can say I've *finally* played Woodward's Gardens!"

From there, Emmaline led us like eager ducklings to America's first public aquarium, a long arcade featuring sixteen large tanks with glass fronts, exhibiting live marine creatures from around the world. When it was time for us to leave, we stopped by the seal pond on our way out to watch afternoon feeding. A half-dozen sleek sea lions paddled, basked, barked, and clowned, as two zookeepers tossed fish to them — an ideal ending to our ideal outing.

Over the next few days, me and my brother were like two sibling ships passing in the night, each preoccupied with our gals. At some point, we'd have to resume playing poker to support ourselves. For the moment, though, I was having too good a time with Emmaline.

Unfortunately for Jake, most of Victoria's long days were devoted to working at the track. Come evenings, she was usually dog-tired, and needed to get to sleep early so she could be back at work with Eddie by daybreak. Jake couldn't help being jealous, but Eddie was so danged likeable, it was hard to gin up any serious hostility toward him. All Jake could do was mope.

I tried to imagine Vic's predicament, stuck between the rival affections of two young men. I knew how my brother felt about her, and I was pretty sure Eddie felt the same, even if he rarely showed it.

Take Tuesday evening, a few days after our Woodward's Gardens visit. I went down to the Carlton lobby with Jake, where he was supposed to meet Vic for supper when she got back after another long day at the track. Eddie came into the hotel with her, even though he was bunking with the horses at Sea Breeze to save money. She had his jacket over her shoulders, slipped it off and handed it back to him. She kissed him on the cheek, turned and walked toward us.

Poor moonstruck Eddie kept watching her instead of leaving. Jake's jaw clenched. By the look on his face, I knew he was about to do something dumb. "Whatever you're thinking," I warned him, "keep your trap shut."

Instead, he confronted Vic. "Why did Eddie come all the way back here with you?"

Well, that was even dumber than I'd expected. But there was no taking it back.

Weary as she was, Vic didn't appreciate Jake's inquisition. "You'd have to ask him."

"No, I don't, because it's obvious."

125

Vic put one hand on her cocked hip. "What is?"

"That Eddie's sweet on you."

"He *is* not."

"He is too!"

"Y'know what? Forget supper. I'm going to take a bath, get room service, and go to sleep — *alone.*" She trudged past us.

My lamebrain brother called after her, "I'll see you at the track tomorrow."

Without so much as a glance back, Vic disappeared into an elevator.

Jake seemed genuinely baffled.

"Great job," I said, short on sympathy.

His eyes widened in oblivious innocence. "What did I do?"

I stared at him. He really didn't know. "When it comes to saying the exact wrong thing to a girl — ? You could write a book."

"Well, maybe I will. And I bet it'll be real popular, too."

I had to hand it to him — there was a certain purity to Jake's cluelessness. "Sometimes you really are a natural-born fool."

"Takes one to know one."

He wasn't altogether wrong, but I'd never give him the satisfaction of admitting it.

11

"Why deny myself anything I can win, buy, or steal?"
∼ Cortland Van Brunt III

American Sport & Spirit, Wednesday, October 1, 1873
★ DEALE'S DEAL
by HORATIO DEALE ★

If you, Dear Readers, are among the thousands in attendance for the heroical finale of the Northern California racing season, be sure to hold onto your hats when visiting the Bay City's Sea Breeze Race Course. Literally!

You may conclude, as Your Humble Correspondent has, that entrepreneurial embroidery and promotional puffery played a leading part in the naming of the track. Utilizing the term "breeze" in conjunction with this otherwise impeccable establishment is to bear profoundly false witness to the fact that the course's location on the San Francisco peninsula is subject to veritable gales off the ocean . . .

Sea Breeze had been conceived by a partnership of a dozen of Northern California's wealthiest horse breeders and owners, who'd signed a ten-year lease on sixty acres and built the best racing facility in the West. Amenities included an imperial owners' box and private clubhouse dining room, making it a sporting venue suitable for financial transactions and escapades.

Despite the wind, the partners believed they had an ideal location, near a stretch of sandy wasteland being transformed into Golden Gate Park. Thousands of trees and acres of grass had already been planted to stabilize the wild dunes. Eventually, it would become San Francisco's answer to New York City's famous Central Park.

Since Jake didn't want Vic to think she'd scared him off the previous evening, we drove over to Sea Breeze the next day. No sooner had we arrived than a fierce gust whipped Jake's hat right off his head. He managed to chase it down and grab it.

Eddie saw us approaching the barns and waved as he examined their gray horse, John

Fremont, while Vic prepared a chestnut named Redwood Forest for the first race at one o'clock. Phoenix had the day off.

"When he wins Friday," Vic said, "he'll be three for three here against Grand Larceny."

Eddie grinned. "I woulda never won *any* races without Vic."

"You're the one who breeds 'em," she said, "so it's okay to brag."

"I may know bloodlines, but you get 'em to run." When Vic reached for Redwood's saddle, Eddie grabbed it first and set it on the horse's back.

"I wanted to try blinders on Redwood this time," Vic said.

"I'll get 'em." Eddie strode off to the barn.

"See? Like I told you," Jake said to Vic.

"Told me what?"

"That Eddie's sweet on you."

"He *is* not," Vic said with a growl.

"You don't believe me, ask Jamey."

I recoiled. "Whoa! Leave me out of this."

Eddie returned with the blinders, put them on Redwood and fastened them.

When I tried to get Jake to go watch the race from the grandstand, he refused. Instead, he spied on all of Eddie's efforts to pamper Vic — seeing if she needed anything, fetching water, making sure she was warm enough. When the wind blew, he tried to give her his barn coat, but she wouldn't take it.

I finally had to drag Jake away with his teeth clenched. "Jamey, did you see all that? Could he be any more obvious?"

"Yeah, I know a lovesick fool when I see one — or two."

Race time approached. We walked to the track with Eddie, Vic, Rafael, and Redwood Forest — and crossed paths with Van Brunt.

"Well, if it isn't Earnest Eddie. Just so you know, I don't make offers like this every day, knowing you are cold-jawed on this subject — but I am willing to kick in another five thousand."

Of course, Phoenix still wasn't for sale. Neither Van Brunt's horse nor Eddie's won that particular race, although Redwood Forest did finish a close second.

Friday, we were back at Sea Breeze, and Emmaline came along with us to see Phoenix run for his third and final time against Van Brunt's champ Grand Larceny. The outcome was closer than their first two showdowns, but Phoenix still won. Emmaline had to leave right after the race, but Vic and Eddie were pleased with their horse as the rest of us headed back to the barns — where Van Brunt was waiting yet again.

Somehow, Eddie remained affable. "You

really don't take no for an answer, do you, Mr. Van Brunt."

"No rich man does, son. Why deny myself anything I can win, buy, or steal? You know I have the money to buy you many times over. But I am not here to sweeten my offer, only to make sure you and li'l Vickie will be at my soiree tomorrow night. Starts at seven, Carlton Presidential Suite."

Eddie ducked his head. "Yessir. I hear it's a tradition when the Sea Breeze meeting's over. But isn't it usually hosted by a Californian owner?"

"This being my first season here, I insisted the Jockey Club let me throw the reception in gratitude for all their hospitality. Allowing as there are no hard feelings between us, I do hope to see you and your associates there." With a charming tip of his hat, Van Brunt strolled away.

Vic watched him go. "Not what I expected."

"Me, neither," Eddie said.

"Maybe he finally *did* take no for an answer," I said, although I was sure none of us believed that.

Next day, Saturday morning, Emmaline took me for a leisurely city stroll and a midday meal at her favorite waterfront restaurant. She was disappointed to miss the horsemen's reception that night, but she had her show to do.

After a stop at her dressmaker's shop to pick up a new outfit, we returned to the Carlton. As we rode the elevator up to her suite, I wondered aloud what we might do together on Sunday. But instead of offering her usual merry list of suggestions, her brow furrowed, and her unaccustomed silence worried me.

She fumbled with her key and opened the door. I followed her in. She hung her new dress on a hook beside a floor-length mirror, then turned to me with her saddest eyes. "Oh, darlin' . . . tomorrow's when I leave."

"Tomorrow?"

"You knew tonight was my last show here."

I did know — and fooled myself into forgetting.

Emmaline sighed. "Damn this vagabond life of mine. I'm due in Omaha for an engagement. Then I head directly to dates in Baltimore. Then Philadelphia, New York, New Haven, Hartford, Boston . . . then south to Washington and Richmond, Charlotte and Charleston, Savannah and Atlanta." She forced a smile. It was not her best performance. "But I'll be spendin' the winter with cousins in Georgia — you can visit me there! It's only a week away by train."

"How long 'til you'd be back gallivanting around the country on your next tour?"

"Well . . . that's not all settled yet. But I go back up north in early spring, then play Midwestern cities, then back to San Francisco for late summer. I lease my own railroad Palace car, Jamey. Travel with me! We can have a lark, seein' the sights, like we did here." The desperate hope in her voice faded. "Oh, darlin' . . . I've broken your heart."

"You knew you'd be leaving when you met me."

"Didn't we both?"

She said it gently, but she was right — and the truth cut deep. I'd known from the start this wouldn't last forever.

She took my hand, and we sat on a coved loveseat. "Life on the road gets . . . lonely. So, when I know I have a longer stay, I like to share the company of a sweet and handsome young man. Is that wrong?"

I didn't know the answer, but I knew how I felt — empty and forlorn.

She leaned close. Her dewy lips grazed mine. "And you, darlin', are many huckleberries above a persimmon —"

A booming British baritone startled us. "Ah-*haaah*! That's *exactly* what you once said to *me*!"

We turned to see a mustachioed man leap out from behind a dressing screen. Tall and trim with aristocratic posture, he brandished a sharp Scottish dirk in one hand and a long-barreled Confederate pistol in the other.

My first thought: *Oh, lordy, I am too young and miserable to die like this!*

The assailant took a hostile stride forward, thrusting a dagger feint in my direction. *"In flagrante delicto!"* he shouted with stage-worthy brio, his diction as chiseled as his cheekbones.

"Oh, *hardly*!" Emmaline fired back. After the initial surprise, she wasn't at all alarmed by this mad invader, and that left me bewildered.

The mad Englishman cocked his revolver. "Do you *deny* that I've caught you in the throes of infidelity with this . . . this . . . loathsome cur?!"

"Hey! Let's not get personal," I snapped. "Who the hell is he?"

His fierce gaze locked on me. "Who in blue blazes are you?"

"There's never a program when you need

one," Emmaline muttered, shaking her head. "Jamey is *mon amour du jour.* Randall Drake is my —"

"— husband!" he roared, stomping on her line.

My eyes widened. "Husband?!"

Randall pointed his dagger toward the ceiling, and emoted: " 'Doubt thou the stars are fire! Doubt that the sun doth move! Doubt truth to be a liar . . . but *never* doubt I love!' "

She took one step toward him and he shrank back, confirming her lack of fear. "Randall the *Hamlet*-quoting fool is my *very* former husband. How did you get in here, anyway?"

"Charm — and a bribe," Randall said as he snatched a flower from a vase and presented it to her with a deep bow. " 'This bud of love, by summer's ripening breath, may prove a beauteous flower when next we meet.' You could never resist *Romeo and Juliet,* my sweet."

"But I *can* resist you."

I was still stuck on one key word. "Husband?"

"*Divorced* husband, permanently disentangled," she insisted. "Pay no attention to him."

"What about his gun and knife?"

"Stage props. He's an actor, not an assassin."

"More like an *over*-actor," I said.

Randall's nostrils flared. "*Now* who's getting personal, sonny?"

Emmaline disarmed him without resistance. "This rubber knife isn't sharp enough to cut melted butter. As for the gun, the worst he could do is throw it at you. And I'd bet gold doubloons he'd miss." She handed me both weapons.

Randall dropped to one knee. " 'If thou remember'st not the slightest folly that ever love did make thee run into . . . thou hast not loved.' "

"Ahh, yes," Emmaline said with disdain. "*As You Like It,* your old standby."

With pleading hands, Randall doubled down on *As You Like It:* " 'Who ever loved that loved not at first sight?' "

Noticing he was off-balance, she planted her hand on his forehead and pushed. He keeled onto his backside, and she stood over him. "And how many lovers at first sight have *you* had lately?"

"None — but not for want of trying! It's been a dry spell."

She helped him up, and steered him directly to the door, which I held open.

" 'How many fond fools serve mad

jealousy?'" Emmaline said, with a fitting line from *Henry VI.* "Out you go, Randall."

He loitered in the doorway, ejected and dejected. Then his eyebrows perked up. "Supper in Boston, my sweet?"

"Good God, Randall, you are hopeless. Against my better judgment . . . yes, supper in Boston. Now get out. And if I spot you prowling around this hotel, I shall call the police, just as I did —"

"— in Baltimore," they said in unison.

Knowing she was about to slam the door in his face, he raised a finger. "Wait — the props! I must return them whence I borrowed them."

I handed him the gun and dagger. And *then* Emmaline shut the door in his face.

"Does this happen often?" I asked.

"Now and then," she said with a sigh. "We had a great love once, when we were far too young. 'Hasty marriage seldom proveth well.' And actors should *never* marry actors."

"Why not?"

"We're not good at sharin' the limelight. But in a marriage, sometimes you have to be the adorin' audience while your spouse hogs the stage."

Randall's melodramatic threat may have been fiction, but my heartbreak was real. I slumped into the loveseat.

Emmaline knelt in front of me. "Oh, Jamey — an actor's life does not easily accommodate lasting love, and I shall never forgive myself for hurtin' someone so dear to me. Nor am I worthy of a moment's regret. You have a wise and gentle heart, and soon it will know that our parting is for the best." She ended her soliloquy with a crooked little smile. "You don't want to end up like poor Randall, do you?"

"No," I said with a short laugh, despite the ache in my "wise and gentle" heart.

"I didn't think so. But — and I have no right to ask — may we have one last night together?"

You have no idea how much I wanted to say yes. But my wounded pride wouldn't let me. I shook my head in silence. We stood, our fingers entwined, and shared a tender farewell kiss. Then she let me go.

I walked away from her door, and didn't let myself look back.

12

> "Immortals are never alien to one another."
> ~ Greek Poet Homer,
> *The Odyssey*

I slunk back to our room, feeling lower than a bow-legged lizard. I took the stairs instead of the elevator, so I could wallow in woe longer and without interruption.

One look at me and Jake postponed any teasing. Instead, he asked what was wrong — and actually listened when I flumped onto my bed and told him. "What do I do now?"

"We go to Van Brunt's party," Jake said. "At least it'll be a distraction — with good food. Since nothing's gonna make you feel better anyway, you might as well eat."

I stared at the ceiling. "This thing with Emmaline . . . I only knew her for a couple of weeks. It's stupid. *I'm* stupid."

"Well, if you think about it, isn't *love* stupid?"

"Yeah — love *is* stupid! Letting a girl twist your insides? She's right. Parting *is* for the best." Not that I believed that for a second.

Jake tried to be encouraging. "That's the spirit! Speaking of which, I hear there's gonna be a spiritualist at the party."

I sat up. "Hmm. Watching people fall for nonsense could be good for a laugh."

"Hey, this Madame Aurora Killegrew is the real deal."

"Says who?"

"Says *Harper's Weekly*. And I doubt they'd waste space writing about a charlatan."

"*All* mediums are charlatans."

"They say she can really talk to dead people, and predict the future. What makes you so sure she can't?"

"The fact that my brain still works."

"Oh, you always think you're *sooo* smart."

"Smart enough to know humbug when I see it."

"Wanna bet? Ten bucks says she's for real."

"You're on."

By the time we got dressed up, I was too listless to resist taking the elevator. There was always the possibility it might crash and end my torment, but we made it upstairs to the festivities. The Presidential Suite took up much of the hotel's top floor, aside from the space occupied by the Eden Terrace. A herd of finery-festooned revelers filed in through the double doors, eager to celebrate the racing season, which would end on Monday. Party host Cortland Van Brunt buzzed around, greeting his guests.

Out of curiosity, we wandered through the elegant suite. In addition to a big bustling kitchen, we counted four bedrooms, two parlors, a dining room spacious enough to double as a ballroom, a library, and a sitting room with huge bay windows, all with high coffered ceilings and gas chandeliers. Rooms facing west opened to a broad terrace with a view of a fiery-gold autumn sunset.

We grazed on delicious appetizers and hors d'oeuvres, and bumped into Victoria and Eddie coming in from the terrace. Vic wore her favorite blue gown, while Eddie looked every inch the dashing gentleman rancher in a black frock coat trimmed with satin. He got all bashful and embarrassed by congratulatory attention from other horsemen, none of whom would've known him from a backstretch roughneck two months ago. But his horses had proved their fortitude at Sea Breeze, and opened lots of eyes in the process.

We felt like four out-of-place peas in that

extravagant pod. Judging by snippets of overheard conversations, the Rich Folk around us seemed consumed by such economic shenanigans as the still-unfolding Panic of 1873, and the associated bankruptcy of Jay Cooke, the renowned railroad tycoon, banker and Union Civil War financier. They wrapped themselves in delusions of monetary omnipotence, certain they were exempt from the laws of fiscal gravity — even as they gossiped about who could be next to fall from grace.

They were still gamblers at heart, no less than the card players I'd been observing since me and Jake were kids in Texas. And their whistling past the graveyard reminded me yet again that most gamblers are prone to unwarranted overconfidence.

Van Brunt came up behind us: "Well, Earnest Eddie and dear li'l Vickie . . . and friends. You clean up nicely, if I do say so."

"Howdy, Mr. Van Brunt," Eddie said. "I half-expected to see Grand Larceny up here."

"I tried, but he didn't fit in the elevator," Van Brunt said with a sozzled wink. He commandeered a passing waiter and made sure we all took goblets of red wine. "I say good for the horses that they forget right after they lose, but I do not. That Phoenix of yours is a blue-chip world-beater, and I don't mind saying at the present time, he beat Larceny fair and square — and I bet you expect I'm about to reiterate how much I want to buy him."

Eddie rubbed the back of his neck. "That did cross my mind, sir."

"Well, not here in these august premises, son." He smiled at Victoria: "Now, li'l lady, don't cut my throat, for I may want to do that myself later. But seeing as you are the youth of America, and how this is your first entry into these high ranks of the equestrian *haut monde,* have yourselves a grand time."

Van Brunt toddled off to mingle, and our quartet went out to the terrace — and smack into the middle of a lusty debate between Horatio Deale and Leland Stanford. Deale was the *bon vivant* editor of the widely read periodical *American Sport & Spirit.* Stanford, of course, was the imperious former Governor of California, future senator, Central Pacific Railroad founding president, and the man who completed the transcontinental railroad by personally hammering the famous Golden Spike at Promontory, Utah. Most recently, Stanford had been applying his wealth to horse breeding and racing, mainly harness trotters.

Deale resembled a lanky scarecrow, resplendent in a yellow-plaid frock coat and blue velvet cravat, adorned with a red carnation in his lapel, his face all clean-shaven angles around a sharp nose. Governor Stanford, bearded and dark-haired with a prominent brow, was the very model of the modern industrialist, corpulent and clad in conservative black — and insisting that when a horse gallops, at some point *all four hooves* are off the ground at the same time.

Deale snorted in good-natured derision. "My dear Governor, without benefit of divinely bestowed wings, that is impossible for an equine beast weighing a half-ton."

With a wry chuckle, Stanford addressed the crowd like he was stumping at a campaign whistle-stop. "I shall prove my thesis, once I find a photographer able to capture incontrovertibly — on photographic plates! — what the human eye is too slow to see ... and Horatio's brain is too slow to imagine."

The surrounding group laughed.

"I, for one, cannot wait to see Governor Stanford's evidence," Deale parried, "proving beyond all shadow of doubt that the great steed Pegasus is *not* mythological after all."

Stanford backslapped Deale. "When I have proof, I dare you to print it."

"May the Gods of photography help you

deliver unto the world validation of Saint Augustine's admonition that 'Miracles are not contrary *to* nature, but only contrary to what we know *about* nature.' And I vow — witnessed by all here this evening — that I shall trumpet your findings to the heavens," Deale said with a courtly bow.

"My money's on Stanford and his flying horse," Vic said to us.

Eddie nodded. "Me, too."

My eyebrows arched. "Really?"

"It ain't easy to see," Eddie said, "but I have seen it."

Deale came over to us. "Ahhh! The underdogs who have upended the racing establishment! Mr. Lobo and Miss Krieg, I am consumed by this recent rivalry between you and Mr. Van Brunt, and my readers love a good rags-to-riches tale. I must interview you before I return to Baltimore next week."

Eddie hesitated. "We kinda like to keep our heads down, Mr. Deale."

"That is precisely what makes you catnip to the racing aficionado. Nary a soul had heard of Fernando Farms prior to these past weeks. Your horses, especially Phoenix, have beaten the best, and soundly thrashed Van Brunt's Grand Larceny — a stallion rarely defeated, let alone thrice by the same horse."

"Excuse us a minute, Mr. Deale," Vic said, pulling Eddie aside to confer. "Why hide our light under a bushel? Publicity could help us get more breeding opportunities with the best bloodlines."

Eddie nodded. "Makes sense, I reckon. Okay."

Vic turned back to Deale with a smile. "We can arrange something."

"I am staying here at the Carlton," Horatio said. "I shall be leaving on Wednesday. Name a time that is convenient for you."

Vic suggested late Tuesday morning, at the Sea Breeze barns. Deale agreed, clicked his heels together and went off for more hobnobbing.

A little before nine, Van Brunt herded his guests into the large dining room for the evening's presentation of what I predicted to be necromantical claptrap. Spiritualism, occultism, communing with the dearly and not-so-dearly departed, divining the future — call it what you will, none of it was new. Why, even the Bible tells us King Saul asked the Witch of Endor to raise the spirit of dead prophet Samuel when the Israelites needed some timely counsel before fighting the Philistines.

I imagine people have been trying to get a leg up on the Afterlife by talking to the dead since humans first started talking at all. Our latter-day incarnation of Spiritualism first sprouted in 1848 in Hydesville, New York, an upstate crossroads hamlet. There, in a humble rented cottage, young sisters Maggie and Kate Fox claimed to be communicating with the unquiet spirit of an itinerant peddler. They insisted the ghost told them by means of rapping noises that he'd been murdered some years prior in that very house.

The movement then blossomed throughout America and Europe, entangling with religion when churches didn't provide the answers people wanted. Séances, readings, and trances became as common as Sunday services in some circles. There may be more than a pinch of irony in the fact that British physician and author Sir Arthur Conan Doyle — who would achieve fame as the creator of Sherlock Holmes, the fictional detective and devotee of logic and reason — would become one of the best known spiritualists of all.

Men of science tried to experiment and investigate their way to the bottom of the whole craze — and some of them ended up converting to the beliefs they'd tried to debunk. There's a head-scratcher for you.

For all the practitioners unmasked as

frauds, others like Madame Killegrew became society darlings and counselors to the rich and royal. According to overheard party gossip, not only did she travel with Van Brunt and attend his business meetings, but he hardly went to the privy without her advice.

Our host cleared his throat with great fanfare at nine on the dot. "Ladies and gentlemen! May I present Madame Aurora Killegrew, celebrated psychic medium and my personal spiritual guide."

A shapely and striking woman wearing a flowing emerald gown, the red-haired, green-eyed Madame Killegrew made her solemn entrance through the French doors from the terrace. Like many long-legged beauties, her age was hard to determine — she could've been anywhere between thirty and fifty. She sat in the lone chair at the long oval dining table, and partygoers gathered around. A young assistant in formal footman's attire shut the doors to the terrace and hallway. When he turned off the chandeliers, two silver candelabras on the table cast dancing shadows on the walls.

With her looks and English accent leavened with a dulcet Irish lilt, she embodied worldly-wise elegance. "I am Aurora Killegrew. If there be non-believers among us this night, ye are still welcome to witness the wonders of the spirits."

Her assistant struck a reverberating Chinese gong.

Among her assorted props, she dipped a quill pen into a jade inkwell, and wrote tiny lettering on a strip of parchment. "Though I neither speak nor comprehend Greek, I've learned to write enough to send messages to my spirit control Kleon. He shall introduce himself when he arrives." She rolled the parchment into a tiny scroll, lit it with a match, and placed it in a silver bowl. "By this method, the Egyptians of antiquity contacted the spirit world."

A mesmerizing tendril of smoke swirled toward the ceiling. Madame Killegrew closed her eyes. "Kleon, my dear spirit friend — we invite your presence."

We all waited, barely breathing for fear of disrupting the enchanted ethers (yes, even me), not knowing what to expect or what form her spirit familiar might take. Horatio Deale scribbled non-stop in his reporter's notebook.

After ten long seconds of stillness, Madame Killegrew beckoned again. "Kleon! Join our circle. Bring us your all-knowing visions from the Infinite Beyond. Be our guide to Olympus, Hades, Elysium — and the future."

Kleon seemed to be taking his sweet time. Her assistant banged the gong again.

Then the poor woman shivered from head to toe, as if seized by a sudden fit. When it subsided, she let out a keening wail, alarming some of the ladies. She spewed a gaggle of clashing voices, babbling so quickly it was hard to isolate a word, or a single language. Her body shuddered, and the chatter ceased, leaving a lone voice — gruff, deep, resonant, speaking English with a crotchety Mediterranean accent. "I am here, Aurrrooorrra. Why do you wake me from ages of slumber?"

Madame Killegrew and Kleon chatted as if over tea, their alternating accents flawlessly controlled, without a stumble. "Please tell our gathering who you are," she said.

"I am Kleon, Alexander the Great's stable master. I tended his royal herd of horses, especially the noble steed Bucephalus — black as midnight, wild as a whirlwind." Then, with a wheezing laugh, he added in a mock-confidential tone: "Had I not trained Bucephalus when Alexander was a lad, the little fool would never have survived to rule the world. That horse would have killed him!"

"And tell us of the legend, if you please,"

Madame Killegrew said.

There was Kleon's gravelly laugh again, somehow *overlapping* her voice. "By Zeus! That horse was of the best Thessalian strain. As the *legend* goes, when the little Macedonian was but a boy, his father King Philip was offered in tribute a horse which no man could ride or restrain — and for an outrageous price. The boy wagered with his father: 'If I can tame him, you shall buy him for me. If I cannot, I will pay the princely sum myself.' "

"Tell us more," Madame Killegrew said.

"As the *legend* goes, Alexander soothed the beast with sweet words and — surmising the cause of his angry distress — the boy turned him to face the sun so the stallion could no longer see his own shadow. And so the boy won the horse, and proved himself to his father, who said, 'My son, look thee out upon a kingdom equal to and worthy of thyself, for Macedonia is too little for thee.' Thus was born the *legend* of Alexander . . . *the Great*!" Kleon paused for effect. "That did not really happen, in that way. But every great ruler needs a *legend* — is that not so?"

"Does the great king mind you telling tales on him?" Madame Killegrew asked.

"Heh-heh-heh! We are long dead — what

matters pride?"

"Do you have any messages for those present here, my friend?"

"Hnnnh. Let me look upon them." The candles almost flickered out, as if fanned through time by the breath of an ancient zephyr. Many in the room gasped. I had to admire Madame Killegrew's theatrical gifts. Judging by awestruck expressions around me, Jake and quite a few others gobbled up every bit of the well-seasoned hogwash she and Kleon dished out.

"The monarch you know as Van Brunt," Kleon said. "He shall find a great treasure in the West. As Homer wrote: 'Immortals are never alien to one another.' "

"If so, ol' King Cortland's running out of time!" someone heckled, prompting a ripple of laughter among the guests.

"Where is the big one?" Kleon said. "The one named for the wolf."

All eyes turned toward a startled Eduardo Lobo, who stood a head taller than the crowd and wasn't hard to find.

"The new kid on the track, at the present time," Van Brunt taunted in that room filled with button-busting egos. "I would have to say he thinks because he won a few races, he's already sitting pretty up there on Mount Olympus."

Eddie gulped and blushed. Victoria prayed he wouldn't take the bait, but Eddie's pride won out. "Well, sir, my best horse beat your best horse — three times."

"For you, boy," Kleon said, "there is a future warning from ages past. Mind your place in the world. You shall have your time, but as your Christian Bible says, 'To everything there is a season.' "

"No disrespect intended, your spiritship. But what if this is my season?"

"Take things in turn." Kleon's words sounded a little bit like a threat.

"And if I don't?"

"Then you may lose all. Even Alexander died."

"Kleon," Madame Killegrew said, "do you sense any skeptics?"

"There are many among you. But there is one above all." Still in her trance, Madame Killegrew's left hand levitated with a palsied tremble. Like a forked twig dowsing for water, two fingers pointed — straight at me. "*That* one."

"Me?" She wasn't wrong, but I wondered how she'd reached that conclusion — or was it a random stab?

"You," Kleon said.

"What do you know about me? Not much, I'd reckon."

Madame Killegrew's trance deepened, but instead of Kleon's rough Greek accent, her next words came out in a man's genteel drawl — pure performance artistry. "I am now speakin' through your dear friend . . . from the war."

After a moment, this new spirit's reedy voice sang in a funereal cadence:

When Johnny comes marching home
    again — Hurrah, hurrah!
We'll give him a hearty welcome then —
    Hurrah, hurrah!
The men will cheer, the boys will shout,
The ladies they will all turn out
And we'll all feel gay, when Johnny
    comes marching home.

Jake gaped in self-fulfilling recognition: "Kirby . . . ? *Johnny Kirby*?!"

"So many dead," the mournful spirit intoned. "Am I . . . dead?"

Jake stared, as if seeing our late Confederate comrade instead of Madame Killegrew.

"Yeah. We buried you. You were the only one we had time for."

Madame Killegrew's prowess at deception had Jake reliving the worst day of our misbegotten Civil War service, after we'd gone off in our dimwitted youth to play rebel soldier. It was the spring of '65 — in our only real action, most of our threadbare Texas infantry company got slaughtered by Yankees in a short, pointless skirmish. Johnny Kirby, our amiable sharpshooter and friend, had been the first to die that afternoon.

As for Jake and me, we survived by hiding in the underbrush. After the shooting stopped, and the bluecoats left, Jake wanted to skedaddle without burying the dead — and without retrieving Kirby's final letter to his wife and kids back home. I convinced him we had to bury at least Kirby, and take his letter. I never forgot Jake's annoyance over me carrying that letter for months before finally mailing it to Kirby's widow.

I'd been scared witless that day, while Jake seemed to take our terrifying war experience in stride. Seeing him so unsettled by Madame Killegrew's act surprised me, but now I knew how witnessing such senseless killing had truly afflicted him.

"So many families," Johnny Kirby's voice lamented, "so many heartsick families . . ."

Like an expert fisherman toying with a hapless trout, Madame Killegrew was a master at dangling the vaguest of bait to catch gullible subjects. With her keen powers of observation and interpretation, she patiently teased out threads to weave into a narrative my dopey brother believed. First hand, it was easy to see how people could fall for spiritualist mumbo jumbo.

Jake was hooked. "Your letter . . ."

"My letter," Kirby echoed.

"To your wife — dammit, what was her name? Claire! We found it. Well, Jamey did."

"My letter . . . to Claire . . ."

"Jeezus . . . I wish we'd've told you we'd send it if you got killed, like Jamey wanted to. But we did, we mailed it. We never knew if your wife and girls got it."

"My girls . . . my babies . . ."

Jake dredged his memory for their names. "Ummm . . . M-Molly, and . . . Grace!"

"Molly and Grace . . ." Kirby's soul-deep sigh of grief sent a chill down quite a few spines (including mine, much to my dismay).

Overcome by guilt, Jake fessed up: "Aww, Kirby . . . I didn't care about mailing your letter. But Jamey said we had to."

"Bless you, Jamey."

I rolled my eyes. I wasn't buying what Madame Killegrew was selling.

"You boys helped me rest easy," Kirby said. "I gotta go now. That ol' heavenly choir's waitin' for me."

"Playing your harmonica, I bet," Jake said

with a sniffle.

"So long, boys . . . so long." The voice faded, as if disappearing over the Hereafter's eternal horizon.

"Kirby — wait!" Jake called out. "What's heaven like?"

But the only response was Kirby's whispery singing, ever more distant and slow as his supposed spectral presence dissolved from our earthly realm:

Get ready for the Jubilee . . . Hurrah, hurrah!
We'll give the hero three times three . . . Hurrah, hurrah!
The laurel wreath . . . is ready now . . .
To place upon . . . his loyal brow . . .
And we'll all . . . feel . . . gay . . . when
  Johnny . . . comes marching home.

I felt like applauding Madame Killegrew, but figured it wouldn't be appreciated. With a mournful sigh, like a death rattle deep in her bones, her head drooped. Her ragged breathing seemed to stop. The rapt crowd of onlookers leaned closer — *did she die?* After twenty seconds that felt endless, her eyelids fluttered. Even I was relieved.

Nothing could outdo Madame Killegrew for an encore, so the party broke up soon after her séance. Since Eddie was heading back to Sea Breeze to stay with the horses, we made our way down to the lobby, taking the stairs instead of waiting for overcrowded elevators.

"I'll admit it," I said, "she put on a good show."

Jake stared at me. "A *show* — are you kidding?"

Vic nudged Eddie. "This should be a pretty good show, too."

I sneered at Jake. "How can you possibly think she's for real?"

"How can you possibly think she isn't?"

"Jesus, Jake. How come an ancient Greek guy spoke such good English?"

"Hey, he had an accent." Jake thought for a second. "Okay, smart guy. Then how'd she know Kirby's name? Huh?"

I shook my head. "His *first* name? Half the boys in the country are named John!"

"So she just guessed?!"

"She didn't have to — you *told* her!"

"I did not!"

"You *did*."

"I *didn't*." Jake appealed to Vic for support.

"Sorry, Jake," she said. "You did."

Jake doubled down. "Well . . . even if I did, how'd she know his *last* name?"

I laughed in disbelief. "You told her that, too!"

He was determined to go down fighting. "Well . . . if she wasn't for real, how else could she know about Kirby's letter? Nobody alive knew about that but you and me!"

"She *didn't* know — until you told her."

"I did not." But Jake looked at me all slantindicular as the truth seeped into his thick skull. "Did I?"

"Yeah," Vic confirmed gently, "you did."

That took most of the wind out of Jake's sails. Me, I'd been well-schooled by Mississippi Mike and knew chicanery when I saw it. "You fell for professional flimflam, pure and simple. That's what a talented charlatan does — she fools people."

Jake wasn't quite ready to fold. "Oh, like how *you* got fooled out of fifty-grand by Gideon Duvall on the *Queen of New Orleans*?"

"That was 'cuz you didn't tell me he was cheating, you slack-jawed idiot!"

"You're the idiot!"

Vic snickered. "How 'bout we stipulate you're both idiots, and move on?"

Jake challenged me to tell him *exactly* how Madame Killegrew tricked him. So I obliged. I (mostly) resisted sarcasm, but it wasn't easy. As the details piled up, what remained of my brother's accustomed piss and vinegar evaporated.

"I coulda sworn I heard Kirby playing his harmonica," he said with a rueful sigh. "It was . . . all in my head?"

"Where there's plenty of empty space," I said, giving him a fraternal pat on his shoulder.

"Jeezus. I really am a slack-jawed idiot."

"Aww, I bet she suckered half the people in that room." I could've made the case that Jake owed me ten dollars on our bet, but I didn't have the heart to collect. And despite my conviction that Madame Killegrew was a two-hundred-proof phony, I did have the *tiniest* doubt. Doing what she did as well as she did would've taken lots of work, and my skepticism couldn't completely explain everything — but I'd *never* admit that to my brother.

When we reached the lobby, there was Van Brunt holding court with a bunch of the rich horse folk (and ever-observant Horatio Deale) in front of the Market Street Tavern. Van Brunt saw us. "Well, if it isn't Mr. Lobo. You certainly got an earful from the spirit, didn't you?"

"Let it go," Vic warned in Eddie's ear.

But he still felt stung by his hazing during

the séance. Before she could grab him, he strode across the lobby. Van Brunt came straight at him — two trains on one track, collision imminent.

"Never mind Kleon," Eddie said. "Not only did my horses beat you and the other old-timers, but I got a mind to take 'em east next year, and beat you there, too."

"I say bring it on, son. But why wait? Take Phoenix to Baltimore for the fall meeting at Pimlico, and we can settle this in a few weeks."

"Maybe I'll do that."

Vic had no patience for bullies like Van Brunt, but she knew the risks of letting them get under your skin. She grabbed Eddie's arm and tried to drag him away. "We don't have the money to take a horse east."

But, like a horse, Eddie was too big to budge if he was of a mind to resist, which he was.

Van Brunt went for the kill. "Just now, at the present time, I'm thinking — why even wait for Pimlico? Before I pack up and head for Maryland, why not a one-mile match race Monday morning, right here at Sea Breeze — Grand Larceny versus Phoenix."

"My horse already whipped yours three times," Eddie said. "What makes you think one more race'll end any different?"

"Then you've got nothing to lose. The youth of America versus an old-timer."

"Okay . . . let's say I'm interested," Eddie said, to Vic's horror.

Van Brunt's entourage included a trio of Sea Breeze owners, who huddled with Van Brunt like Macbethian witches hunched over their boiling cauldron. They toiled and troubled over adding another race to their last day of competition, then consented to a match run Monday morning at eight.

Van Brunt suggested the stakes — five thousand dollars put up by each horse owner. Eddie's jaw tightened. "I don't have that much loose cash, Mr. Van Brunt."

"No, I don't suppose you do. I would say your worth is tied up in those horses, and that quaint little farm of yours." Van Brunt gnawed on his Dutch pipe. "Then I reckon we won't have our race, after all." He turned away, as if to leave.

"Wait," Eddie said. Vic punched his shoulder with all her might. It hurt, but he ignored it. "You don't need the money anyway."

Van Brunt turned back. "Not need, so much as want. Hmmm . . . what matters more to me than money? If you really want to run this race —"

"I do."

"Your pride's at stake, I get that. I'd never stand in the way of man's pride. So, let's say if you win, you get my five thousand."

"And if you win?"

"If I win?" Van Brunt let the question hang in the air. "I get Phoenix."

Vic managed to drag Eddie away from Van Brunt. "Are you loco?! Back out now, before it's too late!"

"If I do, these rich horse people'll never respect me."

Vic stood toe to toe with him. "And you think they're gonna respect you if you lose your best horse on a dumb bet?"

I tried to help. "Eddie, rich people's respect is highly overrated. But the only way to get it is by beating 'em at their own game, on the track — and you already did that. So you gotta ask yourself why you're doing this — what's in it for you?"

"We win that money, we could do things we can't afford now," Eddie said. "Vic, isn't that what we want?"

Jake interrupted. "Why're y'all tryin' to talk him out of this?"

"Because," I said, more to Eddie than Jake, "it's not what happens if you win — it's what happens if you lose."

"A man's gotta stand up for himself," Jake said.

Vic looked from Jake to Eddie, shaking her head. "I swear to God, between the two of you, you don't have half a brain!"

"Can you really afford to risk losing your best horse?" I said, hoping to force Eddie to focus on that very real possibility.

"Five thousand dollars means nothing to Van Brunt," Vic said. "But Phoenix means *everything* to us."

Eddie stopped for a deep breath. "Jake's right."

I waved my hands. "Jake is hardly *ever* right — and he sure as hell isn't now!"

"Phoenix beat Grand Larceny easy before," Eddie said. "He'll beat him again, hands down."

With that, he went back to Van Brunt, and agreed to terms.

"Phoenix will have a fine home at my Elysian Fields Farm, son," Van Brunt said. "I promise you that, and I keep my promises. You can look it up. Maybe you'll come to Maryland and visit him."

"Don't count your horses before they run, Mr. Van Brunt. We'll see you Monday morning."

As we watched Van Brunt lead his pack into the tavern, I wondered whether Vic would commit murder before Monday. And if she did, would she kill Van Brunt? Or Eddie?

Or, who knows . . . maybe she'd kill 'em both.

13

"Temper is what gets most of us into trouble. Pride is what keeps us there."
~ Mark Twain

Sunday morning, I bolted awake from what had to be a nightmare: By nefarious means I couldn't recollect, I'd dreamed that Van Brunt had roped Eddie into risking his great horse Phoenix in a pointless match race. But that was no bad dream — it was reality.

When Victoria went over to the Sea Breeze barns, me and Jake came along for moral support (and to keep her from clobbering Eddie). It was another in a stretch of unusually warm days for early October, begetting a blanket of unseasonably heavy fog over much of the city, including the race course.

Normally, with no racing on Sundays, it would've been a lazy day of pampering the horses and maybe having the jockeys take them out for light exercise. But thanks to

Eddie's foolish pride, he and Vic had to make sure Phoenix was ready. So that's what they did, with hardly a word between them.

Hoping for cooler weather and a stiff wind to blow away the mist, I had a premonition that something evil might happen if it was this foggy on Monday morning. I didn't share my worry with anybody, but I wondered how Madame Killegrew would appraise my inexact clairvoyance.

No more nightmares Sunday night, but not much sleep, either. I woke up early Monday and peeked out through the curtains. Instead of the bright sunrise I'd hoped for, I couldn't see across the street. If anything, Monday's fog was worse.

By the time me and Jake got to Sea Breeze, all involved had decided to wait and see if the weather might improve. By nine o'clock, with the fog still hanging low, Eddie and Van Brunt agreed the race would go on. When the starter called for riders up, Rafael recited the Lord's Prayer in Spanish and crossed himself, as was his custom, and he and Champagne Charley Fly mounted their horses.

At the tap of the starter's drum, they were off and disappeared into the fog. With visibility no more than a few yards and all sounds around him muffled, Rafael felt like he was wearing a gauzy blindfold and earmuffs. He held Phoenix on the inside, hugging the white rail so close he could almost touch it. Without that guide, he doubted he'd be able to tell up from down, and feared getting lost in some netherworld, never to be seen again.

Rafael let Phoenix take a slight lead, to see how Charley Fly would answer. To his surprise, Grand Larceny dropped back, falling far enough behind that Rafael lost sight of him, and the muted thudding of enemy hooves receded. Was Grand Larceny hurt? Or did Charley Fly have some voodoo up his silk sleeve?

For a few seconds, as Phoenix came out of the turn into the backstretch, Raf heard only the hoofbeats of his own horse. Where was Grand Larceny? Then, defying senses and reason, he heard his opponent's hooves again digging into the damp dirt, still behind.

Afraid to drop his guard, Rafael pushed Phoenix to pick up speed. They swept into the far turn — and for a few fleeting strides, disoriented Raf thought he heard a *third* horse. It had to be the fog playing tricks on him. Phoenix barreled wide off the rail and into the homestretch.

Out of nowhere, Grand Larceny came up on the inside, passing Phoenix and pulling away. In a panic, Rafael flailed the whip he hated to use. Always game, Phoenix sailed down the homestretch — too little, too late. They lost by a length. In under two minutes, the world inhabited by Eddie, Victoria, and despondent Rafael — in which the better horse should've won — had crumbled.

We ignored Van Brunt's gang parading in triumph past the grandstand and clubhouse, back toward the paddock. Rafael hopped off Phoenix and our little group surrounded him. By the distraught jockey's account, what happened out there was inexplicable. Did he really see and hear what he said he did? Or had he imagined it?

"I let you down," Raf said, man enough to look Eddie in the eye.

"Not your fault."

"Then whose fault is it?"

I weighed every factor I could think of. Track conditions and pace were middling, both horses healthy. Both had the same rest since Friday, the last of their three previous matchups, none of which Grand Larceny came close to winning. Something didn't add up — but what? I needed more time to figure it out. Good egg that he was, Eddie wanted to do the honorable thing and surrender Phoenix to Van Brunt right then and there.

I literally stood in his way. "What's your hurry?"

"Waitin' won't make it any easier."

"But what if Rafael didn't lose?"

"But I did," Raf said in confusion.

"Not if they cheated," I said.

Vic looked as low as a puppy kicked into the mud. "How? How did they cheat?"

"I don't know — yet."

"I gave the man my word," Eddie said. "He won the horse —"

"*Don't* say 'fair and square,' " Jake said. "Listen to Jamey. He's got a nose for shady shit like this."

I wanted to strangle my brother. Where was his support when Vic and me were trying to talk Eddie out of this race in the first place? "Eddie," I said, "you can keep your word tomorrow. It won't kill Van Brunt to wait a day."

I circled Phoenix, checking his hooves, assessing the mud and dirt on his legs and chest — as if any of that mattered. I mumbled something about wanting to inspect Grand Larceny, too, so we left Phoenix with Rafael and went to pretend-congratulate Van Brunt and his minions.

Van Brunt looked surprised to see us.

While Eddie, Vic, and Jake kept him occupied, I gave Grand Larceny the once-over — twice. Charley Fly sidled over to see what I was up to. Both he and his horse had some dirt and mud on them — but all that proved was that they'd been on the track and running behind for part of the race.

My brain raced through the possibilities: Had Rafael really stopped hearing the other horse — or only imagined it? Was there a phantom third horse? Did Charley Fly somehow take a fog-shrouded shortcut?

I wandered across the infield, to see if my rudimentary tracking skills (learned from our Indian friend Thomas Dog Nose during my brief career as a Union Army scout) might reveal anything. But after two weeks of racing, and dozens of horses tromping back and forth, there were so many prints and ruts in the grass, gravel, and mud that even an actual Indian might've been stumped.

It's tough to find evidence of duplicity when you don't even know what you're looking for. In the end, all I had were half-baked questions without answers. And that, unfortunately, is what I reported when we got back to the barn to find teary-eyed Rafael hugging his beloved horse.

"No point in waiting," Eddie said, looking

at me. "Is there?"

"I *still* think I'm right," I said, with a discouraged shrug.

"That ain't enough," Eddie said. He gently pried Raffie and the horse apart, and led Phoenix over to Van Brunt's barn. The rest of us marched a few despairing paces behind. The only thing missing was the accompaniment of a somber dirge.

Van Brunt greeted Eddie with feigned sympathy. "Son, some days you eat the bear, some days the bear eats you. You could look that up."

"When're you leaving?"

"Tomorrow. Once he's aboard my custom-built horse transport, he'll hardly know he's gone three thousand miles, riding in style any man would envy. Then I'll let him rest a week before a *real* trainer starts working with him."

I saw incendiary fury flare in Victoria's eyes at the offhanded insult, but she kept quiet and refrained from shoving Van Brunt's long-stemmed pipe someplace it didn't belong.

"I'll keep him under wraps," Van Brunt continued, "until I introduce him in a special two-and-a-half-mile match race the last day of Pimlico's fall meeting. Friday the twenty-fourth, if I rightly recall. That new

Pimlico is quite the jewel, the absolute pride of Baltimore, at the present time."

"I'm a little confused, Mr. Van Brunt," Eddie said. "Since Grand Larceny beat Phoenix today, why not enter Grand Larceny in that match race?"

I knew why. "Because Phoenix'll be an unknown back east, and he's gotta travel across the whole country to get there, so he's likely to be a real long shot — and you might clean up big on the betting."

"Smart thinking, son," Van Brunt said. "Though I suspect Larceny and Phoenix are even-steven in any given race, a once-in-a-lifetime wagering opportunity should not be frittered away. Plus, I would say part of the fun of acquiring a new treasure is showing him off. When he wins, they'll know I now have *two* horses they can't beat."

One of Van Brunt's stable boys led Phoenix away. The horse glanced back, as if to say goodbye. Eddie looked as forlorn as any soul I ever saw.

But Van Brunt wasn't quite done. "Miss Krieg, may I appeal to the common sense of the gentler sex?"

Vic clenched her teeth, and her fist.

Van Brunt enjoyed needling his victims. "I could soften the blow of losing Phoenix by paying you a king's ransom for that fearsome Arabian of yours. Why, with that much spirit, he'd be the toast of Maryland, Virginia, *and* Kentucky."

Eddie stepped in front of Vic, mainly to keep her from punching Van Brunt. "I don't think so," he said in a deathly quiet voice.

"Suit yourself," said Van Brunt.

Back at our barn, the empty stall where Phoenix should've been felt like an open wound. Lucifer stood in the next stall, hanging his head, knowing something was wrong. Vic's earlier white-hot rage at Eddie had burned itself down to ice, which might've been worse. She spoke in a bitter whisper. "You let Van Brunt *sucker* you —"

"Vic," Jake said, "the boy feels bad enough —"

She cut Jake off. "Eddie, you *should've* been smarter. You *should've* protected your best horse. How am I ever going to trust you again?" Without waiting for an answer Eddie didn't have, she walked away.

Despite my own ineptitude at deciphering women, I knew Victoria was talking about more than losing a horse. Head down, broken-hearted Eddie shuffled off in the opposite direction. Rafael tagged along, leaving me and Jake behind to ponder the wreckage.

"Your girl really skewered Eddie," I said.

"I don't know if she's anybody's girl."
"Maybe that's for the best."

14

> "Nothing is impossible to a determined woman."
> ~ Author Louisa May Alcott

The day after disaster, Jake and me spent an awkward morning helping Vic and Eddie get their horses and gear packed up for the sad train trip back to Fernando Farms, without Phoenix. We worked in sullen silence, broken only when Vic told Eddie she and Lucifer wouldn't be going with them — she needed time to think.

In my limited experience, when ladies stop to deliberate about the men in their lives, it's usually bad news for the men. Could it be that she and Eddie were done for good?

On one hand, Jake hoped they were, since courting Victoria would be easier without a formidable adversary. On a few other hands, he felt sorry for Eddie; he had some healthy fear of Vic's angry side; and even a blockhead like my brother could tell she was hurting, too.

Back at the Carlton, without telling Jake, I visited Vic's room. She didn't look like she'd been crying, but her sparkle was gone. "I know racing may be the last thing you want to think about right now," I said, "but can I ask you something?"

I took her dispirited nod as permission.

"How does Lucifer stack up against Phoenix — as a racehorse, I mean?"

"Lucifer isn't a racehorse," she said, "not by any jockey club rules."

"So he's not allowed to run in sanctioned Thoroughbred races, right?"

"Yeah. And — ?"

"When we went to Eddie's farm, you said they sometimes raced each other for fun — and up to two miles, Phoenix has a Thoroughbred's speed, so he'd always win. What happens over two miles?"

"Well, Arabians were originally bred for desert stamina. Plus, Lucifer's bigger and faster than most Arabians. So, at longer distances, he's got a potential advantage."

"Enough to beat a Thoroughbred at, say, two and a half miles?"

"Maybe. But he's not even allowed to enter."

"Unless it's a match race — where regular

rules don't apply. And maybe there's a way to get Phoenix back."

"How?"

"What if we take Lucifer to Baltimore, and enter him in that big match race? At two and a half miles, whether Van Brunt runs Phoenix or Grand Larceny, Lucifer *could* win — right?"

"Say he does — how does that get Phoenix back?"

"We lure Van Brunt into a side bet — if Lucifer wins, he has to give back Phoenix."

"And if Lucifer loses?" Vic guessed the downside. "Then Van Brunt gets him, too?"

"That might be temptation enough to get him into the game — on our terms."

"But I'd have to risk losing my horse!" She didn't like that equation.

"How good a horse is Phoenix, anyway?"

"He's a *great* horse. But this isn't one of your confidence schemes, Jamey. Unless you're planning a sure-fire cheat, there's no guarantee Lucifer'll win."

"Oh, there's never a guarantee. Even with your father, that whole railroad play was a gamble."

"How did you know he'd take the bait?"

"We didn't. But we knew pretty quick how greedy your father and brother were, knew what they wanted — and calculated what they were willing to do to get it. Not that there weren't a few scary twists and turns."

"Knowing how nasty my brother was — I mean, he *did* try to burn down your town — what made you even try it?"

"Serenity Falls was done for if we didn't. The potential reward was worth the risk."

"So, I have to decide if the *risk* of losing Lucifer is worth the possible *reward* of winning back Phoenix — ?"

"Pretty much."

Vic took a deep breath. "Yes. It's worth the risk."

"What if Eddie doesn't agree?"

"Don't forget — nobody says no to a Krieg." She frowned. "But why does it matter so much to you if we get Phoenix back?"

"Because I don't like bullies, or cheaters. And I don't like seeing good people get fleeced."

"But you hardly know me, and you know Eddie even less."

"I know you enough. And — don't you *ever* tell Jake — but I like my brother, he likes you. And you like Eddie." I had another reason I kept to myself — righting a wrong and saving Serenity Falls was good for my soul, and I liked how that felt.

"Speaking of things we're not telling Jake," Vic said, "*never* tell him I said this . . .

but I don't know what to do about him."

"Or Eddie?"

"Yeahhh . . . or Eddie."

"You like 'em both." A statement, not a question.

She tilted her head to one side, with a troubled furrow between her eyebrows — the first time I'd seen her bewildered. "Jake? He's all . . . sparks and fireworks."

"Not the first girl to say so. But . . . you might get burned."

She tipped her head the other way, with a serene hint of a smile. "And Eddie? He's like one of those big ol' redwoods."

"Rock-solid steady."

"Or so I thought — until he let Van Brunt skunk him."

"Nobody's perfect, Vic."

"I suppose not."

"And don't forget, his family roots go deep on that little *rancho* of his."

Vic nodded. "And we both *get* horses, y'know?" She groaned in frustration. "I never felt this way about any boy before. So — why two at once?"

"Never rains but it pours."

"Jamey, I don't want to hurt anyone."

"Well, you're not sneaking around, or lying to anybody. But you know somebody's gotta end up hurt."

"There's always polygamy," she said with a half-hearted laugh. "Dammit. I came out here to paddle my own canoe —"

"Which you're doing."

"— *not* to find a man to tie me down. And I am in *no* hurry to start popping out babies — which is all men seem to want. My mother died when I was born, my one brother died *before* I was born, my other brother's a monster. Seems like kids're nothing but trouble."

"Well, when it comes to matters of the heart," I said, "I'm not one to give advice —"

"And I'm not one to ask."

"— so I got nothing to say, one way or the other."

"And I appreciate every word."

"But right now we gotta get to Eddie —"

"— before he leaves for Redwood City!"

Which is exactly what we did, and none too soon. We grabbed Jake on our way out, dashed the buggy across town like we were in a pell-mell Roman chariot race, and reached Sea Breeze just as Eddie's caravan was about to clear out for the train depot.

Horatio Deale was there, too, for the interview we'd forgotten about in all the turmoil of the past few days. "I'd still like to write a story about the human side of recent events — your plans now that you've lost your best horse, how you're feeling."

"How're we feeling?" Vic echoed. "Like horse manure. What're our plans? We're going to get our horse back."

Eddie blinked in confusion. "We're gonna do what, now?"

With a nervous swallow, I explained my belief that Van Brunt had somehow cheated to steal Phoenix out from under Eddie. Then me and Vic explained our bug-crazy plan to go to Baltimore and enter Lucifer in the Pimlico match race, and how we *might* be able to devise a means of winning back Phoenix.

Horatio's eyes lit up. "Ahhh! Now, *that* has the makings of a glorious story. Once my readers get a taste, they'll salivate for more — and be rooting for you classic underdogs."

"Mr. Deale," Vic said, "you know more about racing than any of us. Is it even possible to enter my Arabian in that race?"

"I do believe such an entry would be 'according to Hoyle,' as they say. Indeed, with a match race, Hoyle holds little sway, since the rules are whatever competitors agree upon."

"Meaning," Jake said, "almost anything goes?"

Horatio nodded. "It's certainly not unheard of for Thoroughbreds to compete against other breeds, outside official code and canon. The usual motivations, of course, are pride and profit."

But if Victoria had warmed up to the notion of beating Van Brunt at his own game, on his own turf, Eddie didn't embrace the idea of going all that way for the sole purpose of exacting reprisal. He raised some practical questions Vic and me had glossed over in our quest for justice — for starters, how would we even go about entering a race only two weeks yet three thousand miles away?

I knew who could help us find out — our friend Mississippi Mike Morgan in Baltimore. Eddie agreed to wait at the track until we could wire Mike and ask him to find out the particulars. Once he replied, we could decide if a cross-country trek was worth the gamble.

Vic's determination wavered. "Mr. Deale, be honest — are we crazy?"

"Well, as Louisa May Alcott wrote, 'Nothing is impossible to a determined woman' — such as you. Baltimore is my home base for *American Sport & Spirit*. If you go, I should like to travel with you, file reports by telegraph *en route,* and whip up interest in the race. Your dauntless fellowship may end up nationally famous."

We agreed to keep him posted. Jake and me rushed back to the Carlton's Western Union office and wired Mike. I prayed for a fast reply — because the longer I had to think about this idea, the crazier it seemed.

In Baltimore, a Western Union courier climbed the stairs inside a red-brick building and knocked on the second-floor office door with its frosted window stenciled:

MICHAEL MORGAN, ESQUIRE
ATTORNEY-AT-LAW

"Come in," Mississippi Mike said from inside.

The kid opened the door and saw a round-shouldered little man with a wispy fringe of gray hair, sitting at his desk, reading *The Sun* newspaper. Mike peered over his specs. "Can I help you, young fella?"

The courier delivered the telegram, happily accepted a dollar tip and left. Mike read the message, got up, grabbed his derby, locked the door behind him, and walked to the livery stable three blocks away. He saddled his gray gelding and set out for the Pimlico race course five miles northwest of his Bolton Hill neighborhood.

Leaving the tidy streets of rowhouses, shops, and offices behind, Mike rode out into the countryside, past estates and farms. The lane skirted the newly-preserved six hundred green and wooded acres of Druid Hill Park, set aside for Baltimore residents to enjoy as the city grew around it.

Forty-five minutes later, Mike reached Pimlico's manicured grounds. He tied his horse to the fence outside the three-story Victorian clubhouse with its wraparound veranda, lacy gingerbread trim and green shutters. A cupola topped with a galloping-horse weather-vane crowned the red roof.

Mike went inside, up to the second floor, and entered the reception area outside the office of Chief Steward Emmett Pitt. He waited while a frantic young assistant ransacked his own desk until he pulled a single piece of paper from his jumbled pile.

"Hallelujah!" the assistant sang out — and abruptly noticed he had a visitor. "I'm so sorry! I'm Stanley — may I help you?"

"I were hoping for a moment of Mr. Pitt's time. I'm seekin' out facts about the upcoming match race."

Stanley led Mike into Pitt's office, where the rail-thin and equally agitated steward bounced up from behind his desk. Pitt's bony fingers snatched the document out of his assistant's hand. "Praise the Lord, Stan! Without you, boy, everything would be higgledy-piggledy — and then what?" Pitt raked his other hand through his rumpled brown hair and whisked muffin crumbs out of his beard. "Who's this, now?"

Mike introduced himself and stated the reason for his visit. Pitt confirmed that horses other than Thoroughbreds could enter the match race — but the owners had to show up *in person* no later than three days before the race to submit entry forms and pay a five hundred dollar fee.

"Even for folks coming from California by rail?" Mike asked.

"Rules are rules," Pitt said. "Without 'em, why, everything goes all —"

"— higgledy-piggledy?"

"That's the hardshell truth of it, Mr. Morgan."

Mike asked if Pimlico had a telegraph office on the premises. Stanley escorted him downstairs, where the operator tappity-tapped a concise summary of Mike's fact-finding results to us in San Francisco.

Riding out the main gate, Mike heard a voice equal parts gravel and honey calling him from the shade of a big oak tree resplendent in russet and gold foliage. "Howdy there, Mister Mike!"

Mike turned to see two black men wearing timeworn work clothes, selling fruits and vegetables from under the canvas canopies of their brightly painted one-horse carts. Baltimoreans knew them as "arabbers" (pronounced with the accent on the first long-A syllable — *AY-rabber*). These colorful peddlers and their wagons were stitched into the very fabric of the city, roving streets and alleys, enticing customers with melodic "hollers," as their chants were known.

Even well before the Civil War and Emancipation, free Negro men had been working as arabbers, since hawking produce was one of the few independent businesses open to colored folks. As to the name, some old-timers thought they were once called "street arabs," but nobody knew for sure.

Mike got off his horse, and he and the grizzled older man greeted each other with a hug. "Solomon Carver, you ol' dog. How's my favorite arabber?"

"Doin' fine, Mike. What brings you up to Pimlico?"

"Racing business. Haven't seen you in Bolton Hill lately."

"Sorry 'bout that. Been runnin' out of merchandise early, before I get on over to your neighborhood. I'll change my route for ya." Solomon nodded toward his glowering younger partner. "This here's Hub Robinson."

Robinson grunted and frowned. If Solomon Carver's genial manner radiated sunshine, his friend was a walking storm cloud.

Mike tried to engage him in conversation. "Are you new to arabbing?"

Taciturn Hub seemed disinclined toward chit-chat, so Solomon answered for him. "Hub's been strugglin' through some hard times lately, with his boy bein' sickly. Figured he could use some extra scratch, so I'm sharin' some of my best sellin' spots."

"This here's a good one," Mike said. "You get local city folks, plus the clubhouse dining room."

"Clubhouse chefs do like gettin' fresh fruits and vegetables without havin' to go to the wholesale markets."

"Not to mention," Mike said, "selling lots of carrots and apples to the grooms and trainers for all them racehorses."

"Like the Good Book says, a righteous man's supposed to take good care of his animals."

"Yours sure look healthy and well-fed."

"Some of that's the good Lord's doin', but we also get help from Champagne

Charley Fly."

"The jockey? Is he a friend of yours?"

"More like a friend to the horses. He spends some of his own prize money to make sure we arabbers got enough feed and doctorin' for these ol' ponies. He even helped us find barns in town where we can keep our horses an' wagons at a fair price."

"Mighty kind of him," Mike said.

"Well," Hub said, "I don't trust him."

"Why's that?" Mike asked.

"I don't think highly of the likes of Charley Fly. I saw him winning horse races for 'massah' Julius Caesar Pryce back before the war, when we were both slaves in Virginia. While the rest of us were gettin' worked to death in the fields, Charley Fly was livin' like a king just 'cuz he stayed scrawny and never outgrew that saddle."

"Now, Hub," Solomon said gently, "you know all that boy done was use the gifts God give 'im to make his way in a mean world. No cause to distrust a man showin' us some brotherly goodwill."

Hub grunted again and busied himself arranging the colorful fruits and vegetables displayed in his cart. But he did make a grudging effort to be sociable. "How long you boys known each other?"

"We go waaay back," Solomon said.

"Early '40s," Mike said, "when I were a poor kid studying the law. Kind soul that he were, Sol saved bruised fruits and veggies to sell to us broke students for half-price."

Solomon chuckled. "I forgot all about that."

"You knew that were all we could afford. Thanks to you, we had more than stale bread and water to eat. Why, even back then, you seemed to me like the oldest arabber in town."

"And now I really am!" Solomon said with a grin.

"When were you born, anyways?" Hub asked his friend.

"Born — blessed to be free — right here in Baltimore in aught-nine. Same year as President Lincoln. Edgar Allan Poe, too."

"I always loved reading Poe's stories and poems," Mike said. "I recall you telling me he was one of your customers."

"Gospel truth — back in the early '30s, when he lived here for a few years. Then he come back, passin' through, and up and died young. Nobody ever did know exactly what happened to him."

"A mystery," Mike said, "worthy of one of his dark tales."

Hub gestured toward two cooks in white kitchen aprons, approaching from the clubhouse with empty wooden crates. "Hey, Sol — customers."

"You take 'em, Hub. Mike an' me still got some fat-chewin' to do. Don't forget, the Good Book says a man that's got friends must show himself friendly. So smile and chat 'em up, and they likely to buy more."

Solomon and Mike watched as Hub made a game effort at good cheer and showed the kitchen workers the best selection from his wagon bins.

"You're an angel on earth, helpin' him out," Mike said.

"We all need a hand sometime, right?"

"You sure you're not getting too old for this work, Sol?"

"Hah! Do I look old to you?"

Mike laughed. "You *always* looked old to me."

Solomon swung his arm around to take in the immediate world. "All this keeps me young. I get to be outside, breathin' fresh air, talkin' to folks, spendin' time with my horse. It don't get no better, Mike. Ain't always been easy, but I always been free." Spoken like a man humble enough to count his blessings often.

"Not like poor Hub?"

For a rare moment, Solomon's smile faded. "Don't get no worse than bein' a slave. Hub told me he was about twenty-two when he escaped and come up north to Pennsylvania, first year of the war. Maryland wasn't no safe place for runaways."

"Did he have to leave family behind?"

"Like most. Can you imagine? Not knowin' if your kin got sold somewhere, or died?"

"It's a shameful stain on this here country. I only hope it'll wash out someday."

Solomon beamed again. "With time. I feel it my bones. Why, it's already better down South. Imagine — colored men gettin' *ee*-lected to Congress! I never thought I'd live to see that. God blessed this country, He'll help heal it."

"You got more faith than I do. Hub's lucky to know you. But with all he's been through, can a body like him ever be convinced the world's better than he sees it?"

Solomon pondered the question. "I can't tell him he's wrong if I never walked in his shoes. But I *can* keep showin' him what I see. Maybe someday he'll see it, too."

15

> "There ain't no surer way to find out whether you like people or hate them than to travel with them."
> ~ Mark Twain,
> *Tom Sawyer Abroad*

While Jake and me waited for Mike's reply at the Western Union booth in the Carlton lobby, it struck me what marvelous times we lived in. Instead of letters taking weeks, telegraphic messages could fly from coast to coast in minutes, across thousands of miles of wire strung up on countless poles.

The telegraph clerk translated all those dots and dashes and handed us the paper. We read Mike's news and hurried back to Sea Breeze to tell the others. The requirement that horse owners had to register in person meant we'd have to reach Baltimore and arrive at Pimlico, cash in hand, no later than noon on Tuesday, October 21.

Thanks to the transcontinental railroad, a grueling passage that once took months could be done in a week. If we left within the next couple of days, and the prairie didn't swallow up the train in some Biblical conflagration, we'd arrive with a few days to spare. That allowed for inevitable delays on a means of transportation still rough around the edges, especially in the western deserts where the Union Pacific and Central Pacific rushed to see which would claim bragging rights by reaching Promontory, Utah first.

Knowing we'd be able to get there in time should have cheered us up. But Eddie sat slumped on the bench in front of the barn, arms folded, unconvinced we should even try. "Vic, I know what Lucifer means to you."

"Phoenix means a thousand times more to you — and to us. You had that horse because your *papi* saved him from a fire."

"And you have Lucifer because you tamed an untamable Arabian, and your daddy bought him for you."

"But your *papi* built a way of life — he *gave* his life — so you could carry on. Mine? His own greed ruined him. So if it's a contest between which horse means more, yours does! And we should try to get him back."

"Not if you have to risk losing Lucifer, too."

"He's mine to risk."

"Eddie," Jake urged, "take yes for an answer."

But Eddie shook his head. "What if we go all that way, only to find out Van Brunt won't take any chance at all on losing Phoenix?"

"Fair point," I said. "We don't know for sure if Van Brunt's willing to risk Phoenix for a chance to win Lucifer, too. But I got a real strong hunch he won't be able to resist."

"Eddie," Vic said, "there's nothing men like Van Brunt and my father enjoy more than kicking a man when he's down."

"That ain't no guarantee," Eddie insisted.

"You're right," I said. "If we go, we might not get Phoenix back. But if we don't go, we *can't* get him back. *That's* a guarantee."

Vic knelt in front of Eddie. "Phoenix is the future of your *rancho*. We have to do this, to honor your father and grandfather." She stood up. "If you won't go, I'll take Lucifer and Raf, and go without you."

Eddie looked at the little jockey. "You'd go?"

"Damn right," Rafael said.

The big man took a deep breath. "Well, okay then. We'll go."

With Eddie's agreement, Victoria took charge. She and Eddie put up half the entry fee. Me and Jake kicked in the rest, which was only fair since I'd instigated the whole idea. Vic said she'd hold onto the money for security.

"Where're you gonna hide it?" Jake asked.

"For me to know — and none of you to ever find out."

We had barely two days to get ready. Vic stayed at Sea Breeze with Lucifer. Eddie and Rafael took the rest of their horses and equipment back to Fernando Farms, and packed what they'd need for the long trip.

Jake and me went to the Central Pacific office at the Carlton and bought tickets for Thursday, October 9 — Pullman sleeper compartments for the humans, and a livestock stall for Lucifer. Horatio Deale booked passage on the same train, nicknamed the *Twilight Flyer* because its five P.M. departure left the setting sun behind as it forged ahead into the night.

God, Mother Nature, and the railroad willing, we had reasonable expectations of arriving in Baltimore a week later, on Thursday, October 16, with time to spare. I tried not to think about how often "reasonable expectations" ended up not worth a tinker's damn.

■ ■ ■ ■

Eastbound transcontinental trains left not from San Francisco, but from Oakland across the bay.

With capitalism giving Christianity a run for its money as America's true religion, San Francisco's geographic disconnection had long bedeviled city power brokers who worried about losing out on trade and commerce. Notions for a bay bridge had been tossed around like a proverbial "hot potato" since Gold Rush days, but nobody could figure out how to build (or finance) a bridge over three miles of troublesome water.

In the grand American tradition, this civic puzzle attracted colorful crackpots like fleas hopping onto a hound dog. My personal favorite was Englishman Joshua Abraham Norton, who'd lost a fortune trying to corner the rice market, and then proclaimed himself Norton the First, Emperor of these United States.

Norton ordered the politicians to fund construction of a bridge *and* a tunnel — or he'd have the whole lot of 'em arrested by the army. While his decrees proved popular, no bridge or tunnel was ever built, and the city fathers escaped incarceration. Meanwhile, the insurmountable obstacle of an unbridgeable bay would keep the ferries in business for decades to come.

Leaving the Carlton laden with carpetbags, satchels, and a wheeled trunk containing Lucifer's gear, we and our horse sailed across the bay to the Oakland train depot. After a conductor punched our tickets, Jake tucked them back into the leather wallet he kept secure in his inside coat pocket.

While he, Eddie, and Rafael got our baggage aboard the train, I went with Victoria to load Lucifer into what turned out to be a modern livestock car designed to carry horses with less discomfort than riding in older cattle cars. Racehorse owners found them to be an acceptably quick, affordable, and safe way to ship valuable animals to and from far-flung racing venues. After we got Lucifer settled, we rejoined the others.

The *Twilight Flyer* left Oakland right on time — dare we hope a good omen? Casting our fate to the rails, it was Baltimore or bust.

16

"The one remedy for every evil — social, political, financial, and industrial — the one immediate vital need of the entire Republic, is the Pacific Railroad."
~ *The Rocky Mountain News,* 1866

American Sport & Spirit,
October 9, 1873
★ DEALE'S DEAL
by HORATIO DEALE ★

The attention of horse racing aficionados such as you, my Dear Readers, will soon turn to the dazzling new Maryland cynosure known as Pimlico. There, in roughly a fortnight, four wondrous Eastern steeds shall meet in a match race to be known far, wide, and henceforth as "The Great Baltimore Brawl" (courtesy of the fertile imagination of Your Humble Correspondent).

Yet one more last-minute entry is *en route.* This white California stallion called Lucifer is the quintessential dark horse — not a Thoroughbred, but a crotchety Arabian. And he is eastbound on the Transcontinental Railroad because of the outcome of an unwise personal wager in San Francisco, and the surrender of a superlative racehorse under suspect circumstances.

Neither the soothsaying powers of the Ancient Greek Oracle of Delphi nor the Sibyls of Classical Rome could have foreseen how the competitive results of one foggy Western morn would launch a grudge-fueled, arduous, Odyssean quest for justice, the denouement of which remains to be written.

From Oakland, the *Flyer* headed northeast through California's central valley, making a quick stop in Sacramento before chugging on into the night. The train boasted luxurious appointments throughout — polished wood and brass, lamps lighting each car, brocade upholstery everywhere, and sumptuous furnishings fit for royalty in the parlor and dining cars.

Soon enough, it was time for our first meal. Allow me to quote a far superior writer on the transcontinental dining-car experience. Mississippi Mike's friend Mark Twain wrote this:

> Upon tables covered with snowy linen, and garnished with services of solid silver, Ethiop waiters, flitting about in spotless white, placed as by magic a repast at which Delmonico himself could have had no occasion to blush; and, indeed, in some respects it would be hard for that distinguished chef to match our menu; for, in addition to all that ordinarily makes up a first-chop dinner, had we not our antelope steak, our delicious mountain-brook trout, and choice fruits and berries, and (sauce piquant and unpurchasable!) our sweet-scented, appetite-compelling air of the prairies?

After our own mouthwatering "first-chop" meal, we played cards and talked until the soothing rhythm of the train made us drowsy. We retired to our sleeping compartments — one for Victoria; Eddie and Rafael sharing a second; and me and Jake in a third. Splendid touches in each included inlaid woodwork, framed mirrors, and plush carpeting. Couches slid out to form beds, and the smartly engineered upper berths folded down at night and up to the ceiling by day. Snug and comfortable under crisp white linens, we all fell asleep moments after laying our heads upon downy pillows.

By morning, the train began its long climb into the Sierra Nevada Range, studded with peaks soaring 15,000 feet into the clouds. The terrain had challenged the Central Pacific's intrepid army of mostly Chinese workers with grades so steep that they had to use dangerous explosives to bore tunnels right through the great granite heart of the mountains. Even so, our train needed the power of a second locomotive to conquer them.

Over the formidable High Sierra, we rolled on down to Reno, and across the sunbaked deserts of northern Nevada and Utah. As we crossed the miles in speed and comfort, I wondered: How many pioneers dependent on horses, mules, and oxen to reach their promised lands had instead ended up as forsaken heaps of bleached bones?

The Overland Route curved north of Utah's Great Salt Lake and then southeast. As we skirted along the churning Weber River, the train slowed so passengers could get a good look at Devil's Slide, a narrow canyon between a pair of sharp limestone ridges rising up like Mother Earth's backbone.

On up through the river gorge, we passed the iconic Thousand Mile Tree. This ancient hundred-foot-tall pine had been spotted by Union Pacific workers as they laid track through Wilhelmina's Pass in early '69. Surveyors determined that the tree stood a thousand miles from the Union Pacific's eastern terminus at Omaha, and added a sign attesting to that fact.

The tracks then straightened east through the rolling prairies of southwestern Wyoming Territory. Small outposts had already sprouted alongside the rails, though most were little more than a depot, water tank, and a few cabins, and looked like they might not stand for long.

But steam locomotives were hungry fire-breathing beasts, and needed places where they could replenish their finite supplies of fuel and water. By the early '70s, most railroads preferred coal to wood, since coal yielded more efficient power and became less costly and more readily available as new deposits were mined. Wood, in turn, was in high demand for railroad ties and construction of towns.

Things sure had changed since the summer of '66, when Jake and me were desperate enough for a paycheck that we'd signed up to work for the Union Pacific. It only took us a few days of laying track in Nebraska to conclude that harsh physical labor was more likely to break backs than build character, and we moved on.

The *Flyer* continued east at a steady pace, and we got our first glimpse of the majestic Rocky Mountains in the distance. Comprised of many ranges bearing distinct names, the Rockies stretched all the way from western Canada to New Mexico, reaching 14,000 feet up into an endless sky.

While Chinamen had to surmount the Sierra Nevada in the west, legions of Union Pacific navvies in eastern Wyoming found the daunting Laramie Range blocking their way. That's where U.P. engineers decided to diverge from the trails first blazed by Indians long before the arrival of white men and their wheels, then used in succession by fur trappers, Mormons, Forty-niners, and pioneers. Instead, the railroad saved time and money by carving out a new route that proved shorter by a hundred and fifty miles.

At Evans Pass, west of Laramie, the Union Pacific reached its highest elevation at 8,200 feet. From there, the tracks descended through heartland hills and prairies and approached Cheyenne, which had been christened in 1869 as Wyoming's territorial capital. Springing up seemingly overnight, Cheyenne had been proclaimed by Eastern newspapers and local boosters as "The Magic City of the Plains," and owed its existence and growth entirely to the railroad.

When trains stopped to refill their tanks and tenders, passengers could find refreshment at local establishments. And the railroad brought newfound prosperity to formerly isolated farmers, with Cheyenne as a transportation hub connecting them to the marketplaces of a wider world.

The *Flyer* had scarcely stopped rolling when our conductors announced a one-hour Cheyenne layover — and warned passengers to return promptly or get left behind. Comfortable as the train was, most travelers were eager to stretch their legs and see what nearby restaurants and saloons had to offer. Vic went to check on Lucifer, and we promised to fetch her some food.

Broadsides and signs promoting this and that papered the depot walls and pillars — including, to my chagrin, advertisements for Emmaline Rose's upcoming shows at the Omaha Academy of Music. Never one to miss a fraternal opportunity to rub a little salt into recent wounds, Jake made sure I saw them.

A jumble of humanity crowded the platform — rugged miners, families bound for new homesteads and farms, wayfaring drummers hauling suitcases filled with samples of their wares for sale, all hoping to find their fortunes in America's untamed West. We trotted across the street to beat the rush, ducked into the first café we saw, and came out with a sack of ham sandwiches, a jug of cider, and time to kill.

Ambling back to the depot, we saw a knot of passengers and townsfolk gathered around a performer using the platform as his stage. Propped against a post, a brightly lettered sign proclaimed:

THE AMAZING ALBERTO & His Mighty Miracles of Magic, Fire & Strength!

We wedged our way into the herd and found a spot behind some short kids even Rafael could see over. The bearded man with olive skin entertaining on his makeshift stage was even bigger than Eddie — taller, with muscles where Eddie still carried some baby fat. He had his long black hair bound into a ponytail with a leather tie, and I guessed his age at around thirty. His *Mighty Miracles* included bending an iron bar, expertly juggling four sharp daggers, and fire-eating — all accomplished with a grin, and each feat earning cheers from spectators. Some tossed coins into a collection hat set down near the sign.

As we whistled our approval, Jake and me were surprised to hear a familiar voice right behind us: "Eight years later, and you're still letting Indians sneak up on you."

We turned to find our old Indian friend Thomas Dog Nose grinning at us. "Did I teach you nothing?" he teased.

Like Vic had said — big country, small world. How else to explain encountering an *amigo* we hadn't seen in so long? He looked good, dressed in purposeful trail clothing rather than Indian buckskins. A weathered brown Stetson shaded his bronzed face.

Thomas was about our age, and we'd met him during our short, inauspicious career as civilian Union Army scouts in northeast Texas at the end of the war. We'd been assigned to spy on this particular band of Indians and report their activities. Instead, we ended up learning that "redskin savages" weren't so different from us. Going about the daily business of living, not bothering a single white soul, they didn't deserve to be hunted, trapped, or exterminated.

When Jake and me learned of new army orders to forcibly drive Thomas's group into

Oklahoma's Indian Territory, likely killing a bunch in the process, we'd risked our necks to alert them and give them a chance to escape before the army could bring its brutality to bear.

Even though our commander didn't discover what we'd done, he was so furious at our general incompetence that he booted us out of camp — without horses. Since we really were incompetent scouts, we got hopelessly lost trying to get home, and probably would've died had Thomas not rescued us. His people fed us, and even gave us two horses. So we had a history of mutual friendship and respect.

With few other choices, Thomas and his kin had moved to Indian Territory voluntarily, but he knew life there wouldn't be great, and would only get worse. So he left to find work as a scout and guide all around Wyoming, Montana and Dakota, with Cheyenne as his home base.

"Guiding who, where?" I asked.

"White eyes who'd get as lost as you did. Homesteaders, trappers, prospectors. Some think there might be a new gold rush in the Black Hills. But they're too afraid of the Lakota to go up and see, which sounds smart to me. Then there's the bone-diggers."

Jake gave him a quizzical look. "Bone-diggers?"

"Ever heard of dinosaurs?"

"Yeah, I read about 'em," I said. "Scientists're digging up fossils of these giant beasts that died off millions of years ago."

Thomas nodded. "They're finding big fossil beds up in the Badlands. So these Eastern college boys and museum professors come west on expeditions to dig up whatever they can find."

"Have you seen 'em?" I asked.

"You bet! These critters were *waaay* bigger than horses. It's hard work, but pretty interesting. Sometimes they even get a cavalry escort."

"If they got soldiers," Jake said, "why do they need you?"

"If they do run into hostiles, I reckon it's not a bad idea to have an Indian face in the bunch," Thomas said. He dug into the deerskin pouch on his gunbelt and handed us a business card:

THOMAS DOG NOSE
Scout & Guide to Western Hinterlands
Wire Cheyenne, Wyoming Territory

"Did you boys settle down anywhere?"

"San Francisco, for now," Jake said. "Classy hotel called the Carlton."

"Then what're you doing out here?"

"Long story," I said. "We're heading to Baltimore for a horse race. Maybe we'll look you up when we come back through."

"Maybe I'll visit you in San Francisco."

The magical show ended when the locomotive bell clanged, and the conductors marched along the platform rounding up stragglers.

With nimble efficiency, The Amazing Alberto stowed his props and sign in a rolling trunk and got back on the train. Thomas went his way and we went ours. Victoria returned from visiting Lucifer in the livestock car, and we boarded the *Flyer* for the next long stretch of our journey — twenty-two hours and five hundred miles to Omaha.

The train left Cheyenne and headed into the gathering dusk. We went to sleep that night expecting an early morning breakfast stop at Grand Island in central Nebraska, and then a five P.M. arrival at Omaha on Monday, October 13.

The swaying of a railway coach can be as hypnotic as the gentle rocking of a cradle. Should that motion cease, sleeping passengers tend to wake up — and that's what

happened around five the next morning.
All because of the train wreck . . .

211

17

"Man plans — and God laughs."
∼ Old Yiddish Proverb

Fortunately, the derailed train wasn't ours, but a long freight train that had been barreling through the night until meeting its doom in the dark grasslands between the towns of North Platte to the west and Grand Island to the east.

Aroused from slumber in the middle of Nebraskan nowhere, passengers peering out into the pre-dawn darkness could see railroad workers with lanterns up ahead, and not much else. Our conductors spread the word — the wreck had happened six hours earlier and a couple of miles ahead of us. We'd be delayed for hours until track damage could be repaired by a wrecker train and crew dispatched from Grand Island.

We were about two hundred miles past Cheyenne, which left us nearly three hundred miles (and twelve hours) away from Omaha. Fortunately, the extra days we'd allowed for travel meant we should still get to Baltimore days before our deadline.

With a warning not to stray far, the conductors hung out lanterns so passengers could go outside, get some fresh air, and stretch their legs. Others stayed inside, reading, napping, or gabbing. Some quietly contemplated the immensity of the American continent.

As hours passed, we learned more of what had happened. Seems the buffalo grass covering hill and dale appealed not only to the few remaining buffalo, but also to wandering cattle. You might think any collision between a hundred tons of Iron Horse and some cows would favor the train. But when cattle crossed railroad tracks at the wrong time, the encounter posed a mortal threat to trains as well, especially at night when engineers could not see far ahead. It was left to railroad workers to clear away derailed cars and accidentally butchered beef.

Before long, the eastern sky turned from star-spangled onyx to indigo as a coral sunrise painted clouds on the horizon. I thought back to when we were kids in Serenity Falls, reading classic books Mama had collected for the town's school and library. I was captivated by the epic yarn of long-wandering Odysseus and his crew, who saw their own "rosy-fingered Dawn" in Homer's ancient verse.

With daylight, Vic and Raf went back to visit Lucifer in the livestock car. Jake and me tagged along. Whenever our train stopped for any extended length of time, they'd seize the opportunity to bribe Lucifer with apples, carrots, peppermint candies, and sugar cubes, hoping that horse and jockey would become friendly enough that Lucifer might allow Raf to ride him.

As to whether their plan was working, Rafael remained dubious, while Vic chose to be optimistic. At least Lucifer was more interested in eating the treats than biting the hand that fed him. With half our trip ahead of us, plus days of practice once we reached Baltimore, they'd keep at it.

"So," Jake said to me, "have you figured how Van Brunt cheated?"

My jaw clenched. "No." Jake knew damn well few things annoyed me more than a puzzle I couldn't solve.

After a delay of almost three hours, the locomotive's bell clanged. Conductors rounded up their wandering flock, then waved to the engineer. With three moans of the steam whistle, we got slowly underway, and saw the toll those overmatched cattle had exacted on the mighty machinery that killed them. The wrecker train had winched five derailed freight cars off the torn-up tracks, and the ill-fated locomotive lay on its side where it gouged a long scar into the prairie sod. Three blanket-covered bodies of train crewmen on the grass were a sobering reminder that this modern means of transportation could still be unpredictably hazardous.

Our train tiptoed along a mile of new rails laid in a hurry by the repair crew. The *Flyer* could not resume its usual speed of twenty to twenty-five miles an hour, since we had to follow the hulking wrecker train back to Grand Island, where we stopped for a quick meal.

Vic and Rafael paid another call on Lucifer. To their surprise, the horse nuzzled his prospective jockey without trying to bite him, so Rafael insisted that Vic return to our coach while he'd keep Lucifer company until we reached Omaha. Despite concern for Raf's safety, she reluctantly agreed.

The engineer telegraphed news of the delay to the Union Pacific office in Omaha, with arrival now expected at around eight P.M. instead of five. Now that consistent schedules had been established — thanks to accurate clocks and near-instantaneous telegraphic communications — timeliness was truly next to godliness for railroad men. So our engineer left Grand Island determined to make up for lost time. The *Flyer* spread her express wings, exceeding twenty-five miles an hour with ease — Omaha, here we come!

All was well — until the train braked so suddenly that passengers walking the aisles were thrown off their feet. What new disaster had we encountered?

18

"We humble Reivers thank thee for these gifts of jewels and money, and leave ye with a blessing: May your byways all be sunny."
~ Sir Robin Nettles, Gentleman Highwayman

There we were, becalmed again, this time a few miles past North Bend in eastern Nebraska. It was a bit after five P.M., still more than two hours from Omaha. Was there another obstruction on the tracks? More suicidal cattle?

Gazing out a window, I thought of all the vast acreage along the Union Pacific's route which had been delivered unto the grasp of railroad boss Thomas Durant and his corporate leeches in the form of federal land grants. This enormously valuable exchange had been central to the original Pacific Railway Act signed by President Lincoln on

July 1, 1862.

Lincoln believed railroads would be crucial not only to preserving the Union and defeating the seditious South, but also to the future of a reunited nation. He knew that generous land giveaways were a necessary evil, and worth the price if that's what it took to complete such an audacious project. In addition to being paid for construction progress by the mile, the railroad companies were free to develop all that granted property themselves, or sell it to other developers or directly to homesteaders. Any which way, the arrangement made assorted robber barons staggeringly wealthy.

And speaking of robbers, we could see in the late afternoon shadows that our train was being held up by nine bandits on horseback, who had blocked the tracks with rocks and logs. Gossip spread among the crew and passengers that we were at the mercy of a gang known as the Border Reivers. Their leader was a courtly man in his thirties.

"That's Sir Robin Nettles," our conductor said as he looked out the window with us.

"How do you know?" Jake asked.

"From reading the papers. Nobody dresses up like Robin."

As desperadoes go, he was decked out like

an old-time highwayman in a black slouch hat with a long pheasant plume stuck in a red-ribbon hatband, burgundy cutaway coat, and a dashing crimson silk scarf. Some of his men hid their faces behind bandanas, others didn't bother — a sign of confidence in their skill at eluding the law.

"He ain't really a lord or a duke or anything, is he?" Jake asked.

"Sure," I said. "I bet Queen Victoria knights train robbers all the time."

Jake didn't appreciate my sarcasm, and I didn't really care. The only thing that mattered was yet another delay due to this latest bit of bad fortune.

According to the conductor, the Border Reivers had gained notoriety for holding up stagecoaches and small-town banks on both sides of the Nebraska-Iowa border. Train robberies were not yet common at the time, but the more railroads that got built, the more they got robbed, which stands to reason. So the Border Reivers had expanded their criminal bag of tricks to keep up with the competition.

Sir Robin's voice boomed out, with an accent mixing Cockney, Scots, and Irish. "Sorry for the inconvenience, ladies and gents. If everyone cooperates with me merry men, you'll be on yer way in no time. Y'have me word."

Jake started to slide his revolver out of his holster. But the conductor shook his head. "The Reivers are known for being peaceable, so nobody gets hurt."

"Just one shot," Jake grumbled, leaving the gun holstered. "That's all I wanted."

And that's all he'd have gotten, since the outlaws were well-armed with pistols, Winchesters, and shotguns — odds lopsided enough to discourage resistance.

Robin put his fingers in his mouth and chirped out two loud whistles. "Makepiece, Piggot, Sprottle — on the fly now, lads!"

Like well-trained troops, the Border Reivers commenced their assigned tasks. Three of them — one burly, one skinny, one squat, and probably the aforenamed Makepiece, Piggot, and Sprottle — jumped off their horses and trotted down the tracks to the mail-express car where the safe and assorted valuable cargo would be. Three other men spread out to keep the coaches under surveillance, in case any passengers harbored heroic intentions. One more escorted the engineer and fireman out of the cab at gunpoint, assuring the train wasn't going anywhere.

Robin himself and a flinty-eyed tenderfoot too young to shave made their way through the first-class cars. They politely relieved the wealthiest passengers of personal valuables, including jewelry, watches, and anything that might contain money — pocket books, bill books, purses, pouches, and wallets of varying descriptions were all deposited into a pillowcase held open by the young robber.

When he got to us, Jake said, "Kid, do you mind if I just —"

But the kid gestured with his pistol and cocked the hammer. "Easy, now."

"There's something I gotta —"

"Take out that shiny Colt barker with two fingers, nice an' slow, and empty the chambers onto the floor."

With gritted teeth, Jake obeyed. The cartridges fell out of his gun and rolled under the seat.

"Now yer money, sir."

Jake reached into his coat and pulled out his tan leather wallet. "You're welcome to the cash, but first I gotta —"

"Nope. All of it, into the bag."

Jake grimaced and dropped his wallet into the pillowcase. The kid moved on down the aisle.

Robin bantered with passengers as he went: "That's a lovely brooch, *mad'moiselle* — an heirloom, no doubt? Keep it. Sorry for the bother . . ."

Robin's efficient gang members made quick work of the robbery and soon reconvened near the locomotive. The engineer with a walrus mustache called out, "Robin, you're my first robbery!"

"Well, we're still new at this ourselves. What's yer name?"

"Friends call me Greenie. Sorry we didn't have no gold for ya."

Robin shrugged. "Win some, lose some. As a wise man said, 'Just so long as we come out ahead.' Makepiece! Piggot! Sprottle!" he bellowed. "We're on the bloomin' clock here, mates!"

Greenie the engineer looked disappointed. "Hey, Rob! You're leavin'? Without a song?"

I gave our conductor a confused glance. "A song?"

"Robin's trademark, I hear. Makes the robbery go down easier."

"No, it doesn't," Jake muttered.

"Well, Greenie," Robin said, "this bein' yer maiden robbery, how could I fail to oblige?" He cleared his throat, and crooned a spry tune in his pleasant tenor:

> Ye ladies fair and gents, kind comrades of
>   the road
> May your travels fly much faster as we've

lightened up your load.
We humble Reivers thank thee for these
   gifts of jewels and money,
And leave ye with a blessing — may your
   byways all be sunny!

Greenie and some passengers applauded. Robin tipped his hat.

Jake shook his head. "A robbery — and a floor show."

"He enjoys his work, I'll give him that," I said.

"Rob!" the tenderfoot called out. "Here they come!"

"About bloody time," Sir Robin said. But his irritation quicksilvered into delight when he saw why his three chums were tardy, in addition to lugging two heavy sacks liberated from the express car. "Well, well! What've ye got there, Makepiece?"

"Some bang-up horse, eh, Rob?"

But it wasn't just *any* horse being led by a rope tied to his halter. It was Lucifer. Robin looked pleased by such an unexpected treasure.

Victoria pounded on the window. "Those buggering bastards're stealing my horse! Why is he just *going along*?!?"

Taking compliant Lucifer with them, Robin and his men rode away to the north.

It took me, Jake, and Eddie to restrain Vic from rushing out after them. Once they were out of sight over the hills, we let go of her.

She slumped into the seat, shaking her head in angry astonishment. "Damn that horse! He just prances off without so much as a kick?! The *one time* he needed to put up a fight . . . that *goddam* horse." But her anger took a sharp turn to worry. "Uh-ohh."

We all thought the same thing at the same time: If Lucifer didn't put up a fight, Rafael probably did. We scrambled out and ran back to the livestock car, where we found Raf crumpled and groaning in the straw near Lucifer's stall. He'd been laid out by a couple of haymakers and blood trickled from his nose. Jake grabbed a bucket and dribbled a handful of water over the jockey's face until his eyes flickered open.

Vic sat next to him and cradled his head in her lap. "Poor Raf — are you okay?"

Rafael sat up, saw the empty stall, and groaned. "H-h-how did they steal him? He didn't kick or bite? I tried to stop 'em."

"You got more grit per pound than anybody I know," Eddie said, "but how were you gonna beat three guys?"

Rafael sighed. "What're we gonna do?"

Vic's jaw tightened. "We're gonna get our horse back. *That's* what we're gonna do."

19

> "No matter how bad things get,
> they can always get worse."
> ~ Jamey Galloway

With the train underway again, another hour behind schedule, we five huddled in Vic's compartment. Eddie sounded hopeless. "How're we gonna get him back?"

"I don't know, but we will," Jake said, as if trying to convince himself. "Right, Jamey?"

All eyes on me. "Uhhhh . . . yeah. Yeah, we're gonna get him back."

"You got some ideas in that head of yours, right?"

My brother generally liked to mock my ideas. Now — when I didn't have a single one — *now* he couldn't wait to hear them.

Jake tried to brighten our collective mood. "Jamey's a good tracker."

"I'm not *that* good a tracker."

"This is no time for honesty," Jake said.

"We got other problems," Eddie said. "They stole all our money."

"Not all," Vic said.

"The entry fee?" Jake asked.

"The entry fee," Vic confirmed.

"You kept it hid?"

"I kept it hid."

"Where?"

"Stitched inside my corset."

Bless Victoria for her foresight in protecting that precious five hundred dollars. Of course, we all knew the entry fee meant nothing without the horse. And some of that cash would have to be spent to retrieve Lucifer, which we were not going to do on foot. So, even if we got him back and made it to Baltimore, we wouldn't have enough funds left to enter the race. But we had other treacherous bridges to cross before we got to that one.

Our conductors announced that the *Flyer* would make an unscheduled stop around seven o'clock at the next town — Fremont, Nebraska. Arrival time in Omaha had been pushed back to nine at the earliest. It hadn't been a great day for us. And if life had taught me anything, it was this: *No matter how bad things get, they can always get worse.*

We knew the road to retrieving Lucifer

would begin with hopping off the train at Fremont — but that and equipping ourselves for a search were the easy parts. After that, all our goals were in serious doubt. With no idea where Robin and his bandits had gone, how would we find them? If we were relying on my tracking skills, we could be in big trouble.

Even if, by some miracle, we were able to find them, how were we going to convince them to return our horse? We weren't going to overpower them, and we didn't have a lot of surplus cash to buy him back. We could try charm, but nobody was betting on that.

Horatio Deale ducked into our compartment to check on us. When we told him our plan, he blanched. "I admire your optimism, and may Fortune favor the foolish." He said he'd wire a story about our travails from Fremont to his magazine's Baltimore office, and then he'd have to travel on without us. He hoped to see us and our missing horse soon in Baltimore. "At least your tickets will allow you to resume your journey." Then he left to finish writing his dispatch.

"About that . . ." Jake said with a queasy look on his face.

That's when I realized he'd been acting twitchy ever since the robbery. "About *what?*"

"Our train tickets . . . ?"

We all stared at him. He tried not to squirm. He failed.

"What *about* our train tickets?" I asked, pretty sure I wasn't going to like the answer.

"I — uhhh — they — mmm — what I mean is . . . well, I tried to —"

I leaned in, nose to nose. "Just say it."

Jake shut his eyes. "They got stolen." The compartment wasn't that big — he had no place to hide.

"Why would them robbers want train tickets to Baltimore?" Rafael said.

"Wellll," Jake said, "I . . . I don't think they necessarily *wanted* 'em."

I groaned. "They were in your stupid wallet."

"Hey, it's not like I could've stitched 'em inside my corset!" Jake looked like he wanted to jump off the train.

I'd have been happy to push him. "Why would you keep 'em in your wallet?"

"Where else would I keep 'em?"

"Anywhere else!"

"Jamey, he didn't know we'd get robbed," Vic said in Jake's defense.

She was right. But that and Jake's obvious contrition didn't solve our newest problem, which Rafael summed up: "If we get off in Fremont, and we got no tickets, how do we get back on and get to Baltimore?"

I buttonholed a conductor passing by our compartment and explained our predicament. Under the circumstances, with the robbery and all, might the railroad show mercy and allow us to continue through to our original destination? Or issue replacement tickets? Even though he sympathized, his hands were tied by strict railroad policy. We'd have to buy new tickets, which meant dipping into our entry-fee money.

Vic looked grim. "Without Lucifer, it doesn't matter if we never get to Baltimore. So, first things first — find our horse, figure out the rest later."

Right around sundown, the *Twilight Flyer* steamed into Fremont, passing a big sign proclaiming it as the Dodge County Seat. We hauled our belongings off the train and walked down the platform, where we saw posters announcing Emmaline Rose's Omaha shows, and The Amazing Alberto performing there in Fremont at the Elkhorn Theatre.

Most towns near the railroad consisted of a few dirt streets with some ramshackle cabins, shanties, and businesses, maybe a tiny church. They often appeared so fragile that a strong prairie wind might just blow 'em away.

Flourishing Fremont had managed to put down deeper roots. Located on the north bank of the Platte River, about forty-five miles northwest of Omaha, it was named for John C. Frémont, trailblazing western explorer, first Republican Party presidential candidate, Union Civil War officer, and later U.S. Senator from California.

Anticipating western expansion of the Union Pacific, the town started out in 1856 with a dozen or so log cabins. Once the railroad got there ten years later, along with transcontinental telegraph wires, Fremont developed into a full-fledged regional rail nexus. By '73, it was home to two thousand residents, ten times the size of tiny North Bend twenty miles to the west. All in all, Fremont would be a suitable base for us as we set out after the Border Reivers and Lucifer.

We checked into the Chittenden House Hotel three blocks from the rail depot. So new it still smelled like fresh wood and paint, it was Fremont's most imposing building, with sandstone exterior walls that glittered when the sun hit it right. It had a colonnade veranda surrounding a landscaped courtyard with lawns, trees, benches, and flower gardens. Rooftop carillon bells chimed each hour.

It was all rustic elegance inside, with simple furnishings, high ceilings, and sturdy oak beams. The lobby had a wide staircase to the second and third floors — not an elevator in sight. We could only afford one room, but all we needed was a place to sleep and stow our bags. Once we'd settled in, I dashed over to the telegraph office and wired Mississippi Mike in Baltimore:

Nebraska train robbery. Horse stolen. Stuck in Fremont. More soon. J and J

20

"Step right up, folks! What'll it take to put ya on some horses today?"
~ Oley Bergstrom, purveyor of fine used horses

Thanks to Chittenden House hospitality, in addition to the two beds, we shoehorned three cots into our room, but our sleep was fitful at best. Early the next morning, Tuesday, October 14, we left Rafael at the hotel to guard our baggage like a tough little junkyard dog. The rest of us went out to buy supplies for our mission.

We didn't know how long our search for Lucifer might take, but learning of a few towns with general stores north of Fremont and North Bend meant we could travel lighter and replenish provisions on the way. What we truly needed was a change of luck, which we couldn't buy in any emporium.

Seeking four riding horses and a pack

animal, we made Bergstrom's Livery our first stop. If you love horses, a well-kept barn or stable feels like a cathedral — but Bergstrom's worn and weather-beaten establishment fell far short of that ideal. Cracked, graying boards and fence rails hinted at too many seasons with too little upkeep. Good horses didn't come cheap, so serviceable would have to do. Owing to Jake's lifelong misgivings around horses, he hung back as Vic, Eddie, and me sized up Oley Bergstrom's played-out stock.

We found the threadbare proprietor dressed in a drab sack coat and mismatched pants, with a dusty derby atop his scraggly hair. Grinding a generous tobacco chaw in his right cheek, he greeted us with a cock-eyed grin and a jolly Swedish singsong in his carnival-barker's patter. "Step right up, folks! What'll it take to put ya on some horses today?"

"That depends," I said.

"How many are ya in the market for?"

"Four to ride," Vic said, "one to pack."

"Five, ya say?" Bergstrom waggled a handful of fingers, and gestured toward his smelly stalls. "You want horses, I got horses. Five *fine* horses yonder for you *fine* folks — at a *fine* price!"

"How fine a price?" I asked.

"Say, one-fifty."
Vic grunted. "For all five?"
"Ha-ha-ha-ha! For each, young lady. Yah, it's a deal, I can tell ya for sure!"
"Not a *good* deal," Eddie mumbled.
Oley kept grinning. "As my dear mama used to say, *'Smakar det så kostar det'* — ya get whatcha pay for."
His horses were not worth a penny over sixty apiece. Though they'd probably get the job done, his price was outrageous — and beyond our budget. Despite Bergstrom's cheerfully extortionate offer, I had to give him credit for his enterprising enthusiasm. Before I could whittle down the price, Vic took charge — and Eddie and me knew enough to let her.
Hooking Bergstrom by the elbow, she guided him past several of his own raggedy beasts, pointing out a list of physical flaws extensive enough to fill a Sears catalogue. Some were swaybacked. A few stood with stances too close, others too wide. They were variously pigeon-toed and splay-footed, bow-legged, knock-kneed, or cow-hocked. Too skinny, too fat. All had terrible teeth.
Unfazed, Oley grinned and talked fast. "I been around long enough to know nobuddy's perfect, *min skatt*. And I ask ya, which

none of us isn't a little past our prime? But y'know what that's called? *Experience!* Y'know what experience gets ya — knowledge! Doin' more with less — doin' what matters, style be gosh-damned!"

"Twenty each," Vic said.

Oley chin-chucked her. "I see, I see. Yah, I can come down to one-forty."

"Thirty."

"I'll meetcha at one-twenty."

"In that spirit, sixty."

Their flinty gazes locked, like gunfighters poised to draw.

Oley said, "An even hundred."

"Okay . . . fifty."

Oley blinked. "Huh?"

"Fifty. Five-oh," she enunciated.

Jake and me snickered as we recognized the same combative upside-down bargaining tactic we'd seen her ruthless father employ during our railroad-stock swindle. When the seller is desperate enough, rather than a good-faith meeting in the middle, make lowball, bad-faith offers to drive the price down.

"Alrighty then," poor befuddled Oley said. "Ninety."

Vic's eyes narrowed. "Forty."

Sweat beaded on Oley's forehead. He pooled an excess of tobacco juice in his cheek and spat intentionally close to Vic's boots. Instead of a flash of temper, she gave him her sweetest smile.

After several dry swallows, Oley knew he was being outclassed by a young filly. "Ooo-kay, eighty."

"Sorry, Mr. Bergstrom. No deal." Vic shrugged and led us toward the barn door, quietly warning us, "Do *not* look back."

We didn't dare, and one stride before we were out the door, we heard Oley croak, "Sixty."

Vic stopped, without turning. "Tack and saddles included."

"Yah, ma'am."

"That's a deal, Mr. Bergstrom," she said with a coy glance over her shoulder.

So we had ourselves five barely adequate horses. We saddled up and clip-clopped over to Zimmerman's Mercantile around the corner from the hotel, where we expected to spend most of our remaining funds. Vic and Eddie stayed with the horses. Jake and me went inside.

Spanning two storefronts, with twelve-foot ceilings that made it seem even bigger, Zimmerman's had ample space for well-stocked display shelves, cases, and tables. We'd already calculated what we'd need to last us three or four days — canned vegetables and beans, fresh biscuits to eat before they got stale, hardtack (which started stale and stayed that way), pork and bacon, coffee, and dried fruit to snack on while riding.

Among Zimmerman's sundries, we took a few pots and pans, tin plates and cups, forks and knives, a couple of lanterns, boxes of matches, and such necessities as blankets, rope, two compasses, and a large sheet of canvas to hoist as a shelter in case of rain. We'd all brought rugged trail clothing, coats and gloves with us from California to be ready for unpredictable eastern autumn weather.

I deferred to Jake's judgment on what weapons we'd need for a possible confrontation with outlaws. He figured on one pistol and gunbelt for each of us, plus a Winchester rifle, a second-hand shotgun, and plenty of ammunition. We piled all our selections up at the counter, and while ol' Mr. Zimmerman tallied up our purchases, Jake scuttled off and came back with a half-dozen cans of peaches.

I shook my head. "Nope. We already got dried fruit."

"Canned is better."

"Canned is heavy."

"If I'm gonna have to ride a horse for

days," Jake said with righteous indignation, "I am gonna have canned peaches to look forward to."

No sooner had I surrendered with a long-suffering sigh than Jake's furtive gaze scanned a shelf behind the front counter, stocked with spices in cans and bottles. They ranged from allspice to thyme and turmeric, with a cook's treasury of alphabetical ingredients in between.

But I knew what he wanted. "Nope. No cinnamon."

When it came to sincere innocence, nobody faked it better than Jake. "What makes you think I want cinnamon?"

"You're looking right at it."

"I could be looking at . . . at marjoram."

"You don't even know what marjoram is."

"Do you?"

"No. But I know you love cinnamon. Our funds are limited."

He could practically taste it. "But it's *so good* with peaches."

"Be glad you got the peaches."

"Everybody loves cinnamon," Jake grumbled.

"Not me," Mr. Zimmerman said. "Burns my gut somethin' awful."

After parting with much of our cash, we moved our purchases out to the boardwalk.

Eddie and Vic got everything stowed and secured on the horses, and we were as ready as we could be. With Sir Robin's trail leading who-knows-where and growing colder by the minute, we rode out of Fremont at eleven that morning.

We had a horse to find.

If Lucifer was the needle, Nebraska was one hell of a big haystack.

21

"Horses're dangerous at both ends, and uncomfortable in the middle."
～ Jake Galloway

It took us 'til noon to ride back along the railroad tracks to where the train had been robbed. The next chore was trickier — identifying the gang's trail with certainty.

Maybe it was a sign of improving luck, or the blessing that it hadn't rained since the Border Reivers stole Lucifer the day before. Or my having actually learned something about tracking from Thomas Dog Nose eight years back. Or (and this would be my guess) the tracks were so obvious that a blind man could've found them. Whatever the reason, we picked up their trail and set out after them.

Because Vic thought it was better for his feet, Lucifer never wore horseshoes. He also tended to lead with his right front hoof.

Those factors made it easier to follow his distinctive tracks among all the hoof prints left by the gang's other horses.

Still, at best, tracking is slow going. We kept at it all afternoon, across open fields, along roads, through woods and brush. Nearing sundown, knowing nothing of the terrain ahead or how far we might have to go to find the robbers, we decided to stop while we still had some daylight and make camp in a clearing by a brook.

After we ate, we left the fire burning and nested in our bedrolls and blankets. As I tried to fall asleep, Jake next to me whispered, "Admit it."

"Admit what?"

"You're glad I talked you into the peaches."

"Shut up and go to sleep."

But Jake wasn't quite done: "Have you figured out how Van Brunt cheated?"

"No. But thanks for reminding me, so now I'll be up all night thinking about it."

Of course, I already had plenty of reasons for not sleeping — comfort, for starters, or the lack thereof. Like the finicky gal in the fable of "The Princess and the Pea," I felt every pebble under my bedroll. I also heard every noise in the woods — including a rude gaggle of geese that spent *hours* shuffling their webbed feet through crunchy fallen leaves, honking as they went.

By the ripe old age of a quarter-century, I'd already been spoiled by our staying in hotels and deluxe Mississippi riverboats. The worst hangdog hotel room was preferable to bedding down on cold hard ground. I never, ever wanted to sleep out under the stars again.

Unsettled thoughts rattled around my brain, and I wasn't the only one. Vic tossed and turned, and I could only imagine her personal set of doubts and fears. With our kindred love of horses, I knew how frazzled I'd be if my ol' pony Shadow had ever been stolen.

Eddie rolled over, sighed, and repeated the cycle. He knew Vic had put her beloved horse at risk for the slimmest of chances to win back Phoenix. If we failed to rescue Lucifer, that'd be two lost horses — and a hefty burden of guilt saddling Eddie for the rest of his life.

Only Jake slept like a snoring baby, proving there were actual benefits to not being overly contemplative.

By the calendar, at least, we still had time to retrieve Lucifer and reach Baltimore by October 21. But we didn't talk about it over our Wednesday breakfast of beans, biscuits, jerky, and coffee. We were only too aware of how much could still go wrong.

We packed up and hit the trail again. Tracking the bandits remained unexpectedly easy — until an hour later, when their trail forked. They must've split up, but which way did Lucifer go? Vic said he tended to prance sideways when he was uncertain, and that quirk helped us decide which tracks to follow.

"We better find this horse soon," Jake said as we rode. "I signed on for sitting in a train, not a saddle."

"Ugggh, not this again," I moaned. "Y'all are free to ignore him."

When Vic and Eddie said they didn't mind, Jake continued. "No, really — what is so great about horses? They smell, and that's just the horse, never mind the horseshit. They attract flies the size of buzzards. They bite, they kick. Just admit it — horses're dangerous at both ends, and uncomfortable in the middle."

Vic and Eddie snickered and sat back to enjoy our little "Jake and Jamey Show."

Jake wasn't anywhere near done. "And why do saddles have to be so damned hard? Would it kill 'em to put in some padding?"

"It's a saddle," I said, "not a featherbed."

"All's I'm saying is, does it have to be

torture?"

"If you bothered to learn how to ride right —"

"I know how to ride!"

"Oh, really?"

"I'm ridin' right now, ain't I?"

"You ride like an ol' lady."

"Says who?"

"Says me."

"Says you — Mr. Knows-everything-about-horses?"

"Okay, Jake, since you're *such* a good rider — every time you bounce up, the horse goes down, and then you meet in the middle, right?"

"Yeah. So?"

"Are your balls getting crunched?"

"Damn right they are."

"Then you're *not* riding right."

"I'd rather not ride at all."

"Old lady."

"Know-it-all."

We followed clear tracks north along a rocky path that was more trail than road, meandering past homesteads, farms, fences, and meadows before reaching Maple City around mid-morning. The "maple" part was accurate, surrounded as it was by a forest of maple trees showing off their fiery October blaze of foliage, but it fell far short of qualifying as a city.

With twenty rickety buildings on a few muddy streets, and more saloons than anything else, it was barely a one-horse town — and we hoped the one horse would be Lucifer. At the "city" limits, his hoof imprints got lost in a jumble of tracks and wagon ruts, so we decided to scout the itty-bitty town on foot first, which wouldn't take long.

"While we're doin' that," Jake said, "we can ask around about Robin's gang."

I glared at him. "You are just itching for a shootout, aren't you?"

"Not itching, exactly," Jake said. "But I wouldn't mind one."

With an exasperated shake of my head, I led the way. We kept alert for any signs of Lucifer or the outlaws, and couldn't help noticing the boarded-up town marshal's office, which looked long abandoned.

"That can't be good sign," Eddie said.

Not if we were hoping to recruit the local law to our side. On the other hand, in a town unencumbered by law enforcement, Robin and his men might not feel a need to hide. Still, the smart play was to try and find our missing horse first. We split into pairs, peeked over fences, poked into barns, peered across fields — and detected neither hide nor hair of Lucifer.

Next, we asked a few shopkeepers if they might've seen our unusual white horse — and came up empty. But when we mentioned Robin and his men, we got a surprise. Not only were they well-known, they were genuine folk heroes for regularly coming to town and spending their loot on whiskey, whores, gambling, and grub. The townsfolk of Maple City had no quarrel with these desperadoes, and considered them a boon to the town's economy, such as it was.

We approached a bald fellow with a billy-goat beard, rocking his chair on the boardwalk outside the tiny general store, contentedly chewing tobacco and spitting. "As long as you ain't the law," he said when we asked about Robin.

"What if we were?" Jake said.

"Well, then, we'd be of a mind to shoot you," the storekeeper said, in such a kindly voice it was hard to tell if he was joking. "Nothin' personal, y'see. But Robin and the Reivers, they's like a Wall Street investment — Maple City's nest egg. Without them spreadin' their wealth around, this town woulda gone to ghosts years ago."

Vic pointed at a scruffy storefront bank across the street, hardly an imposing financial fortress. "Do they ever rob that bank?"

The storekeeper chortled. "Lordy, no! Matter of fact, they keep some of their own treasure in there. And other bandits wouldn't dare rob it, for fear of the Reivers goin' after 'em. So it works fine for us city folk."

"Well, we're not the law," I assured him. "We just need to talk to Robin, is all."

"Try the Maple Sap Saloon, down at the end of the street."

"Much obliged," I said.

But Jake wasn't quite done. "Mind if I ask you a question — you got all these maple trees around, right?"

The storekeeper spat and nodded. "Yessir, we do."

"Have you folks ever thought of, y'know, making maple syrup and selling it? You can fetch a pretty penny."

"Used to. But it's a lot of work. Caterin' to the Reivers is easier."

That's human nature for you, I suppose. We headed down the street to the Maple Sap Saloon, a two-story building wearing faded green paint on its weathered wood. A sign decorated with a red maple leaf hung over the door. The saloon was freestanding, with alleys on both sides. Stairs on one side led up to the second floor.

"What now?" Eddie asked.

"Barge in, guns drawn," Jake said. "Element of surprise."

Vic stared at him. "We have no idea who's inside, or how many of Robin's *armed* men might be with him. Is that really your best plan?"

"Jamey's the plan man."

All eyes shifted to me and my blank expression.

"Well?" Jake prodded. "You got one, or not?"

"Mmm . . . maybe."

We peeked over the swinging doors, one of which leaned off its hinges.

"I don't see him," Jake said.

"Doesn't mean he's not in there."

We couldn't see the whole room from our vantage point. It looked like a shabby joint with a simple plank bar, no polished wood or brass, no mirror behind it. A handful of bored patrons and whores sat scattered around a room with mismatched stools, chairs, and tables. A staircase with a landing halfway up led to a balcony and a few rooms used by whores and customers, or travelers unlucky enough to be stranded overnight in Maple City.

I walked around the outside of the saloon, casing it on all sides. Jake, Vic, and Eddie followed, wondering what I was looking for.

By the time we came back to the splintered boardwalk in front, I had a plan. Sort of.

22

"I thought about shootin' him — but then I'd have a dead horse to move, and I'd *still* have the hole he kicked in my barn."
~ Canute Nystrom,
Maple City Livery Owner

I took my gunbelt off and handed it to Jake. Then I entered the saloon by myself, obviously unarmed. The lone bartender, with his wild gray head of Andrew Jackson hair, looked up as I approached. "What'll it be, *señor?*"

"I'm looking for Robin Nettles."

He pointed toward a poker game at a table on the far side of the stairs. There was Robin, seated facing the front door, though not paying much attention to anything but his cards. Four other gang members were in on the game, including skinny Piggot and squat Sprottle. Burly Makepiece sat with his boots propped up on a nearby table.

Jake stood watching me from just outside the swinging entry doors. I gave him a directional nod to indicate where the outlaws were. Jake nodded back and disappeared.

I approached Robin's table. "Room for one more?"

"Sure thing," Robin said with an amiable grin. He pushed out the empty chair next to him with his foot. I took the invitation and sat as they settled their current hand. Robin threw down his cards with good-natured disgust. "Piggy, she's all yours."

Piggot cackled and gathered up the thin pot of maybe twenty dollars. Sprottle collected the cards for the next deal.

"New here?" Robin asked me.

"Just passing through."

"Right nice little town. Hey, Santiago!" he called to the bartender. "Another round o' pints for me mates, including me new friend here."

The bartender filled glasses with beer from a keg and carried them over on a tray. Robin looked me up and down. "What're ye called, friend?"

"Jamey Galloway."

Robin lifted his beer. "Welcome t' ye, friend Jamey." We clinked our glasses. He gulped his down. I took a tiny sip of mine and set it on the grimy table. Robin called out to idle Makepiece, "Tommy — to the ivories, mate!"

Makepiece ambled over and sat at a battered upright piano. He cracked his knuckles and his fingers hovered over the keys. "Which tune, Rob?"

"Shillings."

Although the piano was grievously out of tune, Makepiece played it with passable skill, and Robin sang with exuberance. As if on cue, his men knew when to pound their glasses on the table to punctuate each verse:

> Ohhh, it's shillings an' pence, me ladies and gents!
> How many coins fer an ale?
> Farthings an' cents, to hell with me rents,
> How many drams before jail?
>
> Ohhh, the night is so cold, I've silver and gold
> Weighing me poor pockets down!
> Innkeeper fine, bring us some wine!
> We've so many sorrows to drown!
>
> She's a lassie so fair that's filled me with care
> So I'm throwin' me fates to the storm!
> Me broken heart's bare, I do solemnly

swearrrrr . . .
'Til a new bonnie lass keeps me warm!

Robin laughed and shouted, "Big finish, mates!" and his men joined in on a lusty final chorus:

Ohhhhhhh — the night is so cold, I've silver and gold
Weighing me poor pockets down!
Ohhh, innkeeper fine, bring us some wiiiine! We've so many sorrows to drown!

"Never heard that one before," I said to Robin as other patrons applauded and thumped their tables.

"Composed it meself. Done a bunch. I make me boys learn 'em. Keeps 'em sharp up in the brain pan," he added, tapping the side of his head.

"Not as bawdy as most drinking songs, though."

Robin looked affronted. "No need — I write 'em so me Mum can sing 'em."

Sprottle's pudgy hands shuffled and dealt the cards. I did my usual, quietly winning two out of three hands. With each fold, Robin's face got a little redder. Then I caught him palming a spare ace he'd slipped out of his vest.

"Mmmm . . . I think there's something stuck to your hand," I said with an earnest smile.

"Heh-heh. You weren't supposed to see that, friend Jamey. Must be losin' me touch."

He didn't sound angry, but he put down his cards, slid his chair back and stood. Folks behind me scattered as Robin pointed his gun at me.

I stayed seated, my empty hands above the table, out in the open. With one thumb, I pointed over my shoulder. Robin glanced up and saw Jake, Vic, and Eddie perched along the balcony and stairs — with a revolver, rifle, and shotgun pointed down at the Reivers gang. Positioned on the landing, Jake aimed his Colt square at Robin.

"Yer daft," Robin said to me, "if y' think anybody's close enough to save ya."

"You shoot me, my brother up there shoots you — and he's a very good shot."

Jake waved at him.

Robin assessed his position with a sniff. "*How* good?"

Jake gauged his geometry, waving a few people out of the way. When he nodded, I flipped the nine of diamonds in the air. Jake eagle-eyed the pinwheeling card and fired. The boom echoed — the smoke cleared —

the wounded card fluttered to the floor.

Robin picked it up by a corner between the tips of his thumb and forefinger and showed it around. Instead of the expected hole burned in the middle, the only damage was a singed notch on one edge. He did not look impressed.

I flashed a testy glance up at Jake and got a sheepish shrug in return.

Robin held the card aloft. "Not to be dispertatious, but he barely winged it, mate. Not as good with that iron as y' think."

Without warning, Jake fired again — piercing the heart of the card a *teensy inch* from Robin's fingertips and tearing it from his grip.

Robin belatedly yelped and yanked his hand back. "Y' daft ratbag! You coulda killed me bloody trigger finger." He picked up the card — now a mortally maimed eight of diamonds, with a hole dead center where the ninth diamond had been. "Hah! Well, bugger me sideways."

"It's easier when the target's not moving," Jake said.

"And you're not moving," I said to Robin. "Plus, you're bigger than the card."

"So, ya got the drop on us, mate. Please elukidate on how you're gonna turn us in for some reward."

Jake, Vic, and Eddie came downstairs, firearms still ready.

"You got us wrong," I said. "All we want is our horse. Y'know, that white Arabian from the train?"

"Hnnh. So, I prognostigrate, if we admit we nicked this horse, we get strung up as horse thieves . . . ?"

"Aww, horse thieves hardly ever get hanged, except in dime novels. Besides, who said anything about stealing? Maybe the horse, y'know, followed you home."

"Much as we'd love to help, we don't have *El Blanco Loco*. He's a bleedin' topper, all right, but he's stark ravin' moonstruck. We sold the daft bugger bright 'n' early."

Vic squinted. "Bright and early *today*?"

"Aye. Nobody could get close t' ridin' him."

Fearless Victoria stepped right up to Robin, eye to eye. "Sold him *where*?"

"Maple City Livery, right here in town, *mad'moiselle*. Took what we could get. Go see Nystrom."

"We also want our train tickets back," Jake said.

Robin looked blank. "What'll we be wantin' with train tickets? Sorry, mate. Anything we couldn't spend, bank, or sell, we burned."

We rushed out of the saloon and Vic led our charge to the livery stable down the street, where we found sandy-haired owner Canute Nystrom skewering a hay bale with a pitchfork. When we explained why we were there, his eyes opened wide — and he was not a happy man.

"Oh, yah! I bought that *El Blanco Loco* this morning. Come see what he done!" Still wielding the pitchfork, he led us to a barn stall — with a horse-sized hole kicked in the splintered back wall. "He wasn't here but an hour, come waltzin' in nice an' easy — and then I hear this God-awful crashin' like a sledgehammer. So I come back here and see him bangin' his way out."

"Did you try to stop him?" Eddie asked.

Nystrom gaped. "Try an' stop a demon? You'd have to be as loco as that horse! I thought about shootin' him — but then I'd have a dead horse to move, and I'd *still* have the hole he kicked in my barn."

"When did he run off?" Vic asked.

"Two hours, maybe."

Dammit. We'd just missed that infernal horse, and now he had a head start. We found Lucifer's distinctive tracks outside the stable, saddled up and resumed our hunt a little after noon. The rugged road north wasn't heavily traveled, which made it easier to follow him. Every so often he seemed to wander off for water or grazing, but mostly stayed on the beaten path, for which we were grateful.

With us perpetually a step behind him, Lucifer had in the meantime turned up on the property of a German farmer named Fritz Erdmann, ten miles north of Maple City. Tall and lean, with a sweep of silver hair under his floppy hat, Farmer Erdmann at first thought he was seeing an apparition when the white horse moseyed into his corral and helped himself to a drink at the water trough.

Erdmann approached with caution, but the horse didn't seem wild or threatening, and didn't object when the farmer clipped a rope to his halter and led him into the barn. He even allowed himself to be saddled. Erdmann thought this must be his lucky day as he climbed on.

Of course, they'd no sooner left the barn than Lucifer bucked him off. For the next hour, the horse led the farmer on a less-than-merry chase around his fields, evading capture and shaking off the saddle. Erdmann gave up, hoisted the saddle over his shoulder and returned to his cabin.

He put his other horses and livestock away

— and prepared some special feed for *El Blanco Loco,* laced with his own herbal mellowing formula. All that dodging must've worked up Lucifer's hunger — when Farmer Erdmann dumped a couple of buckets in the feeding trough, the unruly horse sauntered up and ate all of it.

Later that afternoon, once Erdmann's special recipe had worked its magic, he tethered the dazed and placid horse to his buckboard and took him two miles up the road to the runty town of Weaver's Crossroads. There, he tried to make quick work of selling the regal Arabian to yet another unsuspecting livery owner, red-haired and rawboned Hank Rasmussen. Rasmussen examined Lucifer and concluded the horse would be a prize acquisition.

"I'll sell him for two hundred," Erdmann said.

Rasmussen laughed. "I won't pay a penny over seventy five."

"That's robbery!"

"I have plenty of horses, Erdmann."

"Not like this. Have you ever seen a handsomer stud?"

"I have not, but that's my top offer. Why do you want to get rid of him, anyway?"

"Too much horse for me," Erdmann said in feigned shame. "Too handsome for broken-down farm work."

"You never were much of a judge of horseflesh."

"Not as the likes of you, Rasmussen. I'm just a farmer." He winced. "I can come down to one-fifty."

"Mmm . . . one hundred," Rasmussen countered.

"All right — one hundred it is."

Transaction completed, Erdmann climbed into his buggy and drove away, satisfied to have made a hundred dollars on a gift horse.

Back at his farm, he went into the kitchen, fetched himself a china cup-and-saucer of hot coffee, came out and settled into a porch chair. He poured some coffee into the saucer to let it cool, then slurped it from the plate.

He looked up when he spied me, Jake, Vic, and Eddie riding up toward his house. We asked him about our missing horse, and he snorted when he heard the name Lucifer.

"Right name for a horse that was all possessed-like." He told us how Lucifer had wandered onto his farm. "But I didn't need another horse," he lied, "so I took him to Weaver's Crossroads and sold him to Hank Rasmussen's livery."

Jake smirked. "He tried to kill you, didn't he?"

Erdmann admitted nothing.

"One thing," Eddie said. "How did you get him to go with you?"

"He et my secret feed."

"Ahhh." Eddie nodded. "I'm bettin' it was a mixture of valerian, chamomile, and . . . hops?"

The farmer looked impressed. We thanked him, turned our horses, and cantered toward Weaver's Crossroads — hoping to get there before anything else went sideways.

23

"Every sense is open to misdirection, and thus may be made to serve the ends of a skillful magician."
~ Nevil Maskelyne,
British Magician & Inventor

By mid-afternoon, Lucifer had shaken off the last of his stupor induced by Erdmann's hypnotic elixir, and found himself in an unfamiliar corral. He looked around for something to destroy, and targeted the perimeter fencing. A couple of well-aimed kicks shattered the upper rails and sent wood chips flying. Then he went to work on the next fence section.

Hank Rasmussen heard the ruckus and rushed out of the barn. He saw the broken fence rails, and the big white horse refreshing himself at the water trough. Then Lucifer ambled past the stupefied Rasmussen and into the barn.

The livery owner and a stable boy followed and witnessed Lucifer starting a new project — liberating other horses by kicking in their stall doors. Some stayed inside out of confusion, while others filed out to the corral where they skipped over busted-down fence rails and made a break for freedom.

Riding into Weaver's Crossroads, we saw loose horses roaming down the street — and it was a pretty good bet this had something to do with Lucifer. A couple of stable boys ran after the escapees, trying to round them up. At the livery, we found an apoplectic Rasmussen surveying the damage, and cussing out both Farmer Erdmann and the evil white beast.

"Problem?" Jake said as he got off his horse.

Rasmussen winced at alarming sounds of demolition from inside the barn. "You see and hear my problem!"

"We could take *El Blanco Loco* off your hands. How much did you pay for him?"

"I gave that thief Erdmann a hundred dollars in good Uncle Sam greenbacks."

"I'll give you seventy-five."

Frantic Rasmussen dredged a handful of cash out of his pocket and shoved it at Jake. "Here! Here's fifty! Just *take* him, before he wrecks my whole entire place!"

Vic slid off her horse and hurried into the barn. The crashing noises stopped. Out she came a minute later, with Lucifer meekly following her past flabbergasted Hank Rasmussen.

With Vic and her horse reunited, we made it back to Fremont a little after five that evening. We sold our horses and gear back to Oley Bergstrom for a quarter of what we paid — and some of that went right back into Oley's pocket to board Lucifer for the night.

Vic tucked her horse into his stall and gave him a peppermint candy. "*Don't* wreck anything, okay? We can't afford it." With a purring nicker, Lucifer pressed his head and muzzle against her for reassurance, the way a skittish foal would huddle under its mother. She kissed him on his nose. "I'll see you in the morning."

"Y'know what really gets me?" Jake grumped as we walked back to the hotel. "While we're marooned here, that bastard Van Brunt is probably back in Maryland by now."

"We'll get there," I said.

"I ain't so sure."

Truth be told, we were plumb dragged out and looked forward to a better and more comfortable night's sleep at the hotel. We clumped upstairs to our room and found Rafael worried sick. Dispensing with greetings, he blurted, "Did you rescue Lucifer?!"

"More like we rescued Nebraska," I said, "but, yeah, he's safe and sound."

Not that we weren't thankful for that, but now we faced a decision: Tomorrow, should we continue on to Baltimore — and pray nothing else kept us from arriving in time? Or give up, and go home? *If* nothing else went wrong, we still had a shot at reaching Baltimore before the match race entry deadline. What we didn't have were sufficient funds to cover railroad fare for five people and a horse to get us there, or back to San Francisco. We could afford the excursion from Fremont to Omaha, but that would leave us stranded a long way from either coast.

"We might have another way to get to Baltimore," Jake said, "with Jamey's lady friend."

"*Ex*-lady friend," I said.

"That doesn't mean you can't ask her."

"Ask her what?" Eddie said.

"If we can catch a ride with her," Jake said, putting me on the spot. "She travels in her own private railroad car, right? Didn't you say her last western shows were in

Omaha, and then she's headed for Baltimore?"

"We don't know her schedule," I protested, "and we don't know if she's got room for us."

"Well, Jake's right," Vic said. "You're going to have to ask."

"I don't even know if she'll speak to me."

"Only one way to find out," Jake said, savoring my discomfort. "Besides, it's the least she can do after breakin' your poor li'l heart."

My face reddened. "Let's call it a last resort."

Jake patted me on the cheek. "You got 'til Omaha to think of a better plan, plan man."

I hated when he was right. It was the evening of Wednesday, October 15, and we'd get to Omaha the next day, but no further.

"Since we don't have enough money to get to Baltimore anyway," Jake said, "I think we oughta spend a little on something to take our minds off our troubles."

"Like what?" Eddie asked.

"Well, we got a free evening, and that magician we saw in Cheyenne, The Amazing Alberto? He's doing his show here in Fremont tonight."

"Y'know," Vic said, "that's not a bad idea.

And then we can have a decent supper here at the hotel restaurant. We've earned it."

We all agreed — except Rafael, who insisted on going to the livery to keep Lucifer company. "C'mon, Raffie," Eddie said. "The way you stood up to those horse thieves, if anybody deserves a night on the town, it's you."

Raf shook his head. "I gotta do this if I'm gonna ride him. And we wouldn't be in this fix if I didn't lose at Sea Breeze."

"Everybody knows it's my dumb bet with Van Brunt that got us here," Eddie said. "So if anybody's gonna babysit Lucifer, it oughta be me."

"No," Raf said, "me."

"Okay, how 'bout we both go for a while? The rest of you, go have fun."

Vic shook her finger at them. "No sleeping at the livery, you two."

"Yes, ma'am," Eddie and Raf said together.

After they headed out, Vic, Jake, and me freshened up, went down to the lobby and saw a magic show poster pinned up behind the front desk. The clerk gave us directions and we walked a few blocks to the Elkhorn Theatre. Compared to the magnificent Excelsior in San Francisco, the Elkhorn was small and bare-bones. Even though the two-hundred-seat house was only half-filled, spectators from kids to grandparents seemed eager for the show.

At seven sharp, *The Amazing Alberto & His Mighty Miracles of Magic, Fire & Strength* began when purple velvet curtains parted to reveal a stage lit by a half-dozen flickering torches in front of a black backdrop. Props rested on three black-draped tables. An off-stage piano player provided accompaniment suitable to the mood of any moment.

Alberto Palazzo strode onstage, juggling four daggers, his hands moving too fast to follow. He wore black britches, high black boots, and a billowing red shirt that bared his muscular arms. "To prove there is nothing up-a my sleeve," he said with a twinkle, "I have no sleeves!"

He sequentially caught one knife at a time and — seemingly without aiming — threw it at an archery target on the wall behind him, while the remaining knives were still in the air. All four daggers hit the bulls-eye with split-second precision — *Bang! Bang! Bang! Bang!*

He turned to us with a flourish and a big smile. "Good?" he said in Italian-accented English. "Good! We say, *tutto bene!*"

The show varied between astonishing stunts of strength and dexterity and intimate illusions performed with the help of audience members summoned to the stage. Now, some skeptics claim stooges are planted in every magic-show audience, and that may often be true. But Jake, Victoria, and me all took turns as assistants — not accomplices.

Throughout the show, Alberto kept up a lyrical patter in mixed Italian and English, combined with nimble spins, bows, and gestures. It was all part of his charming theatrical presentation, intended to misdirect our attention — and it worked. Each lady he called upon to assist him got a chivalrous hand up the steps at the front of the stage, and a flower conjured from behind his back.

Alberto chose Victoria to help with one trick, asking her to rip up a sheet of paper and drop those small pieces into a glass. He then spread out a folded-paper Chinese fan horizontally, and had Vic sprinkle the paper shreds on top of it. As he shimmied the fan like a chef shuffling a skillet over a hot stove, all but one piece fluttered to the floor.

Then, before our very eyes, he somehow transformed that single remaining shred of paper into an egg. The magician handed the fan to Vic, and to prove the egg was real, he cracked the shell open. He poured the yolk and white into an opaque cylinder and capped it with a snug lid. He swirled it, and then asked Vic if she'd allow him to pour the contents into her hands. Her squeamish expression made the audience laugh, but she played along. He removed the lid, tilted the cylinder — and a live downy chick tumbled into Vic's cupped palms!

"Good? Good!" Alberto called out. *"Tutto bene!"*

He did a series of rope tricks while singing snippets of Italian opera, bent an iron bar, and intertwined and pulled apart a pair of solid iron rings. He chose a *bella bambina* from the audience, had the girl lie down on a table — and made her levitate above the stage.

He lit a cigarette with his fingers, drew in a deep breath, then exhaled four puffs of smoke, and from each one he produced a ball out of thin air — and then made them vanish again! Except for the one ball he turned into a lemon. He ended that smoky sequence by inserting the cigarette into his closed fist — from which it simply disappeared.

With the help of a wide-eyed ten-year-old boy, the magician made silver coins appear in one empty glass fishbowl and — *"Presto fantastico!"* — transformed them into live, swimming goldfish in a second water-filled bowl. As the crowd cheered, Alberto called out, "Is good? *Tutto bene?*"

"*Tutto bene!*" we all answered, on cue.

When he announced a trick called "Any Card, Any Number," I volunteered. I hadn't figured out a single one of his illusions. But maybe I could catch him in a card trick, thanks to what I'd learned from Mississippi Mike Morgan about detecting poker cheats.

Alberto handed me a sealed pack of playing cards, which I opened, inspected and confirmed to be a complete and normal deck. He asked me to shuffle them thoroughly, and noticed my card-handling skills. "Ahhh! You are a gambler, no?"

"I play a little poker."

He laughed and instructed me to place the deck face down on the table, and name any card.

"Queen of diamonds," I said.

Then he turned to the audience, pointed to a lady at random, and asked her to choose any number between one and fifty-two. "Thirty-six!" she said.

Alberto nodded toward me. "This gambler gentleman, he's a-gonna count out the cards, one at a time. Please, you all count with him, out loud. And I promise you, the thirty-sixth card? She will be the queen of diamonds."

I took one card at a time, face-down from the top of the deck, calling out the count and setting them aside in a pile. The piano player added tension with softly drumming notes as the audience joined me in counting. "Four! Five! Six . . ."

When we sounded off at thirty-five, Alberto held up his hand. The piano player struck an ominous chord and fell silent. "Next card," Alberto said, "she's a-gonna be number thirty-six. Will she be the queen of diamonds? Turn it over, my friend — and tell everybody what card she is."

I turned the top card up — and damned if it wasn't that queen of diamonds! I held it up for Alberto to see. He heaved an exaggerated sigh of relief and pretended to wipe sweat from his brow. When I showed the card to the audience, they burst into wild applause.

"Tutto bene?" Alberto asked.

The entire audience shouted back, *"Tutto bene!"*

For his finale, Alberto related the tragical tale of Pompeii, the ancient Italian city buried eighteen hundred years ago when the great volcano Mount Vesuvius erupted in the year 79 A.D., entombing Pompeii and nearby Herculaneum under ash and stone.

He promised to do what the ancient gods could not — tame the primordial element of fire.

After lighting a pair of torch sticks, Alberto put one into his mouth and smothered the flame. Then he put the other still-burning torch in his mouth, removed it, breathed out a fiery jet to re-ignite the first one — and blew three fireballs from his mouth.

Next, he juggled the burning torches, caught both, inserted them into his mouth, and extinguished them. Then he exhaled a flare to relight both. He threw them straight up in the air. As they came down, he caught the flaming tips, one in each fist, and snuffed them out.

He stretched out his arms, bowed, and ended his show to a standing ovation. It was a shame he didn't have the full house he deserved. But for Vic, Jake, and me, the magic show was exactly the tonic we needed.

"Let's invite Alberto to join us for supper," Vic said. "It'll be fun talking to him."

We waited at the back of the theatre as the audience filed out. Soon, with just a few house lights on, we were the only ones left in the eerie, empty gloom.

Alberto stowed the last of his gear into his

two big wheeled trunks, then called out into the darkness. "*Signor* Doyle? I am ready to go."

A rotund man in a pinstriped suit strutted down the center aisle toward the stage, bouncing on the balls of his feet. "Good show, Mr. Palazzo. Nicely done."

Alberto sat on the edge of the stage and smiled.

"There's just a wee problem, though," Doyle continued.

Alberto's grin clouded. "What kind of a problem?"

"Half the seats went empty, as you could see. So I can only pay you half of what we agreed, boyo."

"But, *Signor* Doyle, we have a contract."

The theatre owner patted Alberto on the shoulder. "And Paddy Doyle honors his contracts." He took some folded papers out of his coat and sorted to the last page. "Looky right here — you've got to pay attention, so you're not surprised in the end."

Alberto read the page and bowed his head. Doyle held out a canvas sack of money, and Alberto reluctantly took it.

"Also, since you didn't draw enough, I'm exercising my clause that lets me cancel your next two shows."

Alberto frowned. I don't know about you,

but I would never want to anger a man that big. If it came to blows, Doyle was doomed.

"*Signor* Doyle, I'm a-gonna need those two shows."

"No arguing with the printed word, such as we both signed."

We didn't like what we were overhearing. The Amazing Alberto was getting stiffed by this Paddy Doyle character.

"*Per favore* — you got to let me do those two shows. I settle for half of whatever my share is a-gonna be."

"Sorry. Out of the goodness of my heart, you can store your trunks here overnight before leaving town tomorrow."

Alberto stood to his full height, and towered over Doyle. Angry as he was, his soft voice was unnerving. "I spread the word about how you treat people, *Signor* Doyle. Soon, nobody gonna wanna play your joint. Then you gonna make half of nothing."

Doyle edged back a step. "Are you threatening me, Mr. Palazzo?" Without waiting for an answer, he shouted: "Wiley! Boys! Out front — on the double!"

Four stage hands materialized from the dark corners of the Elkhorn. "Problem, Boss?" said Wiley, the shaggy leader of Doyle's pack of roustabout thugs. He was the biggest of the bunch, rough and battle-scarred, with an unkempt beard. The others were no more appealing.

"Wiley, would you please escort Mr. Palazzo out of the thee-ay-ter?"

"Sure thing, Boss," Wiley said with a grin that revealed some missing teeth.

I looked at Jake and Vic. "Should we help him?"

"Maybe," Jake said. "But I don't think they're gonna lay a hand on him."

Any altercation would've been like rats attacking a buffalo — they might get in a few bites, but even four of 'em couldn't take down this particular prey. They gathered in a baleful semi-circle around Alberto, staying out of reach, preferring not to tangle with a giant who could bend iron. They looked relieved when he left by the backstage door.

24

> "A friend may well be reckoned the masterpiece of nature."
> ~ Ralph Waldo Emerson

We went outside and around to the theatre's side alley in time to see disheartened Alberto wheeling his trunks toward the street.

"He doesn't look like a fella who wants company," Jake said.

"Yeah," I said, "maybe we —"

"— we should offer to treat him," Vic said. She ignored us and intercepted the magician. "We just saw your show, and you were truly amazing!"

Alberto brightened when he recognized Vic as the girl who'd helped him with the egg-and-chick routine. "Ahh — *la mia bella donna. Grazie!*" He kissed her hand. "Alberto Palazzo, at you service."

"We saw what happened in there with Doyle."

Alberto made a face like he'd just swigged castor oil. "Ehhh . . . Doyle! A *figlio di puttana* — how you say — son of a whore."

When Vic asked him to be our supper guest, he was so touched that he teared up. "You are as kind as you are beautiful — *bellissima.*"

"So, *tutto bene?*" Vic said with a smile.

"*Si. Tutto bene!*" Alberto laughed — and wrapped all three of us in a surprise bear hug. "You are a blessing in the world, my new friends."

We introduced ourselves, learned he was also staying at the Chittenden House, and walked there together. "Think you coulda taken those guys?" Jake asked him.

Alberto shrugged. "I no like to find out. Fights, they are . . . no good."

"Does that sort of thing happen often?" Vic asked. "Theatre owners not paying what they promised?"

"I think most people, they are honest. But, *si,* it happen sometimes."

At the hotel, Alberto took his trunks to his room, carrying them effortlessly upstairs like they were mere satchels. "Yup," Jake said, "he could've beaten all four of those guys."

Alberto came back downstairs and we were seated at a round table in the hotel's gracious restaurant. The Chittenden's food was superb, and Alberto reveled in our company.

"When I am traveling all over," he said, "it can get — how you say — lonesome." He told us he'd been born in a tiny Italian hamlet called Velva, in a northwestern region known for its olives and grapes. "But I leave home when I am a boy, only fourteen."

"How come?" Vic asked.

"I knew God meant for me more than to spend my life growing olives and grapes, like-a my father . . . and grandfather . . . and great-grandfather."

"Where did you go?" I asked.

"All to go around Italy, and then to go all over Europe. I walk, I work — I even go to school where I can. I learn to speak a little bit French, German, Spanish, English."

"Still, it does sound lonely," Vic said.

"I was too young and *stupido* to be lonely," he said with a chuckle. "Too much to do, too much to learn — too much to see!"

"Was it dangerous for a boy out on his own?"

"I was a big boy, so nobodies bother me too much."

"Is that when you started doing magic?" Jake asked.

"No — I begin with circus! I do balance, trapeze, tightrope — and I learn you can break-a you neck like that. So I decide to try magic, it seem safer."

Jake gaped at him. "Fire-eating is safe?!"

"For me, is safe. Not for you."

"Did you go straight from circus acts to magic?" Victoria asked.

"No, no! I want more to be scientist, or engineer. To know how things work, how they are put together." Alberto recalled how he'd talked his way into one of Europe's oldest universities, the seven-hundred-year-old *Università degli Studi di Modena* in northern Italy. "I study for a year, then I go apprentice for chemists and builders."

"So, when *did* you start doing magic?" I asked.

Alberto smiled at the memory. "Ahh! Everywhere I go, big cities, little towns, I see traveling magician shows. Some people think they are witches. But every one, I ask the magicians how they do, and I beg to learn their art. Some say, 'Bahh! Go 'way, *ragazzo.*' But a few, they take me as assistant, and they teach me. And then I start my own show."

"Why did you leave Europe?" Vic said.

"I hear about America, how big she is. My home, Velva, she is a long day's ride south of seaport city Genoa, where Cristoforo Colombo — Columbus — he come from. And he discover America! So I think to follow him. I come five years ago, I am glad to miss your Civil War."

"I gotta know," Jake said. "How do you do those tricks? How do you eat fire?"

"Ahhh. The secret is . . . it is magic!"

"Aww, c'mon," Jake pleaded. "Tell me at least one trick!"

"If I tell you, it is no more magic."

We were so wrapped up in good food and conversation that we didn't notice Wiley and two of his theatre rowdies entering the restaurant — until they stepped up to our table. In better light than the darkened theatre, Wiley was an even uglier mutt with his spiky hair and grubby beard. He stared at Alberto. "We got us some unfinished business with you."

Alberto gestured with open palms. "There is-a no need for troubles, *Signor* Wiley."

But Wiley circled around and jabbed a pocket pistol into Alberto's back. "C'mon outside so we can settle this like men."

My brother reached for his own revolver on his hip — forgetting he'd left it in our room. Instead, we tensed in our chairs, unsure of how or whether to intervene.

But, just as we'd been startled by them

sneaking up on us, they failed to notice a tall, broad-shouldered man wearing an impeccably tailored suit approaching from behind. He grabbed Wiley by the scruff of his neck, plucked the gun from his hand, and slammed his head into our table at an empty place-setting, knocking him silly. Food and plates went flying, and we four diners jumped and scattered. So did Wiley's two pals, who vamoosed at top speed.

The well-dressed man hauled Wiley out of the restaurant. "*Mister* Wiley," he said in a commanding British accent, "you know guns are never permitted in my establishment. Nor do I allow such disruptive behavior." With that, he propelled the interloper out the front door.

Then he brushed off his hands, straightened his coat, and returned to our table. "I am Percy Chittenden, the owner. And I do so apologize for this incident. As amends, please join me at my personal table as my guests."

Vic spoke for us. "Thank you, Mr. Chittenden. We'd be delighted."

We followed him to a private corner of the restaurant, sheltered behind Oriental bamboo screens decorated with vistas of ponds and cherry blossoms. Chittenden conferred with his chef, and soon waiters served us a feast that rivaled the best of the Carlton's Eden Terrace.

After chicken giblet soup, our main-course offerings were fresh and steamed vegetables, custardy mashed potatoes, baked ham with cranberries, and filet mignon in a delicate wine sauce. Even overstuffed as we were, we couldn't resist dessert platters laden with pies, cakes, pudding, fresh-baked scones, and lemon ice cream.

As we ate and chatted, Percy Chittenden told us of his mission to civilize the West, the Wileys of the world notwithstanding. He planned to build grand Chittenden House hotels and restaurants all along major rail lines, so weary travelers would have fine places to stay and to dine. This hotel was his fourth, with two more already under construction.

He listened to our tale of how we'd come to Fremont, and sympathized with our situation. When we couldn't eat another bite, we thanked him for his hospitality. He wished us *bon voyage,* and gave us a handful of his personal business cards bearing the hotel's crest. "You are welcome at any Chittenden House property. Merely present one of these cards to the manager, and you shall be treated as royalty."

Mr. Chittenden bade us good night, and

we went upstairs. Though late to bed, we'd be early to rise — Baltimore was still over a thousand miles away, with the race entry deadline in five days. As Jake delighted in reminding me, our cross-country crusade would likely grind to a halt at Omaha unless I asked Emmaline Rose for help. Humbling as that might be, if the woman who'd trampled my heart was to be our last best hope, well, I'd have no choice but to throw myself on her mercy — assuming we could even find her.

Next morning, after breakfast, when we packed up and went downstairs to check out, we poked our heads into Percy Chittenden's office to thank him once again. And Vic, Jake and me didn't want to leave without saying farewell to our new friend Alberto. While we waited for him to come down, Vic went to fetch Lucifer from Bergstrom's livery, Jake ran over to the railroad station to buy our tickets to Omaha, and I told Eddie and Rafael all about The Amazing Alberto and our dining adventures the night before.

I never expected what happened next.

The magician maneuvered his trunks down the stairs — just as the Dodge County sheriff and his curly-haired young deputy strode into the lobby to intercept him. The sheriff wasn't a tall man, and with his thinning gray hair, lined face, and specs perched on his nose, he looked more like a gruff uncle than the long arm of the law. "You are Alberto Palazzo?"

"*Si,*" Alberto said.

"I am Sheriff Walter Rhule, and I am here to tell you that you are under arrest, sir."

Alberto blinked in confusion. "For what did I do, *Signor* Sheriff?"

"You are suspected of murder."

25

> "Always do right. This will gratify some people and astonish the rest."
> ~ Mark Twain

The sheriff's declaration stunned me into several seconds of befuddled silence before I blurted, "Murder? *Alberto?* That's impossible!"

Jake returned with our tickets. "What's going on?"

I told him. He turned to the sheriff. "Murder? *Him?* That's impossible."

Vic came in from tying Lucifer up out front, saw the sheriff, and asked Jake, "What's all this?"

Jake told her. Her jaw dropped. "Sheriff," she said, "that's impossible."

Sheriff Rhule squinted at us. " 'Impossible' seems to be the consensus. However, if you don't mind my asking — who are you folks?"

"Friends of his," I said, as the deputy handcuffed Alberto.

"Since you are in this very hotel with baggage," the sheriff said, "I take it you are all transients?"

"Well, yessir, we are. But we know him!"

Sheriff Rhule pursed his lips. "For how long, if you don't mind my asking?"

"Since . . . well, since . . . last night."

"That is one feeble character reference, son."

"Sheriff," Vic said, "who did he supposedly murder?"

"Paddy Doyle, owner of the Elkhorn Theatre. And not just murder. Also theft."

"Of what?"

"Cash receipts from an as-yet undetermined number of recent theatre performances."

Vic wasn't done. "Says *who?*"

"Four witnesses. They claim Mr. Doyle and the accused had an argument last evening over money — and that Mr. Palazzo threatened Mr. Doyle with bodily harm."

"No, no, no!" Jake said. "We were there, and those so-called witnesses are lying."

"These 'witnesses,' " Vic said, "were they a man named Wiley and his stagehand *amigos?*"

"Yes, ma'am. And they reported finding

the deceased, well, deceased. Strongbox and cash missing from his office."

"Sheriff," Jake said, "we wanna give our witness statements, too."

"Dandy," Rhule said without enthusiasm. "But first, I have to lock up Mr. Palazzo. You are welcome to tag along."

That's exactly what we did, leaving Eddie and Rafael to keep an eye on our gear, horse, and Alberto's trunks. We had two hours before the train to Omaha.

At the sheriff's office a block away, we followed the lawmen and their suspect inside to a pair of cramped jail cells in the back. By that time, Alberto had freed himself from the handcuffs and gave them to the dismayed sheriff.

"Don't be doing that, son," he said, guiding his prisoner into a cell and clanging the barred door shut. He sat at his desk, took a little leatherbound notebook out of his vest pocket and picked up a pencil. "All right, what do you know about the suspect's whereabouts yesterday after seven P.M.?"

We told him about Alberto's magic show, and his *non-violent* dust-up with Doyle when the theatre owner sharped him out of his rightful pay. We described in detail how Doyle and his rowdies threatened Alberto — at the theatre, and later at the restaurant

— *not* the other way around. We swore to spending the whole evening with Alberto, and Percy Chittenden could verify that and the fact that we all went up to bed around midnight."

"I cannot be certain when Doyle got strangled," Rhule said. "Your magician friend could've slipped out during the night. From your statements, he had motive and opportunity. And he's sure as shootin' strong enough to choke the life out of any man."

"Except he's *innocent,*" Vic said, waving her hand back toward the cell — the door to which was now wide open, with Alberto sitting on the cot inside.

"*Signor* Sheriff," Alberto said, "your jail, she needs better locks."

"*Quit* doing that," said the exasperated lawman.

"If he was guilty," I said, "wouldn't he have bided his time and waited for an opportunity to head for the hills, instead of demonstrating that your security needs an upgrade?"

The sheriff went back to the cell. "I don't suppose there's much point in locking this again. You promise to stay in there and not absquatulate?"

That last word had Alberto perplexed.

"He means, 'Don't run off,' " I translated.

Alberto nodded with absolute sincerity. "I give-a my word. Also . . . that I am innocent."

"If you step foot outta this cell, I will shoot you. Is that clear?"

Alberto nodded again.

Sheriff Rhule escorted us to the front door.

"After what we told you," Jake said, "aren't you gonna look for other suspects?"

"I am not a detective agency like Pinkerton or Bannerman," he said. "I got me a suspect with a good justification for murder. I will hold him over for trial, and let the judge and lawyers sort it out."

"When?" I asked.

"Circuit court judge is due next Wednesday."

Vic, Jake, and me trudged back to the hotel. "What're we going to do?" Vic said as we crossed the dirt street.

Jake shrugged. "What *can* we do?"

"We can stay," I said.

"And do what?" Jake asked.

"Either prove Alberto didn't do it," Vic said, "or prove Wiley and his boys did."

Jake shook his head. "And how're we gonna do that? Last time I checked, we ain't wearin' badges."

We stepped onto the boardwalk outside the hotel and leaned on the railing. "I don't know," Vic said, "but we have to try. We *know* Alberto didn't kill Doyle."

"Do we?" Jake countered. "We've known him for a day. And the sheriff's right — we don't know what Alberto did after we all went to sleep."

Vic glared. "Do you really think he went out in the middle of the night and choked Paddy Doyle?"

Jake backed off a step. "We like the guy, I get it. And, no, I don't think he did it. All I'm saying is, it's *possible.*"

"No, it's *not,*" Vic said. "And we can't let him go to prison — or worse — for a crime he didn't commit."

"Just bein' devil's advocate now, if we stay and play detective," Jake argued, "what if we don't make it to Baltimore, and we never get Eddie's horse back?"

Vic stared at him. "We're talking about a man's *life.*"

We went into the hotel lobby and told Eddie and Rafael what we were thinking. Maybe this crazy odyssey of ours was simply predestined to be a bust. We had a stark choice: Do we leave? Or stay — for however long it might take — and try to clear Alberto?

Since we five were in this together, we decided to vote. Even though Eddie and Rafael hadn't spent time with Alberto like Jake, me, and Vic had, they agreed that trying to help him was the right thing to do, damn the consequences. It was unanimous.

Eddie's generosity impressed me, and by the look on her face, I reckoned Vic took notice — as did my oft-clueless brother. But convoluted love affairs weren't uppermost in our minds just then. We had a crime to solve.

Percy Chittenden came over and asked us what was going on. We told him — and he immediately gave us a room, including meals, at no charge, for as long as we needed. Then he marched over to the sheriff's office with us to confirm our testimony.

Not only had Chittenden kept company with us and Alberto in his restaurant, he also confessed to being a night owl who'd spent the rest of last night at the front desk, catching up on work. "Walter, I never saw Mr. Palazzo sneak out. As he's rather a large chap, he'd have been difficult to miss."

"You barely know these young folks," Rhule said. "You sure you want to vouch for them, if you don't mind my asking?"

"They barely know the accused," Chittenden said. "Yet they are vouching for him.

The Greek philosopher Epictetus said 'It is not what happens to you, but how you react to it that matters.' That they are attesting to Mr. Palazzo's innocence, to their own detriment, tells me they are of good character."

Rhule rubbed the back of his neck. It was hard to tell if he was annoyed, intrigued, or both. "Well, it may not be an entirely new kettle of fish, but you've added seasoning to the stew. Mr. Palazzo may have had monetary motive, but from what you've said, he did not have opportunity."

According to both the sheriff and Chittenden, Doyle was a notoriously contentious citizen of Fremont, known to curry favor with (and even bribe) local officials. Rhule assured us he was not among them — but he now had a problem, thanks to us. "Somebody killed Paddy Doyle. And if Alberto Palazzo is not the right man, then there's a murderer loose in this very town."

"Or, about to *leave* town," I said.

"With the dead man's money," Jake added.

Vic played inquisitor. "Have you found Doyle's money?"

Rhule shook his head. "No, ma'am."

"Have you searched Alberto's trunks for that money?"

"Not yet. Mr. Palazzo, the keys, if you please."

Alberto tossed his key ring to the sheriff. The curly-haired deputy stayed behind to guard the prisoner. The rest of us went back to the hotel, where Sheriff Rhule opened Alberto's trunks and rummaged through their contents. He found nothing incriminating.

"Doesn't prove anything," he said. "He could've hid it — or passed it off to you as accomplices. But you are not suspects, and I do not have a search warrant."

"We got nothing to hide," I said. "Feel free to search our baggage and our room."

He accepted, and that's how we spent the next hour — turning up nothing, of course. By then, that day's train to Omaha was long gone.

Sheriff Rhule allowed Jake, Vic, and me to accompany him to the bank, where he quizzed a pinch-faced manager with the unlikely name of Fitzhugh Fitzsimmons about the dead man's monetary habits. According to the banker, Doyle habitually hoarded as much as a month's worth of box-office proceeds, rather than making more frequent deposits.

"Did I warn him? I certainly did!" the scandalized Fitzsimmons said, thumping his fist on his desk for emphasis. "Did I tell him sitting on piles of cash made him a temptation to robbers? I certainly did! Did he listen? He certainly did not!"

Convinced the bank manager was certainly certain, we followed the sheriff back to his office, where I floated a theory. "Other than the banker, who else knew Doyle kept an overflowing strong box?"

"I see where you're going," Sheriff Rhule said. "Doyle's employees at the theatre might well have known. And if he treated other acts like he treated Mr. Palazzo, withholding payment and such, Doyle may have had no shortage of disputes."

There was a catch — any potential suspects had to be in Fremont the night of the killing. Sheriff Rhule knew of some local residents who'd performed at the Elkhorn, and we went around town with him as he questioned a pretty singer, a rotund orator, the piano player from Alberto's show, and a shifty manager of dancing girls. All confirmed Doyle's penchant for fleecing performers, claiming the box office take had fallen short, and whittling down contractually promised fees, as he'd done to Alberto.

Back at the sheriff's office, we chewed over this new information. Since Doyle's shady business practices were common knowledge,

I wondered why artists kept playing his theater. It came down to supply and demand — too few theatres for too many itinerant artists. If more competing theatres opened as the town grew, performers might gain the leverage to demand better treatment from the likes of Doyle — although that particular problem was now as past-tense as Doyle himself.

If none of the local performers struck Sheriff Rhule as likely suspects, who else might have been stung by Paddy Doyle's duplicity — enough to want to rob him, kill him, or both?

"How about his own employees," Vic suggested.

"I myself was leaning in the direction of those backstage ruffians, ma'am," the sheriff said. "Except for that reprobate Wiley, they do tend to be transients."

"If Doyle treated his stagehands as bad as the performers," I said, "they might start thinking of ways to get even."

"Let's say you're onto something," Rhule said. "How do we flush 'em out?"

Jake and Vic looked at me. "Just so happens," I said, "I do have an idea."

Wiley opened the envelope hand-delivered to the Elkhorn and addressed to him. He sported a ripe bruise where Percy Chittenden had banged his forehead against the restaurant table. He unfolded the letter, neatly handwritten on linen hotel stationery, inviting him and his three co-workers to discuss an opportunity in Denver:

> We seek experienced theatre professionals to manage our new Grandview Theatre, an 800-seat operation opening soon in Denver. If interested, please join us for dinner at the Chittenden House Restaurant at 7 o'clock sharp this evening. Please dress appropriately, bring your three esteemed Elkhorn Theatre associates with you & present this letter to Mr. Chittenden upon arrival.
>
> Sincerely,
> John & Polly Oakwood

Wiley and his dandified mates showed up on time, uncharacteristically neat and clean, hair combed, ties and starched collars in place. They stood stiffly at the entrance to the dining room, where Percy Chittenden greeted them with a chilly glare. Wiley showed him the letter, and Chittenden escorted them to the table where Vic and me waited, dressed in our Sunday best. Even if they'd seen us the evening before, they had no idea we weren't John and Polly Oakwood.

We introduced ourselves and invited them to sit. "I hope you don't mind," I said, "but we've asked Mr. Chittenden to provide a splendid supper, compliments of the Grandview Theatre."

Looking like they'd won a lottery they hadn't even entered, they dug right into the free food and drink as we told them about the opportunities and pay coming their way if they joined our Denver organization.

What Wiley and his trio of theatre thugs didn't know was this — when they left the Elkhorn to freeload a meal, Sheriff Rhule, Eddie, and Jake entered the empty theatre and went into the basement to search their dingy dormitory quarters. It didn't take long to find Paddy Doyle's locked strong box bearing an engraved brass plate — *Property of Elkhorn Theatre.* The sheriff pried it open and found it contained a load of cash, divided and tied into bundles tagged by date and performance.

"We got what we came for," Rhule said.

Jake cocked his head. "I hate to quibble — but is this search legal?"

The sheriff scowled. "Didn't you pick a fine time to ask, son — nothing like shutting the barn door after the horses have already run off. These men are domiciled within the confines of the theatre. Therefore, I believe these premises are not their private quarters, and are not protected by the Fourth Amendment of the United States Constitution against illegal search and seizure. Paddy Doyle would've had the right to come in here and turn it upside down, had he so desired."

Jake nodded. "But seeing as he's dead —"

"— I am exercising that right in his stead, as a sworn officer of the law, possessing ample suspicion and justification. I think a judge will agree."

"Sheriff," Eddie said, "is this enough to charge 'em with murder?"

"Well, that is my problem, not yours. But finding this evidence is enough to spring Mr. Palazzo. You've done him a good turn."

Next, Sheriff Rhule and his deputy strolled into the Chittenden House restaurant, arrested Wiley and his collaborators in mid-meal, handcuffed them, and hauled them in for interrogation. They did miss out on some tasty desserts.

As for "just deserts," well, I don't know if honor among thieves even exists, but there wasn't any that night. Questioned one at a time, the other three fessed up pronto and swore they didn't know Doyle would be killed. While Wiley squawked about being railroaded, his pals tripped over themselves incriminating him as mastermind and murderer. With that much corroboration, Walter Rhule had confidence these charges would stick.

Alberto happily relinquished his jail cell to the true criminals, and wept upon his release. He also crushed Sheriff Rhule and his young deputy in a hug of appreciation. Then Alberto, Jake, and Eddie got back to the hotel in time to share pie and lemon ice cream with me and Vic.

26

> "One's own private railroad car is not an acquired taste, darlin'. One takes to it instantly."
> ~ Actress Emmaline Rose

Next morning, Friday, October 17, we checked out of the hotel. Alberto hugged Percy Chittenden in gratitude and shed farewell tears on the Englishman's well-tailored shoulder. We all thanked him again for his kindness (though, in truth, we could not thank him enough), and Alberto and his trunks went to the Fremont depot along with me, Jake, Eddie, Vic, Rafael, Lucifer the horse, and all our gear to await the eastbound train.

"Where's your next show?" Vic asked Alberto.

"It is nowhere. Fremont, she was my last bookings."

"Then where are you going?"

"Where you go, I think," Alberto said with a shy grin.

"We're aiming for Baltimore, but we only have enough money to get us to Omaha."

"Then I am aiming also for Baltimore, and go with you to Omaha." Alberto's eyes moistened. "You are my American friends. You save my life from being hanged. Maybe I help you somehow — even if it is cleaning after the horse. Is good for me to go?"

Vic stood up on tippy-toes and kissed him on the cheek. *"Tutto bene."*

When the train arrived, Vic and Eddie got Lucifer settled in a cramped livestock-car stall, then rejoined the rest of us in the coach where we'd found seats. At long last, we left Fremont and embarked on the two-hour leg to Omaha.

That was how long I had to think of other ways to raise the money we needed to continue on to Baltimore — or to accept that I'd have to hunt down Emmaline Rose and beg for hobo's sanctuary in her private Pullman Palace railroad coach.

After the turmoil of recent days, most of our group stared out the windows or napped. I decided to stretch my legs walking from car to car. When I reached the club car, I found four amateurs playing poker. Was there any possible way I might win enough from these men to pay for the rest of our trip, saving me and my dented pride from having to ask for Emmaline's help?

It was worth a try, so I asked if I could join the next hand. They said fine, and I sat myself down. But they were so unskilled, and the stakes so low, the venture seemed both dull and pointless. I won my first hand easily, and felt miserable for collecting the pitiful pot. It really wasn't fair of me to take their money, and I'd never win enough to ease our shortage of funds. So, thinking I'd excuse myself, I surrendered my winnings.

Unfortunately, what I considered to be a generous gesture offended one of the players, who was the spittin' image of President Ulysses S. Grant, down to his beard and the stogie clamped between his teeth. "By God, what do you mean by that?" he roared as he stood — and whipped out a long, sharp hunting knife.

I threw up my hands. "Whoa! I'm only trying to be considerate."

"*No,* sir. *You,* sir, are pissin' on our honor."

His waving that lethal pig-sticker in my direction sharpened (so to speak) my awareness of the imperative to be diplomatic, and I did try. "Now, fellas, that was not my intention." I slowly slid my chair back from the table, wondering if I could escape without shedding blood (mine, not his).

"Then *why*, sir, are you *insultin'* us?"

"It's nothing personal. It's . . ." And that's where my patience petered out. "Aww . . . well, see, it happens you fellas aren't very good at poker, and I am. So it doesn't seem fair, and that's all on me."

"Then give us an honorable chance to *win* it back."

"Again, nothing personal . . . but I'd have to be asleep or dead for you to win."

"*Dead,* sir, could be how your day ends."

Man and knife advanced one step toward me. I retreated — and bumped into someone behind me. It was Jake — and I have *never* been happier to see my brother, with his frock coat tucked back to clear his holster and his fingers curled around his Colt's polished wood grip.

President Grant took notice. "You know how to shoot that thing, sir?"

Jake grinned. "I do."

"Do I wanna test you?"

"You don't."

"How much of that did you see?" I mumbled sideways to Jake.

"Most of it. Well . . . all of it, really."

"And you couldn't've spoken up sooner?"

Jake ignored me and addressed them.

"Gentlemen, what my little brother meant was, he's not gonna be on the train all that long. So if I was you, I wouldn't look a gift horse in the mouth." He squinted one-eyed at the man with the knife. "Anybody ever tell you, you're a dead ringer for President Grant?"

"Grant" must've known the old saying about the futility of bringing a knife to a gunfight, so he tucked his blade back into his belt scabbard and sat down.

With an affable nod, Jake steered me toward the door at the end of the car, savoring my predicament. "Jamey, all these years we've been related, have you ever counted how many times you'd've been doomed without me?"

"You could enjoy this a little less, y'know."

"Why deprive myself?"

By early evening, *finally,* the train steamed into the Union Pacific depot in Omaha, a certified railroad boomtown of twenty thousand people — ten times the size of Fremont. Although the streets were still mostly dirt, the city's bright future as a gateway to the West was guaranteed by its location on the Missouri River — and its position as the terminus of three eastern railroads, and the beginning of the westbound transcontinental railroad.

We got off with our baggage, sprung Lucifer from the livestock car, and gathered outside the passenger terminal. I'd failed to devise any brilliant alternative scheme to get us to Baltimore, and Alberto had no magical miracles to offer. So it was time for me to stop beating the devil around the stump, and seek out Emmaline.

"We should all go," Jake said, "to make sure you don't turn chicken."

We asked the ticket clerk for directions to the Academy of Music. Then, like a nomadic caravan, six motley humans and a horse walked several blocks to the theatre on Douglas Street, amid the commercial center of town.

With over an hour until show time, I tried talking my way in to see the star. Even though I told the whole truth and nothing but, nobody at the theatre — not the lady selling tickets, the head usher, or the manager — bought my story. The manager did allow me to write Emmaline a note he promised to deliver to her dressing room. Next, I tried sneaking in the stage door, but didn't make it past a beefy guard dozing in a chair.

We were down to our final option — buying two tickets for me and Jake, and hoping

I'd be able to catch her eye from the audience. We scurried to the ticket booth, where a chart showed the theatre's eight hundred seats included a mezzanine tier of exclusive boxes. If we could get a pair of those seats, maybe we'd have a chance. But, of course, they were all sold out. Best we could do was the balcony, last row. We took what we could get, went in, and hiked upstairs to our seats.

"Jeezus," Jake said. "We're so far back, we're practically in Iowa. The odds of her spotting you up here are —"

"— not good."

"Unless we set you on fire."

I checked my watch. "We got thirty minutes 'til she starts. Let's go."

"Go where?"

"To try and bribe somebody to trade seats with us."

Jake's eyes narrowed. "*That's* your best idea?"

He wasn't wrong — it wasn't a great idea, but we had nothing to lose. Hurrying down to the lobby, we looted our wallets, scraped together fifty-three dollars and stood at the foot of the carpeted stairs leading up to the deluxe boxes. We politely accosted every pair of well-dressed patrons headed to their seats and offered to swap our tickets plus cash for theirs.

Most of them brushed past us, and we were ready to concede — until one grumpy short man in a tall top hat seemed curious. "Show me," he said.

We held out our cash.

He didn't reject us outright. "My lady friend has already absconded with a man of exceptional height," he sniffed. "So I no longer need to impress her. I'll take it."

"Where, exactly, are your seats?" I asked.

Jake stared at me. "*Now* you're being picky?"

I looked at the short man's tickets, saw the words *Mezzanine Box,* and took the swap before he could reconsider. Then me and Jake raced up the steps two at a time. We ended up in the front of the second box, stage right — not bad. Though the Academy of Music couldn't compare to the Excelsior, it was magnitudes beyond Fremont's Elkhorn Theatre in size, furnishings, and frills.

Jake enjoyed the show, but I was too intent on drawing Emmaline's attention. Maybe I tried too hard, but she never looked our way, even when I stood and clapped as loud as I could after each song and scene.

I had one last chance. When she came out for her final curtain call, I abandoned any pretense of dignity. I cheered, whooped and hollered — but she left the stage without a single glance our way. The audience began filing out. I slumped into my chair.

"Maybe she didn't like you as much as you thought," Jake said.

"Is this you being helpful?"

"Maybe let's try the stage door again."

"Why bother?"

"Maybe a miracle'll happen."

I didn't move until we were pert near the last ones still seated. With a dejected sigh, I stood, turned to leave the box — and bumped into our miracle in the shape of a stocky usher. He had a familiar perfume-scented envelope in his hand, with *Jamey* written on it.

"Hnnh," Jake said. "Looks like makin' a fool of yourself worked."

I gave the kid a half-dollar tip, grabbed the note and read it while Jake peered over my shoulder:

Darlin' J,
Of course I noticed you, you clown! Come backstage.
       Emma ♡

The usher led us down to Emmaline's dressing room, where she met us with a smile. Not sure we should kiss, we settled for an awkward embrace. I explained our complicated pickle, and how we needed her help.

Before she gave us an answer, she asked, "Darlin', where are your friends? You must bring them in for refreshments." She pointed at a serving cart laden with pastries. "I've got all these sinful delights from Susanetta's *Patisserie* around the corner. When in Omaha, I simply cannot resist. But if I eat them all, my costumes will not fit, and my little Millie will get downright cross with me."

"They're outside the stage door," I said, "with the horse."

Emmaline laughed. "Then we shall go to them." She cinched her robe, and nodded toward the pastry cart. "Jamey, if you'd do the honors . . ." She led. We and the pastries followed.

Emmaline greeted Vic with a more passionate hug than I got. "Victoria, my darlin' girl! And Eddie and Rafael, I am pleased to see y'all again." Her eyebrows rose as she beheld Alberto, standing shyly with his head down. "And who might this be? Hercules?"

Alberto held her delicate hand and brushed it with a chaste kiss. "Alberto Palazzo, at you service, s*ignorina*."

She looked from Alberto to Eddie, and back again. "You two are the most colossal

311

gentlemen I have ever had the pleasure of meetin'." Then she addressed all of us. "I am so sorry you've had to stand around outside. If I had only known you were comin'." She flashed a tart glare at me, then relented. "But I understand this was an unscheduled stop on your odyssey. As for the remainder of your trip, now playin' the role of Good Samaritan is — me!" She bowed.

Vic laughed with relief. "So, we can ride with you?"

"I could never deny a request from Jamey. I'm glad for the company, my ragged little stowaways. It'll be such fun, like boardin' school when I was a girl — except with boys!"

"Thank you, Miss Rose," Eddie said. "We're more obliged than we can say. And I promise, we'll pay you back for the ride."

"Nonsense, darlin'. Y'all are my guests."

Emmaline approached Lucifer, who at first arched his neck in a display of lordly indifference, then bowed his head so she could pet his nose.

"You seem to have a way with horses," Vic said in admiration. "He doesn't usually warm up to new people so fast — or at all."

"I took my equestrian endeavors quite seriously as a girl, and I'm eager to hear all about this horse of yours, and this match race. Oh, and I will make sure he is well accommodated on the train."

Our weary band of nomads could breathe a little easier, knowing we'd at least be able to complete our journey to Maryland. Emmaline had one more Omaha show on Saturday night. Our scheduled departure would be Sunday morning at eight. Then it would be twenty-two hours to Chicago, where her Pullman Palace coach would be switched to a Baltimore & Ohio train to carry us the rest of the way.

If all went according to plan, we could expect to arrive in Baltimore by ten in the morning on Tuesday, October 21, barely in time for us to jump off the train, rush to Pimlico, and beat the noon entry deadline with minutes to spare — and little allowance for any more unforeseen detours or delays. While there's not much point to fretting about random chance, recent history had us worried just the same.

When Emmaline learned we'd had no time to secure lodgings in Omaha, she insisted we stay with her at the newly opened Grand Central Hotel a block from the theatre. Five stories tall, with a hundred and fifty rooms, the Grand Central was Omaha's first truly elegant hotel.

After we'd quartered Lucifer at the nearby livery stable, Emmaline swept into the lobby trailed by her bedraggled entourage. She arranged for sufficient folding cots and linens, brought us up to her suite, and got us settled like a mother hen looking after her chicks. She overheard us talking about our next big problem — scaring up five hundred dollars for the Pimlico entry fee. I figured on wiring Mike in Baltimore to ask for a loan.

"What about me?" Emmaline said. "I can lend you what you need."

"You've already done enough for us," I said.

"Jamey," Jake said, "it's the least she can do after stomping on your heart."

I blushed. Everybody else laughed, including Emmaline. "He's right," she said. "It *is* the least I can do."

I started to protest but she shushed me with a finger on my lips. "Besides, darlin', I know your poker skills. I'd 'wager' you could win back that li'l bit in no time. Or you can repay me when Lucifer wins his race."

Vic frowned. "But what if he doesn't win?"

"Hush, now, Victoria. Think positive."

Early on Saturday, October 18, we sent

telegrams to both Mississippi Mike and Horatio Deale in Baltimore with our latest bulletin, promising updates as time permitted.

Time. Would it be our enemy — or our friend? *Time* was now our all-consuming obsession. Every passing minute, every tick of every clock reminded me that *time* was growing ever shorter for us to reach our goal.

Emmaline provided welcome distraction by showing us around town during the day, and promised to leave tickets for all of us at the Academy box office so we could see her final Omaha performance. Then back to the hotel, get some sleep, up at daybreak Sunday, and board the train.

As much as Victoria wanted to see the show again, Rafael begged her to help him work with Lucifer, and she agreed. At a small corral behind the stable, Raf mumbled his prayer and crossed himself before stepping into the ring like a wary boxer facing a foe with a notorious knockout punch.

Vic and Rafael tried their best, but Lucifer had other ideas. He stole the entire bunch of carrots Raf had intended to offer one at a time as rewards, chased the jockey around while nipping at his backside, and knocked him down with a head butt. After Vic saddled the horse, he displayed his irritation with a few bucks and kicks, and Raf got no closer than arm's length.

When Vic decided to end their lesson before anybody (meaning Rafael) actually got hurt, she tried to sound optimistic. "We'll still have time when we get to Baltimore."

"A coupla days at most — that's never gonna be enough."

"Sometimes horses can surprise you."

"That's what I'm afraid of."

And that, right there, was Victoria's biggest concern: What if Rafael's confidence was shot to hell? What if his funk made him unable to ride not only Lucifer, but *any* horse? What if he couldn't ever again be the same jockey who'd guided Phoenix to so much summertime success?

They say the best thing after falling off a horse is to climb right back on. But what do you do if you never even got on him in the first place?

We left the hotel early Sunday morning. For all our travails, with the ultimate outcome still uncertain, there was some comfort in knowing we were heading into the homestretch of our hard-luck journey.

After Vic and Eddie loaded Lucifer into

the livestock car, Emmaline made sure we felt at home in her first-class suite on wheels. Gaily painted screens partitioned the car into three sections — a bedroom at one end, a central salon with soft chairs and sofas, and a dining area. At Emmaline's request, porters had delivered extra pillows, mattresses, and blankets for her guests. The car never felt crowded, even with seven occupants.

"How long did it take you to get used to traveling like this?" Jake asked.

Emmaline laughed. "One's own private railroad car is not an acquired taste, darlin'. One takes to it instantly."

After we ate that evening, Emmaline pulled out a battered old guitar she'd had since childhood and led us in a sing-along of tunes old and new. Alberto sang a little opera for us, and performed some magical feats. The only thing missing was a campfire. For the first time in days, we allowed ourselves to believe all might turn out well — until our locomotive went lame and limped into Chicago.

After a repair crew wasted a futile hour working on the machinery, our train was hitched to a fresh engine, which hauled us out of Chicago almost two hours behind schedule. Fortunately, the long-established eastern railways allowed faster speeds, and (other than one stretch of track undergoing repairs) our engineer pushed his steam-powered steed to its limits to make up for lost time.

By now, after so many ups and downs, we'd settled into a stoic quietude. We'd done all we could. Either we'd reach Baltimore in time, or we wouldn't — our destiny was out of our hands. Whether we felt the peace of the penitent man putting his trust in God, or of the condemned man knowing his fate was sealed, that I couldn't tell you.

27

> "Mud ain't nobody's friend if you're in a hurry."
> ~ Mississippi Mike Morgan

On the rainy Tuesday morning of October 21, our train pulled into Baltimore's Camden Station, an imposing three-story red brick building. With its gabled windows and a hundred-foot-tall tower, the station looked regal enough to pass for a state capitol.

The depot clock told us it was ten-thirty-three. Late — but was it *too* late? We thanked Emmaline again for rescuing us, she promised to be at the big race, and we hurried about our immediate business of hauling baggage, springing Lucifer, and rushing to Pimlico.

A steady downpour drummed on the shed roof over the platform as we stood with our gear and our horse — and no time to spare. If we tried to hail carriages to take all of us, we'd never beat the noon deadline. Wearing pants, her Stetson, and her coat collar turned up against the rain, Vic decided on the spot to ride her horse straight to Pimlico, alone and without delay.

While Vic and Eddie got Lucifer tacked up and ready to go, I ran inside, got scribbled directions and a hand-drawn map of the route from the stationmaster, and rushed back out. "It's about ten miles and an hour away," I said as I handed the folded paper up to Vic already in the saddle.

Jake gave her his pocket watch and a compass, which she stuffed inside her coat with the directions and the envelope with the entry money.

"Be careful," Eddie said. "You're gonna run into wet cobblestones and muddy roads. If Lucifer slips and gets hurt —"

"— then we came all this way for nothing, I know," Vic said. "But if I don't get there before noon . . ."

"She'll be as careful as she can," I said. "Vic — go!"

She steered Lucifer away from Camden Station and pointed him north. As if heeding Eddie's warning, Lucifer did not like the wet cobblestones paving some of the main avenues, and refused to go faster than a deliberate walk. For once, Vic wished he was wearing studded horseshoes for better traction. Then again, Lucifer didn't much like the narrow, mucky side streets either. Riding "hell-bent for leather" was not an option.

They navigated Baltimore's busy downtown streets not far from the waterfront teeming with skiffs, schooners, and steamships. With its dense jumble of homes, hotels, and boardinghouses, and chockablock with all manner of businesses and factories, Baltimore ranked as America's sixth largest city back then. It felt to Vic like most of its 270,000 residents were out in the rain and determined to get in her way.

On every block and corner, they encountered work carts and wagons, horse-drawn omnibuses and bigger street-cars, not to mention swarms of cattle and pigs crossing back and forth. Especially pigs — *lots* of pigs. All those animals meant piles of stinking manure everywhere, attracting squadrons of flies, and turning any attempt to make your way on foot into a perilous adventure. "Welcome to the big city," she said to Lucifer. "Or more like *pig* city."

She couldn't shake the queasy feeling she was already lost. She felt like an inept Paul Revere, bumbling her way through *terra incognita,* the entire fate of our cross-country quest weighing heavy on her damp shoulders. She hailed a man harrying a herd of porkers west through a muddy intersection. "Hey, mister — why are there so many pigs here?"

The man peered at her through rain-streaked specs. " 'Cuz Pigtown's over thataway, hon. Slaughterhouses and butchers galore."

"Pigtown, huh? I'm looking for Greene Street. The way to Pimlico?"

The pig wrangler waved in a different direction from where she'd been heading. "Coupla blocks back yonder, hon. Then follow yer nose."

"Much obliged."

Vic altered course and maintained a prudent pace. She referred to the stationmaster's notes and map, and dug the compass out of her pocket to confirm their northwest heading. She found Greene Street, and followed the street-car tracks onto Pennsylvania Avenue, which pointed her toward Pimlico.

Once out of the heart of the city and on to more countrified byways along the sprawling green oasis of Druid Hill Park, Vic stopped gritting her teeth and relaxed her death-grip on Lucifer's reins. Though the roads were all muddy dirt out that way, they were also less traveled and offered somewhat better footing. Lucifer still resisted cantering, but agreed to trot.

Victoria was a skilled rider, and if anybody could make this journey safely, it would be her and her eccentric horse. But a glance at Jake's watch told her she was running out of time.

Wearing a Mackintosh coat to ward off the stubborn rain, his furled umbrella under his arm, Mississippi Mike Morgan paced the Pimlico Clubhouse's covered veranda. He checked his watch — six minutes to noon — then went inside and upstairs to Chief Steward Emmett Pitt's office. There he found the gaunt track official hunched over his desk, head bowed in his hands.

"Mr. Pitt?"

Pitt looked up. With worry creasing his forehead, and dark circles under his eyes, a bedraggled bloodhound would've looked chipper by comparison. "Mr. Morgan. Have your long-lost entrants arrived yet?"

"No, sir, but they are on their way. I were hopin' to prevail upon you to hold the entry window open just a wee bit longer."

"Sorry, but rules are rules. Where would this country be without rules? I'll tell you where — *nowhere* is where. We can't have everything going off half-cocked and —"

"— higgledy-piggledy," Mike said, making an educated guess.

"Not to mention, topsy-turvy and cat-awampus. It would be mayhem, Mr. Morgan — sheer and utter *mayhem*. And we cannot have that."

"No, I suppose not."

"My bigger problem," Pitt said, "is this infernal rain. We have us a schedule to keep — four days of racing. But we can't race in mud and slop, from start to finish and pillar to post! What in the Sam Hill am I supposed to do?" Wrapped up in his personal tizzy, Pitt went to the window, as if staring at the rain could make it stop.

Mike went back downstairs. A massive grandfather clock in the foyer struck twelve and he returned to his porch lookout post. A few minutes later, a soggy rider on a white horse approached the clubhouse. It was Victoria. She slid down from her saddle and wrapped Lucifer's reins around the fence rail. Mike opened his umbrella and came down to meet her.

She hadn't checked Jake's watch, but she knew. "I'm too late . . ."

"I tried to get 'em to bend a little, but . . ." Mike's sad shrug said the rest. "You've come a long, hard way, Victoria. I am sorry for the outcome."

"I need to sit on something that isn't moving." They took cover on the veranda and she slumped down in one of a row of wood-slat chairs.

Mike sat next to her. "The rest of 'em?"

"They'll be coming along. We thought if I rode alone, I might make it." Her weary voice trailed off. "But the rain . . . all that mud slowed us down."

"Mud ain't nobody's friend if you're in a hurry."

They sat and listened to the rain spatter against the porch roof until our two hired carriages rolled up a half-hour later, carrying Jake, Eddie, Rafael, me, Alberto, and our bags. We joined them on the veranda and Mike confirmed the bad news — there'd be no match race for us.

We'd made our grueling coast-to-coast trek for naught. We sat quiet, damp, and doleful. Then Vic walked back to her horse and climbed on.

"What's she doing?" Eddie said.

Nobody knew, so we all followed. Slogging through puddles, Vic guided Lucifer to the muddy track and made a somber pass by the empty grandstand. I reckoned she was trying to make her peace with knowing her horse would not race there, and they wouldn't get the chance to win back Phoenix.

Alberto broke the mournful silence in a voice so soft we almost didn't hear him. "I am so sorry."

"For what?" I said.

"I cause you too much trouble. You lose too much time to save me."

"Aww, that's not what sunk us. It was a lot of things."

Eddie gave the magician's shoulder a reassuring squeeze. "This was always a long shot. Maybe gettin' Phoenix back wasn't ever in the cards. But I'll never be sorry we helped you."

Alberto wiped away a tear. "I will do for you anything, my American friends."

Over more than a week of struggles, what had kept us going through thick and thin was the goal of getting to race, and delivering the comeuppance Cortland Van Brunt III deserved. To travel so far, stumbling through one improbable scrape after another, only to fall short by a matter of minutes? That was close to unbearable.

I thought back to Mama's Bible lessons at her Sunday morning saloon-church meetings when me and Jake were kids. Like Job, we almost always tried to remember how blessed we were, and to lead righteous lives.

But I never quite understood how Job didn't cuss out God for all the pain and loss he'd suffered, and instead accepted his fate as God's will.

Even though he despaired over not knowing the reasons for his misfortunes, Job still kept his faith. He never begged for favor — and that's why God restored him to a life even better than before. Like the Bible says, "Behold, the fear of the Lord, that is wisdom; and to depart from evil is understanding."

If there was some comforting moral for us in that Old Testament tale, I had no clue what it might be. But this much we knew — there was no silver lining hiding in the bleak clouds that wept upon Baltimore.

28

> "The rich and powerful always have their thumbs on the scales of justice, and there's no shortage of shady lawyers happy to help 'em."
> ~ Mississippi Mike Morgan

Had we succeeded after so many trials, our spirits would surely have been lifted. But failure left us exhausted and crestfallen, not to mention wet. Mike suggested we retreat to his house and rest a spell, since there was nothing more to be done at Pimlico.

Mike, Alberto, and me climbed aboard one carriage, with Mike's gray horse tied to the back. Jake, Eddie, and Rafael took the other carriage, and Vic rode Lucifer. By then, the rain had eased to a heavy mist. As we were about to leave, there was a flurry of activity on the clubhouse veranda. Emmett Pitt and four other Pimlico officials came outside under umbrellas, huddling and harrumphing their way from clubhouse to track.

Signaling our drivers to wait, Mike climbed down and followed the officials as they conferred with two groundskeepers. They walked up and down a section of the homestretch in front of the grandstand, scrutinizing conditions. Then they huddled and harrumphed their way back toward the clubhouse.

Mike stood in their path. "Mr. Pitt, what may I ask is the outcome of your confabulation?"

"Due to rain and track conditions, the Jockey Club has decided to postpone the start of the autumn meeting. No racing today, or tomorrow. Thursday the twenty-third will be opening day. Subsequent dates, if the weather holds, will be Friday, Saturday, and Monday. No racing Sunday, as that is God's day."

"Well, sir," Mike said, "that means the great match race, which were supposed to be on the final day of competition, is going to be pushed back to your *new* final day of Monday."

Pitt and his colleagues pursed their lips and grimaced, like they'd all sucked on a lemon at the same time. They moved onto the porch for additional huddling and harrumphing. Mike stayed close. The rest of us wondered what was going on.

Pitt turned to Mike. "We do not want such an outstanding event as this match race to be on a Monday —"

"— with many fewer spectators and much less betting going on," Mike said.

"Exactly. Therefore, we are rescheduling it as the third race of four on Saturday, October the twenty-fifth. More spectators will attend, including many from Washington. With this week to drum up publicity in the Baltimore and Washington papers, we can expect a huge crowd. And that will mean even more betting, which is all to the good, and not at all higgledy-piggledy."

"All to the good," Mike agreed. "But with the match race now pushed back, and your entry window previously declared as closed *three days* before the race, we should now be able to enter our horse."

Pitt blinked. "How so?"

Mike made his lawyerly case. "Point one: Originally, your four-day autumn meeting were to begin *today* and end on *Friday,* the twenty-fourth. Two: The match race were going to be on that final day. Three: Your rules for the match race specifically set an entry deadline at noon *three days* before race day. Are you with me, so far?"

"So far," Pitt said, scratching his gray beard.

"Good. To point four: *Now,* match race day is to be *Saturday,* the twenty-fifth, all for good and fit reasons of weather and commercial aspects. And, last, point five: To maintain consistency of the Jockey Club setting the deadline for match-race entries at *three days* before race day, the final day and time for entering that race should now be *tomorrow* at noon, not *today.* Therefore, the rain delay means entries should be reopened."

After Pitt and the other officials huddled and harrumphed some more, the steward turned to Mike. "Mr. Morgan, we shall discuss what you have presented, behind closed doors. Shouldn't take too long. You're welcome to wait."

"Well, sir, we'll do just that."

Pitt and the others went inside the clubhouse. Mike came over to us and explained his argument. If he was persuasive enough, we might get Lucifer into the match race after all. Left for dead and buried, our hopes had been revived — only to be dashed again twenty minutes later, when Emmett Pitt came out to the veranda and announced: "Rain or not, the original entry deadline stands."

"I plan to appeal that," Mike said.

"Fine. Appeal denied," Pitt said, and went back inside.

Like a listless funeral procession, our two hired carriages and Vic on her horse left Pimlico and headed down to Mike's house. On the way, I told him the details of our transcontinental odyssey. Once he knew, he got lost in thought. Knowing Mike's devotion to the pursuit of righteous justice, I thought he'd try to help — but what could he do?

His Bolton Hill neighborhood, on the northern edge of Baltimore City, was a recent development of three-story rowhouses that were handsome but simple, with red brick façades and white marble stoops. Their uncluttered architecture was a welcome change from the fussy ornamentation and Victorian follies so common at the time. His house stood on Eutaw Place at the corner of Wilson Street, facing a verdant median where three blocks of manicured shrubs, trees, flowers, and fountains imparted the feel of living in a park.

We unloaded the carriages, and their drivers returned downtown. Mike assured us he'd make arrangements with his local livery for any transportation we'd need. After more than a week of jumbled travel, we were grateful for a hospitable haven to catch our breath.

Seeing Jake unbuckle his gunbelt and hang it over a coat rack, Mike hinted, "I know you're handy with a shooting iron. But it's uncommon for Baltimore city folk to walk the streets carrying a big ol' Colt."

"Mike's got a point," I said. "When in Rome . . ."

Since he wasn't from Baltimore or Rome, Jake reasoned, he'd keep on carrying his pistol, if it wasn't outright against the law, which it wasn't.

With big windows and spare furnishings, the house felt airy and pleasant. After Vic browsed Mike's well-stocked library bookshelves, she stood for quite a while in front of three framed oil paintings hanging in the parlor — outsized portraits of George Washington and Thomas Jefferson, signed by the acclaimed Independence-era artist Gilbert Stuart, and a smaller work that was unmistakably Da Vinci's Mona Lisa. To me, they looked much more at home in this gracious rowhouse than they had in his dim basement flat in St. Louis, where I first saw them.

"Aren't these famous?" Vic said to me.

"They would be."

"Would be?"

"If they were real. These're copies — well, forgeries, if Mike tried to pass 'em off as the genuine article. Which he doesn't, and they aren't."

"Who painted 'em?"

"Mike did. Like he says, he's got an eye."

"Enjoyin' the artwork?" Mike said after he brought out glasses and a pitcher of cider.

Vic shook her head in wonder. "What else're you good at?"

"This 'n' that," Mike said with a modest smile.

"Me and Jake were surprised you went back to Baltimore," I said. "What happened?"

"Well, by the time Gideon and me got home to St. Louis after our Texas railroad caper, I started thinking there were better ways to spend my days than looking after a gambler who's good enough to win honest-like but prefers to cheat." Mike paused for a sip of cider. "Since I settled here, I been cultivating contacts, doing what I like to call special legal consultation."

"I'm guessing Gideon didn't let you go without a fight," I said.

"He did kick up a fuss. But he were sufficiently appreciative of my years being his mentor and confidant that he gave me a tidy cash sum. That, plus savings, were enough to come back to the ol' hometown and buy this place."

"Now, I distinctly recollect you saying that when you got out of law school years ago, it took you all of a week to figure out —"

"— that the law weren't about justice, so much as winning and losing? I were right then, and still am."

"Then what's different?"

"Me," Mike said. "I know more than in my younger days about what needs doing, and how to do it. The rich and powerful always have their thumbs on the scales of justice, and there's no shortage of shady lawyers happy to help 'em. Regular folks need somebody on their side to balance things out."

"But how *do* you balance things out?" Vic asked. "Don't people like my father and Van Brunt have all the advantages?"

"They think so. Funny thing is, that can play against 'em. It's about knowing how the human mind works. I learned years ago that greed bewitches men — always has, always will. The trick is knowing how to use that fact for good."

"Why does it matter to you?"

"I been on the upside and the down, Victoria. Nobody deserves to be run over by this here Gilded Age."

Vic excused herself to freshen up, and I took that opportunity to pow-wow with Mike in private. "You're already planning something, aren't you?"

"Keep this between us. Knowing the circumstances, I believe your friends have been victims of injustice. And you know nothing riles me more."

"Whatever you're thinking, count me in."

"I have to find some fertile soil first, plant a few seeds, see what grows on short notice. So don't get your hopes high just yet. And don't say anything to anybody else. This may fail."

"What am I supposed to do in the meantime?"

"Help Victoria have that horse of hers ready to race."

"But he can't race if we can't enter him. How can we possibly get the Jockey Club to change their minds?"

"We can't."

"But the whole point was to get Lucifer into this race, and rope Van Brunt into a side bet to try and win back Phoenix."

"Don't hang up your fiddle yet," Mike hinted. "Opportunity sometimes knocks at unexpected doors. There's some people I need to go see. I'll tell you more when there's more to tell."

Since our frustrating day hadn't given us any time to eat, Mike brought us into the kitchen and scrounged up some supper. We sat around the dining room table, and Mike got to know how Eddie and Vic had become racing partners. Then he turned his attention to Alberto, noting they had something in common. "I sometimes create illusions in my line of work, too, convincing folks they see what ain't really there."

We told Mike how the big magician ended up with us, recounting our efforts to clear him of that murder charge in Nebraska, and Alberto got all teary again. "If they no save me," he said, "I would be hanging in the gallows."

"You kids should be proud of what you done," Mike said. "Alberto, how did you happen to come to America?"

"Ohhh, *mamma mia,*" Alberto moaned. "Is a tragic tale, like an opera. I am playing magic all over Europe, even for Queen Victoria in-a London one time. Ahhh, but I fall in love with a beauty." He closed his eyes and sighed.

Vic found herself caught up in the story. "Who was she?"

"*Bellissima* Violetta. I first see her all alone at famous Teatro La Fenice opera house in Venezia. For us, it was love at the first sight.

We dream of running off together. And then . . . I find out Violetta is married to a count, he is cruel to her. He challenge me to a pistol duel, for honor. But I could not kill him — and I did not want to be killed! So I must leave. I go to America, for new life."

Vic reached across the table and gave his hand a sympathetic squeeze. "Poor Alberto."

After supper, Mike excused himself, saying he'd be out for a spell. The rest of us sat around the table for a while. Jake found a deck of cards and asked Alberto to do the astounding "Any Card, Any Number" trick again, like we'd seen in Fremont. Which he was happy to do, while my brother drove himself buggy trying (and failing) to figure out how Alberto could possibly name the right card every time.

"You gotta tell me," Jake pleaded.

"Easy," Alberto said. "It is . . . *magic!*"

"Awww, c'mon!"

"Jake, if I tell you, it would no more be magic."

"Well, can't you at least tell me how you do fire-eating without burning your mouth? There's gotta be a trick to it."

"There *is* a trick," Alberto whispered as Jake leaned closer. "It is, how you say . . .

science!"

"Science? Not magic?"

"Fire, she needs oxygen to burn, yes? Take away oxygen, and fire she goes out. Poof!"

"So . . . like when you stick the torch in your mouth, there's no air in there?"

"Something like that. And I am burned when I first learn. So do not try, Jake."

I snickered. "You already know my brother well — the maestro of leaping without looking."

"Okay, gimme those cards," Jake said. "I got a few tricks, too."

With Jake and Alberto occupied, and Eddie and Rafael spectating, Vic led me to a pair of armchairs in front of the parlor fireplace and interrogated me for the whole story of how me and Jake first met Mississippi Mike and Gideon Duvall, and how they'd helped us bring down the crooked conspiracy hatched by her father and banker Silas Atwood.

"Okay," she said when I was done, "I know *what* Mike does, but I still don't get *why.* Why tilt at windmills?"

"Well, he told me once how he'd never cheat an honest man. But scoundrels were fair game — 'men too mighty for the law to touch,' is how he put it."

"Like my father and Silas Atwood. But

that wasn't Mike's fight, and neither is this. What's in it for him?"

"If you're looking for some ulterior motive, there's isn't one."

"You trust him?"

"Yup."

"And he knows what he's doing?"

"Yup."

Vic's eyes glowed with eager fascination. "Do you have *any* idea what he's planning?"

"Nope."

Whatever it was, nobody wanted to know more than I did — and I couldn't wait to play my part.

29

"For every action, there's an equal and opposite reaction."
~ Mississippi Mike Morgan
(& Isaac Newton)

American Sport & Spirit,
October 22, 1873
★ *DEALE'S DEAL*
by HORATIO DEALE ★

My Dear Readers: The Weather Gods have decreed that Baltimore shall have persistent precipitation sufficient to knock the Pimlico Race Course's autumn meeting schedule into disarray. However, even Noah got his reprieve, and the fifty-odd horses present at Old Hilltop offer the prospect of brilliant competition.

The Great Sweepstakes match race (better known as "The Great Baltimore Brawl"), which so many have anticipated as a highlight of the week, will now take place as the third of four races on Saturday. Unfortunately, the field will not include late-arriving Lucifer, the enigmatical white Arabian from California.

Instead, the race pits three great champions against one dark horse. These splendid competitors are: Virginian Julius Caesar Pryce's chestnut Aries; Southern Cross, the handsome bay owned by Kentucky's Nantura Farm impresario John Harper; Black Swan, the Fabulous Filly from Gotham owned by August Belmont, the German-American financier and politico; and the formidable but little-known challenger Phoenix, Maryland horseman Cortland Van Brunt III's newly acquired California-bred palomino.

All but Phoenix are familiar to Eastern aficionados of the Sport of Kings. Thus, we ask: Does the betting man make the safe wager on one of three known quantities, and reap "small potatoes" at best? Or put his money on Van Brunt's Western interloper, and go for the big score?

Whatever seeds Mississippi Mike Morgan planted, we only had a few days for them to sprout. Come Saturday, barring more rain, Horatio Deale's "Great Baltimore Brawl" would be run between those four Thoroughbreds, without Lucifer.

Horse racing being America's first true national sport, going way back to Colonial times, this match race was a fevered topic of conversation in the papers and on the streets not only in Baltimore and Washington forty-some miles to the south, but over much of the country.

As the frenzy developed, members of America's House of Representatives and Senate had decided to suspend the nation's business on the originally scheduled Friday of the big race. That would free them to set aside contentious quarrels over post-war Southern Reconstruction, ride the rails to Baltimore for a long weekend, and channel factional feuds into rooting for horses from rival regions.

Despite the weather-induced delays, Congressional leaders stuck with their plans. With the race shifted to Saturday, Friday evening would now present the perfect opportunity for pre-race drinking, politicking, parties, arguing — all activities at which Congress excelled, as opposed to the actual business of running a fractious country fast becoming ungovernable. There were even rumors that President Grant himself would take a special presidential train from Washington to Baltimore for Saturday's races.

If the sun wasn't exactly shining on Wednesday, at least the rain had stopped. With a day for the track to dry out, racing would begin as planned on Thursday. And even though conditions weren't perfect, horses were able to take their exercise runs.

Early Wednesday, Mike rode up to Pimlico alone to see Chief Steward Pitt, who granted permission for Eddie and Victoria to keep Lucifer at Pimlico until they left for California. When Mike relayed the word, Vic and Eddie immediately liberated their horse from his cramped livery stall and took him straight over to the race course. The rest of us — me, Jake, Rafael, and Alberto — went along for the outing.

To give you the lay of the land, the track itself was oriented on a slight northeast to southwest diagonal. The main grandstand with its spires flanked the homestretch on the west side of the track. The clubhouse and main paddock were a short walk south of the grandstand.

Barns with peaked roofs and haylofts stood in rows scattered about the property wherever there was room to build them. Each one was divided into twelve-by-twelve stalls with solid walls in between, and room for stowing feed and equipment. Their roofs extended far enough to create a covered arcade protected from sun and rain, providing trainers and grooms with workspace for tending horses outside their stalls.

Lucifer's temporary home was one of seven barn buildings out behind the grandstand, farthest from the track, with eight-foot-high fences separating the barn area from the city streets beyond. Cortland Van Brunt paid a call, inviting us to visit Phoenix. I thought seeing their lost horse might be hard on Eddie, Vic, and Raffie, but they went anyway, and we took Lucifer along so he could see his horse pal again.

Phoenix and Van Brunt's other horses were housed closer to the track. When a groom brought Phoenix out, Eddie looked sad and the palomino looked confused. Raf gave Phoenix a hug, and looked even more woeful than Eddie, knowing he'd never get to ride his favorite mount again.

At least Phoenix and Lucifer seemed happy to see each other. I reckon horses don't overthink things the way we do. After the bittersweet reunion, on the way back to our barn, Jake whispered to me, "So, have you figured out —"

My jaw clenched. "No, I have *not* figured out how Van Brunt cheated. When I do, you'll be the first to know — if I haven't already strangled you."

"You are one grouchy bastard."

Vic rode Lucifer out to stretch his legs. After an easy lap, satisfied he was in good shape, she and Eddie cooled him down and checked him over. That's when Mike arrived with Horatio Deale, who was eager to talk.

The sportswriter knew of our failure to enter Lucifer. "It would've been a marvelous story. But the glorious thing about this sport is that there's always something else a-brewing." His voice lowered to a conspiratorial murmur. "There are rumors that the Jockey Club is planning to triple the fees they charge the bookmakers to ply their trade."

The way wagering on horse racing worked in those days, the bookmakers paid the track management for the right to organize the betting, establish and post odds, take in cash at the betting pools at a local hotel the night before the races, and on track premises at the betting ring on race days. The bookies did all this hocus-pocus by complicated mathematical formulae, guaranteeing themselves a suitable percentage of monies wagered as their commission.

I glanced at Mike, who radiated the meek innocence of a newborn babe. Had Horatio's reported scuttlebutt sprouted from one of those seeds Mike talked about planting? And if so, to what end?

"Why would they raise bookie fees?" Jake asked.

"Because they believe they can," Horatio said. "With the expectation of a record crowd and record betting, Jockey Club czars must believe the market will bear the cost."

"Figuring, even with a big fee increase," I said, "the bookies still stand to make so much from Saturday's racing that they wouldn't dare rock the boat?"

Horatio nodded. "A boat sure to be filled with an abundance of filthy lucre."

"What say the bookmakers?" Mike asked.

"Yet to be determined," Horatio said. "I am about to plumb those depths right now."

After he left, me and Jake cornered Mike, with Alberto listening behind us. "Was that your doing?" I asked.

"Let's call it a test," Mike said.

"Of what?"

"Isaac Newton's third law of motion — for every action, there's an equal and opposite reaction."

Alberto got all excited. "Ahh — science!"

"Now, if you boys don't mind," Mike said, "I'm going to tag along with Horatio."

And, just like that, Mike left us in the dark in broad daylight.

■ ■ ■ ■

Horatio and Mike located a wrathful herd of bookies at the Quarter Pole Pub across the street from the track's main gate. Rounds of drinks came fast and furious, even though it wasn't yet noon. A man named D. H. Galantier held court. The acknowledged top dog of the brotherhood of Baltimore bookmakers, Galantier was a big man with thinning hair and a walrus mustache. Despite his imposing height and heft, he was surprisingly light-footed in step and turn as he prowled and paced in front of the bar like a caged wolf.

Mike and Horatio entered the tavern in time to catch Galantier declaring, "These gilded overlords of the Maryland Jockey Club? My friends, I don't know who they *think* they are, but I swear to you they are *not!*" Even when outraged, Galantier's wily smile revealed a durable inclination toward winking at life's absurdities.

"Dave," one long-haired bookie called out, "what're we gon' do about this?"

"Larry, first we need to reconnoiter — are they serious, or just bluffing?"

Heads bobbed in indignant agreement.

"And if they's serious?" Larry asked.

"Then we walk. Without us, there's no betting," Galantier said. "And if they think tens of thousands — and President Grant himself — are going to turn out merely to see horses run? Without being able to bet on 'em and try to win their piece of the pie?"

"They're crazy!" a dozen angry voices shouted together.

Galantier grinned. "Right you are!"

"What do we do in the meantime?" said a thickset bookie.

Galantier's voice softened and his colleagues leaned in to listen. "We go about our business, fellas. We bide our time. But —" He paused for dramatic effect, then bellowed: "— we will *not* be buffaloed!"

The bookies cheered and stomped, pounding fists and glasses on tables and the bar. Galantier looked mighty pleased with himself as Horatio and Mike approached. "Horatio Deale!" he said, with a clap on the writer's bony shoulder. "The finest gossipmonger — and most colorful dresser — in the sports-writing game. Welcome back to our little den of thieves. What do you think of our aborning insurrection?"

"It would certainly change the game," said Horatio, notebook open and pencil scribbling. "If the Jockey Club did raise fees, would you really go on strike and deprive yourselves of a great deal of money?"

"You bet. We have to show those High-and-Mighties we can't be pushed around. Here, write this: 'Whilst the *heroic* D. H. Galantier generally displays elfin affability in the face of all but the worst mortal dreads, that warm and generous coat of good humor conceals an iron determination to never be bested — least of all by the —,'"

"— gilded overlords of the Maryland Jockey Club?" Horatio guessed.

Galantier belly-laughed. "You were listening!"

"I never met a memorable turn of phrase I didn't like."

"I've got a million of 'em," Galantier said, with a puckish half-smile. "Mr. Deale, chase your story, and consider me at your service as a ready source of juicy quotations."

30

"Never underestimate the power of a blue-ribbon rumor."
 ~ Mississippi Mike Morgan

If the bookies were incensed, so were track officials and Jockey Club potentates. That much became clear to Horatio and Mississippi Mike as they neared Pimlico's clubhouse. They heard argumentative voices rumbling out open windows on the second floor, so they followed the tumult to an upstairs conference room aboil with righteous indignation.

The French doors were half open, so Horatio and Mike walked right in. The big dogs of the Maryland Jockey Club — a dozen extravagantly wealthy men — sat around a long oak table. To be more accurate, eleven sat while one stood at a lectern and roared at much the same volume as D. H. Galantier had at the Quarter Pole Pub.

This other speaker with thinning hair and a prodigious mustache was none other than The Honorable Oden Bowie, who'd lately served a term as Maryland's governor from 1869 to '72, and whose family tree first took root when the state was but a fledgling English colony.

His comrades around the table also carried aristocratic ancestral names dating to Maryland's earliest settlement, their lives enriched by endeavors ranging from tobacco to railroads, mining to manufacturing, and investment speculation to banking (which were often interchangeable). Some, including Bowie, had owned slaves right up 'til Maryland's tardy ratification of Emancipation in 1864.

Governor Bowie was the reason Pimlico existed at all. A breeder of esteemed Thoroughbreds himself, he was one of a number of racing luminaries attending a swanky 1868 dinner party in upstate New York at Saratoga, one of the nation's premier racing venues. Someone suggested establishing a special stakes race, to be run in 1870 between horses then owned by the men at that Saratoga soiree. Bowie claimed the prestigious race for Maryland by pledging to build a grand new track in Baltimore. Terms of their gentlemen's wager were simple enough — each year, the winner would host the losers for dinner, and that's how the two-mile Dinner Party Stakes was born.

True to his word, Bowie had Pimlico ready in time for the inaugural event on October 25, 1870, won by a valiant colt called Preakness. Another notable annual race for three-year-olds would be established three years later and known henceforth as The Preakness Stakes, in perpetual honor of that crack racehorse.

And that's how imperious Oden Bowie came to be president of the Maryland Jockey Club, thundering to his minions about the greedy duplicity of the bookmakers. "They are grumbling about an increase in fees, my friends — an increase we have not even discussed, nor *intended* to discuss. But the fact that we were not contemplating raising those fees should not preclude us from doing exactly that!"

With steely nerve, Horatio Deale interrupted Governor Bowie from the back of the room. "Sir — if I may?"

The intrusion of a voice other than his own threw Bowie off stride. "What? Ahh, it's you, Mr. Deale."

"If you were not contemplating a fee increase before, why now?"

"Why?" Bowie said with the tight smile of an alligator keen to clamp its jaws on helpless prey. "To demonstrate to the bookmakers the perils of vaulting ambition."

Once Horatio had the Jockey Club's side of the dispute, he and Mike left the clubhouse and walked the grounds as the sportswriter tried to make sense of what they'd learned. "I concede that I am mystified as to the wellspring of this brewing storm."

It's a good thing Mike had a peerless poker face. "Care to make a guess?"

Horatio pursed his lips. "I pride myself on my ability to solve any puzzle. In this matter, however, my skills are being sorely tested — and that is *very* frustrating."

"I can see that."

"We have these facts in hand. First, the bookmakers had *no* thought of striking — until they heard rumors that the Jockey Club would more than triple the bookmakers' fees, from thirty dollars a day to a hundred. Second, the Jockey Club had *no* prior intention of raising those fees — until the bookies threatened to strike. Whence did this conflict arise?"

"Damned if I know," Mike lied with immaculate sincerity.

Their walking and talking and thinking had led them back to Pimlico's main gate, where Mike's arabber friend Solomon Carver and his partner Hub Robinson had their produce carts parked. Several grooms and trainers from the track were filling burlap sacks with apples and carrots for their horses.

Solomon waved Mike and Horatio over and tossed them each an apple.

"For us, or the horses?" Mike said.

Solomon laughed. "Depends who's hungrier."

"I'm hungry," said a small black man as he strolled up wearing a derby and a made-to-measure suit.

"Howdy there, Mister Charley Fly!" Solomon said.

Charley's gold tooth glinted as he slapped Solomon's back. "Solly, you ol' dawg. Good to see ya."

"You, too." Solomon turned to Mike and Horatio. "You boys know Charley Fly?"

"Only by reputation," Mike said as he shook the jockey's hand. "I've seen you race, sir."

"And Mr. Deale's been writin' about me for years," said Charley.

Horatio held his pencil poised over a clean notebook page. "Any comment on the upcoming match race?"

"Only that I'll be ridin' the winner," Charley said with a sly smile.

Hub Robinson grunted and scowled. "Someday, you won't. Someday, somebody's gonna swipe that grin off your face."

"I don't believe we've had the pleasure."

Hub looked down at the jockey. "Ain't no pleasure."

"This here's Hub Robinson," Solomon said.

"I was working to the bone in the fields," Hub said, "while you were riding for Pryce."

Charley looked over Hub's fruit bins and tried to be cordial. "You from Virginia, then?"

"Yup, born a slave."

"Same as me." Charley filled a paper sack with apples and carrots.

"Not the same. You got to live high on the hog, just 'cuz you stayed scrawny enough to be a jockey. How's that fair?"

"I ain't claimin' it was. But bein' a jockey and bein' a *winning* jockey — two different things, Mr. Robinson. But you're right, I was lucky . . . in some ways."

"I watched you winnin' races when you were still Charley Pryce."

"Pryce was my slave name. I dropped it when I had the chance."

"You got chances most didn't. And what did you do to help all the other colored folk who weren't so lucky — nothing."

Solomon gave his partner a gentle scolding. "Now, Hub, that ain't called for."

"Why not, if it's true?"

Charley took out a twenty-dollar bill, and handed it to Hub as he held up the paper sack. "This should cover it, Mr. Robinson."

Hub snatched the money, crumpled it, and threw it in the dirt at Charley's feet. Then he stalked away.

"Sorry 'bout Hub," Solomon said to Charley. "He got some anger he can't shake off. It ain't about you."

"Some of it is. I don't blame him. He thinks I'm all high-and-mighty. So do some white folks. Nothin' I can do about it, just livin' my life, y'know?" Charley picked up the twenty, smoothed it and pressed it into Solomon's palm. "For the arabbers at the barn."

"Much obliged."

"Mr. Fly," Horatio said, "I've never asked you this — but is there a story behind your chosen surname?"

"Story behind everything, ain't there? I was a kid and started winning, and when I tore past people watchin' me, I heard 'em holler, 'Lookit that kid go! *Fly, Charley, fly!*'

Seemed as fine a name as any."

"But Pryce had dubbed you Champagne Charley long before that."

"He did. One of my first races, they bet a case of imported French Champagne. I won, Pryce got the Champagne, and I got the name."

Horatio continued jotting in his notebook. "But doesn't it remind you of being a slave?"

"Color of my skin's all the reminder I need. But I liked the sound of Champagne Charley, so I kept it." He tipped his hat and headed for the barns.

That Wednesday evening, back at Mike's house in Bolton Hill, he called us all together. Me, Jake, Victoria, Eddie, Rafael, and Alberto gathered in the parlor.

"Jamey and Jake already know this," Mike said, "but before I say more, remember — you don't go duck-hunting with a brass band, so nothing we discuss leaves this house."

We nodded in solemn agreement.

"All righty," he said. "Working to win back your horse, here's the long and short of it. Thanks to well-placed hearsay, the bookmakers are getting mighty heated about what they think are Jockey Club threats to raise the bookie fees. Other side of the coin, the Jockey Club thinks the bookies are threatening to strike. I expect these embers will get fanned into full blaze tomorrow."

Eddie's eyes widened. "You started all that?"

"Never underestimate the power of a blue-ribbon rumor."

We cocked our heads like perplexed puppies, trying to fathom what Mike was up to. Though I was still uncertain as to exact direction, I began to sniff out the general trail — and knew these were only the first steps of a longer dance.

Vic spoke up. "How does any of that help us get Lucifer into Saturday's match race?"

"It doesn't," Mike said.

"Then what good does it do us?" Vic asked in frustration. "Our whole plan was entering Lucifer and hoping we'd get Van Brunt to agree that if his horse won, he'd win Lucifer, too. But if Lucifer won, he'd give Phoenix back."

"And that was a good Plan A," Mike said.

"But now it's a dead Plan A," Vic said, "and there *is* no Plan B."

"Oh, there's always a Plan B, even if it don't jump up and shake your hand. Jamey — do you see it yet?"

That sure put *me* on the spot. With a deep breath, I tried to remember everything I'd learned from Mike about constructing a justifiable swindle. First, size up your opponent (the mark), figure out what he wants, and calculate what he'll risk to get it. Second, keep your eye on your own goal. Third, take advantage of the mark's greed, ambition, vanity, and anger. Fourth, with some skill and a little luck, you can transform what the mark believes to be his strengths into weaknesses, like alchemy.

We'd originally set out on our journey intending to offer Van Brunt a shot at capturing a one-of-a-kind irresistible trophy — Lucifer. But our failure to enter the Great Sweepstakes race looked like an insurmountable wall. What Plan B did Mike have in mind? And how was his ginned-up squabble between the bookies and Jockey Club supposed to help?

Then, like a magical bolt from the blue cutting through the fog, I started to see the shape of the puzzle. "Hnnh. Okay, so . . . first, Van Brunt doesn't care about bragging rights. And a winner's purse is peanuts to him. He needs a bigger payoff — a bigger thrill."

Vic caught on. "Ahhh! Like cheating to steal Phoenix — or winning a huge betting windfall on a long shot!"

Which Phoenix was, and the famous

Grand Larceny would never be here on his home turf. The fortune Van Brunt stood to reap if Phoenix won the Great Sweepstakes would never materialize if there wasn't any betting. Which, thanks to Mike, looked more likely by the hour — and which would surely make Van Brunt furious. The greater his outrage, the higher the probability he'd bite on our bait and enter a *second* match race, his horse against Lucifer.

Vic's eyes lit up. "We know how much he wants Lucifer."

I nodded. "So we offer him what *he* thinks is a surefire way to win something he values way more than money."

"Because," Vic said, "he thinks there's no way an Arabian could ever beat his Thoroughbreds."

Mike saluted us. "That, my friends, is our Plan B. First, make sure Van Brunt loses something he thought he had in the palm of his hand — that betting windfall. Then we capitalize on his vexation by dangling an even more tempting prize, with only one way to win it."

"That second match race," I said.

Vic wrinkled her brow. "Can this really work?"

"Won't know 'til we try," Mike said.

Now Jake looked dubious. "What if Van

Brunt doesn't agree to another match race?"

"Then we're no worse off than we are now," I said. "But it's our only chance to get Phoenix back."

"Now, don't chop my head off," Jake said, "but even if Van Brunt *does* take the bait, he probably runs Grand Larceny. Are we sure Lucifer can beat him?"

"Nothing's a sure thing," Eddie said, "even in an honest race."

Jake turned to Victoria. "Are you *absolutely* sure you're willing to take this big of a risk?"

She answered with quiet certainty. "If it's over two miles, Lucifer can beat a Thoroughbred — even Grand Larceny. Mike, what happens next?"

"I'll make sure Van Brunt's apple cart stays upset. Stir the pot, keep it boiling, see what cooks up. Horatio provides good cover — I tag along, he asks questions, I hear who's sayin' what. Meanwhile, you need to make sure Lucifer's as ready as he can be."

"That means he's gotta let me ride him," Raf said with a nervous swallow.

"He will," Vic said. "I promise."

Unless Lucifer had other ideas.

31

"You do not want to count me as an enemy, and you can look it up."
～ Cortland Van Brunt III

By Thursday morning, the looming war between the bookmakers and the Jockey Club was the talk of the track — and the town. Oden Bowie and Emmett Pitt sat outside on the Pimlico clubhouse veranda, attempting to enjoy cups of coffee and muffins on a platter.

Mississippi Mike and Horatio Deale walked toward the clubhouse to take the temperature of the situation, but Van Brunt got there first, charging up the steps in a rage. Horatio and Mike stopped far enough away to avoid inclusion, but close enough to hear the commotion.

"What is this poppycock I'm hearing about a bookmakers' strike for Saturday's races?" Van Brunt fumed.

Bowie waved a dismissive hand. "We have things under control. It's not your concern, Van Brunt."

"The hell it isn't! I demand a guarantee that there's betting on Saturday."

"And if there ain't?" Pitt said.

"I will boycott this track for God's own eternity. I will convince others to do the same. I will do everything in my considerable power to ruin Pimlico. You do not want to count me as an enemy, and you can look it up."

Watching Van Brunt storm off toward the barns, Mike suppressed a smile — his seeds just might bear the fruit he'd hoped for.

"Good morning, gentlemen," Horatio said as they approached Bowie and Pitt. "Mr. Van Brunt did not seem happy. May I ask what the Jockey Club is doing about this bookmakers' foofaraw?"

Unruffled, Oden Bowie sidestepped the actual question. "Betting will be available as usual for today's races. I expect the bookmakers will come to their senses."

"Does that mean you will not be raising their fees for Saturday's races?"

"That issue remains pending."

"Then the fee hike *is* still on the table?"

Bowie stood up. "Good day, gentlemen." And he and Pitt retreated inside to partake of their muffins and coffee in peace.

Horatio and Mike walked over to check on the other side of the dispute at Pimlico's betting ring, a sprawling shed shaped like a horseshoe, covered by a roof and open on the sides. At their booths around the perimeter, a score of bookies busied themselves setting up operations for that afternoon's slate of races. A few early birds had already gathered, as interested in the latest news as in placing their bets.

Horatio and Mike found D. H. Galantier trading tall tales with his colleagues, while using his pocketknife to nip bite-size chunks off a wedge of Monterey Jack cheese wrapped in a cloth. He spotted Horatio and called out, "Hey, Mr. Deale! Did you hear? The Jockey Club wants to stick it to us."

"How do you feel about that, Mr. Galantier?"

"We dare 'em. People come to the track to bet. They're expecting great multitudes on Saturday — and then we'll see how they like it when they find out my betting pools and ring are shut tighter than Governor Bowie's lily-white arse."

"May I quote you on that?"

"I'd be insulted if you didn't. Without betting, the Jockey Club will look like fools. Bowie would *never* cut off his nose to spite his face."

"Are you quite certain of that?"

"We'll know soon enough."

Horatio and Mike turned around and went back to the clubhouse for the official Jockey Club response. Governor Bowie laughed when told of Galantier's commentary. "We dare them to go on strike for the biggest race of the season, instead of growing fat and sassy on all the betting. Galantier would *never* cut off his nose merely to spite his face."

Of course, Mike was counting on the dependably vainglorious and boundless human aptitude for folly to lead *both* sides into doing just that.

Despite simmering tensions, betting went on as usual for opening day on Thursday. But the bookies took every opportunity to warn their customers that unless the Jockey Club backed down, there would be no betting on Saturday, the day everyone most cared about.

The two sides continued firing potshots back and forth in the form of public statements and private backbiting. Neither the Jockey Club nor the bookmakers seemed inclined toward conciliation, and every volley only escalated their animosity. Each side had lit its fuse, and the only real question was, who would toss their bomb first?

The answer came just before the start of racing on Friday afternoon, when Chief Steward Pitt delivered Governor Bowie's ultimatum to Galantier and his bookie brethren: They had thirty minutes to agree they would not go on strike under *any* circumstances, or the Jockey Club would most certainly raise the bookmaking fees for Saturday. They didn't really want to, but what choice did they have?

Galantier's reply? He and the bookmakers did not cotton to being ordered around. Therefore, the Jockey Club had the *same* thirty minutes to renounce their impending threat to hike fees. If they refused, the bookmakers would most certainly declare a strike and ensure there'd be no betting for Saturday's races. They didn't really want to, but what choice did they have?

Thirty minutes came and went. Neither side blinked. The Jockey Club jacked up the bookie fees from thirty to one hundred dollars for Saturday and Monday, payable before Friday's final race. And Galantier and his bookies declared their strike — there'd be no betting pools auctioned for the Saturday or Monday races, and the betting ring would be closed.

And that's how Mississippi Mike Morgan

cobbled together the standoff we needed to derail Van Brunt's best-laid plans for the Great Sweepstakes match race. Word spread quickly among the Maryland racing establishment, through the Baltimore and Washington newspapers, and in Horatio Deale's news-flash telegraphed to editors far and wide.

Van Brunt's demand for a resolution failed to persuade either Bowie or Galantier to surrender. Nor were fellow horse owners John Harper, August Belmont, and Julius Caesar Pryce overly bothered by the betting uproar, since they knew wagering on their own horses would not deliver any bonanza. They found Van Brunt's umbrage entertaining, and they were content to compete for glory and a middling purse.

Throughout Friday, Horatio Deale and Mississippi Mike kept watch on the warring parties, though for different reasons. To the sportswriter, these *dramatis personae* were sources for colorful quotes. To Mississippi Mike, they were chess pieces in our game who could be influenced, but still retained the capacity for independent moves. And he knew from long experience with confidence schemes that you never wanted to be caught by surprise. People had a bothersome knack for unpredictability, and total control of any cast of characters was pert near impossible. So you had to be alert for unforeseen twists and turns.

With the bookies sidelined and betting off for Saturday's Great Sweepstakes, our next task was angling Van Brunt toward a second match race — with him none the wiser, of course. To accomplish that, Mike enlisted Horatio's unwitting assistance. "Looks like Van Brunt is your story now, eh?" Mike said as they watched Friday's races from the grandstand.

"He's about as angry as any man I've ever seen."

"He does seem to fancy himself a victim of some terrible injustice, the poor soul."

"Should Phoenix win tomorrow," Horatio said, "most people would embrace the glory of beating three great horses. It's not as if Van Brunt needs such money as he might've recouped betting on his own long shot."

"For rich folks, though, is it ever enough?"

"Ahh, the curse of Midas. While I'd never cause intentional misery, when it happens on its own, it does make for better stories."

Far from the spotlight, Eddie and Victoria tackled their most critical problem, which so far had defied solution — if we managed to lure Van Brunt into a second match race, would Lucifer let Rafael ride him? Despite his bruised self-esteem, Raf mumbled his prayer, crossed himself, and spent all day working with *El Blanco Loco.*

Under Vic's watchful eye, the jockey engaged in some of Lucifer's favorite self-centered pampering — mainly, feeding and grooming, accompanied by a bottomless supply of peppermint candy rewards for good behavior. Jake, Alberto, and me watched — and applauded when Lucifer allowed Raf to saddle him.

There they were, ready to ride.

We held our breath as Raf attempted to climb aboard — and gasped when Lucifer let him. *El milagro!* Nobody seemed more shocked than Raf himself. But when he prodded Lucifer to circle the paddock, the horse wouldn't move. Vic tried to pull him by his halter, proving only that when a half-ton animal refuses to budge, you can't lead him to water or anywhere else.

An instant after Rafael dismounted, Lucifer trotted around in a mischievous circle. Vic clung to her dogged optimism, but hope dimmed with each failure to make progress. And Raf didn't have enough confidence left to fill a thimble.

32

"There's many a slip 'twixt cup and lip."
~ Olde English Proverb

American Sport & Spirit,
October 25, 1873
★ DEALE'S DEAL
by HORATIO DEALE ★

Despite the betting ban, Dear Readers, today is the Great Sweepstakes/Great Baltimore Brawl match race at Pimlico! This epic duel pits Maryland native son Cortland Van Brunt III's newest treasure, the great & mysterious palomino Phoenix (lately imported from California) against three proven champions.

Defending Southern honor are the elegant chestnut Aries, pride and joy of Julius Caesar Pryce, the Virginian Pirate himself (complete with eye patch); and Southern Cross, the stunning bay gelding owned by

Kentucky's equestrian pasha John Harper. The North is represented by New Yorker August Belmont's Black Swan, the ebony filly with her penchant for defeating the boys at such Empire State racing meccas as Saratoga and Jerome Park.

Adding spice is the longstanding animosity between Van Brunt and arch-rival Pryce, who first owned stupendous jockey Champagne Charley Fly, born enslaved on the antebellum Pryce plantation. Nowadays, there is no doubt that Charley Fly, a wily artist of consummate skill, is the brightest star in any saddle.

Starting early Saturday, a stream of horse-drawn conveyances clogged the roads leading to Pimlico. Baltimore's hotels and boardinghouses overflowed with racing pilgrims from near and far. And when the great multitudes showed up at the race course twenty thousand strong — including most of Congress and President Grant himself — they found the betting operations as deserted as an abandoned fort.

While some who came to the races that day had already heard of the spat between the bookmakers and the Jockey Club, and weren't deterred by the betting embargo, many others were unhappily surprised, as

D. H. Galantier had predicted. The ban spawned a frenzy of unauthorized wagers, accompanied by sporadic fights due to the helter-skelter nature of such transactions.

Despite smug assurances by Galantier and Bowie to the contrary, both sides proved willing — even eager — to cut off their own noses to spite their faces, as Mississippi Mike had expected. Neither stubborn faction had anything to gain from a quarrel that hadn't existed until Mike's sorcery conjured it, but that didn't stop them from staying the course.

Throughout Saturday's earlier races, skies grew ever more threatening. At precisely 3:30, under somber clouds pierced by a few heavenly golden rays, the four horses of this particular apocalypse walked onto the track. Emmaline arrived in the nick of time to join us in the grandstand. Obviously, we'd be rooting for Phoenix, even though a defeat might've made Van Brunt more likely to accept our challenge to a second match race.

The race would be two and half laps around the one-mile oval, so the horses assembled at a starting line midway down the backstretch. The riders in their white britches, knee-high black boots, colorful silk jackets and caps tried to calm their horses as they lined up. Champagne Charley Fly was the man to beat, and of the four jockeys only Englishman Richard Sharp riding Aries was white. John Sample on Southern Cross and Jimmy Hawkins on Black Swan were Negroes and both well-known.

In fact, the ratio of black riders to white wasn't unusual in those days. Because American racing had its deepest roots in the agrarian South, Negro jockeys and trainers would dominate the sport for most of the 19th century, first as slaves and then as free men after Emancipation and the war. Of fifteen horses to be entered in the first Kentucky Derby in 1875, *thirteen* would be ridden by blacks — and black riders would win fifteen of the first twenty-eight Kentucky Derbies. Thanks to the telegraph sending horse racing news almost instantly all over the country, many black jockeys would become national celebrities.

The other riders kept glancing at Charley — while he gazed straight ahead, as if envisioning the entire race unfolding in his mind's eye. Tension spiraled through three false starts, none caused by the easygoing Phoenix, until his twitchy competition held still long enough for the starter to wave his flag, shout "Go!" — and they were off and running.

Though track conditions were good, they

lollygagged through a pokey first lap as if no one wanted the early lead. Such experienced jockeys knew races were rarely decided in the early going. Around the clubhouse turn — into the backstretch — entering lap two — and the beautiful filly Black Swan moved to the rail and took a two-length lead over Kentucky bay Southern Cross, just ahead of the Virginian chestnut Aries. Phoenix lagged behind, with Charley Fly crouched above his saddle.

Eddie and Vic looked worried. Was something wrong with their beloved palomino? Did his long railroad journey drain him? Had Van Brunt's trainers already ruined their magnificent horse?

The field passed the grandstand for the second time. A mile to go. Crowd noise swelled. Black Swan faltered and her lead disappeared. But it wasn't Southern Cross passing her — it was Aries, with Phoenix in hot pursuit.

They pulled away, with Phoenix close enough to put the bite on Aries' tail.

Black Swan and Southern Cross faded.

It came down to a two-horse race, around the far turn for the final time.

Charley Fly on Phoenix slapped two urgent snaps of the whip against his horse's rump. Phoenix edged to the outside and moved up on Aries — past his tail, to his flank.

A few more lightning strides, and Phoenix trailed by only a neck.

Into the homestretch! Phoenix bounded into the lead — by a nose — a head — a length. The crowd roared as he crossed the finish line three lengths ahead of Aries. Our little group exploded in such cheers and hugs, you'd have thought he was still Eddie's horse, and we'd struck it rich betting on him.

Of course, there'd been no (official) betting. Down at the front of the grandstand, Van Brunt accepted congratulations from surrounding friends. Judging by the grim set of his jaw, the $2,500 check he'd get from the Jockey Club would not mitigate his fury over the betting fiasco. He was a man known to risk ten times that on a single wager, so his snit was understandable, even if nobody would ever feel sorry for him.

But his bad temper gave us hope. We'd have an opportunity to advance Mike's plan that evening at the gala shindig Van Brunt would be hosting at his Elysian Fields Farm in the hunt-country hills of Greenspring Valley, north of Baltimore. Despite gossip predicting he'd cancel the party after the betting blow-up, he couldn't resist showing off his estate.

Rafael insisted on staying at Pimlico to continue his efforts at making friends with Lucifer. Alberto volunteered to keep him company, and magician and jockey headed for the backside barns.

The rest of our traveling troupe — me, Jake, Eddie, and Victoria — went back to Mike's house and dressed to suit the occasion. Horatio Deale met us there to drive up with us, and the six of us set out in a big covered carriage for Elysian Fields.

On the way, Horatio filled us in on the life and times of Cortland Van Brunt III. His ancestral family presence in the New World went way back to 1647, when three Van Brunt brothers sailed from the Netherlands with other Dutch settlers bound for the New Amsterdam colony. Though the trio became prosperous merchants, ugly jealousies led youngest brother Hendrik to sell his shares and take his new wife south to Maryland.

He bought land, raised tobacco and horses, and eventually achieved greater wealth than his embittered brothers, whose enterprise faltered after the 1664 British takeover of New Amsterdam, soon to be renamed New York. Generations of lineage led from Hendrik Van Brunt to Cortland, born in 1818, a true "Knickerbocker" descended from the intrepid forefather who had established a new family empire in colonial Maryland.

"Wait 'til you see his mansion," said Horatio, who'd been there on several occasions.

He wasn't kidding. We'd seen some fine and fancy homes in San Francisco, but nothing compared to Van Brunt's baronial manor. It wasn't any mere mansion — it was a castle, rising up against the dusky sky as if Camelot had somehow been transported through time to America.

As Horatio related, when Van Brunt was a boy, he'd traveled with his parents to Europe and Merrie Olde England, where he became entranced by the history and romance of castles and cathedrals. Decades later, he used his inherited wealth and investment fortune to build his own personal Gothic chateau. Constructed of granite, marble, and titanic timbers, the fifty-foot-tall main house was framed in front by a pair of round keep towers, complete with slotted openings through which archers could've shot their arrows in times of siege.

The castle's architecture incorporated a bell tower, arches, fearsome gargoyles, and a shallow moat with a working drawbridge that led to fifteen-foot-tall entry doors salvaged from a decaying medieval French church. After we parked among dozens of carriages on a vast lawn, we followed Horatio inside for a tour of Van Brunt's remarkable citadel.

From the vaulted entry hall, he guided us through two round rooms occupying the ground floor of the towers, one a library, the other a gallery displaying armor and weapons of the Middle Ages. Among his prized antiquities was a human skull said to have belonged to a mariner who'd sailed to the New World with Columbus!

Horatio showed us a map room, a huge Renaissance dining room with a thirty-foot-long table and twenty extravagantly carved chairs, secret passageways, and stained-glass windows everywhere. We threaded our way through a hidden portal and stone corridor behind a bookcase, and emerged into a salon with a domed ceiling trimmed in gold leaf. Furnishings included leather and velvet-upholstered seating, and an oblong dining table with eight chairs for more intimate gatherings.

"This," Horatio said, "is where Van Brunt hosts monthly meetings of the Spiritualist Society, with readings and séances conducted by none other than his personal guide to the spirit world, Madame Killegrew."

Mike's eyebrows rose. "*Aurora* Killegrew?"

"The one and only. In fact, she shall conduct a session right here, at nine this evening."

"You know her?" I asked Mike.

"Years ago, in another lifetime."

"We saw her do her medicine show at Van Brunt's party in San Francisco."

Mike's eyes crinkled with amusement. "Not a believer, eh, Jamey?"

"Van Brunt is," Horatio said. "Madame Killegrew reputedly wields considerable influence."

At the heart of the castle, we came to an atrium with a glass-paned roof, filled with the warm, musky smells of a greenhouse. Using real 15th century European building façades of stone and wood, dismantled and shipped at great expense, Van Brunt had recreated an Old World courtyard around a rectangular pool and fountain, complete with Roman mosaics.

Throughout the castle, wherever we turned, there were authentic medieval statues, paintings, books, and tapestries. And we'd only seen the main floor — there were two private floors above, rumored to contain fifteen bedrooms and stored treasures too numerous to be displayed.

Last stop on our tour — the Great Hall, a cathedral-like sanctuary a hundred feet long, with a three-story vaulted ceiling and a stone fireplace big enough to hold an entire bull, on the hoof or on a spit. The crowning touches were stained-glass windows and a massive pipe organ that must've shaken the walls when played.

The party was well underway, and Horatio scanned the crowd. "Ahh — I see some racing eminences with whom I need to hobnob." He drifted off to mingle and fish for news and gossip.

If we hadn't been intimidated by Van Brunt's wealth before, we were now. No wonder he could afford to transport horses in a custom rail car. Or offer twenty-five thousand to buy Phoenix and another ten grand for Lucifer, like those amounts were pocket change. Van Brunt wasn't just any old bastard — he was a colossally *rich* old bastard, as rich as the Rockies were high.

Waiters in white tunics circulated about, serving drinks and various hot *hors d'oeuvres*. Catering cooks tended enormous food platters and chafing dishes set out on long buffet tables. But before we could help ourselves and find seats at one of the many small tables around the hall, Mike pulled Eddie, Vic, Jake, and me into a huddle.

"Time to set things in motion," he said. "We got a solid plan, but there's many a slip 'twixt cup and lip. If things jump the track, follow Jamey and Jake's lead. All righty, then — ready to play your parts?"

We nodded.

"Good. This mark is ours for the taking."

If only I'd shared Mike's certitude. Instead, I expected the evening ahead to be like a twisting kaleidoscope, with pieces tumbling every which way, and no assurance how they'd fall into place. Still, we knew what we had to do. So Eddie, Vic, Jake and me we went one way — to find Van Brunt. Mike went another — to find Governor Bowie and his Jockey Club cronies.

But first, he took a detour.

33

"Seeing is believing — and believing is seeing."
~ Madame Aurora Killegrew

Dressed in a gossamer red and black gown, alone in the salon, Madame Killegrew precisely arranged the mystical props that were the tools of her trade on the dining table. When she reached for them later, even the slightest distraction could derail the illusion of a séance, what with all the voices and cues to keep straight.

She heard a gentle knock at the door. Hinges creaked as someone entered. "Sorry, you're a tad early," she said without looking up. "Please come back no sooner than eight-forty-five."

"Why, if it ain't Frenchy Muldoon," Mississippi Mike Morgan said.

Aurora froze for a heartbeat, then turned to see Mike with a little smile on his face. "I don't go by that these days," she said carefully.

"I'd heard that, and that you were in this new line of work. By God, it's been a dog's age."

She couldn't help smiling back at him. "A month of Sundays, Mickey my dear."

"Quite a few blue moons."

She pursed her lips in coy amusement. "What are the odds —"

"— we'd both end up here tonight?"

"Incalculable," Frenchy said.

"Last time we laid eyes on each other, it were . . . '58 in St. Louis."

"*Au contraire.* It was '59, in New Orleans."

"Well, I'm positive it were a Saturday around midnight."

"Sunday, at eight."

"I *know* we were on a riverboat. I remember it well."

"St. Charles Hotel — *near* the river, I'll grant you."

Mike's brow wrinkled in mock frustration. "Then I must've walked you home."

"You called me a carriage."

"I said goodbye."

"You never did," she said with a touch of sadness.

"That's not how I recollect it."

She arched one eyebrow. "Your recollections are a wee bit fuzzy."

Mike chuckled. "Well, we had us some high times. *That* I do remember."

She brushed his cheek. "As do I."

"Ain't it strange to be closer to the end than the beginning?"

"I find it's not so much the time passed, as the distance traveled. Any regrets?"

"Any man claiming no regrets is either a liar or a fool — or both."

"Ever the philosopher, Mickey my dear."

"Biggest regret, other than losin' track of you? Not graspin' sooner how the older we get, the faster time flies."

"It's a sure sign you're getting on when you know more dead people than live," Frenchy said wistfully. "But if someone had told us that when we were young —"

"— we'd never have believed 'em. Ahhh, to be young and foolish again. But I always knew you and your nine lives would land on your feet."

She fingered the satin-trimmed lapel of his bespoke frock coat. "And you as well, it seems."

"Not without some rough times cuttin' me down to size. I reckon I ain't as handsome as I were way back when. Nor as tall."

"You weren't all that handsome then," she teased, "and you were never tall."

He laughed. "And you are still both — not to mention sassy."

"Flattery will get you . . . somewhere. Are you still working with that blackguard Gideon Duvall?"

"We had an amicable parting of the ways."

"Good. You were better than that, Mickey. I hated when you went off with him."

"If I hadn't, I expect I'd've been dead long ago."

"What brought you to Baltimore?"

"Born and schooled here. So I come back to where I begun. But lookit you — some cushy life you've made for yourself."

"I found a good role, so why not keep playing it?"

"The Frenchy Muldoon I knew thrived on variety."

"After a certain age," she said, "I found variety to be overrated."

"Do you ever get 'em right? The prophesies, I mean?"

"Close enough, often enough, to keep my patrons happy. At risk of being immodest, I give them better advice than their spouses, preachers, barristers, and bankers."

"You always did have a level head. I imagine a lot of it comes down to presentation?"

Frenchy nodded. "Giving the appearance

of being precise, while leaving enough latitude for them read into it what they will. I think of it as a kind of dancing."

"Speaking of which, I will never forget the first night I saw you dancin' up a storm at the Parisienne Club in New Orleans."

She laughed. "Trying in vain to introduce the can-can to you colonists."

"The curse of bein' ahead o' your time, Frenchy."

"It's Madame Killegrew now," she said with mock snootiness. "Aurora, for an old friend."

"To me, you'll always be the gal who made her way from Dublin to Gay Pa-ree by her wits. Never met a better singer, dancer, dealer, or master of disguise and dialect. You had talent comin' and goin'. So, where did this spiritualism bunko come from?"

"Oh, ye of little faith!" she quipped. "I come by it honestly. Ever since I was ten, I've communed with my late Granny Muldoon. She's delivered unto me signs and portents that got me out of numerous scrapes. It was she who told me to move to France, and then America."

"She told you, flat out?"

"She speaks to me in dreams. It's up to me to interpret their meaning."

"So you believe this hoodoo's real?"

"Seeing is believing — and believing is seeing," she said with a beguiling aura of mystery. "There's much we don't understand about transcendental planes of existence. What do you think happens to us when we die? To our bodies — to our souls?"

"I don't rightly know."

"No one does. Yet, the ancients would entomb their dearly departed with possessions they'd need beyond this mortal veil."

"Well," Mike said with a wry smile, "I'm convinced that *you're* convinced."

Frenchy laughed again. "That's half my craft, Mickey. Not unlike the challenge of running a confidence game. Read people quickly, glean their hopes and fears, find captivating means to tell them what they want to hear."

"Or what they already know, but can't face," said Mike.

"I provide comfort in a wild, wicked world that offers all too little of that." Frenchy closed her eyes and tipped her chin high, as if receiving enlightenment from the Great Beyond.

Mike played along. "Are them spirits telling you something now?"

"Indeed," she purred. "They are suggesting . . . that you've come to ask a favor . . . for old time's sake."

"Well, I'll be buggered, Madame Killegrew," he said with a wink.

He related our tale, how Van Brunt likely cheated Eddie out of his racehorse, and why we'd come all this way. "So my young friends are not out to swindle Van Brunt. They just want a fair shake to try and win back their horse."

"If they're planning to gull him —"

"Just an honest race between two horses."

"And you're certain Mr. Van Brunt bamboozled them in San Francisco?"

"I weren't there. But I taught Jamey how to spot a shifty scheme, and he's as perceptive and honest a lad as I ever knew. If he says it happened, I'll bank on it."

"So they're going to propose this second match race to Mr. Van Brunt . . . and you want me to nudge him toward accepting the challenge?"

"In a nutshell."

"And all he stands to lose is this horse of contention, this Phoenix?"

"That's all they want. And if Van Brunt's horse wins, he not only keeps Phoenix, he gets Lucifer, too — a horse he's begged to buy."

"Mr. Van Brunt can be . . . mercurial. If he blames me for giving him ill-fated counsel, I could lose a generous patron."

"Oh, I have faith the spirits'll show you a way around that."

"Over the years, I've developed a strong instinct for self-preservation. You're asking me to risk my reputation, which keeps me well able to afford the finer things . . . and for whom?"

"My friends."

"But not *my* friends. Of course, should I not go along, you know my past, and if you shared that knowledge with Mr. Van Brunt . . ."

Mike looked hurt. "Do you really think I'd try to blackmail you?"

Frenchy shrugged. "Why not?"

"Because of all them years we go back," Mike scolded. "You said yourself your foretellings don't always pan out — but here you are, still smellin' like a rose."

"That's because I keep failures to a minimum."

"Don't you just blame your spirit guides?"

"How gullible do you think Mr. Van Brunt is?"

"Enough to believe in talkin' to spirits beyond the veil." Mike frowned. "You thought there were more to me than teaming up with Gideon Duvall."

"And you think there's more to Frenchy than Aurora Killegrew's reputation . . ."

"I do. Or I wouldn't be asking you to do a right thing."

"Ahhh. Now, there's the rub," she said. "Doing right isn't always as easy as it sounds, is it?"

"If it were, more folks might give it a whirl," Mike joked. "It's up to you . . . Aurora."

"I suppose it is."

"I'm lookin' forward to seeing your work later." Mike bussed her on the cheek, and left Frenchy Muldoon alone with her moral dilemma.

Van Brunt's mood that evening careened between residual wrath over the Pimlico betting mess, and button-busting pride over showing off his castle. We had no way of knowing which frame of mind we'd encounter with our proposal.

Before we could find out, Julius Caesar Pryce and his eye patch intercepted our host and steered him into the library. We followed at a discreet distance, and got a lucky break when they didn't shut the door all the way, enabling us to eavesdrop.

Pryce didn't mince words, immediately revealing his "dire financial excruciation." To hear most rich men tell it, fortunes *gained* were due entirely to their personal genius, while fortunes *lost* were always somebody else's fault. Pryce blamed his troubles on the autumn stock market swoon (to go down in history as the Panic of '73), rather than his own dereliction coming home to roost.

Van Brunt struck a match to fire up his ever-present clay pipe. "Are you as bad off as Jay Cooke and Company?"

"Sweet Jesus, no!"

"Yet you fell into the common trap."

"Pray, enlighten me," Pryce said in his baritone drawl.

"While markets soar, even the world's worst investor deludes himself into believing he's brilliant, and forgets that what goes up must come down."

"Gloat all you like. You know what your enemies say about you, Van Brunt?"

"Hah! I have no enemies."

"Ahh, but you are intensely disliked by your *friend*s. As God is my witness, one of these days the bell will toll for thee."

"Supplication does not become you. What do you want, Pryce?"

"I need cash — fast."

"Why would I help you?"

"To have the better of me, sir."

Van Brunt puffed a cloud of smoke into Pryce's good eye. "Not out of the goodness of my heart?"

"An organ we both know you lack, you pirate."

"Says the man with the eye patch."

"We are men of the world. We seek gain. There are always things we must have, by hook or by crook, as you like to say. I have things you want."

"If the times are laying you this low," Van Brunt said, "I expect to have my pick at the crack of an auctioneer's gavel soon enough."

"By then, there may not be much left worth the takin' — whereas now you might gain your heart's desire. Is it not sufficient sport that I am at your mercy?"

"It is entertaining, I'll grant you that. And as long as we're confessing, you do have something I want, at the present time. Would five thousand dollars help you?"

Pryce's voice dripped suspicion. "In exchange for which precious bauble?"

"Merely a horse."

Pryce winced, fearing the answer. "*Which* horse?"

"The one I just beat."

"Aries?! Dear God — he's worth ten times that! He's my top stallion!"

"Why else would I want him? Of course, if you don't need the five grand . . ."

"Burn in hell, you buggerin' bastard."

"A fate we're both tempting. But if you're not interested. . ." Van Brunt turned to leave, but Pryce grabbed his arm.

"I'll take it," Pryce said. "In *cash*, you brigand."

"Cash it shall be, you beggar. We'll complete our transaction tomorrow at the track. Done?"

"Done," Pryce said, his voice a dismal croak.

To avoid being caught spying, we scurried down the hallway and stared at a ten-foot-square tapestry hanging on the stone wall, illustrating some valiant crusade. Pryce brushed past us.

Van Brunt came out of the library looking like the cat who'd just reduced the canary population by a dozen. He noticed us admiring his artwork. "Sixteenth century, found it in Edinburgh. Every journey's a treasure hunt."

We might never get a better moment to make our pitch, so I started with flattery. "Quite a stronghold you have here, Mr. Van Brunt."

"I'm sure you young folks have never seen any place like it. That's because there *isn't* any place like it."

"Gosh, it's got just about everything a man could dream of," I said.

His eyes narrowed. "Just about everything?"

"It's missing . . . something."

"I'm here to say, I think not — unless it hasn't been invented yet."

"A horse, sir," I said. "One particular horse."

"My Arabian," Victoria said.

"Ahh — the grandiferous Lucifer," Van Brunt said. "As I recall, I offered you ten grand for him, which you turned down, bottom fact of the matter. Is he suddenly for sale?"

Vic shook her head. "No. But he could still be yours."

Van Brunt was both intrigued and bewildered. "How?"

"We propose another match race," I said. "Grand Larceny, or any of your racehorses, against Lucifer. Three miles, on the last day of the Pimlico meeting."

"Betting might be back on by then," Jake added.

"Betting?" Van Brunt scoffed, grinding his molars on his pipe-stem. "If this proposed race happened, I'd be running a famed Thoroughbred against an unknown long shot, and not even a racehorse at that. So there'd be no betting motherlode for me to claim."

"Well, what about side bets?" Jake said.

"Who would bet on Lucifer, son? Nobody, and that's a straight-up fact."

We'd dangled a singular prize we knew Van Brunt coveted, then presented the one and only path for him to claim it. Without the promise of an actual pot of gold to distract him, we had him right where we wanted him. Or did we?

"Then let's make it more interesting," Vic said. "You don't really care about the money anyway — do you, Mr. Van Brunt?"

He laughed. "My dear, everyone cares about money. Especially those who claim they don't. The gentler sex, of course, may not be aware of that."

Victoria's voice lowered to a bewitching purr. "Isn't it *really* all about the horses?"

"It's true the purse is a drop in my very deep bucket. So, li'l lady, what can you offer me that means more than money?"

"You win the race? You win Lucifer." Vic spotted an avaricious sparkle in Van Brunt's eyes. We had our mark roped. "You've begged to buy him for outrageous sums."

"Which you have refused."

"We know you have Arabians in your stable," I said.

"Three mares, as fine as any."

Vic batted her eyelashes. "Then imagine

what kind of foals Lucifer would sire with your mares."

"I could reinvent the breed."

"He's yours for the taking," said Vic, "*if* your horse wins."

Van Brunt puffed on his pipe. "And if you win?"

"If we win?" Vic let the question hang in the air for a moment. "We get Phoenix back."

The greedy gleam in Van Brunt's eyes dimmed. Had we broken the magic spell? "Three miles? Too long. No more than two."

Whew. If he was negotiating race terms, we still had him hooked.

"Compromise at two and half," Vic said, "same as today's race. Unless your horses are too fragile . . ."

Van Brunt mulled the particulars. "Two and a half miles . . . I win Lucifer and keep Phoenix. An intriguing proposition — *if* I was interested, which I am not at the present time."

He turned and walked away.

"What the hell," Vic said, completely befuddled. "This was supposed to be irresistible. He was supposed to say *yes.*"

Jake looked for the bright side. "Well . . . he didn't *exactly* say no."

"Jake's right," I said, "and how often do I

admit that? Sure, this could've gone better. But the game's not over. Not when pieces are still being put in play."

"What pieces?" Vic fretted.

"Ummm . . . whatever Mike's up to."

"And what *is* he up to?"

"I don't know, exactly."

"Whatever it is," Vic said, "he'd better be more successful than we just were."

34

> " 'Will you walk into my parlour?' said a spider to a fly."
> ~ Poet Mary Howitt,
> *The Spider and the Fly* (1829)

You'd be hard-pressed to find a beaver busier than Mississippi Mike was that night, as he sought to direct the flow of events our way. After leaving Madame Killegrew to decide whether she'd help or not, he rejoined Horatio Deale. The sportswriter knew an intriguing story when he smelled one — though he hadn't sniffed out Mike's covert role in the entire betting hullabaloo.

Together, they entered the Great Hall, where they found Governor Bowie and his Jockey Club pooh-bahs encamped within easy reach of the bar. For his part, Mike suspected that both the Jockey Club and Van Brunt might be more amenable to a second match race if the betting battle could be settled, and all parties had a chance to put any residual bad blood behind them.

So he presented himself as a go-between who *might* be able to arbitrate the dispute. "I heard the bookies are begging for a quick rapprochement, having belatedly determined they've painted themselves into an unproductive corner."

That got Bowie's attention. "Heard from whom?"

"Mum's the promised word on that," Mike said in a confidential hush, "but I can tell you, human pride being what it is, you must not let on that you know your opponent's desperation — or else they will chew off their own foot to escape the trap. Are you interested in having me pursue these delicate matters with Galantier's gang?"

Bowie and the others conferred, nattered, and buzzed for a few minutes. Then they gave Mike their nothing-to-lose blessing.

"I will keep you apprised," Mike said, and he and Horatio left.

"How are you going to maneuver implacable foes into an accord?" Horatio asked.

"By making each side think all the good ideas were theirs."

Horatio chuckled. "Ahh, the delicate art of utilizing human vanity in the service of good. I like it."

Jake, Vic, Eddie, and me met up with Mike and Horatio in the salon where Madame Killegrew was ready to enact her séance for forty or fifty party guests. With all the chairs and couches in the room filled, quite a few of us had to stand.

Madame K was already seated at the table, and the tall candelabras on either side of her had been lit. "I . . . am . . . Aurora Killegrew. If there be non-believers among us this night, ye are still welcome."

Her show went pretty much the way it had in Frisco — the gong, the burning parchment strip, summoning her ancient Greek pardner Kleon, showing off her full repertoire of physical and vocal gymnastics. You have to admire any trouper who can deliver consistently polished performances — and also tailor her spectacle for different audiences.

"Speaking" through Madame Killegrew, Kleon alluded to the Pimlico betting rhubarb, warning the Jockey Club to come to terms with the "moneychangers at the Temple of Mammon" — phrasing which drew laughs from otherwise respectful witnesses. Kleon also singled out Cortland Van Brunt. "Who is the *vasiliás* of this palace?

The king, bestriding his world like Alexander?"

Van Brunt puffed out his chest. "That's me."

"You have lately returned from a distant campaign, and brought back spoils of that war — a great stallion, yes?"

Kleon's knowledge flabbergasted Van Brunt, and I heard gasps of astonishment around me. It's a good thing eye-rolling is silent, so nobody caught me marveling at how easily rich folks could be hoodwinked.

Kleon continued: "You have been offered the opportunity to win yet another great treasure, yes? Is it gold, or jewels?"

"No, no. It's another magnificent horse."

"Then *why*," Kleon thundered, "have you not seized the day?"

Van Brunt pulled out a handkerchief and blotted sweat off his forehead. "B-because I'd have to risk losing the other stallion I just won in California."

"Are you a conqueror, like the great Alexander? Or a mewling infant?" Kleon mocked. "Do you quake at challenge? Or vanquish all foes? *Answer this!*"

Unaccustomed to being called out by anybody anywhere, let alone in his very own castle by a rude Greek ghost, Van Brunt pulled himself together. He pounded his chest: "I conquer, like Alexander! And you can look that up, you dead Greek sonofabitch."

"Good! Good." Kleon's voice turned weary. "I tire of this visit, Aurorrrra. I must return to the realm whence I came. Farewell . . ."

Madame Killegrew closed with her standard routine — the long death rattle, slumping limp in her chair — leading the uninitiated to fear she'd expired. Right on time, twenty seconds later, her eyelids fluttered, and spectators cheered her revival. A knot of admirers surrounded her, gushing with praise.

As we shuffled toward the door, Mike mumbled in my ear, "We got what we needed."

I shouldn't have been amazed, but I was. "Let me guess," I whispered back, "Madame Killegrew's an old friend of yours?"

"By another name. But I asked, she delivered. Now let's see —"

Van Brunt intercepted us and pulled our group aside. "Well, now, in view of recent advice, I've reconsidered. I accept your challenge — if you're still batty enough to stand by it."

"We are," Vic said. "But what about the Jockey Club? Don't they have to —"

"I'll handle them. In fact, let's hash this out right here and now."

How much influence did Van Brunt have, anyway? We were about to find out. Horatio joined the parade to the Great Hall and up to Governor Bowie and his pals, still abiding close to the bar. Several of them had made impressive progress toward getting roostered up on free liquor.

Cortland Van Brunt III didn't make requests. He *told* them to schedule this two-horse match race on Monday afternoon, just before the last race on the final day of Pimlico's fall meeting. "Two and a half miles. Me and Grand Larceny against them and their Arabian. *No* other entrants."

With a gubernatorial harrumph, Bowie informed Van Brunt they'd have to deliberate. He gathered his comrades into a tight scrum (still within reach of the bar). Once again, they conferred, nattered, and buzzed for a short spell — and agreed to allow the race.

Van Brunt looked at us. "Five hundred dollar entry fee for each horse goes into the pot, same as before. Other terms as agreed upon: My horse wins, Lucifer is mine. Your horse wins, I give up Phoenix, even though his brightest future is here with me."

Eddie and Van Brunt shook hands. And

just like that, we'd wangled our way into the grudge match we'd come three thousand miles for — thanks to Mike. The more I watched him work, the more I couldn't help thinking of the old poem about the spider and the fly.

Sunday dawned cloudy and gray. Early drizzle turned into yet another steady rain. Mike put on his Mackintosh, grabbed his umbrella, took out a covered buggy, and began a day of shuttling between the bookmakers' haunt at the Quarter Pole Pub and the Jockey Club's lair at Pimlico's clubhouse.

Even though we'd lined up our race between Lucifer and one of Van Brunt's Thoroughbreds, we still hoped for a resumption of betting, since we thought longshot Lucifer had a good chance of winning. So we had our fingers crossed for Mike's negotiations to succeed.

The tavern was empty except for the sidelined bookies, for whom an appreciative innkeeper stayed open even on God's sanctified day of rest. Mike presented D. H. Galantier and his buddies with a mirror image of the conversation he'd had the evening before with Governor Bowie and his *compadres:* "I heard tell the Jockey Club is eager for a quick settlement, having concluded they have painted themselves into an unproductive corner."

"Heard tell from *who*?" Galantier asked.

"Mum's the word on that," Mike said, "but I caution you: human pride being what it is, you'd best not let on knowing your opponent's desperation, or they will gnaw off their own foot to escape the trap. Are you interested in having me pursue these delicate matters with the Jockey Club?"

Galantier and a half-dozen of his mates took their turn to huddle, natter, and buzz for a bit. Then they gave Mike the nod. They didn't see him smiling ever so slightly as he left the pub.

At noon that rainy Sunday, the Jockey Club and track stewards made the decision to postpone Monday's final day of racing until Tuesday. That gave Vic and Eddie an extra day to coax Lucifer into allowing spooked Rafael to ride him. They weren't ready to give up. They *couldn't* — they needed a jockey, and Raf was it. As much as Vic loved Lucifer, she was running out of patience, and wondered if Alberto had a mood-improvement spell to cast over her surly horse.

By mid-afternoon, Mike had persuaded both the bookies and Jockey Club bigwigs to meet for talks in the clubhouse conference room. Jake, Alberto, and me went along out of curiosity, to see if Mike could whip up a magical miracle out of thin air. And Horatio Deale was there to follow the story.

Galantier and five fellow bookmakers sat on one side of the long table, Bowie and Jockey Club officials on the other, all staring across the gulf with grim faces. Galantier was not his usual jovial self, claiming he'd already made a concession by setting foot in the enemy's house. That both sides came determined to be bullheaded was no shock. And since Mike had warned each that saying the wrong thing might doom any slim hope of breaking the deadlock, they were like two hounds angling to piss on the same tree at the same time, without getting sprayed themselves.

After twenty minutes of back-and-forth, Mike had heard enough posturing. "Since this here dispute is over betting, I propose to settle it with a simple game of chance."

"What," Bowie said, "a coin toss?"

"No, sir. A cut of the cards. I'll shuffle and cut once for each side. If the bookies draw low, they accept the Jockey Club's fee increase. If the Jockey Club draws low, the fee hike is forgotten. Whichever way, betting will be reinstated for the final race day on Tuesday."

Both sides resisted embracing such a one-shot gamble. After letting them gripe for a while, Mike said, "Or, you can both agree to sit down and negotiate like civilized men, and I'll be happy to referee."

Despite more grousing all around, the idea of protracted haggling had little appeal. Whereas, reaching agreement by a cut of the cards possessed the virtue of being short and sweet.

"Best two out of three?" Galantier suggested.

Mike shook his head. "One out of one."

"Well," Galantier said, "what if the cut turns out to be a draw?"

"Yes," Bowie said, "would the stronger suit win the day?"

Mike raised an eyebrow. "Keeping the cut strictly clean and numerical, should there be a tie, we stipulate that both sides take that as a sign from above, and agree on reversion to terms in effect before all this folderol began — no fee increase, no strike."

"We're all gamblers at heart," Galantier said with a sly-fox twinkle, "or we'd not be in the racing game at all. Let us cast our fates to the cards, and end this standoff here and now. Governor?"

"Done."

Mike flipped a coin to decide who went first. The bookies won. Mike shuffled to Galantier's satisfaction, cut the cards — and up came a lowly four of diamonds. The Jockey Club princes looked smug. They liked their odds of beating a four.

Mike shuffled again. At Governor Bowie's nod, he cut the deck. And what card showed?

Four of spades.

Jaws dropped on both sides of the table. You might marvel at such an outcome — unless you knew what me and Jake knew about Mississippi Mike's mastery of a deck of cards, and his ability to turn up any card at will by means we mortals would never understand.

"The cards have spoken," Mike said. "Nobody wins, nobody loses. Now, I am still available for good-faith mediation. But I strongly recommend both sides in this here matter lick their self-inflicted wounds, and bury the hatchet."

Galantier slid his chair back. "Betting resumes for Tuesday?"

Bowie agreed. They sealed the bargain with a handshake.

"A suggestion, gents," Mike said as he pocketed the cards. "Next time, parley first, before hotter heads prevail."

As the meeting broke up, the Jockey Club men retreated to their private sanctuary for drinks. The bookies headed out to their favorite pub for drinks. And Mike, Horatio, Jake, Alberto, and me left the clubhouse without any drinks at all.

Pausing on the veranda, Horatio gave Mike a sly-eyed glance. "I suspect you are as slick as a whistle, Michael, but I cannot prove it." Off he went to write his improbable story and send it out on the wires.

"Mike," I said, "you outdid yourself."

Alberto shook his head in admiration. "Michael, *la prego* — please! I must know how you do such magic!"

"Well, now, if I told you . . . it wouldn't be magic," Mike said with a wink.

35

> "It is difference of opinion that makes horse-races."
> ~ Mark Twain,
> *Pudd'nhead Wilson's Calendar*

As word of the latest rainy-day postponement spread, some horsemen groused about packing up and leaving. After Saturday's historic main event, wouldn't the final day and the inevitable end of racing season feel anticlimactic anyway?

Competitive as they may have been, for horse owners and breeders their sport was an exclusive silk-stocking brotherhood. Cultural camaraderie was as important as actual racing, which in truth only filled a small portion of the time. The rest was devoted to arguing, bragging, drinking, horse trading, bragging, comparing jockeys, making breeding arrangements — and bragging.

In the lulls between races, a careful observer could see how slavery still shadowed the sport. For many unrepentant Southerners, all the pomp and circumstance stirred nostalgia for their halcyon heydays. Listening to their shameless recollections, you might be deluded into believing that the valiant Confederacy had won, or even that the war had never happened at all.

In fact, many Southerners lost their best horses during the war when invading Union troops seized whatever livestock they could find. Fearing the worst, some Dixie aristocrats had the foresight to sell or ship their most treasured equine stock to friendly horsemen in border or Northern states, to keep them out of barbarous enemy hands.

For former slaves now employed as riders, trainers, grooms, and caretakers — often by the same planters who'd once owned them — there was no pining for that cruel past, only a desperate desire to build a better future for themselves and their kin.

All day Sunday, Victoria made no headway in building a partnership between Rafael and Lucifer. By Monday morning, the rain had stopped, the unfamiliar sun came out, and horses were allowed out on the track in the afternoon for practice and exercise.

Eddie and Vic needed to know once and

for all if Lucifer would run for Rafael. The horse stood idle while Eddie got him tacked up. Raf petted him and fed him carrots, and Lucifer didn't fuss a lick when the jockey recited his prayer, crossed himself, mounted up — and tried to get the horse moving.

You could see Lucifer calculating — and after some deliberation, he moseyed toward the track. Raf grinned, and the rest of us cheered and followed, including Horatio scribbling in his notebook. Lucifer nodded as if to acknowledge well-deserved adulation. It sure looked like we'd been blessed by one of the Good Lord's tender mercies — until we got within ten feet of the track.

And that's where Lucifer stopped.

No amount of coaxing, pulling, or shoving could get him to take another step. If Eddie and Vic looked dejected, poor Rafael was crushed. He was a fine jockey, he'd done everything possible, but Lucifer made it plain he would not run with Rafael in the saddle. Vic and Eddie muscled Lucifer back to his stall, where Raf slid off the horse and hung his head in defeat.

"Great," said Jake. "So now we got a race, we just don't have a jockey. Jamey, how 'bout you?"

"Me? I haven't raced in years. And I only raced on Shadow."

"I'll ride him," Vic said in a firm voice.

"Are ladies even allowed?" Jake asked.

"Not in a normal race," Horatio said. "But those rules don't apply to a match race."

Vic climbed up and settled into Lucifer's saddle. "Let's go, you big dummy." Her horse did as she asked and we followed them to the track.

"Eddie," Vic said, "one warm-up lap. Then time us on the second."

We sat midway up in the grandstand for a better view. After they cantered through a lazy circuit, Vic shifted her weight and Lucifer took off.

I glanced at Eddie. "How's she doing?"

"Good."

"Better than good," Horatio said with an eye on his own stopwatch.

For the few other spectators around us in the stands, in addition to Lucifer's speed, two obvious oddities stoked their curiosity — the horse wasn't a Thoroughbred, and the rider was a girl.

"Did ya hear there's gonna be another match race?" said a stoop-shouldered man in a red corduroy coat. "Gonna be that there 'rabian against Van Brunt's Gran' Larceny."

"That's a joke!" a rotund man in a stovepipe hat scoffed. "No Arabian can keep up with Larceny."

"Not at a mile," said a third man, bushy-bearded and skinny as a fiddle string. "But I heared the match race'll be two and a half miles. And they say those A-rab horses got stayin' power."

"That Arabian'll bust a gut trying to keep up for ten furlongs," Stovepipe Hat said. "After that, he'll be so beat-out, Larceny'll waltz home, and you'll be able to eat your hat or mine before the Arabian stumbles in."

But Lucifer's time for that mucky mile was impressive, and the men kept arguing — as the literal embodiment of Mark Twain's observation that "it is difference of opinion that makes horse-races."

"Heh!" Bushy Beard said to Stovepipe Hat. "You wanna put yer money where yer mouth is?"

"I heared the bookies and Jockey Club smoked the peace pipe," Red Coat said.

Stovepipe Hat's ears perked up. "So there's gonna be betting Tuesday?"

"Yessirree," Bushy Beard said. "But I'll take yer money in a side bet, too."

"Done," Stovepipe Hat said.

The rest of our gang left the grandstand and joined Vic as she rode Lucifer back to the barns at a walk. "How'd he feel out there?" Eddie asked.

"Good enough," Vic said. "Could've gone faster — but there's no point in advertising."

Then we heard Van Brunt's voice shout to us as he approached: "What happened to your jockey?"

"He and the horse had a falling out," I said.

"Well, I don't mind saying, you got a day to find another rider. Otherwise, you forfeit and that handsome horse is mine."

"Don't worry your pretty little head," Vic said. "We've got a rider."

"Who?"

"Me."

Van Brunt could scarcely contain his glee. "Oh-*ho*! Is that so?"

Vic looked down defiantly from the saddle. "Do you have a problem with that?"

"I don't give a hoot if a monkey rides him, as long as there's no weight advantage. I'm fine with anything that makes my winning more likely. And a pretty li'l amateur versus my professional jockeys? Well, I wouldn't want you to get hurt out there — or hurt my Arabian before I take custody."

"Your concern is touching," Vic said, "but he's still *my* Arabian."

"This twist makes Lucifer as good as mine. Or you could give him over now, and save yourself a load of embarrassment, li'l lady." Van Brunt turned to go.

"Wait just a damn minute," Jake said. "Did you say your 'jockeys' — *plural?*"

Van Brunt smiled. "Yes, I did. I was enjoying this here so much, I forgot to mention — I will be running a second horse."

"Ohhh, no, no, no," Jake said, taking a threatening step forward. "That is not what y'all agreed to."

"He's right," I said. "You specified *no other entrants.*"

Van Brunt seemed unperturbed. "Letter of the law, there *is* no other entrant — just you folks and me. But we never said one entrant could not enter a second horse."

"*What* second horse?" Vic demanded.

"Not that it matters," Van Brunt said, eyes wide and innocent, "but it's Aries, the horse I just bought from Pryce."

We were stunned speechless. Aries had finished a competitive second to Phoenix in Saturday's Great Sweepstakes, so he was no pushover.

"Unless," Van Brunt said, "you prefer to forget the whole notion of winning back Phoenix."

"If we need to beat both your horses," Vic said through clenched teeth, "we will."

Van Brunt laughed and tipped his straw

hat. "I'm looking forward to your trying." He walked away and left us stewing.

"This ain't good," Eddie said.

Jake looked up at Vic. "With two jockeys in cahoots, they're gonna gang up on you."

"Thanks for pointing out the obvious," Vic said with a withering glare.

For the rest of Monday, Victoria tried to hide her jitters, and we all tried to pretend she'd succeeded. She and Lucifer had cross-country raced for fun, like I had with my pony Shadow when I was a kid back in Texas. But that was very different from competing with Thoroughbreds on an intimidating race course against seasoned jockeys.

Forced to accept his new role as coach, Rafael talked Vic through as many race scenarios as he could think of. But nobody could predict exactly how Van Brunt's jockeys might team up to checkmate her — or how Lucifer would react. We already knew Van Brunt had no qualms about cheating, so Vic had to expect a nasty race from start to finish. And she'd be out there all on her own.

With too many worries, we lost track of the hours that Monday afternoon. The late-October sun reminded us it was time to head back to Mike's house for a decent meal and as much sleep as possible. As Vic and Eddie got Lucifer settled in we heard shouts of alarm a few barns over, and a word that strikes terror into anyone who's ever worked at a racetrack, with wooden buildings, straw and hay everywhere, and horses stuck in their stalls.

"Fire!"

36

"Ignorance may be remedied. But stupid is forever."
~ Jake Galloway

We smelled smoke. We needed to find the source, and fast.

There weren't many horses stabled on our side of the property, but that also meant fewer people around to fight a fire or move the horses to safety. Eddie, Rafael, and Alberto ran out with me and Jake to join a handful of others looking for the fire.

Vic stayed with Lucifer. He may not have known what fire was, but the acrid air smelled like danger to him. He scuffed at the floor of his stall and gave the wall behind him a tentative kick, as if seeking another way out.

"You stay here," Vic said in her calmest voice as she slipped a halter over his head, in case she had to grab him and flee. "I'll be right back."

She kissed his nose, then went out to follow us. When she latched the stall door behind her, she didn't notice the stout man with a droopy mustache and a beer belly lurking in the shadows nearby.

At the center of the barn area, we found one hay bale ablaze. Flames licked at the nearest wooden shed. We joined a growing brigade, filling buckets from troughs and passing them to two men up front, who tossed water at the burning hay. In the midst of all that, Alberto ran off.

The water buckets kept coming. A second hay bale caught fire.

"Soak the barn," somebody yelled, "before this whole place goes up!"

Vic found us and stood next to Eddie, who had to be thinking of when his father died in the barn blaze at their farm.

One frantic man shouted, "Git all the horses outta their stalls!"

"Go!" Vic said to Eddie. "I'll get Lucifer."

She ran back to their barn, while Eddie rushed off to help save other horses.

Alberto returned with an armload of seven-foot-wide woolen cooling blankets, unfurled two of them across his full wingspan, and leapt like some giant condor onto the burning hay bales. He shouted instructions in jumbled Italian and English, but we understood enough to aim buckets of water around the edges of the fire left uncovered by the blankets.

Embers landing on other hay bales were quickly drenched, and by some miracle the scorched wood boards of the barn did not catch fire.

Vic approached Lucifer's stall — and heard her horse snorting and squealing up a storm. The stall door — which she'd closed — was open. Quick but quiet, she sized up the situation — and saw the stout man in with her horse.

Lucifer had him cornered. The intruder alternately lunged — trying to stick the horse with a glass hypodermic syringe — and reeled back to avoid getting pummeled by lethal hooves.

Vic grabbed a shovel, the nearest thing she could use as a weapon.

After what felt like forever, the main fire was out. Somebody said something about a guardian angel, but we knew it was The Amazing Alberto who'd saved the day. He slid off the charred hay and we kept throwing water and blankets on anything combustible, just to make sure every spark had been snuffed.

Alberto stood up and brushed himself off. I counted it as one more miracle that he wasn't burned. His fellow firefighters surrounded him in admiration. What he'd done seemed both crazy and courageous, but he kept faith with science — he knew that when a flame is smothered and starved of oxygen, it goes out.

"Hey! Get away from him!" Vic yelled at the man in the stall as she charged in, swinging the shovel like a broadsword.

The brutal ballet of two humans and a horse exploded into a full-on melee. The man had to defend against both Lucifer and Vic. He fumbled the syringe and it fell into the straw and muck on the floor. He wrestled the shovel away from Vic, flailing it at her and the horse. She leapt onto the bushwhacker's back, wrapped her arms around his throat, and tried to strangle the life out of him.

He dropped the shovel and struggled to break her chokehold, clawing with both hands like he was caught in a swarm of bees. Gyrating and spinning, he whirled Vic off his back like a rag doll.

Her head and right shoulder banged hard against the wall. She crumpled to the floor.

His chest heaving, the man slumped to his knees next to her motionless body, frantic to find a sign of life. "Ohhh, jeezus lordy! Dammit, girlie!"

He felt hot horse breath on his neck and looked up. Lucifer loomed above him like a death-dealing gargoyle come to horrific life, lips curled, ears pinned back, eyes wild. The man was sure he was about to die. With mad fury, Lucifer reared and punched out with his front hooves.

The fat man skittered and rolled sideways, barely avoiding a stomping. He snatched up the hypodermic and scuttled in a terrified crouch, looking for any fleshy part of the crazed horse where he could plunge the needle in. But there was no way to stab a murderous moving target, so he abandoned his malicious task in favor of escaping alive.

Lucifer swung his big head and knocked the man down, then reared and lunged. The man dropped the syringe again, rolled onto his hands and knees — and screeched in pain as the horse chomped down on his rear end. Lucifer lifted him off the ground and thrashed him from side to side like a terrier shaking an unfortunate rat.

Certain the horse was about to dash his brains out against the wall, the man heard his pants ripping and felt a chill on his nethers. With one more jerk, the seat of his pants tore clean away. The man crashed to the floor and scrabbled out with his life — if not his dignity.

Lucifer started to chase him — then stopped and stayed to guard Victoria.

Alberto and Rafael helped make sure the fire was out and all the horses were safe. Jake and me approached Lucifer's barn in time to see a curious sight — a fat man missing the backside of his britches, his ripped and bloody drawers hanging out, hobbling away as fast as he could.

Hearing Lucifer braying in alarm, we ran to the open stall and found him standing over Vic's body. We feared she was dead until we heard her moan. Jake looked from her to the apparent intruder making his painful getaway.

"I've got her," I said. "Go get him — but *don't* kill him! We need him talking."

"No promises!" He drew his gun and ran after our suspect.

I took a cautious step toward Vic, and spoke to her wary horse in the most soothing voice I could muster. "It's okay, Lucifer. We're gonna take care of her."

Horses don't growl, but this one came close. Then I heard Eddie behind me:

"What the hell?!" He grabbed Lucifer's halter and nudged him a few steps away so I could tend to Victoria.

Rafael came back and saw Vic on the floor. *"Dios mío!"*

"Raffie," Eddie said, "go get clean water."

The jockey grabbed a bucket and darted away to the nearest pump.

I took off my coat, folded it, and placed it under Vic's head. Rafael returned in a flash with a full bucket. I dipped my bandanna in the cold water, and gently patted her face.

Her eyelids flickered open. "Huh?" She was dazed, but recognized our anxious faces hovering over her. "I'm not dead?"

"Nope," I said.

"Did Lucifer kill that bastard?"

"Close, but no. Jake went after him."

We got her sitting up and knew her right arm was hurt by the way she held it. "Can you move it?" I asked.

She wiggled her fingers a little, and her face squinched up in pain. "Never mind me. That sonofabitch was trying to skewer Lucifer with a hypodermic. Raf, fetch the track veterinarian."

Rafael nodded and took off at top speed.

Jake stalked Vic's limping assailant through the maze of barns, catching glimpses only to lose his quarry again when he disappeared between buildings or into a doorway. When the man ducked around the corner of a barn, Jake followed — and froze, caught by surprise. Twenty feet away, the man aimed his pistol at Jake's chest. Nobody with his eyes open could possibly miss at that distance, so Jake expected to die right then and there.

The thug fired his gun. The bullet pinged off the wooden shed, inches from Jake's shoulder. Jake got off one wild shot as he dove for cover behind a stack of hay bales.

Mr. Bloody-drawers cocked his pistol again. This time, it misfired with a feeble click. He cussed and fled.

Jake popped up like a prairie dog and caught up to his cornered prey attempting to scale the eight-foot-tall plank fence at the edge of racetrack property behind the barns. If he made it, he might get lucky and disappear into the dark Baltimore streets beyond. His desperate jumps were hampered by the painful bite Lucifer had inflicted on his sorry ass.

"Stop!" Jake shouted.

Ignoring the order, the thug made one more jump, and managed to hook his fingers over the top of the fence. His shoes slipped as he tried to climb. At last, he hauled himself up, balanced on his beer gut, fixing to tumble over the top — briefly presenting his bloody behind as a perfect target.

Jake aimed. "Get down — *now!*"

The man continued trying to squirm over the fence.

Jake fired, intentionally winging him in the *right* butt cheek, balancing the horse bite on the left side.

The man yowled and fell to the ground with a squawk of pain. Irate at being run ragged and shot at by a dimwit, Jake strode over and stepped on the man's wrist, pinning his gun hand to the ground. "Didn't I tell you to stop?"

Jake snatched the thug's gun away and displayed it like he was holding a dead rodent by its tail. "This is the most disgusting, gummed-up firearm I ever saw. I bet you didn't know a filthy gun doesn't shoot straight, if it shoots at all."

Lying on his side in the dirt, moaning in misery, the man answered in a shaky voice. "Ooohh-owww . . . No, I didn't know that."

"Look at it this way," Jake said. "Any day you learn something new is a lucky day."

"I've had luckier."

"But I bet you have no idea what your *biggest* lesson is for today."

"No, but I bet you're gonna tell me."

"I will do you that favor." Jake held the grimy gun up again. "If you ever took the time to clean this thing, you might've shot me and got away with at least one good cheek to sit on — although, the horse probably did more damage than my little flesh wound."

The poor dumb cluck whimpered. "Ehhh . . . it feels about the same."

"You are a sorry excuse. Is this what your mama raised you for?"

"Mmm . . . yeah, pretty much."

"Ignorance may be remedied. But stupid is forever." Jake shook his head as he tied the prisoner's hands in front of his ample belly. "Can you walk?"

"N-not if I have a choice."

"You don't." Jake pulled him to his feet and poked his gun into the man's ribs. "Move."

It took them a while to get back to the barn. By that time, Lucifer had calmed down, and Jake was relieved to see Vic sitting on a bench, her injured arm in a makeshift sling. She tried to be stoic, but grimaced every time she moved.

"Is this the jackass?" Jake asked her.

Vic nodded. "Unless somebody else got bit on the behind."

The pathetic thug leaned against the wall.

"H-how would she know?"

"Beyond us finding the missing piece of your britches," Jake said, "how 'bout her seeing your ugly mug."

"M-maybe she didn't get such a good look."

"And why not?"

"Well . . .'cuz she spent most of the time jumped on my back and chokin' me."

Jake rolled his eyes. "Every time you open your mouth, you are not doing yourself any favors."

I showed Jake our evidence in addition to the shredded rag matching our captive's pants — a cracked glass hypodermic containing the residue of an unidentified liquid, a leather pouch that looked like a case for the syringe, and a canvas haversack with a box of matches inside. Add Vic's eyewitness account, and we had a strong case. As for who pulled his strings, it had to be Van Brunt. Still, some actual proof would be helpful.

"How 'bout you answer some questions," I said to the suspect.

"Standin' up? In my present condition? I might faint from the fierce achin' in my ass," he whined in a shaky voice. "I got b-b-bit by a horse . . . can I set down?"

I glanced at his bloody backside. "I don't

know. Can you?"

With his hands tied, he slid down the wall toward some soft straw. Before his rear made contact, he tipped onto his side.

I looked down at him. "Comfy?"

"Not really."

"Tough," I said. "Okay, so you tried to poison this horse — on Van Brunt's orders?"

My interrogation got interrupted when Rafael drove up in a buggy with track veterinarian John Holt, a tall, bald, and gentle man wearing spectacles. We told him what we knew, and Lucifer stood surprisingly still while Doc Holt examined him.

He found no obvious injection site, which might have bled a little and been noticeable on a white horse. But he couldn't be sure. Then he held the syringe up in front of our reclining captive. "What was in this?"

"I don't know."

Seeing the doctor's skeptical expression, Jake assured him, "Near as we can tell, he doesn't have enough sense to spit downwind. So he could be telling the truth."

"All right, then," Holt said, "did you manage to inject any into the horse?"

"What horse?"

"When a dunce plays dumb," I said, "is it really playing?"

"Doc," Vic said, "if Lucifer's been poisoned, how long 'til we know?"

"Hard to tell, without knowing the specific substance or dosage. In general, it would likely show by morning, at the latest. Meanwhile, ma'am, I advise you to see a doctor for your injury."

"I'm staying with my horse."

"There's nothing you can do for him," Doc Holt said. "I can bunk overnight at the clubhouse and check on him every few hours."

"I'll stay here in the barn with him," Rafael said. "If Lucifer looks sick, I run to get the doc."

Jake mentioned the need for somebody to fetch the local law to deal with our prisoner. Raf volunteered.

"There's a *po*-leece station not far," Doc Holt said. "I'll show you."

They left in the buggy, and we turned our attention toward Vic.

"We're gonna take you back to Mike's house and get a doctor to check that arm," Jake said.

"And don't bother arguing," Eddie added.

Vic knew when she was outnumbered.

Jake nudged the woebegone thug with his boot. "Hey — what did I tell you to say to her?"

"Oh . . . yeah." He shifted his position to

face Vic. "Hey, girlie, I'm real sorry you got hurt. B-but you was chokin' me to death."

"And I'm *not* sorry my horse took a chunk out of your ass," Vic said. "You're lucky he didn't kill you."

"I'm as good as dead anyway, once the Boss gets wind."

I squinted at him. "Van Brunt, you mean."

"Yeah — *no*! I ain't never said nobody's name! You oughta be ashamed, takin' unfair advantage of a man in m-mortal agony."

A familiar voice came out of the dusk: "What's this I heard about some commotion back here — somethin' about a fire?" Champagne Charley Fly strolled up, well-dressed as usual. He looked into the stall and grinned at our suspect lying on his side. "Why, if it ain't Humpty Bleeker. What're you doin' out on this fair fall evening, and you missin' the seat of your britches?"

Jake stared at Charley. "You know him?"

"No!" Humpty croaked, in vain.

The jockey nodded. "He works for Mr. Van Brunt."

"Including poisoning horses?"

Charley's smile disappeared. "Whoa. I thought it was just a little hay fire that got put right out."

"That was a diversion," Jake said.

"From what?"

"A plot to poison my horse," Vic said.

I showed Charley the syringe and box of matches. "We figure your friend Humpty set the fire to draw everybody away while he snuck into Lucifer's stall to inject him with something."

Jake gave Charley a suspicious stare. "How do we know you weren't in on it?"

"Yeah," I said. "Mighty convenient, you just dropping by — maybe to see if Lucifer's dead yet?"

But Charley looked genuinely troubled. "I don't need to poison no horses to beat 'em. Anyways, Mr. Van Brunt *wants* this horse. Why would he wanna kill him?" He stood over Bleeker while resting a hand on Lucifer's neck.

"Careful," Eddie said. "Lucifer —"

"— bites," Charley said, nodding toward Bleeker. "I reckon that kiss on Humpty's ass is Lucifer's work. But he's okay with me — aren't you, boy?"

Lucifer replied with a soft nicker, which surprised the rest of us.

"Humpty," Charley said, "how 'bout ownin' up to all this chaos."

"Got nothin' to say."

"Last chance." Charley waited a few seconds, but Bleeker stayed mum. "Okay, maybe the horse can kick some sense into you."

Charley took hold of Lucifer's halter and led him a step closer to Bleeker, who quaked in terror.

"You got five seconds 'til I set this horse waltzin' on your sorry carcass," Charley said. "Did you set that fire?"

Bleeker groaned. "Yeah."

"To cover you poisoning this handsome horse?"

"Yeah."

"Boss's orders?"

"Ohhh, lordy . . . I am done for."

"Unburden your Christian conscience," Charley preached.

Bleeker crumbled. "Yeah. B-boss's orders."

"Were you trying to kill the horse?" I said.

"Naaah, only make him sick enough to lose or forfeit."

"That damned cheater," Vic said. "All so he can take Lucifer and keep Phoenix."

Charley shook his head over sad-sack Bleeker. "Humpty's all yours. You, I'll see soon," he said to Lucifer, slipping him a peppermint candy. He looked at Vic. "I hope y'all are okay tomorrow. Forfeits ain't no fun, so I'm eager for the race."

Champagne Charley Fly walked off into

the twilight, leaving us to try and account for his way with Lucifer.

37

"Can't always count on skill or luck — but a good cheat is hard to beat."
~ Champagne Charley Fly

Leaving Alberto behind to keep an eye on Humpty Bleeker until the police could collect him, the rest of us climbed into the big carriage and Jake drove us back to Mississippi Mike's house. After we briefed him on our eventful evening, Mike gave me a note and sent me to get Dr. Franklin Church, who lived around the corner.

The kindly young doc diagnosed Vic with a dislocated right shoulder. There was only one way to pop it back into place, and it was going to hurt. He yanked it. She howled. He apologized, and fashioned a better sling. "It'll be tender for some days, but it'll heal faster if you keep the shoulder immobile for at least a week."

"But I have a race to ride tomorrow."

"A *race*? Hon, I don't even want you riding in an omnibus." The doc turned to the rest of us. "Tie her down, hammer the door shut — but for godsakes, do not let her ride a horse, in a *race* no less."

Eddie and Jake stood together in front of Victoria, presenting a formidable united front. "Got it, Doc," Eddie said.

"Only way she gets to ride," Jake said, "is over our dead bodies."

"Don't tempt me," Vic said.

Doc Church handed her a medicine bottle of laudanum from his leather bag. "It'll help you sleep tonight. But as of tomorrow, it's better if you can gut through without it. Listen to your pain, hon. It'll remind you not to do anything stupid."

After he left, Vic refused to take the medicine, and vowed she'd be fit to ride tomorrow. None of us were looking forward to convincing her otherwise. Alberto came in after handing Humpty Bleeker over to the Baltimore police, and leaving Rafael with Lucifer at the track.

"There's no choice," Eddie told Vic. "With you banged up, Raffie's gotta ride."

"Lucifer won't even *walk* for him, let alone run."

We all knew Rafael would try his best. We also knew that wouldn't be enough. We could revisit our options in the morning, but without some kind of elusive miracle, they'd look no better. Vic finally gave in and downed a laudanum dose. She got wobbly pretty quick, so Eddie carried her to the back bedroom on the main floor. Jake followed to lend a hand. They tucked her in, and Eddie said he'd stay until she fell asleep.

Jake returned to the kitchen to find Alberto juggling two apples. Jake picked up three apples from the fruit bowl on the table, and matched Alberto's rhythm. Alberto added two more and juggled all four. Jake laughed and knew when he was licked.

I wondered about the depths of deviltry required to poison a horse. Charley Fly was right — Van Brunt wouldn't want to kill the horse he coveted for his treasure collection. But he plainly had no qualms about making Lucifer sick enough to lose or forfeit. If the poisoning scheme failed, there was no telling what else a desperate Van Brunt might do to claim his prize — "by hook or by crook," as he liked to say.

And I remembered Mike's cautionary wisdom: *Whatever the game, expect your opponent to cheat.* Between somehow stealing Phoenix in the Frisco fog, and now this, it was hard to imagine a more brazen cheater than Cortland Van Brunt III.

After an uneasy night's sleep, we were all up early Tuesday morning. Jake found that Eddie had catnapped in a chair by Vic's bedside all night. When he tried to help her out of bed, she shook him off. But her shoulder still hurt pretty bad.

She winced as she slipped her arm out of the sling. "Owww. See? Owww. I can ride today."

Jake frowned. "The hell you can."

Eddie mumbled something about needing some air and ducked out the front door.

"What's eating him?" Vic said as she and Jake went into the empty kitchen.

Jake brought her coffee and a plate of muffins to share, and they sat at the table. "He stayed with you all night."

"I know," Vic said, sounding sheepish. "And where were you?"

"Me? Aww, you know how Eddie fills up a whole room all by his lonesome." He nibbled a muffin. "I told you he was sweet on you."

"Wellll . . . maybe he is," she admitted. "Are you?"

Jake hesitated. "I reckon maybe I am."

"Then maybe we're going to have to work this out."

"How?"

She made the mistake of shrugging her bad shoulder. "*Oww.* How should I know?"

On the carriage ride all the way to Pimlico, Vic still claimed she was ready for racing. First, we'd have to determine if Lucifer was ready — or sick. Afraid of what we might find, we got there by nine, under a dazzling blue sky decked out with cotton clouds and bursting with brisk autumn brilliance. We found Doc Holt already examining Lucifer outside the stall. Horatio Deale was also there, adding to his story.

Eddie helped Vic down, like she was a delicate glass figurine. But it was clear she had no intention of giving an inch, no matter how much pain she tried to hide.

Rafael skipped over to greet us. "Lucifer's okay!"

Even Lucifer seemed relaxed.

"Your horse is tip-top," the veterinarian reassured Eddie and Vic. "Whatever that substance was, either the dose was inconsequential, or nothing at all. Broken syringe, hard to know for sure."

"This might be the best story I have ever covered," Horatio said. "I do not want to miss a single detail, with tensions rising, and the outcome very much in doubt."

Lucifer's mood took a quick dark turn.

He snorted and tried to rear, but Eddie had a tight grip on his halter. What roused Lucifer's dander was Van Brunt approaching, with Charley Fly at his side and a couple of his lackeys trailing. Van Brunt wore his usual straw hat, his pipe clamped in his teeth. Charley looked dapper in a tailored blue cutaway suit and blue derby.

But the sight of Lucifer alive and well sure put a hitch in Van Brunt's stride. His expression mixed equal parts surprise and anger. "I heard tell you had some unfortunate incidents last evening. But it certainly appears to me your horse is . . . fit as a fiddle, at the present time."

We didn't need Madame Killegrew's sixth sense to guess what he was really thinking: *Why isn't that horse sick?* If Van Brunt's demeanor was easy to read, Charley Fly stayed as inscrutably cool as an ice house in August, like he was sitting on a secret — and I couldn't figure out what. Unless . . .

I pulled Jake aside and whispered, "Is it possible Van Brunt doesn't know Bleeker got caught last night?"

"Could be. But why wouldn't Charley tell him?"

"No idea. But Van Brunt sure didn't expect to find Lucifer 'fit as a fiddle' today."

I stepped forward, gambling that Van

Brunt was not accustomed to having the rug pulled out from under him. "Mr. Van Brunt, y'know we had the pleasure of meeting your associate last night. Jake, what was his name again?"

Jake played along. "Mmm . . . something with a B, wasn't it? Barker? Blocker? Bleeker! Humpty Bleeker. Not an easy name to forget."

"If you haven't seen him this morning," I added, "that's because he's in a city jail."

By the priceless bug-eyed look on Van Brunt's face, momentary as it was, there was no doubt we'd caught him flatfooted. He chewed on that pipe stem like an ornery horse trying to grind his bit into dust. But all he said was, "What is this world coming to when somebody would try and poison a horse?"

Give him credit — he had a gift for faking sincerity.

"That shoulder looks mighty tender, Vickie," Van Brunt said, his balance recovered. "If nobody but you can ride Lucifer, you don't look in any condition, poor dear. And who ever heard of the gentler sex competing in a big-time race, anyway?"

Rafael stepped forward in full-throated defiance. "*I'm* gonna ride him. I beat your horses in San Francisco. I'm gonna beat 'em here."

Vic confronted our jockey. "You are not risking your neck for this."

"I can get him going!"

"Maybe if you had a month — but we don't even have a day!"

Eddie stepped between them. "*Neither* of you is gonna ride him."

Our plans were going to hell, and Van Brunt couldn't have been more tickled. Jake wanted to flatten him, and I wanted to help.

"Eddie, you gotta let me!" Rafael pleaded.

"You both know he'll only run for me," Vic said.

"And *you* can't ride a race with one good arm!" Eddie yelled at her.

"That's why *I* gotta ride him!" Raf yelled at both of them.

"Whoa!" Charley Fly's booming voice stunned everybody into silence. He aimed a tight smile at Van Brunt. "*I'll* ride him."

Van Brunt's rapture came to such a screeching halt, I thought he might swallow his pipe. He stared at Charley. "You'll do *what?!*"

"I said —"

"I *heard* you!"

Horatio scribbled non-stop in his notebook.

Vic confronted Charley with the suspicion the rest of us were thinking: "How do we know this isn't Van Brunt's plan all along — have you ride Lucifer and then throw the race?"

Charley thumbed a gesture toward the seething Van Brunt. "Does he look like he knew I was gonna do this?"

No, he certainly did not.

"I swear to God, Charley," Van Brunt said, "I will ruin you."

But nothing rattled Charley Fly. "This ain't the South. There ain't no more slaves. Your horses win 'cuz I'm the rider."

"You owe me everything, you little bastard!"

"A dozen other owners'll jump for joy if I say I'll ride for 'em."

"Damn you to hell. I set you free!"

"And I'm free to walk. You go find yourself another jockey. Otherwise, you'll have to forfeit that fine stallion you stole from these folks in San Francisco."

I elbowed Jake. "I *knew* it!"

Van Brunt stomped away. "Go!" he bellowed at his men, who scattered like startled crows. "Get me another goddam jockey!"

When they were gone, Charley found us all gawking at him, like he was the stupefying in-the-flesh visitation of one of Madame

Killegrew's spirits — we could see the apparition, all right, we just couldn't believe our eyes. And if we asked too many questions, we feared he'd dematerialize in a sulfurous flare of smoke.

"You've been riding for Van Brunt for years," Jake said. "Why throw that away?"

"I've loved horses since I first laid eyes on 'em, down on Pryce's plantation, when I was knee-high to a grasshopper. Horses saved me from bein' worked to death in the fields. I owe 'em everything. Hurtin' a horse — any horse — that's my last straw, and the gospel truth."

"But cheating's okay," I said with icy distrust.

"When I first rode for Pryce, I learned real quick nobody gonna give a colored man a fair shake. Can't always count on skill or luck — but a good cheat is hard to beat."

"So, I was right — Van Brunt *did* cheat in San Francisco. But I still can't figure out how."

Charley chuckled. "That's 'cuz we're good at it. Fog gave us the cover we needed. At the start, Grand Larceny keeps up with Phoenix. Then I drop him back a few lengths."

"And get lost in the fog," I said.

"Nobody can see much of nothin'. On the

backstretch, we had our horse Susquehannock waitin' in that fog. He's almost a dead ringer for Larceny, his jockey's wearin' the same silks as me. They glide onto the track behind Phoenix, and me and Larceny, we slide on off."

"Then you cut Grand Larceny across the infield."

"Yessir."

"But why the second horse?" Jake asked.

I knew. "Even if Rafael couldn't see you, he could *hear* you. Without the other horse taking your place, he'd've known he was running alone, that something was squirrelly."

Jake got it. "Hnnh. But as long as Raf hears Susquehannock, he figures it's you on Grand Larceny."

"That's the onliest thing made me feel bad," Charley said to Raffie. "You're a good rider, kid. You ended up thinkin' you messed up."

"Then coming out of the stretch turn," I said, "that's where you switched again?"

Raf gritted his teeth. "*That's* when I heard three horses."

"Yup," Charley said. "Then Susquehannock drops out, nobody's the wiser. Me and Grand Larceny're back in the race, but he's only half as tired as Phoenix. No way a played-out horse can outrun one that took a short cut."

"So you storm past Phoenix like a freight train," I said.

"What happened to Susquehannock?" Jake asked.

"Heads back to the barn," Charley said. "Nobody sees him in the fog, and nobody's lookin' for him anyways. By the time the race is over, he's back in his stall."

"It is like how I do in magic," Alberto said, with a glower in place of his usual smile. "People do not look for what they no expect to see."

"I reckon that's not the first time Van Brunt used that cheat," I said, with grudging admiration for the execution, if not the ethics.

Charley smiled with a glint of gold. "Let's just say, it's in our repertoire. When we see that morning fog, Boss figures it's worth a try, not leavin' things to chance." He came up to Lucifer. "No fog today, boy. You're gonna have to live up to your name and run like the devil."

Vic looked Charley square in the eye. "What makes you think you can ride him?"

Charley petted Lucifer. "Miz Victoria, I've rode every damn kinda horse. Some so mean they make this guy seem like a sweet

Georgia peach. Lucifer and me, we got ourselves an understanding."

"Don't forget," Jake said, "your neck's on the line, too, after jumping Van Brunt's ship."

"Ain't that the truth. I'll be back at ten to give Lucifer some work. Then you can tell me all his secrets."

Rafael bristled and blocked Charley's way. "So I didn't really lose."

"Nope." A second later, Raf's fist clobbered Charley's jaw and he ended up in the dirt, seeing stars. "Whooo-eee . . . I reckon I had that coming."

"You sure did," Raf said.

Charley picked himself up and dusted himself off. "You feel better?"

"Yeah, I do."

"Good." Charley walked away with a spring in his step, looking for all the world like a man eager to level those pesky scales of justice.

38

"Slavery is the next thing to hell."
  ~ Harriet Tubman

Funny thing, when Champagne Charley Fly wasn't riding fast racehorses, he hardly ever rode horses at all. Instead, he loved walking up, down and around city streets. From bucolic byways meandering through parks to downtown avenues, from the waterfront to Mount Vernon's mansions and marble Washington Monument, from scruffy taverns to fine restaurants — Baltimore was his kind of town.

He considered it home, despite Maryland's embrace of slavery going back over two centuries, to the first shackled Africans brought to Lord Baltimore's colony in 1642. Ever since, Maryland's blacks and whites had shared a confusing and contradictory relationship.

In early Colonial times, tobacco became

the foundation of Maryland's economy, leading to huge plantations that rivaled Deep South cotton plantations for acreage and output. Fact was, growing such crops on a grand scale would not have been possible or profitable without slaves. From 1700 to the 1750s, the colony's population leapt from 25,000 to 130,000. Four in ten Marylanders at that time were black, and most of them were slaves. Yet, by the eve of the Civil War in 1860, while Maryland still had nearly 90,000 slaves, it also had almost as many free black citizens, more than any other state in the Union.

Charley knew the stories of two who had been born into slavery in Maryland, fled to freedom and achieved historical distinction for fighting to end what even Southerners called "that peculiar institution." You may have heard of them, too — their names were Frederick Douglass and Harriet Tubman.

Young Mr. Douglass escaped to the North by boarding a train in Baltimore in 1837 and riding to New York City. Within a few years, he would rise to become a famous preacher, abolitionist, orator, and writer — wielding a moral authority that helped convince President Abraham Lincoln to make Emancipation a keystone of his struggle to redeem the Union.

Harriet Tubman, born enslaved around 1822, made her escape in '49 via the Underground Railroad. Unlike the actual rails that carried Frederick Douglass to freedom, the Underground Railroad was a transport web woven by the linked hands and hearts of both free and enslaved black folks, and white abolitionists who'd committed themselves to liberating slaves and ridding the nation of its original sin. The woman also called "Moses" then risked her own freedom and her very life during a dozen or more daring expeditions to help scores of other slaves escape.

By the time Charley had gained his freedom from Van Brunt, Baltimore was home to the largest free Negro population in any American city. Although Maryland did not secede, it was a border state with a Southern soul. Even as secession ripped the Union apart, sympathy for the Confederate cause burned long and died hard there, with Baltimore as a persistent hotbed of pro-slavery sentiment.

When President-elect Lincoln left his home in Illinois in February 1861, on his way to inauguration in Washington, D.C., he did not travel a direct route. Instead, he took a deliberately roundabout two-week whistle-stop tour through several states and seventy Northern heartland towns and cities, hoping to bolster resolve to save the imperiled Union. His most perilous passage would be through Baltimore, where assassination plots sprouted like summer weeds.

Baltimore was particularly dangerous because the train including Lincoln's special rail car would arrive from Pennsylvania at Calvert Street Station on the *east* side of town — but would depart for Washington from Camden Station on the *west* side. And the only way to get from one to the other was for the vulnerable presidential coach to be drawn on rails by horses — *slowly* — through the city, in the dead of night.

To avert catastrophe, the railroad hired detective Allan Pinkerton and his agents, who took extraordinary measures to ferret out conspiracies and assure Lincoln's security. The new president reached Washington safely, but that was the temper of the times. Even years after the war, black and white Baltimoreans lived as uneasy neighbors in Charley Fly's adopted hometown.

After Charley left us at the barns, he walked to the arabber stable a few blocks from Pimlico to see how the peddlers and their horses were getting by. Arabbers based there on the north side of town were able to pick up produce directly from nearby local farmers, paying a lower price than at the city's wholesale markets — savings they could pass on to customers.

As Charley entered the stable, he called out: "Watermelon, watermelon — red to the rind!"

Solomon Carver's gravelly voice sang back from the shadows, and several pairs of work-roughened hands clapped in rhythm: "Apples an' grapes! They lookin' so fine!"

Solomon came over to join Charley, and they finished together: "Holler, holler, 'til my throat gets sore! Them pretty girls come runnin', don't holler no more!"

The old arabber and five fellow hucksters, all younger black men, gathered around Charley. Only Hub Robinson kept to himself, concentrating on hitching up his horse.

"How you doin'?" Solomon said to Charley. "You got a race today?"

"I do." Charley greeted each of the horses with a pat and a sugar cube from his pocket.

"Which Van Brunt horse you ridin'?"

"None. Ridin' rogue today."

Solomon's grizzled eyebrows jiggled in surprise. "You workin' for somebody else now?"

"Not sure who I'll be ridin' for in the future — but it won't be Van Brunt. How y'all doin' here? Need anything?"

"We doin' good, Charley," a young arabber said. "We appreciate you helpin' us."

"Once racing season's done, I'll stop by more often. Anything these horses need, y'all make me a list."

As Hub led his horse and cart toward the open barn doors, Charley called out, "Mr. Robinson, right?"

Hub stopped, but didn't turn or speak. So Charley went up to his horse and looked him over. "Fine-lookin' animal. You take good care of him, I can see. But if he ever —"

"Don't need your help."

"Ain't sayin' you do."

Hub cast a critical eye on Charley's clothing, from his polished black shoes, up to his suit coat and the derby he wore tipped at a jaunty angle. "Surprised you got any money left after buying those duds."

With a curt nod, Hub led his horse out to the street. He hadn't gone far when Charley left the barn and strutted down the block, invigorated by the fresh air, whistling on his morning constitutional. Hub and his horse moseyed in the same direction and fell behind Charley's brisk pace.

But Hub noticed something Charley Fly didn't — a one-horse Brougham Coupe carriage, with its enclosed passenger compartment, side doors, glass windows all around, and the driver perched high on a front bench seat. These rigs were common in cities, often serving as hackney cabs — and usually in a hurry. But this one wasn't, which made Hub all but certain that its occupants were deliberately shadowing the unsuspecting jockey.

The slow-rolling vehicle drew even with Charley. Two brawny white men threw open the doors, hopped out and grabbed him. Despite his flailing limbs, they threw a feed sack over his head, lifted him off the ground, and crammed him into the cab. As the carriage lurched forward, Charley kicked open a door and tumbled out.

Before he could wiggle free and find his feet, both assailants jumped out and caught him again. One clubbed him with a stout shillelagh. The other hoisted the limp jockey over his shoulder like an actual sack of feed. They stuffed him back inside, climbed in and yanked the doors shut.

With a snap of the driver's long whip, the carriage took off south.

And Hub Robinson witnessed the whole incident.

He didn't like Charley. But he also didn't like seeing *any* black man snatched against his will by white men up to no good.

Not wanting to add to the weight of fruits and vegetables their horses had to pull, arabbers didn't normally ride in their wagons as they circulated through the city. This one time, Hub made an exception, sat on the narrow bench at the front of his cart, and followed the Brougham carriage downtown.

39

"For a man hanging on a meat hook, you don't seem overly concerned about your immediate future."
∼ Jake Galloway

Back at the Pimlico barn, Eddie saddled Lucifer while Victoria and her one good arm stewed on the sidelines. It was ten-fifteen — and no Charley Fly.

Eddie and Vic stayed with the horse, in case Charley showed up. The rest of us — me, Jake, Rafael, Mike, Horatio, and Alberto — spread out and asked around. Nobody had seen him since he'd left the grounds early that morning, but everybody who knew him agreed — if he said he'd be somewhere at a certain time, you could count on it.

Expanding our search, we checked out the rooming house where he lived, his favorite haunts near the track — and came up empty. After Charley's early-morning defection, Van Brunt topped our list of likely villains behind this mystery. Mike and Horatio questioned him, and of course he denied everything, other than enjoying our predicament and badmouthing Charley as a lowdown skunk. We didn't believe a word, but all we had were suspicions.

Our dispirited group gathered back at the barn. It was like Charley Fly had vanished into thin air, which was something Alberto knew a thing or two about. As our master illusionist explained, in magic when something *appears* to disappear, it hasn't truly dematerialized in violation of natural laws — it's merely hidden. And hidden things, or people, can be found, if you know where to look.

The ticking clock was our enemy, with the special match race scheduled for three-thirty. If we failed to find Champagne Charley Fly in time, our choices were grim: either one-armed Victoria or shaky Rafael would have to ride, facing probable disaster. Or Eddie and Vic would have to forfeit Lucifer to Van Brunt.

"Hey," Mike said, "did anybody check with the arabbers at the gate? Charley sometimes stops there to get apples and carrots for the horses."

Nobody had, so Mike grabbed me and off we went. Solomon Carver greeted us with his usual good cheer. His partner Hub Robinson occupied himself with rearranging his produce bins.

Solomon told us he hadn't seen Charley since he'd stopped in at the arabbers' stable on his morning walk. "How 'bout you, Hub — you seen him after that?"

"I don't waste my time keeping track of Charley Fly's comings and goings," Hub muttered as he sorted out some overripe fruit and tossed it near the trees for the squirrels.

"All I'm askin' is, did you see him."

"Mr. Robinson," Mike said, "he's missing and we need to find him."

"I got nothin' to tell you."

Solomon went over to Hub, and rested a peaceable hand on his shoulder. "Seems like you got a burden weighin' on you, son. And you got here later than usual."

Hub looked down at the ground. "Had something I needed to do."

"These folks are friends, and they're countin' on Charley. So if you know somethin', now's the Christian time to speak up. Don't forget, the good Lord knows your heart." The old arabber said what he had to say and shuffled back to us at his wagon.

"Hold on a spell. He got some trouble on his mind, I can tell."

Solomon gave Mike and me a couple of fresh apples. We chomped and chewed, waiting to see if Hub knew anything about Charley Fly's whereabouts. By the time we'd munched down to the cores, Solomon shook his head. "Sorry. I thought maybe he'd come around. If I hear anything . . ."

Mike patted his old friend on the arm. "Thanks, Sol."

As we turned to leave, Hub's unquiet conscience got the better of him. He told us what he'd seen, and how he'd followed the carriage and the men who'd nabbed Charley. "All the way down to Pigtown," he said. "They carried him into a slaughterhouse near the freight yards." He even gave us the block where the building was located.

"You can guide 'em," Solomon said.

But Hub Robinson insisted he didn't want to get involved.

He'd been born in a stormy sea of injustice, and there must've been many a time when slavery's relentless riptide had nearly drowned him. Even after swimming free, the terrible memories seared into his soul would likely stay with him for the rest of his days. How could those so enslaved keep from asking: *Where was God's grace when countless numbers of His children toiled in brutal bondage?*

I could understand Hub believing how, there but for fortune, Charley Fly had been delivered from evil and not suffered as so many had. Maybe it was Charley's due destiny to get a taste of the cruelty he'd escaped — or maybe it wasn't. How was any man to know what God had in mind?

Solomon sensed his friend's turmoil, but we couldn't wait for Hub's mind and heart to change. Mike stayed at the Pimlico gate while I ran back to the barn and reported what we'd learned. Jake and Alberto jumped into our parked carriage, and Eddie commandeered a pair of riding horses.

"Eddie, you gotta stay here," I said as I took the reins of one horse. "You gotta make sure Lucifer's ready to race, in case we find Charley in time — or in case Raf or Vic have to ride."

He knew I was right, but didn't like it as he watched us dash away.

Our tiny expeditionary force pulled up at the arabbers' wagons, where Solomon implored Hub one more time. "You may not like Charley Fly, but think on this. You was a slave, and they treatin' him like he still is."

Hub couldn't look him in the eye, but Solomon wasn't done.

"Hub, without you showing 'em the way, what if they get lost? What if Charley gets killed — can you live with that?" Solomon shook his head with more sadness than anger. "If you won't help, I will. You watch the carts 'til we get back."

Alberto gave Solomon a hand up into the back seat of the carriage. Jake got the horse going. I rode alongside. We were almost out of earshot when Hub shouted after us: "Wait!"

Jake pulled back on the reins.

Hub trotted over and looked up at Solomon. "I'll go."

They traded places, and we headed downtown as fast as we could. I could've ridden the horse faster, but without Hub's navigation I wouldn't have known where to go.

It took us an hour to get to Pigtown, where it wasn't hard to figure out how the area got its colorful name. Located a few blocks from the railroad, Pigtown's concentration of stockyards, slaughterhouses, meat packers, and butcher shops processed an endless supply of Midwestern pigs transported east on the venerable Baltimore & Ohio Railroad.

We picked our way around droves of ham-on-the-hoof being herded this way and that, in a part of Baltimore which — well, let's just say it had a distinctive stink in the air. Not like a farm, though — farms (and racetracks) had enough open land, green grass, and fresh air that earthy and pungent smells of animals and their leavings were somewhat diluted. Most big cities smelled *much* worse, owing to their fetid hash of industrial odors and smoke along with mounds of horse manure adorning every street. We curled our noses in futile self-defense.

Hub identified the slaughterhouse building where he'd seen the trio of plug-uglies drag Charley inside. We parked down the street, and Jake and me debated our best approach — stealth, or guns drawn? When I reminded him I didn't even have a gun, Jake argued we had no idea who might be inside, and he wasn't wrong. So we compromised. Hub stayed with the carriage and horses. Alberto, me, and Jake and his revolver snuck up to the building.

Alberto boosted me up so I could reconnoiter through a transom window. It looked empty inside, except for one pudgy little man in a crumpled fisherman's cap waddling toward the door we were about to enter. Instead, we hid on either side and waited for him to come out. Jake decked him with one punch. Alberto slung the dazed man over his shoulder and carried him back inside.

When he came to, he found himself securely tied hand and foot, and hanging from a meat hook by a rope. He sized us up with a shrug, like he was accustomed to ending up this way.

"You work for Van Brunt," Jake said.

The man on the hook shrugged again.

"You got a name?" Jake asked.

"Dirty Ray Craven."

"Well, Ray —" I began.

He cheerfully cut me off. "No, buster, that's *Dirty* Ray."

"You seem right proud of that."

"I am. Been workin' at this since I was born'd. Gawd, if we wasn't in a slaughterhouse painted with pig guts, you'd smell me for sure."

Jake took a cautious sniff. "When's the last time you had a bath?"

"Does walkin' in the rain count? I was out in a real goose-drownder the other day."

"Okay, *Dirty* Ray," I said. "Three of your buddies dragged a little black fella in here this morning."

Ray's face scrunched in thought. "Oh, you mean that bidness wit' Charley Fly, that li'l colored jockey?"

"Yeah. Where is he?"

"Gone."

"Gone *where*?" Jake demanded.

"Don't know. Wouldn't say if I did."

"For a man hanging on a meat hook," Jake said, "you don't seem overly concerned about your immediate future."

"Y'all don't look like killers. So I figger I'll walk outta here when all's said an' done."

We stepped away to confer. "He's right," I said. "We're not exactly menacing."

"If he doesn't think we're gonna inflict pain and suffering," Jake said, "he ain't likely to tell us anything. And we don't have all day."

"Any suggestions?"

"Sure," Jake said. "We could lay a beating on him."

"Any *better* suggestions?"

Preoccupied Alberto glanced around the room. "What if we make him *think* he gonna get pain and suffering?"

"How?" I asked.

Alberto's eyes glowed with excitement. "I'm-a gonna saw him in half!"

"But that's just a trick," Jake said. "Right?"

"Ahh, to us, is a trick. To him, is-a gonna seem real."

In the absence of more promising options,

we agreed it was worth a try.

"Hey," Dirty Ray said, "what're you boys hatchin'?"

"You'll see," Jake said, "assuming you don't mind hangin' around for a spell."

Ray glanced up at the meat hook suspending him above the stained floor. "I reckon I'll be where ya left me."

Alberto told us what he needed, and we split up and scoured the deserted slaughterhouse, adjacent shed, and office. During our scavenger hunt, I found Charley Fly's hat and coat hanging on a hook. When I grabbed them, a handmade tin box about the size and shape of a deck of cards fell from the coat. I had no idea what it was, so I slipped it into my pocket, in case we succeeded in finding him.

Before long, we'd returned with a couple of hammers, a box of nails, and a sharp butcher's saw. Alberto carried a wooden shipping crate, shaped like a child's coffin, about two feet deep and wide, five feet end to end, complete with a lid.

The magician set the crate down on a work table and grinned at Dirty Ray. "How you like to help Alberto to do a magical trick?"

Ray squinted with uneasy suspicion. "Whut kinda trick?"

"Sawing a man in half!" Jake said with a demented laugh.

Ray's eyes bugged out. "You mean sawin' *me* in half? No, no! I would *not* like to help!"

Alberto lifted Ray off the meat hook, carried him over and laid him on his back inside the crate. As Alberto held the lid down, Jake and me nailed it shut, leaving enough of an opening for Ray's head to stick up at one end.

"How do I know you know what you're doing? How many times you done this trick?"

"Oh, lotsa times," Alberto assured him. "Sometimes she work, sometimes she no work."

"Wh-whut happens when she no works?"

"Little blood. Lotta screaming," Alberto said with plainspoken sincerity. "Or maybe other way around. Now, is important, make-a sure you hold *verrry* still."

Then he commenced his deliberate sawing through the top of the crate, right over Dirty Ray's bellybutton. One *looooong* stroke at a time, followed by a pause so Ray could ponder the irony of being butchered in a slaughterhouse. As the saw chewed through the soft pine box, inch by inch, Ray's terror grew, and I thought for sure he'd start spilling his secrets.

But it wasn't until he felt saw teeth grab at his clothing that he screeched, "Stop! For Gawd's sake, stop!!"

Jake leaned over him. "Something you'd like to share?"

"Jeezus — I nearly took a heart attack!" wild-eyed Ray said. "Give a man a minute to collect hisself."

"Time's up. Alberto?"

The magician tightened his grip on the saw handle, ready to resume cutting.

"Wait! Wait — it's comin' back to me," Ray said. "Like it was jes' yesterday."

"It was *today*," Jake snapped.

"It was Schnetter! Yeah — Schnetter and Poke! They took that li'l colored fella over t' the railroad freight yard."

"Why?" Jake said.

"To ship him out of Bawl'mer on a train."

"Ship him where?"

"Do I look smort enough to know every tiny detail?"

I nodded to Alberto. "Keep sawing."

Half a saw stroke later, Ray squealed, "Okay. *Okay!*"

Jake loomed above Ray's face: *"Where?"*

"Richmond, Virginny," Ray whimpered.

Jake patted Ray's cheek. "You were right about us not being killers."

Leaving him boxed up, we headed for the door. "So long, Dirty Ray," I said with a wave.

"Hey — I'm still encoffinated here! How'm I supposed to excape?!"

"Keep hollering," Jake said. "Somebody'll find you — sooner or later."

We ran across the street to Hub and the carriage. Alberto and Jake climbed aboard and I got on my horse.

"Where to?" Hub asked.

"Railroad freight depot!" Jake said.

Hub shook the reins, and we took off.

40

"Better a live chicken than a dead idiot."
~ Jamey Galloway

Instead of graceful Camden Station, where we'd first arrived aboard Emmaline's private rail coach, we raced to the Mount Clare freight yards, a mile west of the passenger depot and cheek by hog jowl with Pigtown.

Mount Clare Station took its name from the estate owned by descendants of Maryland's founding Carroll Family, who gave a ten-acre section of their plantation to the fledgling Baltimore & Ohio Railroad in 1828.

Over the next decades, Mount Clare evolved into the industrial heart of the B & O, encompassing foundries and factories, iron works, machine shops, and roundhouses. Over a thousand men worked on constructing new locomotives, and freight and passenger cars; maintaining machinery;

even manufacturing bridge components — nearly everything related to building and running the B & O, right down to forging new rails. The facility's mainline tracks split off into a half-dozen spurs leading to various structures and yards.

With all that activity, nobody had taken any notice of Van Brunt's squat pair of henchmen named Schnetter and Poke hauling bound-and-gagged Charley Fly down a spur to a train made up of engine and tender, five boxcars, and caboose. The moaning steam whistle and smoke belching from the locomotive's chimney signaled it was about to leave for Richmond.

Charley continued thrashing. Bearded Schnetter threatened to knock him over the head again if he didn't stop. "You're goin' where you're goin', so settle down and enjoy the ride."

They came alongside the middle boxcar with its door halfway open. "This'll do," said baldheaded Poke. He set Charley's tied feet down on the ground so he could slide the door open the rest of the way.

Charley caught Schnetter off-guard, jerked free and tried to hop away. Schnetter stuck out his foot. Charley tripped and fell on his face. The two men heaved him into the boxcar, then clambered up after him to get him situated. Other than some hay, the car was empty. Schnetter propped Charley up with his back against a bale. "Now, don't you look all comfy."

Charley tried to speak. "Hmmph ymmph!"

Poke obliged him by pulling the gag down. "Why're y'all doin' this to me?"

"This here's yer reward for bitin' the hand that feeds ya," said Schnetter.

"I don't owe Van Brunt a damn thing. I already won him enough money for two lifetimes!"

"You may not be no slave no more," Poke said, "but the Boss still owns ya."

"*Nobody* owns me. Where you sendin' me?"

"Down south," Poke said, "where somebody'll find ya and reckon you's just another darky hobo."

"You goddam —"

Schnetter whacked Charley across the head and replaced the gag, cutting off his last angry words. "Yer lucky, boy. In the olden days, instead of findin' you first-class transportation, all we needed was a rope and a tree."

"Bone *voy*-age, Charley," Poke said. He and Schnetter jumped out and rolled the door shut behind them. They left Charley

Fly to his fate in near darkness, with only a few shafts of light peeking through gaps in the boxcar's wooden walls.

We pulled up in front of the two-story red brick station on the corner of Pratt and Poppleton Streets. I hopped off my horse, ran inside, and interrupted a trio of clerks concentrating on their freight scales and bills of lading spread across their desks. "Freight train to Richmond! What time, which track?"

The oldest clerk said, "Track Two, time — now."

I ran out, jumped back on the horse and led the carriage through the busy freight yard. The tracks were marked with numbered signs — and the train on Track Two was just pulling out. Lucky for us, locomotives lumbered off the starting line.

We didn't know for sure if Charley Fly was even on that train. And we didn't know how far Hub in the carriage would be able to give chase along the right-of-way next to the tracks. But we had no time to think, we had to act — *right now.*

Last boxcar before the caboose, the big side door yawned open. I stopped my horse, jumped down, and tied his reins to the carriage. "Jake, Alberto — let's go! Hub, follow as far as you can — then wait for us!"

I grabbed the long rope coiled on my saddle, and we took off running.

The caboose passed us.

But the train hadn't yet picked up speed, so we were able to sprint and catch up. As we drew even with that open boxcar door, we grabbed hold, hauled ourselves up on the sill and rolled inside. A minute later, or a step slower, we'd have missed our chance altogether. We'd accomplished magical miracle number one — getting onto the train.

Hearts pounding, we sat on the rough floorboards and leaned against some wooden shipping crates. "Now what?" said Jake.

I tried to catch my breath. "We . . . search . . . boxcars."

"We also gotta stop the train," Jake panted, "or *we* might end up in Richmond."

On our hands and knees, we three crept to the open doorway and peered along the side of the boxcar. The ladder to the roof was located at the rear of the car, and it was impossible to reach from the door. That problem with no apparent solution meant we couldn't stop the train *or* search for Charley.

"Which is more important?" Jake asked.

"Stopping the train," I said without hesitation.

The only way to get to the locomotive, or any of the other boxcars, was by scuttling across the top of a moving train, leaping from one car to the next. And only Alberto had the circus-daredevil skills to even attempt it. He stood up. "I go to stop the train."

Before we could object, he took my coiled rope, tied a slip-knot lasso loop at one end, and draped it over his neck and shoulder. Lying down on his stomach, he stuck his feet out the door, and lowered himself from the sill. The second the soles of his boots skimmed the gravel, he started running. He lost ground with every stride — but that was his intention.

Could he make it? His timing had to be perfect. He wouldn't get a second chance.

I was almost too scared to watch.

What felt like forever was a matter of seconds. As the ladder came even with Alberto's shoulder, he jump-twisted in midair — and grabbed a ladder rung with one hand, an instant before it would have sped beyond his reach. He swung himself up, like the trapeze artist he'd once been. He secured footing and grip on the ladder, and climbed to the top of the boxcar.

I marveled at our second magical miracle. "How does he do that? I could never do that."

"Oh, I bet I could," Jake said, sounding both serious and delusional, "with a little practice."

I stared at him. "Not if you practiced for a million years."

We heard Alberto's bootsteps crossing the roof of our swaying and bumping boxcar. And then he was gone. All we could do was pray he'd get to the cab without getting himself killed.

"So we just sit here," Jake said, "while he's riskin' his neck?"

"Yup."

"No, really — I can make it to the next boxcar."

My brother had an undeniable talent for denying reality. He crouched and leaned out the door, looking fore and aft. Boxcars had no handrails or ledges on their sides, no doors end-to-end like passenger coaches. Yet Jake still believed he could duplicate Alberto's feat — jump down, climb the ladder, and run across the top of our car to the next boxcar.

"You're nuts," I said.

"And you're chicken."

"Better a live chicken than a dead idiot."

"I'm gonna try this."

Several deadly hazards should've been obvious, but I felt obligated to point them out to my oblivious brother. "Okay, let's say, by the grace o' God, you manage to reach that ladder without falling, breaking all your limbs, or getting run over. How're you gonna get into the next boxcar, smart guy?"

Jake puzzled it out. "Hold onto the edge of the roof . . . and swing down through the side door."

"What if the door's closed?"

"Well, then . . . drop down through the roof hatch."

"What if there is no hatch? Or it's also closed?" Like the one in our boxcar, as my upward glance made clear.

With a sulky grunt, he plunked himself down on the floor next to me. "I still think I coulda made it."

"Have I told you lately you're an idiot?"

"Slack-jawed, or regular?"

"Either."

"Maybe. I wasn't really paying attention."

"Then I'm reminding you, no extra charge."

We fell silent for a few minutes and watched the countryside speed by.

"Alberto's gonna make it to the locomotive," Jake said, though with less blithe conviction than usual. "You think he'll make it?"

"Yeah. Sure." Truthfully, all I could picture was Alberto falling off a boxcar. Maybe that already happened. Maybe he was already dead.

"But . . . what if he doesn't make it?"

"Jake, you just said he'll make it."

"I know, but . . . what if he doesn't?"

"He *will.*"

"But if he *doesn't* . . ."

"Then we got a long ride to Richmond."

I wondered, though: Assuming he didn't fall off and die, how long should it take for Alberto to reach the locomotive, anyway? We got our answer when the train suddenly braked, pitching us ass over teakettle. We hugged the boxcar floor as the train eventually came to a jerky stop.

"Heh-heh! I told you he'd make it," Jake said with an exuberant clap of his hands.

Magical miracle number three.

We jumped down and ran toward the front of the train. Alberto leaned out the locomotive cab and waved to us: *"Tutto bene!"*

The engineer and fireman stood together, back to back, the rope coiled tight around their chests and arms. Alberto must've surprised them from the tender, lassoed the both of 'em, and used his lickety-split rope-trick skills to tie 'em up before they could even think of putting up a fight.

Jake and me commenced searching the train, and soon found Charley in the middle boxcar, still bound and gagged. I wasn't sure who was more relieved, us or him. We cut him loose, helped him out, and walked up to the locomotive.

As Alberto untied the engineer and fireman, I apologized for waylaying their train. I gave them an abbreviated explanation — and it turned out they were horse racing fans and knew of Champagne Charley's exploits on that other kind of track. They had no hard feelings, and wished us luck. With three lusty hoots of the locomotive's steam whistle, they resumed their run to Richmond.

On our hike back toward Mount Clare Station, we told Charley all about the rescue. In a mile or so, we found Hub Robinson waiting for us alongside the tracks with the carriage and horses.

I checked my watch — it was a bit after two o'clock. The race would be at three-thirty.

"Get me there in time," Charley said. "I got a score to settle."

I'm not sure I'd have bet on us, but we

had an outside chance. We climbed aboard the carriage, with Jake and Hub up front, and Charley, Alberto, and me in the back seat. Jake shook the reins and we trotted for Pimlico. I felt bad for the horse pulling us all that way.

I gave Charley his hat and suit coat I'd found at the slaughterhouse. First thing, he checked the inside coat pocket and reacted with alarm when something he expected to find was missing. So I took that little dented metal box out of my pocket and handed it to him. "Looking for this?"

Charley clutched it to his heart. "Oh! Thankya, Jesus!"

"What is it?"

"Tin wallet my daddy made for me when I was a slave, and Pryce started lettin' me keep some of my winnings."

Jake glanced over his shoulder. "You still keep money in it?"

"Nope." Charley slid the lid open and took out a folded two-page document, dated May 15, 1860. "Freedom papers."

"I thought Van Brunt freed you after he won you from Pryce," I said.

"He did. But I wanted to make it all official. Goin' about my business, if anybody doubted I was free, I'd have proof."

"But you don't need that anymore," Jake said.

"Don't matter. I'll keep this on me 'til my dyin' day." Charley leaned forward. "Mr. Robinson, I hear I got you to thank for me not bein' halfway to Richmond by now. I thought you hated me."

"Hate's a strong word," Hub said, without looking back.

I couldn't help noticing they both spoke in voices stripped of passion, at odds with the burdens of anger, fear, and bitterness they each must've carried for so many years.

"You think I had it easy," Charley said.

"You did."

"Not like you think. Not every slave jockey stayed small. Most had the poor luck to get bigger."

"They still didn't have to spend all their days picking crops."

"Maybe not. But y'know what their 'massahs' did to 'em? First they'd starve the weight off 'em. If that didn't work, they'd bury 'em up to their necks in horse manure, under the bakin' sun, to sweat it off."

"When I escaped," Hub said, "I got to Philadelphia, where they weren't hunting so much for contrabands like me. I always reckoned I'd sneak back and help my family escape, but I couldn't figure out how.

Started working in a factory . . . hated myself for being free."

"Why?" Charley asked in disbelief.

"Because nobody's free 'til everybody's free. So I joined the Union army, so I could fight — and maybe hear some news on where my kin were at."

"Did you?" Charley asked.

"Nope. I tried finding 'em after the war, put advertisements in the papers in Richmond and Washington and Baltimore. Never heard a word. Some nights, I still dream I'm waiting to meet 'em at the station. But their train . . . never comes."

This was personal between Charley and Hub. We couldn't help listening, but it wasn't our place to speak — not while two proud black men who'd endured unimaginable cruelty revealed scars branded into their souls by their white masters.

Charley shared the story of how he got his freedom. "In early '60, I rode a race where Pryce and Van Brunt had a five-thousand-dollar bet between 'em. Family feud goin' back years. I'm on Pryce's best horse, and he stumbles in the last turn."

Hub looked back at Charley for the first time. "You lost?"

"Couldn't catch up. So I jump off, and Pryce starts beatin' me with his cane. Van

Brunt stops him, hollerin' how I'm just a kid. Pryce don't have the cash to cover the bet, Van Brunt says he'll take *me* as payment, so I go back to Maryland with him. He never owned slaves, hated slavery. So he frees me, and I go to work for him, ridin' and trainin'. But I still felt like a slave for years. It's all I knew."

"Sometimes I still look over my shoulder," Hub said, "thinking I saw slave-catchers following me."

"Even after I got freed, wasn't a day I didn't think I might still be hanged as a runaway, or sold back into slavery someplace they never heard of Champagne Charley Fly."

"I've had nightmares ever since about the whipping post near the slave cabins, on every plantation," Hub said. "I must've been five the first time I saw slaves tied up and beaten for the smallest sins — for nothing."

"Pryce had the same whippin' post."

"But I'm betting you were never tied to it."

"I wasn't. But when I was just startin' to race? Every day, for months, that white stable boss would order me to lay down in an empty stall, and flog me with a horse whip, just so I'd remember he's God. I was scared how much worse it'd be if I didn't keep winnin'."

After that, Hub and Charley rode in silence for a spell, leaving me to wonder: Could living free for the rest of their lives ever make up for even a *single day* of enslavement? I could see how hard it was for Hub to let go of his belief that Charley had it easy by comparison — and just as hard for Charley to shed his guilt over knowing Hub wasn't entirely wrong.

Then Charley told about the wagon wheel. "It was one freezin' Christmas, there was a mama and daddy, been teachin' their kids to read the Bible, in secret."

Hub reminded us that slaves were forbidden to learn reading and writing — "so we wouldn't get all uppish. As if words on paper would show us something we didn't see every day with our own eyes."

"But they got caught," Charley continued. "Overseer ordered the daddy tied spread-eagle to a wagon wheel, everybody watchin'. Then they made him lick the metal rim of the wheel. His tongue froze right to it, which all the white folks found real funny, 'til they left for their Christmas feast. Poor fella had to rip away part of his tongue to get free."

"But that never happened to you," Hub said.

"I can't say I didn't have it better than most, just 'cuz God kept me scrawny."

"Still . . . that don't mean you weren't scared," Hub allowed, his fierce righteousness yielding a little. "If I was you? Maybe I'd've done likewise, ride those horses as fast and as long as I could."

"Ain't nothin' I can do to make up for . . . not sufferin' more," Charley said. "But I *can* help you arabbers take care of your horses."

Charley offered his hand over the seat, and kept it there for the time it took Hub to reach back and shake it.

"Ain't nobody free 'til everybody's free," Charley said.

"Amen."

They both looked as if they'd stumbled onto some magical means of lifting a wicked hex. Maybe they could banish age-old demons, and see a peaceable light illuminating a new path to a long-hidden patch of consecrated common ground.

Their recollections not only reminded me of the evils of slavery, but also the long and continuing war dedicated to obliterating most of the Indians, and penning up the rest on barren reservations. I felt haunted by the blood on the hands of so many fortunate white men, who had forged a golden nation "conceived in liberty," as Lincoln said, yet always falling short of its gospel promise.

Now, as to the oft-made claim that white folks had also bestowed kindnesses upon blacks and Indians, well, I can agree up to a point, since I'd personally witnessed such acts of grace. But they were a paltry few when compared to numberless atrocities, creating what I feared to be an eternally unredeemable imbalance in the eyes of God.

As one of many slaveholding Founding Fathers, Thomas Jefferson was certainly aware of the contradictory sin as he lived it, yet did not free most of his slaves even at his death. Jefferson must have believed that the Almighty was keeping score, and dreaded the inevitable reckoning when he wrote: "Indeed I tremble for my country when I reflect that God is just: that his justice cannot sleep for ever."

Was the Civil War that squaring of accounts in the Lord's ledger which Jefferson expected to happen someday? Or is there another, even dearer payment still to come due? As dumb kids eager for adventure, me and Jake had served briefly as Texan Johnny Rebs. And though we weren't ignorant of the malevolent Confederate cause — the perpetuation of slavery — we never subscribed to Southern grievances that unleashed so much carnage. Still, I will go to my grave bearing my own indelible shame for having participated at all.

Hub gave Charley a sly glance over his shoulder. "You know what I *really* got against you? You dressing so fancy all the time and putting on airs."

"That's so these white boys don't think they're better'n us."

"That didn't keep Van Brunt's white boys from kidnapping you."

"Ain't that a fact."

As relieved as I was to hear Charley and Hub joking with each other, I knew in my bones that nothing could erase the tragic truth that linked them. For all time, their kith and kin would ask a question mine would never have to ponder: *Who once owned my family?*

41

"It's whether you win or lose, *not* how you play the game."
~ Cortland Van Brunt III

Meanwhile, at Pimlico, Eddie, Victoria, and Rafael did their best to keep Lucifer calm yet ready to run. But their perceptive horse sensed the tensions between Eddie and Vic, what with her bum shoulder and arm in a sling. Horatio Deale and his notebook continued to chronicle the story.

In case there weren't enough jitters already, Van Brunt drove up in his fancy buggy to savor the dire straits of his adversaries. "Closing in on three o'clock and you appear to be missing your jockey at the present time, which is no surprise. It took him years to betray me, but he seems to have buggered you faster than you can say Jack Robinson."

"Whatever happened to Charley Fly," Vic

said, "we know it's your doing."

Van Brunt clucked his tongue. "Remember, no jockey, no race, and you forfeit that feisty Arabian to me. On the bright side, your return trip west will be that much easier without a horse to worry about." He tipped his straw hat, and drove away.

"That's it," Vic said. "I'll ride with the reins in my teeth if I have to."

"Let me ride," Rafael begged.

"Great," Eddie said. "We got us a one-armed cripple girl, or a jockey the horse won't walk for, let alone run."

"My horse, my decision," Vic said, "and *I'm* riding him. Eddie, get him saddled. Raf, help the cripple girl get dressed."

They didn't know how to stop her, short of tying her up. Rafael looked to Eddie for guidance, but all Eddie had to offer was a defeated shrug. Vic steered Raf into the barn. When they came out a few minutes later, she wore the green and white silk shirt and cap of Fernando Farms — just as our carriage pulled up.

Eddie, Vic, and Raf stared, dumbstruck.

"Hey, why're you wearin' my silks?" Charley joked as he hopped down. "How 'bout we give Mr. Van Brunt the beating he deserves."

It was three-fifteen — fifteen minutes to

post time, when Cortland Van Brunt III would get his second nasty surprise of the day.

Charley dressed in a hurry and Eddie boosted him into the saddle as we heard Pimlico's bugler blare out the Call to the Post. Led by Vic and Eddie, Lucifer made three halfhearted attempts to buck Charley off on their way to the track. Charley leaned forward and whispered to the horse, which ended the bucking. But Lucifer still looked jumpy, ears swiveling every which way as he scuffed onto Pimlico's rich brown loam.

That's when Van Brunt saw Charley Fly in the last place he expected him to be — on Lucifer's back. Van Brunt's jaw clamped down on his pipe. Charley saluted his former boss with an extended middle finger.

Victoria walked next to Lucifer, but for once the sound of her voice failed to settle him down. Even the buzz of anticipation from a smaller Tuesday crowd only half-filling the grandstand rattled him.

By contrast, Van Brunt's Grand Larceny swaggered out. His young black jockey sat proud, and the big chip on the kid's shoulder was tough to miss. Aries high-stepped just behind, the picture of equine poise, although his older, pointy-nosed white jockey looked edgy enough for the both of 'em.

Charley sat serene but determined. No smile, though, no gold tooth glinting in the sun. He and Lucifer were underdogs, and Charley wasn't used to that.

"What do you know about Van Brunt's jockeys?" I asked him.

He nodded toward Grand Larceny. "That's Willie Epps. Kid's nineteen, been Van Brunt's second rider the past coupla years. He's good, but thinks he's great. Thinks my always ridin' Van Brunt's best horse was holdin' him back."

"And now that he's on Grand Larceny, he wants to prove himself —"

"— and prove I'm over the hill."

"How 'bout Aries?"

"Richard Sharp, his regular jockey. He's a Limey, been around a long time, knows how to ride — and how to cheat. He likes folks to call him King Richard. But watch this." Charley called out: "Hey, Li'l Dickie!"

Sharp's head twitched, but he resisted looking.

"Yeah, you, Li'l Dickie — you ready to lose today?"

That time, Sharp turned and glared. Then he goosed Aries out ahead of the procession.

Charley chuckled. "Anybody calls himself King Richard, I like to git under his skin. He hates me, and I ain't too fond of him. But I do respect his skill."

"So, Larceny's the better horse, but Sharp's the better rider?"

"Yup. Facing either one of 'em, we win easy. Up against both? They'll do anything to beat me. I expect to use that to my advantage."

The horses finished their promenade in front of the stands and their attendants left the track. Eddie tugged Vic away and we joined Rafael and Alberto in Lucifer's cheering section in the lower grandstand, even with the finish line. We were all too nervous to sit, as were Van Brunt's courtiers occupying a nearby section.

Mississippi Mike arrived with a surprise guest — Madame Aurora Killegrew. Then I heard Emmaline Rose's musical voice call out, "Jamey, darlin'!" I waved and she rushed up to join us. "I bet big on Lucifer," she said with a saucy smile.

Down on the track, brash Willie Epps on Grand Larceny taunted Charley. "Hey, ol' man! You ready to get Chicagoed out there?"

"Then everybody gonna know you're better than I ever was," Charley said. "Van Brunt never gave you the chance, always puttin' me on better horses."

"Damn right! Lookit the nag you ridin' now."

"He ain't even a Thoroughbred. Today's your big chance to prove you the new champ."

"And you the new *chump.* Charley the Chump! Nobody gonna keep Willie Epps down after today, ol' man." Willie and Grand Larceny trotted ahead.

Horatio Deale stood near us, watching and scribbling. This was the first time I'd noticed he liked to dictate his notes to himself, mumbling out loud: "Race Day. Three horses, twenty furlongs. Two favorites — bay Grand Larceny, chestnut Aries — both owned by Van Brunt. Third horse Lucifer — white Arabian, *not* Thoroughbred. Spirited steed, unknown ability. *White horse is truly the dark horse.* Bad blood between Van Brunt and Eddie Lobo makes race the *real Baltimore Brawl.* Speed favors well-rested Grand Larceny. Arabians notable for endurance — will distance favor Lucifer?"

Van Brunt had surely ordered Sharp and Epps to abide by a rigid strategy. Any vengeful agendas the jockeys harbored were nullified by their boss's goal — beating Charley Fly and going home with Lucifer. For all his skill and savvy, Charley would be riding a touchy horse with no true racing experience, for the first time and without so much as a single practice lap, against not one but two implacable opponents.

But Charley heard from Vic that, given a long enough race, Lucifer was capable of outrunning Thoroughbred champ Phoenix — and Phoenix had already beaten both Grand Larceny and Aries. Charley would be counting on Lucifer's inherent Arabian durability over the full distance.

We had several pairs of leather and brass field glasses for our group to pass around. Out on the backstretch, far side of the course, the starter struggled to get the horses lined up — Lucifer on the outside, Aries in the middle and Grand Larceny on the rail. Only Lucifer stood still at the starting line. But did that mean he was calm — or that he'd refuse to run at all? We were about to find out.

Both Grand Larceny and formerly poised Aries fussed and wheeled. Sharp managed to coax his fidgety horse into position, but the starter ordered young Willie Epps to take Grand Larceny back up the track and walk him to the line. The moment he drew even with the other horses, the starter waved his flag and shouted, "Go!"

Spectators rumbled with excitement as Grand Larceny jumped out ahead. Aries reared up, nearly throwing Sharp. Then Lucifer bucked and Charley's left foot slipped from the stirrup. Sharp seized the advantage and muscled Aries forward, leaving Lucifer behind.

But I saw through my field glasses how calmly Charley slipped his foot back into the stirrup, and got his horse moving at a measured pace. The crowd didn't know what to think as Lucifer trailed into the far turn, already ten lengths back.

Up ahead, Aries flew like a bullet, trying to catch Grand Larceny, both running hard — maybe too fast, too early. Despite Lucifer's terrible start, Vic and Eddie watched and timed quarter-mile fractions. Aries and Grand Larceny were competing with each other — which they shouldn't have been, according to any sensible strategy.

As they galloped past the grandstand, Van Brunt's entourage whooped it up, thinking Charley's blunder would cost him the race. But Van Brunt knew the "lost stirrup" was an old trick Charley used every so often to fool rivals into believing they were home free.

Completing their first lap on the backstretch, Aries took the lead. But Willie Epps on Grand Larceny refused to allow Aries to pull away. Both jittery jockeys kept glancing at each other, and back over their shoulders at Lucifer trailing them by seven lengths.

Charley perched over his saddle, rocking with his horse's smooth gallop, sending unruffled signals through the reins. The race played out before him, as if he could see it clear through to the finish. He kept his horse tight to the rail.

"What do you think?" Vic said to Eddie.

"I figured Aries'd be the rabbit. He just ran hard the other day, so he was never gonna go all-out the whole distance."

"But I bet they wanted him to draw Lucifer into a chase, and wear him down," Vic said.

"Leaving Grand Larceny to stay fresh, and come from behind."

Vic nodded. "Which is how he likes to race anyway."

But that wasn't how Van Brunt's horses were running, and his face grew redder with their every reckless stride. He stomped down to the grandstand's front railing, bellowing at his jockeys as they blazed past for the second time: "*Goddammit* — stick to the plan!"

Vic checked her stopwatch. "Brutal pace for twelve furlongs."

One mile to go. If the distance was going to work in Lucifer's favor, he was running out of time.

Emmaline squeezed my hand. "Why isn't Charley catching up?"

"Because he's banking on Lucifer's stamina." Or so we hoped.

The horses thundered into the backstretch. Van Brunt's runaway jockeys tried to salvage the strategy they'd ignored for the first mile and a half. Aries tired and Grand Larceny passed him. But the stopwatches told the tale — both were running out of steam, and the last mile unfolded just this way:

Charley eases his hands forward. Lucifer takes his cue and closes the gap. Seven lengths behind Grand Larceny — then six — now five. Still on the inside, still running third.

Lucifer comes up a neck behind Aries.

Dickie Sharp swerves Aries and sideswipes Lucifer into the rail.

The white Arabian stumbles — and recovers his stride.

But the collision drops Lucifer two lengths behind Aries. And Charley receives Sharp's clear message: *Break for the lead at your peril.*

Charley Fly has no choice. Still on the

inside, he makes his move.

Sharp and Aries crash Lucifer into the rail again.

Charley loses a stirrup for real, and almost tumbles from the saddle.

Lucifer instinctively tries to thread the needle and escape from trouble.

Charley regains balance and control — and holds his horse back. He knows for certain how dirty Sharp is willing to be — and knows Van Brunt's Jockey Club cronies will never call such blatant interference as a disqualifying foul.

As Charley keeps his horse in check, Lucifer flashes a mean glare back at his rider. But seconds later, horse and jockey meld into one formidable force. Lucifer seems to understand that his rider's quick thinking saved them from disaster. Charley feels his horse relax, and knows Lucifer will do whatever is asked of him.

But Grand Larceny holds a commanding eight-length lead. Doubting his good fortune, Willie Epps looks back to see if either horse is gaining. Even though he and Sharp have butchered Van Brunt's precious plans, Grand Larceny is where they wanted him to be — in the lead and heading for an easy win.

Charley and Lucifer gain on Aries. Sharp

knows he's only ahead by a nose. He flogs the fading Aries so he can throw another block if Lucifer tries to sneak past on the inside again.

The horses barrel into their last half mile. It's still Grand Larceny by a commanding seven lengths, but the big bay is tiring. Epps needs Dickie Sharp and Aries to keep Lucifer hemmed against the rail.

Grand Larceny's lead shrivels — six lengths . . . five . . . now four.

Exhausted Aries clings to second place. Charley can hear Aries' ragged breathing, and fears the horse's heart might burst before the finish line.

Lucifer runs with ease. The tide has turned in his favor — but is it too late?

The horses sweep into the final turn. On the outside, it's Grand Larceny by two lengths. To Charley's surprise, Aries drifts back to third on the outside, even with Lucifer's right flank.

Still on the inside, Lucifer closes on Grand Larceny — just a half-length behind.

Nip and tuck, into the homestretch, a thousand fleeting feet from the finish line . . .

Willie Epps shouts back to Sharp: "Now!"

With Grand Larceny barely in front and Aries just behind, Charley's instincts tell him they're about to pin the upstart challenger to the rail. Lucifer will be boxed in with no escape.

Charley goes to his whip for the first time. The Arabian surges — *to the outside.* Through the narrowest of openings, they abandon the rail and catch the competition leaning the wrong way.

An instant too late, Sharp swerves Aries inside to bash into a horse that's no longer there.

At the exact same moment, Epps makes the exact same mistake — he veers Grand Larceny toward the rail to block Lucifer — realizing too late he's already been fooled.

The big white Arabian streaks past on the outside.

Grand Larceny caroms off the rail and loses ground.

Lucifer leaves his fading rivals in the literal dust. Eddie's jaw drops in astonishment: "*No* horse can do that."

Vic smiles. "Mine can."

Lucifer extends his lead with every stride. Three lengths, then five . . . seven . . . ten!

The grandstand throngs are on their feet and roaring.

But all Charley Fly hears and feels are the perfect percussion of Lucifer's hoofbeats and deep, steady breathing.

Aries and Grand Larceny flounder home like they're slogging through mud.

Lucifer rockets down the homestretch like he's soaring over the wide-open Texas prairie where Victoria raised him to run. He and Champagne Charley Fly win by an astonishing twenty lengths. And Lucifer keeps right on running, not because of pride, or promise of rewards, riches or recognition — but for the pure joy of it . . .

"That's no mortal horse," Horatio Deale declared. "That's a supernatural machine!"

The crowd's cheering and stomping shook Pimlico's grandstand from floorboards to rafters. Our jubilant little gang hugged and danced. Emmaline kissed me on the cheek. Victoria threw her arms around Eddie's neck, kissed him smack on the lips, then did the same to Jake.

Van Brunt's humiliated horses wobbled across the finish line. Jockeys Epps and Sharp hung their heads and slouched in their saddles. Even cheating, they still couldn't win.

We rushed down to the track and surrounded triumphant Charley and Lucifer as they circled back from their victory romp up and down the stretch. Charley couldn't stop grinning. "That is the most fun I have *ever* had ridin' a horse!"

Eddie reached up and shook his hand. "You look like you've been ridin' him for years."

"Like I said, Lucifer and me, we got ourselves an understanding."

Two seconds later, Lucifer bucked him off. Charley landed flat on his back in the dirt. The horse lowered his head and snorted. It sounded an awful lot like laughing.

"An 'understanding' — uh-huh," Vic said, trying not to snicker.

"How 'bout we just call that an unscheduled dismount," Charley said from the ground.

Vic laughed as she grabbed Lucifer's reins. "Consider that your initiation."

Rafael helped Charley to his feet. "Lucifer, he likes to have the last word."

We euphoric winners and Van Brunt's morose losers crossed paths in the paddock. And, yes, it did our hearts good to hear Van Brunt swearing at his jockeys, vowing they'd *never* ride *anywhere* on Earth *ever* again, before he turned away in disgust.

Eddie spoke up with new authority, his voice matching his size. "Mr. Van Brunt. We'll take Phoenix now."

Van Brunt fluffed his feathers like a vanquished gamecock trying to salvage a shred of dignity. "Yes, yes, of course." He cleared his throat, signaling an impending pronouncement. "But I could make a rematch next spring worth your while. You still need money to bring your dreams to what we'd call fruition, and you can look that up. And to sweeten the pot — how would you like a chance to steal both Grand Larceny *and* Aries away from me?"

"Knowing you're that desperate to keep Phoenix," Vic said, "and knowing we're taking him home is good enough for us."

Van Brunt's eyebrows arched. "Does the gentler sex speak for you, Eddie?"

"Yup," Eddie said without hesitation, smart enough to know where he stood.

With a grouchy grumble, Van Brunt summoned a groom and told him to fetch Phoenix.

"We'll save you the trouble," Vic said, "and go get him ourselves."

And that's exactly what we did. The groom led Phoenix out to us, and when the palomino champ saw his human friends and Lucifer, he yanked the lead rope out of the groom's hands, and danced a few hoppity-skippity steps over to us. The two equine *amigos* bumped noses in gentle greeting, and entwined their necks in a happy horse hug. Eddie picked up Phoenix's rope. "You boys ready to go home?"

Side by side, they both nickered and swished their tails, leading our parade to the barn. We didn't have to look back to know Cortland Van Brunt III was probably madder than the wettest of hens, or a puffed toad, or any other critters commonly cited for pitching fits.

But he surprised us when he called out with a laugh, "Remember this, my friends: It's whether you win or lose, *not* how you play the game. Today, you won. Next time? Who knows?"

Which brought to mind words of wisdom from Shakespeare's *Henry VIII:* "Heat not a furnace for your foe so hot that it do singe yourself."

Or, to borrow from the Bard of Avon's *Richard III,* we could be forgiven for taking satisfaction in knowing this would be the winter of Van Brunt's discontent.

42

> "What, sir, would the people of the earth be without woman? They would be scarce, sir, almighty scarce."
> ~ Mark Twain

That evening, Mississippi Mike treated the entire extended gang — Eddie, Victoria, Rafael, Alberto, Jake, me, Emmaline, Madame Killegrew, and Horatio Deale — to a victory feast at his favorite restaurant not far from his house.

As desserts were served, Mike announced a big surprise — that he'd been referred by the local law firm of Mikles, Hersey, Smith & Learn to the Keefer, Wilson & Woods theatrical agency. Baltimore's acclaimed "Impresarios of Extraordinary Entertainment" proved eager to book The Amazing Alberto into theatres from Maryland to Massachusetts, and we drank to our friend's unexpected but well-deserved good fortune.

Matter of fact, our celebration included so many merry toasts that most of us were a little tipsy by the time we staggered back to Mike's place for coffee and conversation. By arrangement, bookmaker *meister* D. H. Galantier kindly made a special delivery of our betting proceeds. Lucifer had been the longest of long shots, and our pooled wagers returned more than enough to repay Emmaline's loan, and to finance our trip back to San Francisco in style, for humans and horses alike.

After sorting our winnings, we drifted into pairs and trios for sentimental *tête-à-têtes,* as the French say. Since many of us would soon be going our separate ways, our valedictory recollections of the challenges we'd shared over the last few days and weeks soon turned wistful.

Meanwhile, Victoria, Eddie, and Jake prowled like skittery cats determined to avoid each other. When I asked Jake why, he answered with a discouraged shrug: "Have you ever felt like you knew *what* you should say, but had no idea *how* to say it?"

"Are you asking your little brother for advice?"

"Not if you're gonna make a big circus out of it."

"Just tell her what's on your mind."

"How do you know she's a 'her'?"

"Who else would you be dodging?"

With a sigh of frustration, he went and found Victoria concentrating on a book off the shelves in Mike's library. "Hey, Vic," he said from behind her.

"Oh!" Her startled eyes darted, as if seeking an escape other than the doorway where Jake stood. "Hey."

"Ummm . . . you didn't happen to talk to Eddie."

"About what?"

"You know what."

"Are you still insisting he's sweet on me?"

"Everybody sees how he fusses over you."

"Even if that were true," Vic said with an aggravated edge in her voice, "I figured you'd be the *last* person who'd want me talking to him."

"You'd think." Jake hesitated. "But I keep chewin' on what you told me."

"You need to be more specific."

"About how you build trust with horses — how you promise 'em you'll never let anything bad happen to 'em?"

"Why are we talking about horses?"

"We're not. I'm talkin' about Eddie — he's already made you that promise."

"Well . . . can't you make the same promise?"

"Well . . . I *could*. I'm just not sure you could count on it." Jake expected she'd be grateful for having one less tarnished knight vying for her hand. "You know I'm right — right?"

Vic gritted her teeth. "If Eddie's got something to say," she growled, not at all grateful and plenty fed up, "how come he's not telling me himself?"

" 'Cuz it ain't easy talking to a girl who's as prickly as a cactus."

Vic slapped his face. "Ooooooh! Why are men *all* such fatheads?!" She bolted and stormed out Mike's front door, slamming it behind her.

Jake shuffled into the hall. Between Vic's angry exit, his defeated posture, and the red hand imprint on his cheek, it didn't take a detective to conclude their conversation could've gone better.

He glared at me. " '*Talk* to her,' you said. 'Say what's on your mind.' Thanks for the *grrreat* advice, Jamey." Lost in a hazy muddle, he pushed open the back screen door and went out to the yard.

I followed him. "Look, you've gotta tell him."

"Tell who, what?"

"Eddie, you numbskull." Now *I* felt like slapping him, too. "You've gotta convince him to tell Vic how he feels."

"Me? Since when am I a matchmaker?"

"Just *once,* why can't you do the . . . the *noble* thing?"

"You want noble?" he said, poking my gut. "I'll show you noble."

"Yeah, right — when pigs fly."

"Wanna bet?"

Jake barged back inside, found Eddie and herded him out to the yard. "Eddie, we gotta talk — *now.* And you damn well better get her a piano!"

Eddie blinked in confusion. "Get who what?"

I lurked and listened from behind a tree.

"You like Vic," Jake said, flat-out.

"So do you," Eddie shot back. "I'm not deaf, dumb and blind, y'know."

"Yeah, well . . . she should be with you, not me. And that's what I told her."

"*You* told her?" Eddie got red-faced. "Who elected *you* Cupid?"

"Someday you're gonna thank me for this. I'm tellin' you — go find her, and *beg* her to marry you!"

Eddie's temper boiled over. He could've knocked Jake plumb into next week if he was of a mind to, but all Eddie did was shove him — nearly knocking him off his feet. Then, Lord knows why, Jake shoved

Eddie right back. That's when Eddie popped him in the chin with a quick right jab. More shocked than hurt, Jake crumpled to his knees in the grass.

Lucky for my brother, the big rancher was immediately mortified. "Jake, I am *so* sorry!"

Jake rubbed his jaw, concluded that an actual "Baltimore Brawl" with Eddie wasn't a smart idea, and decided he was safer on the ground.

Vic pushed the screen door open, came out and sized up the scene. "What are you two jackasses doing?" With an exasperated grunt, she stomped back into the house.

Eddie's shoulders slumped and he looked down at Jake. "You're right. If I'm too yellow-bellied to tell her how I feel, she deserves better."

"No!" Jake squawked as Eddie shambled past him. "That's *not* what I said!"

When Eddie retreated inside the house, I stepped out of the shadows.

"Thanks for another great piece of advice, Jamey," Jake groused. "That's it. I *quit.*"

"One little slap, one little punch — and you're all done being noble?"

Jake squinted at me as he got up. "Y'know, sometimes I really, *really* hate you. Like, right now."

Witnessing Don Quixote knocked silly by a windmill, it's natural to wonder whether he can stand, let alone march back into the fight. To my brother's credit, he had one more try in him. But just as he reached for the handle of the screen door, it flew open and smacked him in the face. Vic charged out into the yard, with Eddie in pursuit.

Dazed by the door, Jake narrowly escaped getting trampled. Vic turned and stared at him. If looks could kill, Jake would've been pushing up daisies right there in Mississippi Mike's backyard. "*What* did you tell him?" she demanded, pointing at Eddie.

Beleaguered Jake shook his head. "Jeezus — try to do the right thing, and all you get is grief. Eddie, I'd like to escape this alive, so — *talk* to her!"

Eddie swallowed hard and took a chicken-hearted step forward. "Ummm, well . . . Jake says I . . . I should ask you to . . . to marry me."

"My exact word was *beg,*" Jake said.

I added my two cents. "It doesn't happen every day, but Jake's right."

Eddie looked into Vic's eyes. "Is he?"

"Well, if the Galloway brothers agree," she said with a tart twist of her lips, "who am I to argue?"

Jake raised a tentative hand. "Does that

mean y'all are done hitting me?"

"Probably," Vic said. Then she planted a lingering kiss on Eddie's lips, and he didn't put up any struggle.

"Is there a wedding in the works?" Emmaline chirped from behind us. "You must allow me to sing at the ceremony!"

All that French-farce commotion of stomping, slapping, shouting, and door-slamming had drawn a full-house audience to the backyard — Emmaline, Madame Killegrew, Mike, Horatio, Rafael, and Alberto, all present.

As the kiss continued, Madame Killegrew pretended to enter a trance. "Ahhh, the spirits foretell a future for the happy couple filled with bliss . . . many fine horses . . . and children."

Vic abruptly ended the kiss and waved her hands. "Whoa! Am I the only one who's noticed that Eddie hasn't actually proposed yet?"

"That does it, Eddie," said Jake. "You had your turn. Now it's *mine*." Before Eddie could protest, Jake plowed ahead like an auctioneer, loud and fast: "Victoria! Love being a rare and fleeting thing, we gotta strike while the iron is hot, so will you do me the honor of marrying" — dramatic pause — "Eddie?"

It took us a second to realize what he'd *actually* said, instead of what we *thought* he'd say, and everybody laughed. Sheepish Eddie got down on one knee. "Victoria Krieg, would you do me the honor of . . . of what Jake said, and us gettin' hitched?"

Vic scanned the whole grinning group. "Any other bids? Better offers? No? Then, going once — going twice —"

"Sold!" the rest of us shouted together.

Everybody crowded around, offering congratulations — except Jake and me. "Ha!" he said to me, justifiably pleased with himself. "How's *that* for noble?"

"Don't break your arm patting yourself on the back. Then again, when a pig *does* fly, nobody expects him to stay up there for long."

Vic and Eddie decided to get married right there in Baltimore, on the Pimlico clubhouse veranda, as soon as Mike could arrange for a judge to officiate. Jake was good and surprised when Eddie recruited him to be best man, but the reasoning made sense: "Probably wouldn't even be a wedding," Eddie said, "without you gettin' in the middle of things."

"Not to mention getting slapped, punched, and hit with Mississippi Mike's back door," Jake reminded him.

"And you did kinda give her up for me."

"Naah, she was never mine to give up," Jake said with a bittersweet half-smile. "Vic's her own gal — and don't you forget that."

"Wanna bet she won't let me?"

"Wanna bet you're right?"

"Oh, and don't tell her," Eddie said, "but I already ordered her a piano."

The nuptials took place at eleven on Thursday, one of those sparkling fall mornings when the air is as crisp as a fresh apple, and shadows as sharp as cut crystal. The dearly beloved gathered to witness the joining of Victoria Krieg and Eduardo Lobo in holy matrimony included Mike and Madame Killegrew, Alberto, Rafael, Jake, me, Horatio Deale, Champagne Charley Fly, and Phoenix and Lucifer, of course. Our new arabber friends Solomon Carver and Hub Robinson volunteered to hold the horses.

Although Mike and Emmaline had offered to take Eddie and Vic shopping for wedding finery, they chose to be married in their riding clothes. The happy but nervous couple came out onto the clubhouse porch with best man Jake and maid of honor Emmaline. They say all brides are luminous, and Vic was no exception.

The white-haired judge welcomed everyone and made brisk work of the ceremony. After Vic and Eddie exchanged vows and their first wedded kiss, Emmaline sang " 'Tis the Gift to be Simple" and wished them "many years filled with blessings, and love that will always come 'round right."

We toasted the newlyweds with real French Champagne — a gift from none other than Cortland Van Brunt III himself. When the two bottles first arrived, and Vic read the note, she'd wanted to smash them — but the rest of us convinced her that would be a sinful waste of innocent A-number-one libations. I even indulged in a sip or two myself.

Then Eddie and Vic saddled up and trotted their horses in a jubilant loop up and down Pimlico's homestretch, hailed by our applause and cheers. When they came back and hopped down, Charley approached to say his farewells.

"I can't tell you how much fun I had ridin' these critters," he said. "I'd ride Phoenix again anytime, anywhere."

"Thanks," Eddie said, "but Raffie swears he's never letting another jockey within ten feet of that horse."

Vic held Charley's hand. "Thank you for risking your reputation — not to mention your neck — riding *El Blanco Loco*. Burning your bridges with Van Brunt, that's no small thing."

Charley flashed a carefree smile. "Ma'am, I got so many offers, I'd end up ridin' three horses in the same race if I took 'em all. But next time you got another great horse needin' a jockey, keep me in mind."

"We will," Eddie said. "See you in San Francisco next summer?"

"You bet."

As Charley turned to leave, he spotted Solomon and Hub heading over to their horse carts. "Hey, Mr. Robinson — wait up!"

"Some of us still gotta work," Hub griped.

"I got a proposal," Charley said when he caught up with them. "I'd like to help you try and find your kin."

Hub frowned in silent suspicion.

"I know folks all over the South," Charley said. "We can write letters, send some wires. Nothin' to lose, right?"

"Let me think on it."

"Think on it?!" Solomon scolded. "Offer like that, you say yes!"

Hub threw up his hands in a gesture of surrender. "Okay, okay. I know when I'm licked." They agreed to meet at the arabbers' barn the next morning and get started.

Before Charley left the track, he made a point of shaking Rafael's hand. "It's been an honor, kid. You got a magic touch. Don't forget, you skunked me fair and square a bunch of times, so don't let ol' Lucifer getcha down."

If you're thinking that made Raf's day, you'd be right.

43

"Look on my works, ye Mighty, and despair!"
~ Percy Bysshe Shelley, "Ozymandias"

After the wedding, Mr. and Mrs. Eduardo Lobo honeymooned for a couple of days at the seven-story Carrollton, one of Baltimore's newest hotels. Not only was the name similar to our Carlton in San Francisco, but the Carrollton was almost as elegant. It even had "rising rooms" in the lobby — and, no surprise, Jake couldn't resist riding their elevators, too.

Speaking of Jake, despite this latest love lost, he remained remarkably cheerful — maybe because, deep down, he knew he really had been noble when it counted. Mississippi Mike kept us busy touring around Baltimore, found us a friendly poker game, and we all went to see Emmaline's show, which was always a treat.

Vic, Eddie, Rafael, Jake, and me splurged on the railroad's best Palace Car accommodations for our homebound journey. We also reserved the largest side-by-side stalls in the livestock car for Phoenix and Lucifer. They'd certainly earned the luxury.

Despite feeling a little blue as we packed, we all met up at Camden Station on Saturday morning, November 1. The Amazing Alberto, our courageous Italian magician pardner, would be staying to pursue his American-dream performing career. Emmaline Rose would continue with her eastern tour. And Mississippi Mike not only had his new life in Baltimore, but he and Frenchy Muldoon had so enjoyed their reunion that they promised to keep company now and then.

Before we left, I mailed clippings of Horatio Deale's reports on Lucifer's saga to "Sir" Robin Nettles, in care of the Maple Sap Saloon, Maple City, Nebraska — so he'd know the true quality of the horse he and his Reivers had stolen from the train that day. Back at the Carlton weeks later, I was surprised to get a letter from the outlaw poet himself, including his handwritten tribute called "White Horse, Dark Horse," inspired by Lucifer's Pimlico victory:

When you're riding a dark horse with no chance to win
Never give up! Never give in!
When it's two against one and the enemy cheats
Never surrender! Never retreat!
When they laugh at your dreams and the deck has been stacked
Always look forward! Never look back!
When the race has been run and they've done their worst
They shall be last — and Lucifer first!

Jake and me were glad to be home — although we looked forward to taking the train back to Cheyenne in the spring, joining our Indian friend Thomas Dog Nose for fossil-hunting season. We definitely wanted to see those gigantic bones of antediluvian monsters for ourselves.

Vic and Eddie loved Sir Robin's poem so much that she embroidered it into a sampler they framed and displayed outside Lucifer's stall. They settled down to build their horse business in earnest, and we saw them often in San Francisco and on visits to their *rancho*.

Eddie's protective housekeeper Han Mei slowly warmed up to the new mistress of Fernando Farms — especially once babies began arriving. In what felt like the blink of an eye, they had three smart and spirited daughters, all taking after their mama, growing up to help raise and train the finest horses in California. Our benefactor, Mr. Boone, happily bought two of those horses for himself over the years.

Even today, and for a long time to come, I believe people will still need good horses. Some folks insist these newfangled automobiles and other infernal combustive contraptions will take their place, but I have my doubts. Of course, Jake disagrees, and he desperately wants a car of his own, for the adventurous novelty — and any excuse to avoid horseback riding.

Despite the global market crash of '73, America was embarked on quite the emboldened spree in those early days of the era dubbed "The Gilded Age" by Mark Twain. The country continued expanding from sea to shining sea, thundering headlong like a speeding locomotive into a darkling, unknowable future.

Although the Civil War was a grievous national wound I feared might never heal, there was much to look forward to as the nation neared its 1876 Centennial. San Francisco and Baltimore — both humming seaport cities where Jake and me would spend considerable time — symbolized the tangible advancements of the day, as well as the daring promise of tomorrows still to be imagined.

Of course, Progress is rarely as linear or direct as we poor players strutting and fretting upon the stage might wish — and its bounties are never granted equally to all. As Destiny invents what is to come, it often tramples what once was. If you doubt that, just ask the Indians and the buffalo.

The railroads of the Great American Over-Land Route could never have been constructed without the audacious ambition of men vain and foolhardy enough to believe they could subdue the classical elements of Nature — Water, Wind, Earth, and Fire — bridging gorges, spanning deserts, cutting God's own purple mountain majesties down to size. But in gambling terms, Nature *is* the house — and, as all smart gamblers learn, sooner or later the house wins.

The calamitous Baltimore Fire of February 1904 incinerated much of the city we'd known in the 1870s. Although few died in that blaze, it ravaged a hundred and forty acres in the heart of town, razing fifteen hundred buildings, including businesses, shops, and homes.

San Francisco would be even more tragically devastated in 1906 (the year I write this account) by a catastrophic earthquake. Early on April 18, the Earth heaved with such primordial force that it shattered sturdy modern structures and streets. Ruptured gas mains unleashed rampaging firestorms. Twenty-five thousand buildings fell to rubble (including our beloved Carlton, although me and Jake had long since moved on). Thousands of poor souls perished, and hundreds of thousands more were left homeless and bereft of all possessions.

Though burned and broken to ashes and dust, both San Francisco and Baltimore will rise again, and then some. But such disasters leave indelible scars on human landscapes, hearts, and history — as they should, because they remind us of this eternal lesson: Whatever the hand of man hath wrought cannot stand against the power of Nature or the corrosion of Time, both of which capriciously scour us and our achievements from the face of the Earth.

I've seen many a prideful man like Cortland Van Brunt and Wilhelm Krieg ignore that everlasting truth, presuming their empires of soil, stone, steel, and treasure to be immortal. They cling to the conceit that they can bend all to their whims and iron wills, including any lesser mortals blocking their way.

As a lesser mortal myself, there's a poem that's stuck with me all these years — "Ozymandias," penned by Percy Bysshe Shelley in 1818. His sonnet tells of "a traveller from an antique land" crossing a barren desert and encountering the fallen, fractured ruins of a once-magnificent shrine exalting the monarch of an empire long gone:

> . . . And on the pedestal these words appear:
> "My name is Ozymandias, King of Kings.
> Look on my works, ye Mighty, and despair!"
> No thing beside remains. Round the decay
> Of that Colossal Wreck, boundless and bare
> The lone and level sands stretch far away.

In our own times, when we find ourselves confronted by self-proclaimed kings, the easy choice for us lesser mortals is to yield before we get pulverized. Personally, I've always subscribed to the motto "Better a live coward than a dead hero." So I'd be the last man to try talking folks into suicidal assaults against insurmountable odds.

But if I've learned anything from such acquaintances as Mississippi Mike Morgan, The Amazing Alberto Palazzo, and Madame Aurora Killegrew, it's that things aren't always what they seem. Every so often, magic may be conjured, minds may be fooled, and miracles may be possible.

There's almost always more than one way to skin a cat or best a bully. When compelled to fight for what's right, I reckon most of us are capable of being more resourceful than we think. And (in the eloquent words of Sir Robin Nettles) "when it's two against one and the enemy cheats," it helps to have good friends on your side. I've been fortunate in that regard. I hope you will be, too.

ABOUT THE AUTHOR

New York Times bestselling author **Howard Weinstein** began his writing career at age 19, when he sold his script for "The Pirates of Orion" episode to NBC's Emmy-winning animated *Star Trek* revival in 1974.

His first historical novel, *Galloway's Gamble,* won a Western Fictioneers Peacemaker Award, leading to this sequel. Bestselling Western-history author Jeff Guinn calls *Galloway's Gamble* "the whole package — entertaining, heartwarming, and historically accurate."

Howard's eclectic writing credits include novels, graphic novels, comic books, and nonfiction books; story-development assistance on *Star Trek IV: The Voyage Home; Puppy Kisses Are Good for the Soul,* a charming account of life with his first Welsh Corgi, Mail Order Annie; and many magazine and newspaper articles.

For more information, readers can visit Howard online at www.howardweinsteinbooks.com. They can also find him at www.facebook.com/howard.weinstein.33 on Facebook.

The employees of Thorndike Press hope you have enjoyed this Large Print book. All our Thorndike Large Print titles are designed for easy reading, and all our books are made to last. Other Thorndike Press Large Print books are available at your library, through selected bookstores, or directly from us.

For information about titles, please call:
 (800) 223-1244

or visit our website at:
 gale.com/thorndike